A LADY AT BAY

A LADY AT BAY

by

EDGAR MAASS

TRANSLATED BY

RICHARD *and* CLARA WINSTON

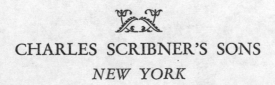

CHARLES SCRIBNER'S SONS

NEW YORK

CONTENTS

A LADY AT BAY

PART I

THE PROMISSORY NOTE

, I ,

ON A SULTRY July evening, when darkness was already beginning to fall, a broad-shouldered and strikingly imposing figure of a man entered the Place Maubert, which is in the Latin Quarter of Paris, on the left bank of the Seine. His face, at once good-natured and serious, was adorned by a martial-looking, bushy mustache twirled at the ends. His gait, self-assured, firm, unhurried, as well as the jingling of his spurs and the cavalry saber hanging from his sword belt, bespoke a person who was used to authority. One hardly needed the silver stripes on his coat collar and the brass shield on the turned-up brim of his hat to identify him as a sergeant of His Majesty King Louis XIV's Paris police force.

As he strode heavily across the narrow triangle of the Place Maubert, he kept looking around him with the penetrating glance of a man accustomed to be always on the alert. This neighborhood did not have the best of reputations. From the Place Maubert many narrow alleys led off in all directions, and their sagging houses offered hiding places for all sorts of unsavory characters. The vicinity was full of stables, taverns of questionable nature, transients' lodgings, and bistros that were the hangouts of criminals. Many prostitutes, the so-called *filles de joie*, walked in pairs, arms locked, stepping with almost military precision as they sought customers for their dubious charms. Here and there, at the entrances to the bistros, where stood green pails for watering horses, groups of young men were gathered in heated discussion, or simply making noise. Many of them were dressed in the dark, semi-clerical garb of students, for the underworld of criminals and the intellectual world of the studious youth of France rubbed elbows in the Place Maubert; which fact was a permanent worry to the authorities and caused them to keep an unusually large force of policemen at the precinct station here.

With clanking spurs the sergeant strode on toward this precinct station, which was located behind a fountain at the southeast corner of the triangle and was marked by two red lanterns. Suddenly he stood still. In a barred niche in the wall of a building was a bright, naïve wooden statue of the Virgin pressing a bunch of tall-stemmed lilies against her breast. Some pious soul, probably from the nearby Carmelite Convent, had lit a small oil lamp before the statue, and though the night was windless the light flickered unsteadily, making the white, contemplative face of the Virgin seem almost alive.

The sergeant crossed himself and solemnly murmured an Ave Maria. Then, sighing, he turned away and walked on. But after a few steps he stood still again, hesitated, and then descended into a cellar over which dangled a signboard showing three heraldic lions— to indicate that the place was a tavern. Some moments later he reappeared carefully carrying a wooden mug in his right hand.

Behind the fountain, which was surrounded by people, he climbed the three steps to the precinct station, banged on the door with his left hand and, without waiting for an answer, kicked it open. Inside, in the dim light of a candle that seemed to be struggling vainly against the darkness, sat a short, white-haired little man with a peaked face, sharp nose, and short-sighted eyes half hidden under bushy eyebrows. "Oh, it's you, Cluet," the man croaked reproachfully. "Can't a person ease up on work even at night?"

"Evening, Père Picard," the sergeant said in a booming voice, and set the jug on the table. "Don't worry, there's nothing on my mind. Just wanted to have a bit of gossip with you, for old times' sake."

"Oh, if that's all, that's another matter," Picard, the precinct captain of the quarter, said in a somewhat less cranky tone. "Why didn't you say so right away, Cluet? What have you got in the mug there?"

"What do you think?" Cluet boomed. "Cider, of course, from the Three Lions. It's a damned hot night."

"Oh, too bad," Picard sighed disappointedly. "I would rather have had *vin ordinaire*. But take your coat off, Cluet, and make yourself comfortable. After all, you're more or less at home here."

"I should think so," Cluet agreed, taking off his coat and sword belt. "I spent nearly five years here battling with thieves, fences, and swindlers before Lieutenant Desgrez got me into police headquarters. But you know, on the whole, it wasn't so bad here. Nowadays I miss being in touch with the boys I'm supposed to chase."

"How is Lieutenant Desgrez?" Picard asked as he rummaged among dusty papers in a cupboard for the glasses he kept there.

"Lieutenant Desgrez?" Cluet repeated, stretching out comfortably on a chair and putting his spurred boots up on the table. "We've been tracking down a gang of counterfeiters. But tonight he wanted to work alone. I wouldn't be surprised if he hasn't got the gang to take him in and is standing at their press right now coining false livres." He chuckled good-naturedly and added significantly, "It's quite an affair—really quite an affair."

"Yes, he's quite a boy, isn't he. They use him only for the big-time stuff—like the time the Duchess of Orléans kicked off so suddenly," Picard said. He placed the glasses, which he had found at last, on the table and filled them. "Well, *mon vieux*," he said, "what shall we drink to?"

"To the things we love!" Sergeant Cluet responded immediately, and he raised his glass so that the light sent a golden gleam through it.

"Then let us drink to pretty little Mademoiselle Jeannette Surfie in Villequoy," Picard said gallantly, and he looked slyly at Cluet, who smiled uncomfortably.

They clinked glasses and drank. Then Picard sat down and began telling the sergeant the latest gossip of the Latin Quarter, sparing none of the spicy details.

⌁ II ⌁

BUT HE did not get far. Suddenly through the open window came the buzz of excited voices. Then the door opened violently, and into the room rushed a plump woman wearing a dirty blue-and-white-striped dressing-gown. An equally dirty coif of the same loud pattern was draped over her disheveled hair, which hung in oily strands around her fleshy shoulders. "Inspector," she gasped, "there's been an explosition in my house." Her enormous bosom rising and falling, she threw a terrified look at the two men, who had sprung to their feet.

"An explosion, Mother Brunet?" Picard asked.

"That's it, Inspector, a terrible explosition," the woman moaned. And then words flowed from her lips like water over a cataract. "I was right there in the kitchen warming milk for Leona—she's my cat, you know. All of a sudden there was a boom that scared the daylights out of me, and I almost burned myself. The windows shook and the pots jumped. Leona, poor beast, was so frightened she scratched my leg."

"Now wait a minute, Widow Brunet," Sergeant Cluet said. "Maybe it was only some pimp shooting at his whore in one of your rooms."

"Sir," the woman replied, "I wish to inform you that I keep a decent house. Of course I rent rooms to students. Where else are young folks to go if they want to be alone with their girls for a while? But pimps and suchlike never set foot inside my door. 'Germaine, my dove,' my sainted husband always used to say to me, 'keep the place clean' . . ."

"Very well, very well, Mother Brunet," Picard interrupted her. "Tell us the circumstances."

"I've told you already, Inspector, an explosion happened."

With considerable difficulty, because the widow was constantly tempted into reminiscences about her deceased husband, Picard and Cluet learned that something like an explosion had actually taken place in the Cul-de-sac des Marchands des Chevaux—the Blind Alley of the Horse Traders. The loud booming sound had been followed by a dull thud, and the house had filled with noisome fumes. Widow Brunet had run to the back room. She found the door locked, and no one answered her knocking and calling. The tenant, who had been renting the room for a full year, didn't live there all the time; he only used the room occasionally. But today she had seen him come into the house.

"Well, we won't get anywhere sitting here," Cluet said, putting on his coat and buckling his belt. Picard took his hat and Cluet an iron crowbar. Accompanied by two guards, one carrying a lantern, and by the Widow Brunet, who alternately chattered and groaned, they hastened toward the Cul-de-sac des Marchands des Chevaux. From the street fountains and houses along the way a large crowd joined their procession.

The narrow hallway of the house was filled with a strong smell of bitter almonds. Picard pounded on the door that the widow pointed out. Everyone listened tensely, but only silence followed his knocking. Cluet inserted his crowbar. Wood splintered loudly, and the door flew open with a groan. The smell became stronger and more pungent. Cluet grabbed the lantern, rushed into the room, and smashed a window to let in some fresh air.

The flickering light of the lantern illuminated a large table massed with bottles, retorts, and mortars and pestles in the middle of the room. Along one wall was a stove in which some charcoal embers still glowed dark red, and on the opposite wall stood an open cupboard, the shelves filled with variously shaped glass apparatus and bottles with illegible labels.

Cluet walked slowly around the table. His foot encountered an obstacle: it was the body of a man stretched out face downward. He knelt down and turned the man over. The wide-open eyes were staring vacantly; the handsome features bore an expression of numbing terror. Over the white face, tied by two ribbons behind the ears, were splintered fragments which Cluet immediately recognized as the remains of a glass mask. The man was dressed in a black habit with a narrow white clerical collar.

Cluet opened the man's waistcoat and shirt and laid his ear to the bared chest. "No heartbeat," he said, getting up. "The fellow's dead, dead as a doornail."

Widow Brunet uttered a high-pitched cry. "Poor man, the poor good gentleman," she sobbed. "Tomorrow he might have become the king's chamberlain."

"Is that so?" Inspector Picard said skeptically. "What was the fellow doing here, anyhow?" He threw a suspicious glance at the retorts on the table.

"What do you want, Inspector," the Widow Brunet sobbed. "He was looking for the philosopher's stone. There's no sin in that. Oh, he was going to be a great man, believe me."

"I don't know, there's something odd about this whole affair," Cluet said, turning to her. "What was the man's name?"

"When I tell you, you'll see how wrong you were to be suspecting him of anything underhanded," the widow said. Triumphantly she pronounced, "Jean-Baptiste Godin de Sainte-Croix."

"Sainte-Croix? Never heard of him," Cluet said indifferently.

"He was from Gascony. An ancient noble line, going way back to the Crusades."

"I see. Did he have any kinsfolk you know of, Mother Brunet?"

"He was married and lived nearby, on the Rue des Bernardins."

"His wife must be informed," Cluet said. "So you know he was looking for the philosopher's stone, Mother Brunet? Did he often have visitors?"

"Some gentlemen came now and then. I suppose the poor man talked about his chemicals with them. And once there was a lady. But I never recognized any of them. Not the lady either; she wore a veil. Maybe she was his wife."

"Is that all, Mother Brunet?"

"No, Sergeant. I mean, common people came often—servants or messengers who ran errands for the gentleman, I guess. He often talked to them for a long time; he was a very friendly sort of gentleman. He used to talk to me, too, and he told me that he was expecting to enter the king's household in a high position soon. I guess he said that about three months ago, before he fell ill. Today he called out *bon soir* to me, friendly as you please, and went right into his room. Oh Lord, the poor good man." She snuffed loudly, again on the point of tears.

"One more question, Mother Brunet," Cluet said. "Where does this door next to the cupboard lead to?"

"Oh, that's a small storeroom that the gentleman rented also. He used it for his books and papers. At least I think that's what it was for; he always kept the room locked and carried the key with him."

Sergeant Cluet stepped back and whispered to Inspector Picard, who nodded vigorous assent. Then Cluet turned to the widow again. "Mother Brunet," he said, "I'll have the body taken to the Châtelet now. Of course we must determine the cause of his death. Meanwhile I'm going to seal the storeroom and laboratory and you must not allow anybody to enter the rooms until we have taken an inventory of the deceased's property. That will probably take a few days."

Widow Brunet nodded. The guards lifted the body and carried it out of the house. After placing the seals on the doors, Cluet went out into the hall, which was still crowded with curiosity-seekers. "Run along home, neighbors," he said, pushing them through the door. "It's just an accident. Only an alchemist whose philosopher's stone blew up in his face."

⟨ III ⟩

THESE EVENTS took place on the night of July 30, 1672.

On August 13, a dreary, rainy day, Inspector Picard, Sergeant Cluet, and Sainte-Croix's widow, a pallid, shy woman, gathered in the house on the Cul-de-sac des Marchands des Chevaux. In addition there were two men present whose reasons for coming nobody knew. One was a Carmelite monk, Father Verron, an intimate of one of the deacons of Notre Dame. The other was Monsieur Breuille, a close associate of a certain Monsieur Pennautier, who was an exceedingly rich man. Cluet noticed that the two gentlemen seemed depressed and rather anxious, although they chatted in a lively manner and made a show of helpful activity.

The two policemen ran into difficulty right at the start: there was no key to the storeroom. None had been found on the dead man's person. When this became clear, Father Verron drew a key from the folds of his gown and asked whether it might not do. The key was tried, and fitted. Everyone was so pleased at the key's having been found that no one thought to ask Father Verron how he happened to have it in his possession.

Meanwhile, still a third unexpected gentleman appeared, a Monsieur Gucheux. He came, he explained, as legal representative of the deceased's creditors, who seemed to be fairly numerous. Thus six persons entered the storeroom, and all eyes at once lit upon a plump sealed envelope which lay on a small table. The words *"Ma Confession"* were written in large letters across the envelope.

With an impetuous gesture Father Verron snatched it up, exclaiming, "Gentlemen, I confiscate this document as a secret of the confessional which only the deceased's confessor has the right to examine." After a moment he added, "On second thought, I consider it best to burn this letter unopened at once, so that it cannot fall into the hands of any unauthorized person."

Inspector Picard protested, though not very vigorously, against the immediate destruction of the document. But the persons principally interested, Madame Sainte-Croix and Monsieur Gucheux, agreed to Father Verron's proposal. Picard was soon persuaded to withdraw his protest. "After all, this is a civil case, not a criminal one," he whispered

to Cluet, "and as good Catholics we must be mindful that the secrets
of the confessional are inviolable."

Everyone therefore returned to the laboratory, where, with the
company as witnesses, Father Verron burned the letter on the hearth.
He placed the charred remnants of paper in a mortar and ground
them to dust, so that the dead man's confession, whatever it may
have been, was now lost forever to the world. Cluet noticed that
from this point on Father Verron and Monsieur Breuille seemed much
more composed than they had been earlier. Nevertheless, both gentlemen continued to watch closely as the inventory proceeded.

Listing the contents of the storeroom was simple enough. It contained, in addition to the destroyed envelope, only a red chest
bound with leather straps. This was about two and a half feet long,
two feet wide, and equally high. Sticking in the lock was a badly
rusted key, which Inspector Picard turned only with considerable effort. Then, after unbuckling the straps, he lifted the lid.

The general disappointment was most pronounced on the faces
of the dead man's widow and Monsieur Gucheux. For, instead of
money, the chest contained only a large number of packages, enve-
lopes, and paper twists filled with powders, some colored but most
of them white. Picard laid them on the table one after the other, in
the order in which he removed them from the chest. There was
also a stoneware pot containing a brown, sticky substance, a wooden
box in which lay a gray stone, and two bottles of different sizes
filled with a transparent liquid.

These materials were evidently chemicals which the unfortunate
alchemist must have been using in his attempts to synthesize the
philosopher's stone. It seemed unlikely that they would have much
value. The widow and Monsieur Gucheux debated whether it would
be worth an apothecary's fee to have the materials assayed. While
they were conferring, Inspector Picard brought out from the apparently empty chest a slip of paper he had overlooked. He unfolded
the paper and in his scratchy voice read aloud, "For value received
I promise to pay Monsieur de Sainte-Croix by January of next year,
at the latest, the sum of thirty thousand livres. Given at Paris the
twentieth day of April in the year 1670. Signed: Daubray."

The widow gave a deep sigh and swayed against the table heaped
with chemicals. Monsieur Gucheux rushed to her side. "Be calm,
Madame de Sainte-Croix," he exclaimed. "That is a huge fortune.

After satisfying the claims of all the creditors you will still be a wealthy woman. Permit me to congratulate you."

Picard stood staring incredulously at the sheet of paper in his shaking fingers. But Sergeant Cluet seemed more excited than any of the others. "Daubray!" he cried out. "It's impossible, absolutely impossible! How could a Daubray have had anything to do with that alchemist?"

"Here it is, read it yourself," Picard said, handing Cluet the paper.

Cluet read the note, murmuring the words under his breath, and his amazement increased. "It really is signed by Daubray," he mused. "And yet I can scarcely believe my eyes. It must be a forgery."

"What are you saying, Sergeant?" Monsieur Gucheux exclaimed angrily. "Thirty thousand livres and a forgery! You have no right to make such an assertion."

"Messieurs, madame," Inspector Picard said, "have you noticed that the signature consists only of the surname?"

"Of course," Monsieur Gucheux agreed, "but remember, the note is valid before the law with or without the Christian name."

"Provided we can identify this Daubray, Monsieur Gucheux," the inspector said. "But, Cluet, what the devil's the matter with you? You look as though you've seen a ghost—and not a very pleasant one."

Sergeant Cluet was standing wide-eyed, his mouth half open, staring vacantly. His face was white under his superficial tan. His forehead was slightly beaded with perspiration, and as Picard spoke to him he slowly began wiping it with his sleeve. "Inspector Picard," he said abruptly in a hollow, official voice, "this puts an entirely different complexion on the matter."

"What do you mean by that? I admit that thirty thousand livres is a great deal of money. But people do sometimes owe debts as large as that."

Sergeant Cluet was unimpressed by this argument. "Inspector Picard," he continued in an almost menacing tone, "a matter like this is out of our province. The Châtelet will have to be informed."

"Why so, Cluet?" Picard asked uncertainly. "Because there is so much money involved?"

"That for one thing, Picard. But mainly because of the signature. How could a Daubray owe a nobody like Sainte-Croix thirty thousand livres?"

"But, my dear Sergeant," Monsieur Gucheux protested, "that is private business. Why should the police stick their noses into everything? Probably neither Madame de Sainte-Croix nor Monsieur Daubray would like to see their personal affairs made public."

"You do not seem to be aware, sir, that there no longer is a Monsieur Daubray," Cluet replied coldly.

"Come now," Monsieur Gucheux said irascibly, "what do you mean by that? That's nonsense, my man."

"Not nonsense to me," Cluet replied. "I know the family very well. And I happen to know that the last scion of the male line of the Daubray family died nearly two years ago."

"There are still the heirs. And they will have to pay. The note is valid before the law." Monsieur Gucheux fanned his overheated face with his hat; he obviously saw the money for his creditors slipping out of his hands. But in a moment he apparently reconsidered his protest, for he said, "As you think best, Sergeant. Perhaps under the circumstances the police ought to take a hand in the matter."

"Yes," Inspector Picard said. "Obviously we must determine the identity of the debtor. We also must find out whether these chemicals have any value. I quite agree with Sergeant Cluet and Monsieur Gucheux. The inventory is ended. I shall take the chest and its contents to the Châtelet, and His Excellency the Prefect of Police will then decide what steps are to be taken."

Madame Sainte-Croix, Father Verron, and Messieurs Breuille and Gucheux bade goodbye and hesitantly left the room and the apartment. Picard and Cluet were left alone. Outside the rain pattered cheerlessly against the dirty pane of the single small window in the storeroom.

"Picard," Cluet said, "let me take that note right with me. It's an important document."

"Certainly," Picard said, handing the paper to the sergeant, who carefully folded it and placed it in one of his coat pockets.

"The prefect will certainly open his eyes when he sees this," Cluet said.

"The prefect? Why?" Picard asked.

"Well, there was one Daubray who was chief of police before him," Cluet said.

"So there was. I hadn't thought of that," Picard exclaimed.

The sergeant glanced disgustedly out of the window and threw his cape over his shoulders. "Au revoir, Père Picard," he said. And he left the room.

◄ IV ►

THE SUMMER RAIN fell in long, fine lines. Deep in thought, Sergeant Cluet crossed the Ile de la Cité, scarcely noticing the water dripping through the open collar of his cape. The ends of his mustache drooped mournfully and the heavy drops of rain ran down his tanned cheeks.

After reaching the right bank over the Pont Notre Dame, he went northeast toward the Faubourg Le Marais. He crossed the Place Grève with its towering black cross in the center, passed the imposing medieval façade of the Hôtel de Ville, and entered the labyrinthine tangle of narrow alleys back of the big building. On his left lay the Monastery of Saint Jean, to his right the pointed turrets and late-Gothic towers of Saint Gervais looked down upon him. The rain water washed along the gutters, and here and there it gushed in a heavy stream from a downspout into the street and swept away weeks of accumulated filth, as though the sky itself had undertaken to give the city of Paris a thorough cleansing.

Sergeant Cluet walked fast and soon found himself in a neighborhood of a different character. First he reached the Rue Saint Antoine, both sides of which were lined with shops in which crowds of women, haggling with lively Gallic gestures and loud exclamations, were buying their daily supplies of vegetables, meat, milk, and bread. Through the crowd pressed peddlers carrying baskets or pulling carts; these had no fixed stand and were crying their wares in their peculiar chants.

Further east, the street became broader and quieter. Large houses, with more modern baroque ornamentation, stood side by side. Some of them were virtually palaces. And everywhere were the spires of the chapels of monasteries, which were particularly numerous in this quarter. The towers rose up above the tops of the trees which grew in the well-kept gardens within the walls.

After a while Cluet turned into the short Rue Royale and reached the Place Royale. This was a spacious square surrounded on all four sides by three-story mansions that closely resembled one another. The houses, built of unstuccoed brick, all had very high, steep gable roofs from which long chimneys protruded. On the ground the walls were set back the width of the sidewalk, and a row of columns formed an arcade. The square itself was a neatly clipped lawn protected by a low, artfully wrought iron fence. In the middle of the grassy area was the equestrian statue of Louis XIII, the father of the reigning king. His sullen face, fleshy and long-nosed, was crowned by a laurel wreath.

The Place Royale had obviously been planned by an architect of genius. It was one of the most successful of King Henry the IV's architectural projects, although Henry himself had not lived to see its completion, for Ravaillac's dagger had put an untimely end to his active and conciliatory reign. Something of the lofty, serene and free-thinking purity of the great king seemed to linger still in the rain-washed grass and the graceful, dignified buildings.

Sergeant Cluet walked faster. He crossed the grass toward a house whose windows on the two lower floors were heavily draped. At the side of the house was a narrow corridor, which he entered. He pushed open a door, tramped noisily up the steep, dim stairway to another door—apparently the entrance to the rooms under the mansard roof —and knocked ponderously.

"Come in, Cluet," a forceful, slightly ironic voice called out. "The door is unlocked."

Cluet went in. He crossed a tiny anteroom, turned to the left, and entered a spacious attic room. Sitting in a comfortable easy chair, his legs dangling over one of the arms, was a man dressed in a voluminous dressing-gown embroidered with large flowers. It must once have been a very handsome garment, but now it was worn out and rather tattered-looking. The man seemed about forty. His dark, slightly wavy hair had no trace of gray, but tiny crinkles around his eyes and the corners of his mouth indicated his age. He gave Cluet a look of good-natured shrewdness and asked, "Well, Cluet, what's that you have in your pocket for me?"

Cluet gaped. "How do you know, Lieutenant Desgrez?" he cried. "And in fact how did you know it was I knocking on your door?"

Desgrez laughed heartily and blinked his eyes. "I was standing at the open window, Cluet, enjoying the cool rain after all these hot days," he said. "Last night at Madame d'Argenteuil's I met a young German scholar who raved to us about pre-established harmony. And as I stood by the window I thought, Really, everything is beautifully

harmonious—the freshly washed red brick of the houses, the gleaming panes of the windows, the green of the grass, the silent bronze
equestrian figure, and even the thrushes pecking for worms. But
then this harmony, this well-constructed fugue, was rudely interrupted by a man who came clumping along out of the Rue Royale
obviously in a hurry. He stepped over the fence around the lawn
instead of walking peacefully under the protection of the arcade, and
while he rushed along he kept clutching at the right-hand pocket
of his coat. And the expression on his face—your face, I soon saw,
Cluet—was one of perplexity. In short, a discord has broken into my
fugue. The harmony, alas, is gone—as so often happens. But sit down,
Cluet. Take that easy chair. Don't mind the book—throw it on the
table. It's Monsieur Descartes's analytic geometry, which I've just
been glancing at to reassure myself that there are other and better
reasons for believing in the world's harmony than the assertions of
a young philosopher. And give me what you've brought for me."

Cluet was used to the ironic tone in which Desgrez spoke, and he
always listened attentively although he usually could not follow all
that the lieutenant said. Now, too, he merely took the folded sheet
of paper from his coat pocket and handed it silently to Desgrez. Then
he sat down and studied the lieutenant's face with tense expectancy.

Desgrez unfolded the promissory note. As he read it, a vertical
furrow appeared between his eyebrows. It gave his thin face, which a
moment before had been amiable and indifferent, an expression that
was somehow menacing. The cheekbones under the bluish, smoothly
shaven skin of his face moved slightly, and each feature tensed, so
that Cluet, who was watching with bated breath, involuntarily
thought of a bow with its string drawn taut.

Desgrez read the note several times. He turned it over and examined the back, holding it up against the light from the window. He
brushed his forefinger lightly over the surface of the paper, then
raised it to his nose and smelled it. Finally, with a little sigh, he let
it drop to his knee and said in his ironical voice, "Cluet, you ought
to get a new tobacco pouch or close your old one tighter. The crumbs
of Virginia tobacco in your pocket are hampering my examination.
All I can tell now is that the paper must have lain in some closed
place for a long time—and, if I'm not mistaken, under or near certain chemicals. It seems to me that opium must have been one of

them, and that the owner was rather careless with it, as this brown spot here indicates."

"Right, Lieutenant Desgrez," Cluet said. "I mean, I didn't know about the opium. But what do you think of the handwriting, and of the signature?"

Desgrez picked up the paper again, examined it once more, dropped it, and then raised it again and held it out in front of him. "The writing and signature are by one and the same person," he said finally. "And a person of extraordinary energy and self-confidence. The letters are large and steep. The writer apparently dashed this off all in one sentence because he was excited . . . possibly angry, I think. . . . He may have been the target of blackmail. What is most extraordinary is that the handwriting is not modern. If it were not for the date, and if the paper were more yellowed, I would say that the writer lived about a hundred years ago, around the time of the religious wars and St. Bartholomew's Night. Since that can't be the case, I must conclude that the writer probably is a person in whose blood the *élan* of the Renaissance still flows. His character is more suitable to that bolder and more active era. And in our quiet times, what could such a person be if not an adventurer, a criminal, or a fool!" Desgrez laughed softly and added, "That is, unless he happened to be a policeman. For what are we, Cluet, if not criminals in reverse?"

"But what about the name, Lieutenant Desgrez? You've paid so much attention to the handwriting, you've disregarded the name."

"Not at all, Cluet. While I've been talking, I've been considering which Daubray the signer of this note could have been. Remember, I served under the old man and his son, just as you did. But neither of them is the author of this note—although I must admit that the writing is rather similar to the old man's." Desgrez fell silent and sat meditating for several minutes.

Cluet made a point of not disturbing him by asking questions. He looked around the big room, which took up all of one side of the building. His gaze paused at a striking bronze statue newly installed between two narrow bookcases along one of the walls. It did not go with the other furniture in the room, the comfortable but far from new armchairs, the large table with curved legs, the flowerpots by the window, and the worn rug which covered only part of the floor.

The statue, whose elegant curves suggested that it was the work

of Goujon or one of the other prominent sculptors of the day, represented a nymph just stepping out of a stream. The reeds at her feet
delicately concealed one foot. The firm, full breasts gave her slender
body a certain amplitude. She stood bolt upright, as though surprised
by a world of light encountered for the first time. But her eyes were
somewhat too round and there was something fishlike about the full,
upturned lips and the stringy hair which hung down around the fine
shoulders as though water were still dripping from it. There was an
air of the unspoken and the hidden about the bronze creature. Although all of her, except for the left foot, stood full-bodied in the
light of reality, she seemed nevertheless to belong to a silent and
primeval world.

Desgrez shook himself out of his thoughts. His eyes followed
Cluet's gaze and he said smilingly, "My forceful friend, the Marquise
d'Argenteuil, pressed the fish-woman upon me. She insisted on seeing it in my room. You know how it is, Cluet, when women get an idea
into their heads." He laughed meaningfully and then added, "Incidentally, it is supposed to be modeled after the Duchess of Valenti-
nois, the Diana of Poitiers, you know. A very lively woman once, but
she's been a long time dead. A fine ornament for an inveterate
bachelor's room, I must say. But come, Cluet, let's stop the guesswork.
Tell me where this promissory note comes from."

Cluet informed him of the death of the alchemist, the inventory
of his property, and Inspector Picard's discovery of the note. Now
and then he halted, groping for words. It was not Desgrez who confused him; the lieutenant sat with bowed head, his fine hands clasped
over his chest, listening attentively. But Cluet kept turning to look
at the statue. It seemed to him that the nymph, too, was listening to
him and watching him with her mysterious, slightly scornful smile.

When Cluet finished his story, Desgrez rose and began pacing
the room. He seemed to have forgotten Cluet's presence. Once he
took the volume of Descartes from the table, opened it, glanced into
it for a moment, and then closed it again. Then he resumed his pacing.
Finally he stopped by a window and stood there for a long time.
Drumming his fingers against the glass, he looked out. Cluet recognized the rhythm of the drumming at once. It was the cavalry march
of the Argenteuil Regiment. His eyes grew concerned.

Abruptly Desgrez turned around. "Cluet," he said, "thank God
you're sitting here and able to tell me all this."

Cluet stared at him in surprise. "What's that?" he whispered. Then, almost inaudibly, he added, "I suspected right away that something was fishy."

"You were right, Cluet. That is, if my reasoning is correct. Tell me, what did this fellow Sainte-Croix die of?"

"Dr. Moreau says he died of a heart attack. That is what he put down in the death certificate."

"But there was that smell of bitter almonds in the apartment, Cluet, wasn't there? You're certain of that, aren't you?"

"Yes. It was much stronger in the laboratory than in the hall. That was why I smashed the window."

"Good," Desgrez said, and he resumed his tapping on the window-pane. "Dr. Moreau was mistaken. Though a heart attack was certainly possible. It must have been a monstrous shock for the man when suddenly, possibly by a clumsy movement, he broke his mask and found himself without protection."

"I don't understand," Cluet murmured.

"One moment, Cluet," Desgrez said. He went up to the sergeant and touched his shoulder lightly. "It was the name Daubray that made you come to me, wasn't it? Or rather the fact that your girl, Jeannette, works for Daubray's widow in Villequoy. If I remember rightly, you told me a few weeks ago that you were worried about the way things are going at Villequoy."

Cluet flushed. "That's true," he said, stroking his mustache in embarrassment. "I just can't stand looking on any more without doing something, Lieutenant Desgrez. Kind as Madame Daubray is, she's driving my Jeannette crazy. Jeannette is already as scared as her mistress."

"Cluet, I'm afraid Madame Daubray's fears may not be so unfounded. Don't misunderstand me, I have no proofs. But tomorrow —yes, by tomorrow I'll know more about it." He paused and brushed back his mane of hair. "But in order not to lose time, let's consider the Daubrays' affairs for a moment. First we must have a drink, though. It stimulates the mind—nothing like combining pleasure with business. I'll have cognac. What about you? Oh, of course, you insist on cider. I've never understood how anyone not dying of thirst can drink that tart stuff. But I still have half a decanter of the vinegar in my cupboard—saved up just for you, my friend."

⸙ V ⸙

DESGREZ HAD not always been the subdued and thoughtful person
he now was. Some twenty years ago his father had been administrator
of the estates of the Marquis d'Argenteuil, who had been rich enough
to supply France, at his own expense, with a regiment of splendid
dragoons. As was the custom, the regiment bore his own name. The
marquis, a great drinker and gambler, with a passion for the cavalry,
had taken a liking to young François Desgrez. Against the wishes of
Desgrez père, he had persuaded François to join the regiment. As a
dragoon, Desgrez had done his best to vie with his well-born companions in carousing and roistering. It required no great effort on his
part, for the handling of horses and weapons, girls and wine flagons,
came to him naturally. And so he had enjoyed a wild, merry, and
thoughtless life until the bleak day on which the marquis was killed
in battle and he himself so badly wounded that it seemed certain he
would remain a cripple for life.

The marquise, Madame d'Argenteuil, had taken the wounded man
into her house. Widowed and childless, she had treated him like a
son, and it was due largely to her somewhat stern kindness and her
ironic encouragement that Desgrez conquered his despair and
learned to walk again after three slow and painful years.

He limped now, and was in all respects a changed man. Everything, even the most common facts of life, seemed an absolute mystery to him. He had a sense of having died and having been born
anew. His old world of easy living had vanished, and a new world
opened before him—a greater one, though it contained anxieties and
uncertainties which he had never known before. The happy dream
of physical well-being, money, high connections, and high station,
which so many people accept as life, was gone for ever. Existence,
by the blessing of pain, had assumed the aspect of a great riddle
and an arduous, never-ending task.

The great difficulty was that this task was not assigned him by an
authoritarian command from someone above, as had been the case
in the regiment. Now he had to define the task for himself. Without
it, his existence would be meaningless.

It happened, by grace of the king, who looked after his veterans,

that he was given the post of lieutenant in the Paris police force.
He accepted the job, though it did not interest him greatly. With
his newly acquired sense of duty, he did his work well enough. And
yet he could never overcome a lurking sympathy for the criminals.
During his slow recovery he had begun to question, in a purely
theoretical way, the basic soundness of his society. And he was now
inclined to see in criminals men who were in reality rebelling against
the injustices of that society.

This attitude led him, sometimes, to a neglect of his strict duty as
a policeman in favor of what he felt to be the higher duty of a
humanitarian. More than once he looked the other way and released
petty criminals with nothing but a sharp warning. Soon he became
known in the underworld of Paris as a friend and silent helper of the
poor, the wretched, the small malefactors. And he found, to his surprise, that this reputation paid dividends. When a murder, a daring
robbery, or some other major crime was committed, the beggars,
vagabonds, and women of the streets came to him with information.
Unwittingly he had mobilized the underworld on the side of justice.

No one else in the police force knew the source of his information,
so that to others it seemed to border on the miraculous. Desgrez
quickly acquired the reputation in Paris, and even in Versailles, of
being a genius at detective work.

As time passed, he began to love his job. And at the same time, he
began to see it in terms of a larger framework. For he happened to
meet, and to strike up a close friendship, with a theologian, a professor at the Sorbonne who was a friend of the great Pascal. Father
Pirot spoke a great deal about the fallen state of humanity and directed Desgrez's attention to an examination of the criminal's men-
tality and its influence upon his actions. The professor was a
scholastic philosopher whose reasoning was highly intricate, though
clear and rational. He presented to Desgrez a far more complex view
of the world than Desgrez had ever arrived at in the course of his
own meditations.

One of the professor's doctrines that made a particularly deep impression upon Desgrez was the thesis that there are multiple causes
for each action. Hitherto, in all his detective work, Desgrez had tried
to find a single motive. Now he saw the possibility of probing for
unconscious motives and of working out a pattern of multiple causes.
He was fascinated by the idea; he saw an enormous horizon stretch-

ing out before him. This, he decided, was truly his lifework—to explore all the causes of crimes, not only for curiosity's sake, not only in order to solve a mystery, but in order to save (in the eternal sense) the criminal, and to protect others who might follow in his footsteps.

Desgrez also gained an intimate knowledge of the life of the nobility at the court of Saint Germain. What he saw there disturbed him; it seemed to him that the corruption of court life was one of the major secondary causes of nearly all crime. This idea became almost an obsession with him. He was doubly interested, and almost pleased, when the investigation of a crime pointed to the upper layers of society rather than to the underworld.

⋆ VI ⋆

THE SUN HAD broken through the clouds and was filling the room with a watery light that seemed to intensify the red of the geraniums on the window sill. Fresh air, the air of the Ile de France which seems to dissolve all sharpness of outline, blew softly in through the open window, and warm flecks of light played upon the bronze skin of the nymph.

The lieutenant, who had changed into high boots, and the sergeant had moved their chairs up to the open window so that they could look out upon the Place Royale with its silent equestrian in the center. The high voices of children at play rang from the street.

Desgrez warmed the large glass of cognac in the palms of his hands. Then he raised it to his nose and with a contented expression inhaled the faintly nutty bouquet of the golden-brown liquid. Cluet raised his cider in a salute to Desgrez and took a long drink. Desgrez sipped carefully. Then he placed the glass on the window sill. "When we were in the Argenteuil Regiment," he said, smiling, "we rode like the king down there, with our big feathered hats and our cuirasses, against the outward enemies of France. Rode, that is, until I found myself underneath the horse instead of on top of him, with a wound in my leg, and you pulled me out of that uncomfortable position. Today we're riding against inner enemies. And let me tell you, they're always the worst."

Desgrez picked up his glass and took another sip of cognac. "To go over it," he said, setting the glass down again, "here we have a

series of mysterious circumstances. Nobody knows whether there has
or has not been a crime. The fate of the house of Daubray is involved,
so I'll begin with Daubray the elder. Please interrupt me at any
time, Cluet, if my memory omits any fact that seems important to
you."

Cluet nodded. Desgrez sat in silence for some time. Then he
gathered up the threads of his thoughts and began: "First, then, we
have Count Antoine de Dreux Daubray, whom I'll call the elder,
since his first-born son bore the same name. He had a string of titles
and offices. Count of Offémont, Chevalier of Villiers and other places,
Councilor to His Majesty the King, Quartermaster, Prevost, Viscount,
and Police Prefect of Paris, and Chief Administrator of the Mines of
France. If memory serves, he came from Amiens and of an old family
of the official nobility—the *noblesse de robe*. He is supposed to have
married early. I don't know what his wife's maiden name was. She
died quite young, after bearing him four children."

Desgrez picked up his glass and this time emptied it. "This elder
Daubray," he went on, "accumulated a tremendous fortune in his
lifetime. Several million livres at least, I should guess. He was high
in the favor of the king, and of Cardinals Richelieu and Mazarin.
And he had an absolute faith in authority—in God's, the king's, and
in his own as well. During the difficult times of the Fronde civil war
he opposed with equal vigor the Paris Parliament's libertarian as-
pirations and the nobility's efforts to recover all their feudal prerogatives. Clearly, such a man would make many enemies. Unlucky rivals
for office, people whom he outwitted in financial matters, but especially political opponents of all groups. What's on your mind,
Cluet?"

Cluet, who had been shifting restlessly in his chair, said, "I happen
to know that the rich county of Offémont was acquired by him for
next to nothing. It formerly belonged to the Duke of Montmorency."

"I see that we're on the same scent, Cluet. The Duke of Montmorency came from a family who feel that they are older than all the
Bourbons, from the old hereditary nobility, the *noblesse de l'épée*.
At Toulouse he was beheaded, and probably Count Daubray had
something to do with that. And the Montmorencys never hesitate
where the honor of their family is at stake. . . . But to get on to the
count's character."

Desgrez paused and refilled their glasses. Looking out on the square, he continued, "I was quite fond of the old man, Cluet. He even helped me out with a loan, once, when I was in a tight spot. In spite of his harsh exterior he was fundamentally amiable, as long as you didn't oppose his ironclad political views or violate his equally rigid concept of honor. On the whole he was a Calvinist, really, a Catholic Calvinist. He was rather close to the group around Port-Royal, I believe, and divided all humanity into two categories—the damned and the blessed. Naturally he counted himself among the latter. As so many people do, he confused his indubitable success, his offices, titles, and two or three million livres, with God's blessing. Against anyone who disagreed with him he could be brutal and un-just. I can just see him sitting there in that old leather chair at police headquarters. I can see him coming every morning punctually at eight and not leaving until nightfall. Remember that stiff gray hair of his, that large, heavy mouth with the missing teeth, that hooked nose that always reminded one of a bird of prey. There was some-thing unbending about the whole man, Cluet. He never changed his mind about anything. And the worst of it was, Cluet, that in spite of all his wide experience he really did not understand human beings and had no sense of humor at all. Whenever I talked to him I felt that I was not speaking to a man but to a principle."

"I liked him all the same," Cluet murmured.

Desgrez smiled. "As I've said, so did I," he went on. "For all his faults he was a personality, the kind you hardly ever meet up with these days. He was like a character out of our old Corneille. But you know, Cluet, I doubt that our affection for him would be shared by the people he condemned to two years in the galleys for some trivial offense. I'm only trying to say that, with his rigid character and the position he held, he couldn't have helped making innumerable enemies."

Cluet nodded gloomily, but said nothing.

"Now to get to the matter in hand." Desgrez picked up the prom-issory note. "A philosopher—Montaigne, I think—has said that our death should be something all our own—'une mort toute mienne.' If I understand that aright, it means that our death should develop organically out of ourselves, with our conscious or unconscious assent. Now what about Count Daubray's death. He was an extraordinarily vigorous, active man of sixty-two who more or less enjoyed life. Sud-denly, in 1666, he fell ill during a summer vacation at his castle of

Offémont. He vomited frequently, suffered acute abdominal pain, could not retain food, and lost weight steadily. Soon his skin was white and he was only the ghost of his former self—all within a few weeks. The doctors thought he must have a stomach ulcer. They prescribed a diet for him consisting mainly of milk. But the stomach pains came more and more often, and finally he was taken to Paris, where the physicians are supposed to be more experienced and more skillful. But no matter what they tried, his sickness grew worse. Within four months of the time he first fell ill, he died, after a frightful death agony lasting for three days. Autopsy showed that he had not died of a stomach ulcer. The doctors, who had to say something, spoke of liver disease. But we could not help wondering whether the doctors were not mistaken—and whether Count Antoine de Dreux Daubray's death was not altogether inorganic, a death by violence produced by one of his numerous enemies."

Desgrez paused thoughtfully, the furrow deepening above his nose. "The strange part of it comes now, Cluet," he said at last. "Old Daubray was succeeded by his son Antoine as Count of Offémont and, by the king's favor, as chief of police as well. A man of thirty-six, happily married to a rich heiress who brought him the fine estate of Villequoy in her dowry. His character resembled his father's, though he was very much more temperate. An honorable man who saw no reason to increase his large inherited wealth, he was also less strict in office and did not possess his father's fatal gift for making so many enemies. Nevertheless, fate struck him down, too. The beginning was about three years ago, when two highwaymen on the main road to Orléans fired several pistol shots at him and his retinue. However, they missed."

"Jeannette told me about that," Cluet put in. "But perhaps they really were mere highwaymen."

"Perhaps so," Desgrez said. "But it might also be a case of a murderer changing his methods. I should think a murderer would, if he had any sense. For if the facts of two given cases are the same, it is less difficult to identify the criminal. But whatever this attack meant, the murderer—assuming there is one—returned to his old method. Two years ago Antoine de Dreux Daubray the younger sickened of the same mysterious disease that had killed his father, or of a disease diabolically like it. He died in June of that year under the same painful circumstances. Once more the doctors could not determine the cause of his death and again they spoke of an unknown liver disease, apparently hereditary in the Daubray family. That is suspicious, Cluet. But the suspicion of foul play becomes a virtual certainty, it seems to me, in the light of the third death which followed the second almost immediately."

"So Madame Daubray says," Cluet remarked. "That is the reason she is so afraid."

"Well, then, the heir of Count Antoine the younger was his brother Jacques, who had previously been Baron of Nouars. He was Councilor of the Paris Parliament and probably would have become chief of police in time—if he had been allowed the time. But he fell ill at the same time as his brother, though not so severely. His constitution seems to have been stronger than his brother's, although I've heard that this was not the case . . ."

"You know, Lieutenant Desgrez," Cluet remarked, putting down his cider glass after taking a long drink, "I saw him often at Villequoy, even after he fell ill. It's queer, he looked a little like you."

"Like me?" Desgrez exclaimed.

"Well, not so very much, I mean, but between the eyes."

"Oh, come now, Cluet, everybody looks the same between the eyes. The man was a highbrow, you know, one of the *Précieux;* he hung around the Hôtel Rambouillet and probably wrote just as bad verse as the rest of that clique. Didn't he have a pen name—or nickname, as you will?"

"They called him Orestes—whatever that means."

"Orestes?" Desgrez looked stunned. "I shouldn't be surprised if his two sisters were named Electra and Iphigenia."

Cluet gaped at the lieutenant. "I don't know about that," he said, "but I do know that his two sisters were very close to him, much closer than to the other brother."

"Hm," Desgrez murmured. "But let us go on with their brother, Baron Jacques de Nouars. He, too, died of the same strange and horrible disease as his father and brother. I think that was in the fall of 1670."

"He died on September 8, 1670, Lieutenant Desgrez. I remember the date so well because his sister-in-law, Madame Daubray, called me to Villequoy on the following day, a Sunday. She was despondent and terrified."

"Yet again, Cluet, the doctors could not determine the cause of death and again talked a lot of Latin nonsense. But this third death, which meant the end of the male line of the house of Daubray, created a stir. People talked openly of poison. Even the king, who was still mourning the death of his sister-in-law, Madame d'Orléans, demanded a report. But after a while the excitement died down. The police could never even prove murder, let alone find a murderer. But as you see I've remembered these three deaths. I was never satisfied with the way the investigation was dropped. My mind kept working on the problem. But now let's get back to the promissory note."

Desgrez picked up the paper again and read it over once more. "Have you noted the date, Cluet? This was made out on April 20, 1670, around the time that Count Antoine Daubray the younger and his brother Jacques began to suffer from the mysterious disease that had carried away their father four years before. Count Antoine died in June 1670, Baron Jacques in September. In January 1671 the thirty thousand livres were due to be paid. Now what does that look like, Cluet? I mean, if we assume that the two brothers did not die a natural death?"

"Good God, Lieutenant Desgrez!" Cluet exclaimed, jumping to his feet. "It damn well looks as though the thirty thousand livres were payment for two murders. And as though Sainte-Croix were the murderer."

"Not so fast, Cluet. We have to feel our way along step by step or we'll be getting lost. The note speaks of 'value' which the unknown debtor admits having received from Sainte-Croix. Note that the phrase is not 'for services rendered.' The person who wrote this note had an accurate mind. I feel sure that he really meant something of value—in other words, some object."

"What kind of object can he have meant? And how could we possibly find out at this late date, Lieutenant Desgrez?"

"I think we can, Cluet. This man kicked off so fast that he had no time to cover up all traces of his activities." Desgrez dropped his tattered dressing-gown to the floor and put on his coat. "Come along, Cluet," he said, carefully brushing the coat to smooth out the wrinkles. "There's no time to lose. The counterfeiters I've been after these past months were arrested this morning in the charming little village of Picpus, just as they were about to take their well-merited rest after a

hard night's work. So I'm free of that affair and can spend all my
time on this new one."

"Where are we going, Lieutenant Desgrez?"

"To the Châtelet," Desgrez replied, covering his head with a
broad-brimmed hat and carefully brushing back his long hair. "Dr.
Moreau and the apothecary will be angry. I have a hunch they will
have to work all night. And then we'll call on the widow of Sainte-
Croix in the Rue des Bernardins. And then, for all I care, we can
play taroc at the Three Lions, although I'd prefer a game of chess."

They left the room. At the threshold, Desgrez paused and smilingly
blew a kiss at the bronze nymph.

⸰ VII ⸰

ON THE MORNING of the following day Prefect of Police Michel de
la Reynie was sitting in his big office in the Châtelet like a spider
in the center of its web. Paris police headquarters was a fortress-
like building in Romanesque style with high, gray, thick walls, solars,
and three bristling towers. Its damp rooms lay in an eternal twilight,
and the entire building had an aura of the forbidden and terrifying.
Citizens of Paris who were called there entered it with hearts pounding, even when their consciences were clear.

Possibly all police chiefs look alike, since they all have the same
cares and responsibilities, whose everlasting pressure ultimately
stamps upon their faces the official physiognomy of distrust and sternness. In any case, the description Lieutenant Desgrez had given Sergeant Cluet of Count Daubray the elder also fitted Michel de la
Reynie. He was a tall man of about fifty, with a bony face and a
permanent look of feeling put upon. His round eyes were keen and
penetrating, though at certain moments there was an air of astonishment and light-shyness about them. Strands of iron-gray hair hung
down to his narrow white collar. The rest of his dress was a colorless
gray. He sat in the same leather chair from which his predecessors,
Counts Daubray, father and son, had guarded the public safety and
the morals of Paris. His fine, slender hands were laid carefully on the
leather top of the huge desk. Leaning back in the comfortable chair,
he was examining his well-manicured fingernails. He had the unpleasant habit of rarely looking at the person he was speaking to, as

though he thought his eyes too good to waste upon such unimportant specimens of humanity, or as if he were afraid his secret thoughts could be read from his gaze.

"It is true," he said in a soft but distinct voice to Desgrez and Cluet, who stood humbly, their hats held in front of them, on the other side of the long stretch of desk, "that I have to deal with more than a hundred thousand possible criminals. And I admit that your theory is logical, Lieutenant Desgrez. The dates on the note fit in very well. Too well, to my mind. For it is difficult to believe that a criminal would so piously preserve such a convincing proof of his crime. Those scoundrels are always afraid we'll use anything in writing to trip them up. No, no, Desgrez, this time you've bent the bow too far."

"It's possible that Sainte-Croix kept the note with intent to blackmail," Desgrez pointed out.

"Possible, yes," La Reynie said in a drawling voice.

"It's possible that Sainte-Croix was afraid of the unknown debtor and considered his life safe only so long as he possessed proof of a crime they had committed together."

La Reynie sighed softly and shifted his gaze from his fingernails to the dim arches of the ceiling. "Desgrez," he said almost in a whisper, "you are overburdened with imagination. We have nothing tangible at all. Nothing but this scrap of paper. You yourself say that Sainte-Croix's widow knows nothing."

"That fact increases my suspicions, sir. The note concerns too large a sum for a wife not to know about it—if it were honestly come by."

La Reynie continued to stare at the ceiling, unimpressed. "But you must admit, Desgrez, that Sainte-Croix had a very modest, almost bourgeois household in the Rue des Bernardins. You saw that yourself yesterday. One steward, two lackeys, a few maids, one sedan chair—not even a carriage. The wife seems quite decent. She says her husband had a modest inheritance and earned a small additional income by writing pious little treatises. 'The Inner Essence of Heaven and Hell,' 'The Nature of the Holy Trinity'—does that sound like a criminal's work? No, Desgrez, I'd say the man was an innocent eccentric. Nothing surprising at all that he should have been looking for the philosopher's stone on the side."

"But suppose all of it, his wife, the household, the pious tracts, even the philosopher's stone, were just a front?"

"I cannot reopen the Daubray case on sheer guesswork—if there actually was a case. We have more than enough to do as it is."

There was an awkward silence, broken by the creaking of the door. A plump, asthmatic man came panting into the room, his hair in disarray above his round face.

"Monstrous!" he cried out, gasping for breath. "We slaved all night, but it was worth it. What a discovery!"

La Reynie's eyes turned toward the man. "Well, my dear apothecary, what have you discovered? Not by any chance the philosopher's stone—we've just been talking about that."

"The philosopher's stone?" the fat apothecary asked blankly. "No, no, Your Excellency. We've discovered poison. Poison! It's incredible, frightful!"

A faint smile passed over Desgrez's face and instantly vanished.

"Control your emotions, Monsieur Sinon," La Reynie said coolly. "Tell me exactly what you have found. I suppose you were working on the contents of the chest from the Cul-de-sac des Marchands des Chevaux?"

"Quite so, Excellency. Yesterday afternoon Lieutenant Desgrez asked me to examine it at once." Sinon's shortsighted eyes blinked timidly at the chief of police. "I set to work right away, although—but that hasn't anything to do with it. Duty is duty, as I always tell my wife, and no pleasures can . . ."

"I want to know what you found," La Reynie interrupted incisively, laying stress on every word.

"Beg pardon, Excellency, I still can't grasp it. I found pulverized arsenic, antimony, calcinated vitriol, and other well-known poisons. Sixty-five pounds of mercuric sublimate alone!"

"Opium, too?" Desgrez asked.

"Yes, opium, too, and lunar caustic. But these were not the worst. Messieurs, there were also two bottles of an odorless, transparent liquid which defied all my efforts to analyze. But I discovered that this liquid was the most terrible poison of the lot. I gave a few drops to a dog and it died within minutes."

"Oh, well," La Reynie said, obviously still unimpressed, "sublimate would have had the same effect, would it not?"

"Very true, Your Excellency. But anyone could have discovered quicksilver and seen its effects upon a corpse. Not this fluid. Dr. Moreau dissected the animal at once. We examined everything—

stomach, intestines, heart, lungs, kidneys. Not a single organ showed
even the faintest trace of the poison."

The police chief's eyes grew round with astonishment. His light-
shy gaze moved rapidly along the top of the desk, as though he were
searching there for traces of the poison that the apothecary and the
doctor had been unable to find in the body of the dog. "So if a man
died from this mysterious elixir," he said softly, "no one could tell
the cause of his death—not even the most skillful physician?"

"Exactly so, Excellency," Sinon replied.

"A bullet in a man's soup," Lieutenant Desgrez murmured.

"Exactly, Lieutenant," Sinon exclaimed. "Or it could be used so if
anyone thought to. And there is enough of the stuff to make Paris a
deserted city—an arsenal of poisons."

La Reynie looked uneasily at Desgrez, then at Sinon. He bent his
gray head and tugged thoughtfully at his lower lip. Then his eyes
turned up to the ceiling again. "It is a discovery, Sinon," he declared.
"You may go now. You and Dr. Moreau will write out the report at
once. I must inform His Excellency the Minister of the Interior."

"Very well, Excellency," Sinon said, bowing low.

There was a silence in the room after the fat apothecary left. Each
of the three men pursued his own thoughts. In his mind's eye Reynie
saw his stern superior, Minister Colbert, and in vague outlines behind
Colbert he seemed to see another, remote personage—the king himself. This vision was so disturbing that La Reynie's forehead became
beaded with perspiration.

"Desgrez," he sighed, "you were right, as usual. Item upon item,
this thing is building up. But who can have been the murderer of the
Daubrays?"

"Obviously the writer of the promissory note, which presumably
was payment to Sainte-Croix for the poison used in the murders.
Therefore a man who, with or without the right to do so, calls himself a Daubray."

"Wait a moment. You say 'a man.' Why necessarily a man?"

"The signature is that of a man, not of a woman."

La Reynie picked up the note that lay on his desk. "So it seems,"
he admitted after glancing at the handwriting. Then he sighed again.
"However, we might be mistaken, Desgrez. In any case it will be wise
to keep an open mind about that. It's always possible that the writer
disguised his handwriting."

"I've thought of that, too, sir. I've considered the possibility that the younger brother, Baron Jacques de Nouars, might have been the author of this note. For example, he might have tried poisoning himself slightly in order to divert any suspicion that he was responsible for his brother's death. Suppose he underestimated the power of the poison and, in spite of his taking only a tiny portion, it carried him off, too, three months after his brother's death."

La Reynie smiled. "Very ingenious, Desgrez," he said, "but extremely improbable. That kind of justice is much too poetic, to my mind."

"To my mind also," Desgrez said, and the faintest hint of an ironic smile passed over his chiseled features. "There is also the possibility that the note was signed by a Daubray of whose existence we know nothing. Possibly an illegitimate son of the elder Daubray's. It's well established that illegitimate children almost always envy the legitimate heirs and frequently try to obtain the family fortune by fair means or foul."

La Reynie shrugged. "You knew old Daubray well," he said significantly, with a faint overtone of reproof.

"Certainly, but not when he was a young man."

"No, no, Desgrez. We're stumbling from one improbability to the next. Let us stick to what we have. You've just said something very important when you suggested that the murderer might have been aiming at the Daubray fortune. *Cui bono?* Who are the Daubray heirs?"

"The father's principal heirs were his two sons. The elder son left almost all his portion to his widow, Madame Marie-Thérèse Daubray of Villequoy. He had no children. The younger brother, Baron Jacques, was unmarried and lived with his brother. His fortune went to his two sisters, who had also received a sizable share of the inheritance upon the father's death."

"Hmm," La Reynie murmured, once again absorbed in contemplation of his fingernails. "Do you know the ladies, Desgrez?"

"No," Desgrez replied. "I know only that the elder sister married a Baron de Gobelin, whom the king elevated to marquis at the time of the wedding."

La Reynie's face became animated for the first time that morning. He literally radiated, and for a moment he looked quite human, as though the rigid mask of office had fallen to pieces. "Aha, the little

Marquise de Brinvilliers; a charming woman," he said smilingly, touching his lips with two fingers of his right hand. Then, looking significantly and gravely at Desgrez, he remarked, "And a very good mother, Desgrez—five delightful children."

Desgrez was unaffected by this sentimental appeal. "I hear the lady lives on a very extravagant scale," he said coldly.

La Reynie was obviously amused. "Why shouldn't she, Desgrez?" he asked condescendingly. "Apparently you don't know that the marquis is fantastically rich."

La Reynie walked wearily over to an open window. Outside, the Seine glistened brightly in the gentle sunlight, and from a window of a house nearby, where a maid was thumping bedclothes, a gay song floated up.

At last La Reynie turned and asked without great interest, "What about the other sister, Desgrez?"

"Mademoiselle Thérèse Daubray. Unmarried. Has been living in a Carmelite convent for some time and is said to be very pious."

"Pious?" La Reynie asked dubiously. Then he seemed to realize what he was doubtful about, for he added quickly, "Recently this Monsieur Poquelin, or Molière, as he calls himself, produced a play called *Tartuffe*. Very entertaining, like everything the fellow does, though scandalous. I must call the man down here one of these days and give him a talking to." He gave Desgrez a questioning look.

"I understand," the lieutenant said, "but Mademoiselle Daubray's piety may be quite real. She may be no Tartuffe at all."

"Possibly not." La Reynie reflected for a while, then added, "So there remains only Madame Daubray, the widow in Villequoy."

Cluet, who had been standing silent all the while like a bearded statue, suddenly burst out with deep conviction: "I'd put my hand in the fire for her. She's such a good and unhappy woman."

La Reynie could not have looked more surprised if the Sphinx had opened its mouth and spoken. But he recovered quickly. "How do you know, Cluet?" he asked.

"I've heard so much about her from Jeannette, Your Excellency," Cluet said, flushing red.

"Jeannette? Who in the world is she?"

"Jeannette is Madame Daubray's tiring-maid," Cluet replied. With embarrassment he added, "And she's been my friend for years."

"Well, who would have thought it!" La Reynie said. "Monsieur

Cluet has a little girl all his own." He winked at Desgrez, who, however, did not notice; the lieutenant was standing lost in thought, his
brow furrowed.

"It's not what you think, sir," Cluet growled. "Jeannette is my
fiancée and I would have married her long ago if Madame Daubray
weren't so confounded timid."

"About what?"

"She thinks someone wants to kill her, too, sir."

La Reynie nodded gloomily. He slowly sat down in his leather
chair again and for a long time stared at the top of his desk. Then he
cleared his throat and said softly, as though talking to himself, "That
is certainly remarkable. That is, if her fear is genuine."

Desgrez started. He looked up at the police chief and said, "It
would be even more remarkable, sir, if her fear were not genuine."

Cluet looked at each of the other men, without understanding. He
opened his mouth as if to say something again, but then thought
better of it and held his peace.

La Reynie struck the table a light blow with his fist. "You'll have
to follow this up, Desgrez," he said firmly. "Perhaps the lady knows
more than she herself realizes."

Desgrez smiled. "I have taken the liberty of anticipating Your
Excellency's decision. The horses to take us to Villequoy have been
waiting outside for half an hour."

The chief's face darkened. For a moment he seemed on the point
of flaring up. But he controlled himself, though his jaw moved as if
he were chewing some leathery substance. Finally he shrugged,
grinned, and said, "You're a thorn in my side, Desgrez. But go ahead,
and take Sergeant Cluet along with you. Since he can set hearts
fluttering at Villequoy, perhaps he can make tongues wag, too."

⌐ VIII ⌐

As LIEUTENANT DESGREZ and Sergeant Cluet rode into Villequoy at
an early hour of the afternoon, the village seemed quite deserted to
them. Like many French villages, it looked as though it were about to
be sold at auction. The gray houses, with their unglazed windows,
their doors hanging askew, and their scabby thatched roofs, would
have looked altogether uninhabited were it not for the manure piles

in front of them. These gave off a sharp ammoniac odor which indicated that they were of recent date. And the hens pecking about in the filth of the village street, as well as a flock of geese that greeted the two mounted men with angry cacklings, suggested that the village was lived in after all. But not a soul was in sight.

Desgrez and Cluet watered their horses at the well and rinsed the dust from their overheated faces. Then, leading their mounts, they turned off the village street into a lane that ran uphill between tall poplars and ended in a high iron gate. The gate was bolted. They rang a bell that hung beside it. Two large, droopy-eared bloodhounds instantly appeared and regarded the men silently, melancholy and distrust mingled in their eyes. Then an aged man shuffled up in heavy wooden shoes. His long blouse, which had apparently once been blue, was now a patchwork quilt. In his gray hands he carried a huge bunch of keys. His gaze was remarkably like that of the bloodhounds.

"Good day, Father Loren," Cluet greeted him. "Hurry up and open the gate."

"That's what I'm doing, that's what I'm doing," the old man grumbled, busying himself with the keys. "Who's the other gentleman, Sergeant Cluet?"

"Lieutenant Desgrez of the Paris police."

"Anyone can call himself a policeman. Don't know whether I ought to let him in."

"Come now, don't fuss and fret, Father Loren. Is Jeannette home?"

"She's always home, poor girl. And Madame, too. Oh Lord, it's a vale of tears, this world."

The rusty hinges of the gate screeched as if in annoyance at the arrival of strangers. Desgrez and Cluet entered the large park, which once must have looked very spruce. Now plantain weeds were growing on the paths, and the shrubs and trees were unpruned. Here and there a stone had come loose from one of the handsome terraces, or a column from a balustrade, and had fallen into the luxuriant grass. Statues of naiads and fauns were tinted green with moss. They stared with blank eyes into a wilderness which, Desgrez realized, had once been a strictly geometric garden with many charming views and prospects.

The old man had taken the reins from their hands and was now clumping along behind them in his heavy wooden shoes. He seemed to share their awareness of the garden's neglected state, for he sighed

and exclaimed, "Oh, how beautiful it was here once. Full of ladies
and gentlemen and torches and music."

Desgrez looked up at the castle itself. It was a two-story structure
with wings on either side. To judge by the architecture, it had been
built in the second half of the last century. The front of the building
and both wings were densely covered with red and white roses in
full flower. So thick were the unpruned roses that the vines covered
the dusty window panes almost entirely. This gave the castle an air
of enchantment, of being turned in upon itself. Above the main
entrance was a small turret with a gilded clock face. The face was
scarred with black marks where the gilt had slivered off, and the
hands stood still—as no doubt they had for years—at five minutes to
twelve.

Decay and disorder—it was all in a mournful minor key, Desgrez
felt. But his melancholy was momentarily banished by a joyous outcry in a high, clear feminine voice. From the doorway a dark-haired,
slender girl in a long striped dress with high bodice rushed out and
threw herself into Cluet's arms. The sergeant smiled in embarrassment as she covered his tanned face with kisses. She paused for a
moment to exclaim, "Jean, Jean, how good that you've come," and
then began kissing him again with redoubled gusto.

The old gatekeeper stood by, watching this tempestuous greeting
without the slightest expression of either interest or amusement on
his wrinkled face. Desgrez, however, bent over his horse's stirrup and
fussed with it. At last he straightened up and turned around. Cluet,
brushing his mustache with an air of mingled pride and shamefaced-
ness, came over to him and introduced the girl. "Mademoiselle
Jeannette Surfie, my fiancée," he said, and the girl took both
Desgrez's hands and shook them with vigorous cordiality.

Desgrez took a liking to her at once. It was true, he noted, that
she was neither young nor really pretty. Her mouth was somewhat
too large, her nose too long, her forehead too bony. But all these
defects formed an ensemble by no means unattractive. She had an
altogether candid face with black, lively eyes that bespoke innate
prudence and intelligence. He liked her, too, for the way she was
frank and unembarrassed toward him, without a trace of boldness or
overfamiliarity.

Jeannette led them into the big cellar kitchen and gave them a
snack and a cooling drink. Then she took them up a white winding

staircase to the second floor. She opened two doors, which she carefully shut and bolted behind her, and led them down a hall to a
spacious room with heavily barred windows that looked out over the
courtyard of the castle and the unkempt gardens. In the whitewashed but smoke-blackened fireplace a small fire was burning, in
spite of the summery heat of the day. The sharp smell of burning
wood mingled with the gentle but spicy fragrance of camomile tea
to produce the characteristic atmosphere of a sickroom. The curtains
were half drawn over the window. A heavy rug covered the floor. In
front of the fireplace, in a low armchair, sat a slender woman with
ash-blond hair above a strikingly white and frail face. She greeted
Cluet with a timid smile of recognition. Then her large gray eyes
turned a searching, almost fearful look upon Desgrez.

Jeannette introduced him. In a fluttery, hesitant voice the lady,
Madame Marie-Thérèse Daubray, asked the two visitors to sit down
in the two chairs near her. As she spoke, she kept her eyes fixed
tensely upon Desgrez. It was obvious that Madame Daubray saw
few strangers, and was upset by them.

Desgrez sat down and began to explain the purpose of their visit.
He spoke in a light conversational tone, with a restraint and un-
emotionality that perfectly suited the muted atmosphere of the room
and the woman's air of timidity. Like a clever fisherman dangling
his bait cautiously before a fish that scares easily, Desgrez limited
himself to unfinished sentences and veiled hints. To his satisfaction,
he soon saw the woman's expression of weary distaste vanish. She
became animated; her eyes filled with concern. At last I have her,
Desgrez thought, and he said, "Madame, I know very well how
painful it must be to you to speak of these things. But we are firmly
convinced that we can solve this case only if you help us. Naturally
we take it for granted that you, too, want very much to help find the
criminal. That is why I have come here to speak with you."

Madame Daubrey stared at him wide-eyed. "What can I do?" she
said in despair. "I have thought and thought about it all these past
two years. Often I awaken in the dead of night, sit up in bed with
my heart standing still, and ask myself, What was that? But I hear
only the trees rustling in the garden. There is no answer. And I lie
down again, relieved to hear my Jeannette's quiet breathing as she
sleeps soundly beside me. I have no idea who the criminal could have
been. But I do know one thing—the murders were political. Both my

husband and his father were strong Royalists. And as you know, during the days of the Cardinal and the Fronde, they sometimes had to employ measures that could be called harsh."

"That's putting it mildly," Cluet growled under his breath.

Madame Daubray half rose from her seat and agitatedly stretched her frail, bloodless hands toward the dying fire on the hearth. "I know that some terrible enemy has sworn to destroy our whole family. Silently, swiftly, out of the darkness, he strikes down one victim after the next." She sank back into the chair, and her hands rested, quivering like two white mice, upon the lap of her gray gown.

Jeannette leaned over the high back of the chair. "Madame, your heart," she whispered anxiously. "Remember the doctor said . . ."

But Madame Daubray paid no attention. "All the men have already been murdered," she moaned. "Now our turn has come. Oh, I feel it, we women will not escape our fate either. Does it help for me to wall myself in? What good will it do my sister-in-law to shut herself away in a convent? There is always a cranny, some unforeseen gap, through which the murderer will reach us." Exhausted, Madame Daubray let her head sink back and her eyelids droop shut, so that her white, wasted face resembled a death mask.

Silence filled the room. Desgrez's eyes wandered thoughtfully about and paused to study a rather large picture hanging on the wall opposite the fireplace. It showed two unclad young women, one dark-haired and mischievous, the other serious and blond, standing in a large tub. In the background several servant girls were busy with jugs of water and towels. The two bathers stood side by side, their tender young faces looking into the room. The dark-haired girl was smiling and tentatively touching the nipple of the blond girl's breast with her slender fingers.

Desgrez smiled, but his face grew grave at once as he turned his eyes toward Madame Daubray and asked, "Madame, you spoke of your sister-in-law, Mademoiselle Daubray. But your husband's other sister does not seem to share your fears. Or does she?"

"Oh, Marie-Madeleine," Madame Daubray sighed, opening her eyes. Her tormented features relaxed and she smiled involuntarily. "She's just a child, Lieutenant Desgrez. Impossible to take her seriously, or for her to take anything seriously. She dances and plays all night long, whenever she's not traveling around on a jaunt as she happens to be doing right now. She's always been a frivolous favorite

of society. Oh, you're right, Marie-Madeleine doesn't know the meaning of fear." Madame Daubray paused, then added softly, "It's
strange, it's hard for me to imagine anything ever happening to her,
and yet . . ."

Desgrez was thinking hard; he seemed to go on listening after
Madame Daubray had stopped speaking, as if he wanted to hear her
unspoken thoughts. Suddenly he asked, "Pardon me, madame, can
you tell me since when your sister-in-law—I mean Mademoiselle
Daubray—has been living in the convent?"

Madame Daubray sighed. "Poor Thérèse, she was once so gay. But
ever since her father died she has been a changed soul. She entered
the convent just after his death—that would make it six years ago."

"I suppose she had been very close to him," Desgrez murmured.

"Oh yes. Though he was actually fonder of Marie-Madeleine—the
Marquise, that is. She was his darling."

"But Madame la Marquise went on living in the world," Desgrez
said.

"Well, she has her children to care for. And then—she has never
been the sort of person to make a show of her feelings."

They fell silent for a while. Then Desgrez shook himself, took the
promissory note from his pocket, and handed it to Madame Daubray.
"This note recently fell into the hands of the police," he said. "Do you
recognize the signature as your brother-in-law's, madame?"

Madame Daubray's fear-filled eyes flickered uneasily across the
paper. "What is this?" she whispered. "Sainte-Croix? I've never heard
the name. Thirty thousand livres?" She seemed feebler than before
as she gave the note back to Desgrez, saying, "No, it is not the
baron's signature. He wrote a finer, more intellectual hand. The note
must be a forgery."

Cluet gave a sigh. If Desgrez shared his disappointment, he did
not show it. "Doesn't the writing seem familiar to you in any way,
madame? Please think the matter over carefully, won't you? It is
very, very important."

Again Madame Daubray took the note, and this time she studied
it carefully for a long while. The fine blue veins on her white temples
stood out with the effort of thought. "I don't know," she said hesitantly. "The writing does seem familiar to me after all. Oh, now I
know. My father-in-law would write something like this when he
was excited."

"You're quite right, madame," Desgrez said, "the writing has some resemblance to your father-in-law's hand. But the count could not have written the note, for the date is, as you must have noticed, April 20, 1670, three and a half years after Count Daubray's death."

"It's all so dreadful," Madame Daubray whispered wearily, and from the exhausted look in her eyes it was evident that she wished her visitors would go and leave her alone with her fear and her sorrow. But Desgrez had evidently made up his mind to get out of her all the information she possessed. He gave no sign of being prepared to leave. After pocketing the note again, he sat for a while in silence and then began circumspectly to bring up the subject of the manner in which the two Daubray brothers had died. He proceeded with great delicacy, with something of the air of a man groping about in total darkness in a strange room. Jeannette answered almost all of his low-voiced questions; she stood all the while—a guardian angel in a maid's uniform—behind her sick mistress's chair. From Jeannette, Desgrez learned that both Daubrays had first fallen ill after the Easter feast two years before, and that the immediate cause of their illness seemed to have been a chicken pie of which the elder brother had eaten more than the younger. "It was my husband's favorite dish," Madame Daubray threw in mournfully. Then she again dropped into silence and let Jeannette do the replying.

"Did any of the other guests have some of the chicken pie?" Desgrez asked.

"I can't say for sure," Jeannette answered. "I was coming in and out, serving the ladies, and I didn't stay in the dining room until Monsieur le Comte suddenly threw up, and shortly afterward his brother, Monsieur le Baron, did the same."

"You don't know who served the pie, Jeannette?"

"No, sir. It was a large party. There were at least twenty people dining and six lackeys serving."

"Well, it's customary for the master of a house to have his own particular servant who attends exclusively to him, or almost exclusively. Wasn't that the case here, Jeannette?"

"Oh yes, sir. La Chaussée, who was really Monsieur le Baron's valet, usually served both gentlemen to give Couthé, the count's old valet, a chance to rest. But I remember distinctly that La Chaussée was not in the dining room and came rushing in when both gentlemen were lying on the floor, writhing with frightful cramps.

He helped carry them to their bedrooms and then prepared hot compresses for them."

"Oh yes, the good fellow," Madame Daubray sighed; in spite of her lethargy she had evidently been following the conversation. "He stayed up all night tending the gentlemen and even prayed with them for their quick recovery."

"He prayed?" Desgrez murmured in thoughtful astonishment, as if the words stirred up some memory. An ironic smile flickered across his face. "How is it, Jeannette," he asked, "that you happen to remember so distinctly La Chaussée's absence from the room?"

Jeannette's candid face flushed. "Because I was glad not to have to see him," she snapped. "I never could stand the ugly fellow."

"How unjust of you, Jeannette!" Madame Daubray cried, offended. "You know he cared for the two gentlemen with such patience and devotion until the end. I really don't know what I would have done without him." In a lower voice she added, "You know, Jeannette, that the count left him a hundred livres for his faithful services. And I will say I have rarely given anyone money with greater satisfaction."

Jeannette's face grew even pinker. She shrugged. "Still and all," she persisted, "that mournful expression and that flat face and pushed-in nose of his—he was disgusting."

"I will admit he was no beauty," Madame Daubray said. "But you cannot judge people by their outward appearance, my child. At any rate I'm very sorry to this day that I turned the poor fellow away when he asked whether he might work for me. But I didn't want to be reminded by his presence of all the horrors I had been through. That was unjust of me."

Desgrez's attention sharpened. "So after the death of your husband and your brother-in-law the man asked for a job with you?" he asked with keen interest.

"For the post of gardener. Oh, I certainly could have used him, Lieutenant Desgrez. You've seen what a state the garden is in. When I refused him, he was terribly downcast. Why, the poor fellow actually wept."

"Well, I must say, Jeannette, you've let your feelings get the better of you," Desgrez observed with a sly smile. "Unless you have better reasons for your dislike than this La Chaussée's unprepossessing appearance."

Cluet went up to Jeannette as though to shield his sweetheart against the combined reproaches of Madame Daubray and Desgrez. But the girl looked boldly at Desgrez and said, "That's just it, Lieutenant Desgrez, I do have better reasons—much better reasons." She turned to her mistress. "Madame, I can't forget that story of the glass of wine."

"Now, Jeannette," Madame Daubray said, shaking her head, "that was all explained long ago."

"Nevertheless," Desgrez said rapidly, "perhaps you will be so good, madame, as to tell us this story Jeannette refers to."

"Why, it's scarcely worth the trouble. But very well, if you think it can help you, Lieutenant Desgrez. I myself have it only from hearsay, since I was in Paris at the time. One day my husband asked for a glass of wine. La Chaussée brought it to him. But as soon as my husband touched it to his lips, he shouted, 'What the devil have you brought me here? The stuff tastes terrible.' "

" 'Like poison!' Monsieur said," Jeannette put in quickly.

"Oh, nonsense," Madame Daubray exclaimed uneasily. "It turned out that Couthé, our groom of the chamber, had taken medicine a little while before and had neglected to wash his glass. La Chaussée, always eager to serve the master the moment something was asked of him, had in his haste taken this glass and served the wine in it. My husband often used to laugh about the incident."

"Laugh?" Desgrez asked tensely. "What was so funny about it?"

"Why you see, Lieutenant Desgrez," Madame Daubray said with a patient smile, "as soon as the poor fellow saw what he had done by mistake, he snatched the glass out of my husband's hand with a really excessive expression of horror, poured the contents into the fireplace, and rushed off to the kitchen as though the devil himself were after him, to get a new glass."

Madame Daubray's smile froze on her face. She had been looking at Lieutenant Desgrez, expecting him to join in her appreciation of the ridiculousness of the scene. But the lieutenant was sitting bolt-upright and staring at her with a cold stiffness that apparently struck the lady as extremely coarse and impolite. Desgrez turned his eyes away, glanced at the barred windows as if inspecting their security, and said lightly, "I admire your husband's sense of humor, madame, but I must confess I cannot share it."

"Oh, it's just because you have never met La Chaussée," Madame Daubray declared.

"We shall do our best to make his acquaintance," Desgrez replied. And after a pause, he added, "I think it will prove worthwhile." "Damn well should," Cluet muttered. "I think so, too."

Madame Daubray rose, sighing. Apparently the others' refusal to share her opinion had exhausted rather than offended her. Her thick, ash-blond hair seemed almost too heavy for her slender neck and her thin, suffering face with its sunken temples. She swayed unsteadily for a moment, and Jeannette hastened to support her with her strong arms. "Thank you, my child," the lady breathed softly. "And thank you, too, gentlemen, for your patience. But I must withdraw now. You can see how unwell I am."

Cluet stood embarrassed. Desgrez, too, had risen. "Just one more question, please," he said. "Permit me, madame."

"If you must," Madame Daubray sighed reproachfully.

"Do you happen to know who recommended La Chaussée when he entered your husband's service? Had he by any chance previously been in the service of your father-in-law?"

"I understand what you are getting at, Lieutenant Desgrez," Madame Daubray said, smiling gloomily as, leaning on Jeannette, she turned toward the door to her bedroom. "But you are quite mistaken. La Chaussée did not wait upon my father-in-law or tend him in his last illness. He died in the arms of his daughter—and she is, I may add, the most affectionate daughter any father ever had."

To Jeannette's delight, Desgrez and Cluet remained overnight in Villequoy. They stayed up till ten over a bottle of excellent Burgundy, playing taroc under the arched ceiling of the big whitewashed basement kitchen. In the course of the evening they made the acquaintance of Monsieur Couthé, the deceased count's former groom of the chamber. To Couthé's surprise the lieutenant questioned him very closely about his health during the past years. But Couthé could not recall ever having been sick, with the exception of an occasional cold.

✦ IX ✦

THE HUNT FOR La Chaussée began the following day. Desgrez had his men comb lists of the names of the servants of noble houses, for he assumed that La Chaussée would have stuck to his occupation and would probably have found a job in some other noble family. But these efforts brought no results. Nor was an interrogation of Sainte-Croix's widow any more fruitful. Madame Sainte-Croix could not recall anybody by the name of La Chaussée, although she gave the names of many of the alchemist's former servants. Desgrez made a point of questioning each one of them himself.

None of the servants knew anything about La Chaussée. But in the course of questioning them Desgrez learned that Sainte-Croix had sent messengers with letters to many families, among them some of the greatest in the land. Among Sainte-Croix's correspondents were noblemen and noblewomen whose homes were in the vicinity of the Place Royale and the Marais, and others who lived in Saint Germain and even in Versailles—all persons who must be counted among the cream of society. But the alchemist's acquaintances were not only of the nobility. He had also been in touch with several members of the wealthy bourgeoisie and even with some persons of the higher clergy. Among the latter were Monsieur Pennautier, Farmer-General of Taxation of the French Clergy, whose enormous wealth naturally aroused questions in the lieutenant's mind as to Sainte-Croix's dealings with him, and Canon Dulong of Notre Dame, reputedly a confidant of the Archbishop of Nantes. Desgrez suddenly recalled that Monsieur Pennautier and Deacon Dulong had, according to Cluet, been represented by two men during the inventory at the house on the Cul-de-sac des Marchands des Chevaux.

The more Desgrez analyzed the far-flung connections of Sainte-Croix, the more important the Daubray case looked to him. He was convinced that if he could solve it, it would explain many of the inexplicable events of recent years. He thought, and he did not hesitate to express his conviction to a still skeptical Michel de la Reynie, that the final result would be the revelation of a ghastly conspiracy in which none of the plotters had known about the others and in which Sainte-Croix alone had held all the threads in his hand. He expected to uncover a sinister picture of a general collapse of morals and piety which was threatening the very existence of the French nation.

"You see everything far too darkly, Desgrez," the police chief said when Desgrez outlined this picture for him. "Murders have always happened. They are as old as the history of mankind. But the State has always survived. It is indestructible."

"I doubt that," Desgrez replied. "There has been more than one chaotic period in history when states collapsed. In fact, history is nothing more than a succession of breakdowns out of which people have emerged to build new orders by fearful efforts. But it isn't so much this single concrete case, this Daubray case, that worries me. Rather it is, if I may put it that way, the aura of this case, the atmosphere surrounding it. There is a kind of smell and spirit of crime and depravity that has spread from the Cul-de-sac des Marchands des Chevaux over the whole city and reached into the houses of the bourgeoisie and the nobles alike, and even into the churches. That is how it strikes me, at any rate, as day after day I keep adding new names to the list of this poison-manufacturer's correspondents. For all I know, those people may have been his customers!"

Around this time—it was getting on toward the end of October, and violent gusts of autumn wind were attacking the orphaned leaves of the poplar trees on the banks of the Seine—a gaunt little man of indefinable age appeared at the Châtelet one evening and asked whether His Majesty's sergeant of police, Monsieur Cluet, would have, as he put it, the gracious condescension to see him.

Cluet was annoyed. He was just about to knock off for the day, and he rudely interrupted the little man's servile bows and pointed out how late it was. "What do you want?" he grunted gruffly.

The creature—he seemed scarcely to deserve the name of man—looked as though his own existence were a great burden to him. He seemed to understand quite well that his appearance was no pleasure to the stern sergeant. He stammered repeated apologies and pleas for forbearance. But he managed to inform Cluet that he was seeking the protection of the police in an urgent matter having to do with money.

"What do you mean, urgent!" Cluet snapped at him. The visitor retreated toward the door with a frightened expression. The little fellow's fright placated the irritated sergeant. "Kindly express yourself more clearly," Cluet said somewhat less gruffly, in a voice that had something of the quality of a fading thunderstorm. "What kind of money matter is it?"

"You see, I gave my money to somebody to keep for me," the dwarf began explaining.

"You look just the sort who would," Cluet interrupted. "You're a fool."

"Begging your pardon, sir," the fellow whispered, coming closer to Cluet again, "how could I guess that the gentleman—a very fine gentleman he was—would so suddenly take leave of this world? Of course we're all in the hands of God, I always say, but still he kicked off so fast I didn't know what to make of it. Just a while before, he'd said to me, 'Come now, Hamelin, give me your money. There are so many bad people today and you're such a trustful soul. I'll keep your money and it will be safe.' "

"Sounds to me like a fine crook," Cluet boomed. "How much money was it?"

"Begging your leave, sir, about three hundred livres."

"Well, now, that's a pretty sizable wad," Cluet exclaimed, scrutinizing the little man from top to toe. "How did you ever make so much?"

"Begging your leave, sir, it's the fruit of long toil. I was in service with the gentleman for many years. He was very generous and the blessing of God rested on the money, too. Commend your ways to the Lord, I always say. And now it's all gone to pot. I cursed fate and finally I couldn't stand it any longer and I talked to Martin about it—you know Martin, don't you, officer?"

"Martin? Of the Rue de la Bûcherie? The one who works for some barber? Do you mean him?"

"The very same, officer. But begging your leave, sir, he works for Monsieur Gaussin in the Rue des Lions—a most elegant establishment, sir. He is court barber to His Majesty—and by his gracious condescension has let me live in his house."

"Oh, I see now. Martin sent you to me?"

"Yes, sir. He sends his regards and he said you would straighten everything out if it isn't too late."

"Hmm," Cluet growled, pleased that he still enjoyed a good reputation in the Quartier Latin. "You say the man who's keeping your three hundred livres is dead? Well then, there's nothing you can do but apply to the Probate Court."

The little fellow gave Cluet a mournful look out of his watery blue eyes and said sadly, "But you see, Sergeant, there's some kind of foolish business. You see, the police have placed everything under seal. You see, there's supposed to be some kind of trouble and mess."

Cluet smiled. "Hm," he said, "that often happens in inheritance cases. But if that's the state of affairs, you have a better chance to get your money. Put in a petition."

"A petition! Oh my Lord, that's awful."

"Why so? There's nothing to it."

"Oh, nothing to it for you, officer. You deal with that kind of legal affair all the time. But not people like me." He looked at Cluet with an air of helpless despair.

Cluet went over to his desk, smoothed out a sheet of paper that lay there, and dipped a pen into the inkwell. "Well, I won't make it hard for you," he growled good-naturedly. "We'll fix it up one way or the other. All right. First of all, what's your name?"

"Oh, a thousand thanks, officer, for your exceptional kindness. My name is Jean Hamelin."

Cluet's pen scratched slowly over the paper. Writing was not easy for him; practicing it was one of the great efforts he made for the sake of his attachment to Desgrez. "And where do you live?" he asked.

"With Monsieur Gaussin, if you please, sir, in the Rue des Lions."

"Oh yes, you told me that before," Cluet said, and he awkwardly began writing down the address.

"Begging your pardon, sir, it just occurs to me . . ."

"Don't keep interrupting me, man," Cluet said angrily, and went on writing. "What is it now?"

"Begging your pardon, sir, but I'm also called La Chaussée. I only wanted to call the fact to your attention, sir. Maybe it's important."

There was a dead silence in the room. Cluet stood numbly at his desk, pen in hand. "What's that?" he demanded in a funereal voice. "Your name is La Chaussée?"

The other man looked at the sergeant with slight uneasiness. "Yes," he said in a placating voice. "That is to say, it isn't my real name, Your Honor. It's sort of a nickname."

There was another silence. Then Cluet placed the pen back into the inkwell—carefully and quietly, as if he were afraid of frightening off some timid game animal. "What was the name of the man you gave the money to?" he asked.

"Monsieur de Sainte-Croix. A very fine gentleman. He lived in the Rue des Bernardins."

Cluet gave an almost imperceptible start, and said softly, "Sit down please. One moment. We have something here for you."

"For me?" La Chaussée asked in amazement. "What can it be?"

"You'll see. Just sit down."

La Chaussée sat down on the edge of a chair, as though he did not feel himself important enough to take up the whole of a seat. Cluet opened a door and, without taking his eyes from his visitor, called Lieutenant Desgrez. The lieutenant's slim figure appeared in the doorway almost at once. "What is it, Cluet?" he asked, yawning.

"There! We have him!" Cluet cried triumphantly, pointing to the seated man.

"Whom?" the lieutenant asked in surprise.

"La Chaussée. There he is."

Without further word, Desgrez went over to where La Chaussée was perched on the chair. First he stared squarely into the little man's face. Then he stepped to one side and studied La Chaussée's profile with equal intentness. "Disappointing," he said at last. "We always imagine these rascals are more important-looking than they turn out to be. Where did you pick him up, Cluet?"

"Didn't pick him up at all. The fellow walked right in here. Into police headquarters, Lieutenant Desgrez—imagine that! Claiming a whole lot of money that he says Sainte-Croix owed him."

"Aha!" Desgrez said with satisfaction. He whistled under his breath. "So that's the way the wind is blowing."

La Chaussée had kept looking from Desgrez to Cluet with growing uneasiness. He half stood up and said in an uncertain voice that rose almost to a squeak, "What is all this about, gentlemen? Please don't play jokes on me."

"How large an amount of money was it?" Desgrez asked, paying no attention to La Chaussée's protest.

"Three hundred livres," Cluet replied.

"Well, now, who would think of it," Desgrez said. "That's a nice, tidy little sum. My respects."

La Chaussée had finally risen to his feet. "That's my hard-earned money," he said, impudence and fear contending in his voice. "I'm only asking for what's coming to me. I've got a right to do that, don't I?"

Cluet made a threatening move toward him and suddenly gave a roar that rattled the windowpanes. "Sit down!" he shouted. "And speak only when the lieutenant questions you."

La Chaussée sagged into the chair and stayed there.

Desgrez walked lithely, almost soundlessly, back and forth in the room. La Chaussée's terrified eyes followed his footsteps. He shrank away as Desgrez came up to him and spoke in a conversational, almost friendly tone of voice: "Well, Monsieur la Chaussée, you will admit that three hundred livres is a very pretty sum. Or don't you think so?"

"Oh, yes, of course, certainly. But I saved it up bit by bit over many long years of hard work. Sou by sou, Lieutenant. And with the help of God. My masters were always kind to me. Monsieur de Sainte-Croix paid me really princely wages at the last."

"Do you think so?" the lieutenant asked with barely perceptible irony in his voice. "Do you think you were well paid for the kind of work you did?"

"Why yes, it's true there was a great deal to do," La Chaussée replied, perplexed. "All the sweeping up. And the cleaning. Everything had to be kept clean as a whistle." He looked up questioningly at the standing lieutenant.

Desgrez was silent for a moment. He uttered a low sigh, and then he said, "I don't mean that sort of work. I mean the work you did for Monsieur de Sainte-Croix outside his home. In Villequoy, for example."

La Chaussée bounced up, then collapsed into the chair again. "What's that? What do you mean?" he whispered hoarsely.

Desgrez studied him, frowning. Then he smiled. "Anyway, Villequoy is quite a charming place, isn't it?" he said chattily. "Such an idyllic garden, especially in its present state of neglect. I was there recently. Oh yes, I've just remembered, I wanted to give you an old friend's regards. You remember the servant Couthé, don't you? We talked a great deal about you. But it's too bad, the good fellow is so old now and I'm afraid his memory is going. He can't remember ever having been sick." Desgrez paused. "And, poor man, he doesn't remember anything at all about a wine glass that he supposedly drank medicine from."

La Chaussée sprang to his feet. "I'm innocent!" he cried in terror. "I'm innocent, I tell you. That was an accident, that business with the wine."

Desgrez stepped back away from him, his face full of disgust. But the expression vanished immediately, and he said in an icy voice, "La Chaussée, I arrest you in the name of the king. You are charged

with having brought about the deaths by poison of Count Antoine
Daubray and Baron Jacques de Nouars."

"Heaven help me!" La Chaussée screamed, his fingers curled and
pressed against his temples. "I'm innocent, wholly innocent. I swear
it by the Mother of God!" He burst into sobs.

Desgrez watched the man's actions with repugnance. At last he
turned to Cluet and ordered, "Take him off to the Conciergerie.
Chains, darkness—and solitary confinement, of course. Tomorrow
we'll loosen his tongue."

X

LA CHAUSSÉE steadfastly refused to admit anything. But the suspicions against Baron Daubray's former valet seemed well founded.
The police therefore did not hesitate to subject him to the first degrees of torture.

In the cellar of the Conciergerie, where the walls always dripped
with water that seeped through from the nearby Seine, La Chaussée
was stripped of his clothes. Heavy iron weights were attached to his
feet, and he was fastened by his hands to a kind of overhead jack
and drawn into the air. The work was done by the henchmen of
Maître Guillaume, a youngish man distinctly amiable in appearance.
He was generally known as le Monsieur de Paris and held the office
of executioner, which was hereditary in his family.

In front of the victim stood Monsieur de Mandat, councilor of the
Paris Parliament, Michel de la Reynie, and Lieutenant Desgrez. At
a candlelit desk sat a scribe ready to record the defendant's confession.

La Chaussée's gaunt white body with its thin, protruding ribs was
a pitiable sight. As he hung by his hands he groaned, but said nothing.
Guillaume jerked his thumb at a basin of glowing coals. One of the
henchmen thrust several pairs of tongs into the basin. Guillaume
stepped up to the helpless man. La Chaussée's goggling watery eyes
stared agonized at the executioner. Guillaume pointed the index finger of his right hand meaningfully at the basin, where the tongs were
beginning to glow as red as the coals. Then, with a teasing smile,
he poked the same index finger into La Chaussée's side. La Chaus-

sée screamed in pain, for the force of the little push had been skillfully measured and had thrown his arm out of joint.

"Well, my friend," Maître Guillaume said, "are we willing to speak
up now? Or will we have to pinch the baby first?"

"Everything!" La Chaussée screamed. "I'll tell everything."

Maître Guillaume bowed to the gentlemen present and gestured,
with a graceful movement of his arm, at the screaming man to indicate that his work was finished, at least for the present. The defendant
was theirs for questioning. He stepped back and loosened a hook on
the wall. With a rattle of chains La Chaussée fell to the damp stone
pavement.

The henchmen removed the heavy weights from La Chaussée's
feet and half led, half carried the staggering wretch up to the three
gentlemen. Maître Guillaume sat down on a water barrel standing
nearby, lit his pipe, and listened with attentive interest to the interrogation—ready at any moment to intervene again if it should prove
necessary.

Questioned by Councilor Mandat, La Chaussée confessed that he
had been ordered by Sainte-Croix to kill the two Daubrays. He had,
he said, mixed the poison beforehand, while he was in the kitchen,
into the stuffing with which the chicken pie was to be filled. Then,
pretending that he did not feel well, he had stayed away from the
dining room in order to divert possible suspicion from himself.

Mandat asked the nature of the poison. La Chaussée said there
had been three different substances, a white powder, a pink powder,
and a colorless liquid. What sort of poisons they were, he did not
know. He was asked about antidotes and said Sainte-Croix had told
him he should take theriac or milk in case he poisoned himself by
mistake.

"La Chaussée," Mandat asked, "did you have any personal reason
for desiring the deaths of the Daubray brothers?"

"No, Your Excellency," La Chaussée sobbed. "The gentlemen
were always very good to me and treated me like one of the family."
He began to weep loudly. "I swear I did it unwillingly. God forgive
me!"

"What motive did Sainte-Croix have for the murders?"

"I don't know, I really don't know. He only said to me that the
Daubray family had done him hurt." La Chaussée threw a terrified

glance at Maître Guillaume, who had taken his clay pipe from his
mouth and was glaring threateningly at him.

"What was your payment, La Chaussée?"

"Three hundred livres, Your Excellency. But as I said, I gave it
back to Sainte-Croix. Oh, my God!"

"How did you ever get the position in Villequoy?"

"Sainte-Croix—he sent me to the baron, with a letter of recom-
mendation, Your Excellency."

"What! Was that letter written by Sainte-Croix?"

"I do not know, Your Excellency, the letter was sealed."

The interrogation went on in this fashion, and the questioners had
the feeling that the wretch was telling the truth. It was in any case
to his own interest not to conceal anything. He was certain to be
condemned to death and could only hope that a complete confession
would result in his being granted an easier death. Accordingly, he
admitted that he had also planned to poison Madame Daubray. In
order to accomplish this he had applied for the post of gardener at
Villequoy.

La Chaussée's confession created a tremendous sensation in Paris,
and in Versailles the excitement was even greater. The Parliament
of Paris took the matter in hand, and the worthy gentlemen in their
sweeping red robes and flowing white wigs condemned the murderer
to the cruel and by now rarely used death on the wheel. They were
fully conscious of their duty and wanted, as they said, to provide a
spectacular and frightful example of punishment such as Paris had
not witnessed since the terrible execution of Ravaillac, the murderer
of Henry IV. According to the verdict, La Chaussée was a "parricide"
because his innocent victims had been masters whose relation to him
was one of paternal kindliness.

The populace hailed the verdict of the Parliament of Paris. Had
there been merely a bloody murder, the man in the street might
have passed it over with a shrug and gone about his business. The
fact that poison had been used was what aroused so much horror.
And a poison that apparently defied detection. The Daubray case
was talked about everywhere, in the *estaminets*, the market halls,
in offices and monasteries. In the hovels of the poor as well as the
mansions of the bourgeoisie and the palaces of the nobility, wherever people talked together, they brought up the death of some rela-

tive or friend—deaths which had seemed inexplicable at the time.
Now the cause seemed obvious to all. And what assurance did a man
have that the same fate might not strike him down tomorrow? For
everybody had enemies and rivals, even though he might not be
aware of them.

A kind of panic spread over Paris. Innkeepers and lemonade-
peddlers complained that their business was falling off. Everybody
suspected poison in every bite of food and every drink; everybody
saw a possible poisoner in everybody else. This exaggerated fear was
intensified by the fact that the poisoning of the two Daubrays had
only been discovered two years after the deed—and then only by
sheer chance, as a result of Sainte-Croix's death under strange circumstances and Desgrez's persistence. Lieutenant Desgrez's name
was on everyone's lips, of course.

The king, the glorious king in Versailles, was sensitive to the mood
of his people. The public demoralization became a problem of state.
Accordingly the king ordered his Minister, Colbert, to subject the
criminal, La Chaussée, to the severest degrees of torture, to question
him again, and then have him executed at once so that—as he put it
—this carrion whose presence was stinking up all Paris could be
thrown into the offal pit.

This time Maître Guillaume had a free hand, and he proved himself a master of his trade. It was as though all the demons of hell that
Bosch and Breughel had dreamed up were let loose upon La Chaussée in the cellar of the Conciergerie. The victim was filled with water
through a funnel until he almost burst. The nails were pulled from
his fingers and toes. His body was stretched until it nearly snapped,
then crushed together again. He was pinched with white-hot tongs
on the most sensitive parts of his body. But perhaps Maître Guillaume, whose amiable look never deserted him throughout the torture, overreached himself in ingenuity and art. For even physical
pain has its limits. La Chaussée, who had at first uttered piercing
screams, grew quieter and quieter.

Lying on his cot—for he could no longer stand—he whispered in a
hoarse, distorted voice the few facts he had withheld. But the tor-
turers' efforts had scarcely been worth the trouble. He could add
little to what he had already confessed.

He had murdered only the Daubray brothers. If other persons had
been killed by Sainte-Croix's poisons, he could not say who were

the murderers. All he knew was that Sainte-Croix had sent him to many houses to deliver letters. He had also received letters, which, however, he always turned over to his master unopened.

Desgrez, who was conducting the interrogation, pricked up his ears at this. These were details he had received from the other former servants of Sainte-Croix.

Once again the names of Pennautier and Canon Dulong came up. La Chaussée mentioned many great names—the Prince of Conti, of royal blood; Turenne, Marshal of France; Olympia Mancini, a niece of the late Cardinal Mazarin; the Duc de Richelieu; Madame de la Fayette, the famous novelist and friend of the witty Duc de la Rochefoucauld; Baron de Gobelin, the heir of the well-known tapestry manufacturers; and Marquis de Brinvilliers.

Desgrez started. "That's strange," he said to Michel de la Reynie.

"But my dear Desgrez," the police chief replied, "you can't imagine that all these wealthy and powerful persons were in a conspiracy with that low creature."

"No," Desgrez said, "but it upsets me to hear that the Marquis de Brinvilliers was one of the correspondents."

"Good Lord, Desgrez! You've heard enough to know that that fawning rotter toadied up to everybody in France who had money or a name. Probably he tried to get around me, too. Only I can't remember."

Desgrez smiled. "That is quite possible," he said. "But the Brinvilliers are another matter."

"Why? Why should they be?"

"The Brinvilliers are closely related to the Daubrays."

"You're incorrigible, Desgrez," La Reynie said, shaking his head. "But ask him anyway."

"La Chaussée," Desgrez said, bending down to the groaning man's ear, "did you go to the Marquis de Brinvilliers's often?"

"Yes, very—very often," La Chaussée moaned almost inaudibly. "Madame la Marquise—a wonderful woman—always most kind to me. She gave me wine. . . . Oh, if she had known. . . . Me, her brothers' murderer."

"So she knew nothing?"

"No. Sainte-Croix said to me, he said, 'Be especially careful with the marquis and the marquise—they know nothing and must not suspect.'"

"Well, there you have it—just as I thought," La Reynie remarked with a smile of superiority.

If Desgrez was disappointed, he did not show it. He stared thoughtfully into space.

Then, suddenly, he bent down to La Chaussée again. "Listen, La Chaussée," he said urgently, "did you also go to Mademoiselle Daubray—to Madame de Brinvilliers's sister, I mean?"

"Yes," the wretch groaned, "quite often . . . but then . . . she was never so kind."

"Did Sainte-Croix warn you against her also? Tell me, La Chaussée."

"Warn me? No, he didn't . . . he never did, oh, God . . . but he said something else."

La Chaussée was losing consciousness fast. Desgrez touched him gently. "What did Sainte-Croix say?" he asked. "Try to remember, La Chaussée. It is very important."

"He . . . he said . . . she was an heiress . . . worth a great deal. He said . . . the whole fortune of the Daubrays might be hers in the end . . ." He gave a deep sigh and his eyes dulled.

Desgrez looked up, but La Reynie had moved away and was talking quietly to Councilor de Mandat in a corner.

Shortly afterward the rough hands of the hangman's assistants pulled La Chaussée from the cot and dragged him up the stairs into the light of day. In the yard of the Conciergerie the two-wheeled tumbril was ready for him. Amid the howls and menacing shouts of vast crowds, who reluctantly opened a narrow lane for the cart, La Chaussée was driven across the Pont Notre Dame to the Place Grève. There, beneath the many towers of the Hôtel de Ville, the henchmen broke the bones of his arms and legs with a heavy wooden mallet and Maître Guillaume, dressed all in red, broke him upon the wheel. He died after four hours, without having uttered another sound.

≺ XI ≻

DESGREZ'S FRIEND and protectress, the Marquise d'Argenteuil, was a character. She was a big heavy woman with a round face that terminated in a double chin. Her hair, which had been gray for many years, hung down around her face in long, elaborate curls, so that the onlooker was involuntarily reminded of a prize poodle. She affected naïveté and liked to wear clothes much too youthful for her, cut too low in front and decked out with too much lace, too many ruches and ribbons. But she enjoyed a reputation for great cleverness. Under the protective cloak of apparent harmlessness she often expressed ideas so bold that others scarcely dared to think them. Since she was also good-natured, everybody liked her, even at court. Her friends, men and women both, often turned to her in all sorts of difficulties.

When she was in Paris it was her custom to give a soirée once a month in her home on the Place Royale. Her door was open to anyone, no matter who, who could be entertaining or instructive. Among her constant and most welcome guests were the officers of her deceased husband's regiment. She treated these officers almost as if they were her children. But writers, philosophers, mathematicians, and even actors, also came to her evenings. She would take them under her pseudo-maternal wings and often, when they had done something wrong, she would, as she put it, "pin their ears back" with the greatest bluntness.

Lieutenant Desgrez came regularly to these little parties. Madame d'Argenteuil still considered him a kind of adopted son and substitute "man of the house" whose duty it was to receive the guests and make them feel comfortable. He enjoyed this part well enough, but the meetings also served him in another way. When he had a difficult problem on his hands, he liked, as he called it, to air the case in company. He did not betray any state secrets, but he talked enough to stimulate the others. Then he listened attentively. By suppressing his own ideas and suspicions and by balancing out all that was said, he was sometimes able to get a more objective view of his problem.

Tonight—it was a December evening, and outside it was beginning to snow gently—there were no officers in Madame d'Argenteuil's simple but comfortably furnished rooms. The regiment was in the Netherlands at the moment. Aside from Lieutenant Desgrez, the Duke de la Rochefoucauld, and a German scientist named Baron Leibnitz, there were only ladies present at the soirée, and none of them under forty. Among these ladies were Madame de la Fayette, the duke's intimate friend; the seventy-year-old Mademoiselle de la Scudéry, author of sentimental novels; and Madame de Sévigné. She was generally gay and lively. But now, with Christmas so near, she seemed to be feeling more keenly than ever the absence of her daughter, Madame de Grignan, whom she adored. Throughout the evening she was markedly subdued.

At first the conversation revolved around the war which had recently broken out between France and Holland. Not one of the guests approved of the bloody quarrel, instigated by the French government merely for the sake of glory.

"Now it's being brought home to us that our king is Louis the Grand, not a Saint Louis," Madame d'Argenteuil remarked slyly, and all the guests smiled.

"It's not so much the king, it's that damnable Louvois, Le Tellier's son," Madame de la Fayette said sighing. "His ambition will ruin us all yet. And he has the ear of the king, who, alas, is more susceptible to the lure of fame than to the complaints of his subjects."

"Quite true, madame," the duke said, bowing to her. "Things are by no means going well with us. The peasants whose labor supports France are barely keeping alive, when they are not starving to death. And in Paris one frightful crime follows the next."

"For example, the Daubray case," Mademoiselle de la Scudéry said. "I dream of it often and have even been considering barring my windows as Madame Daubray is said to have done."

Up to now the guests had conversed in a casual, easygoing manner. But now a note of tense interest came into the atmosphere. Involuntarily, everyone turned to look at Desgrez. But the lieutenant merely smiled and shrugged his shoulders silently.

"He wants to be coaxed, I know him," Madame d'Argenteuil said indignantly.

"Please, please, my dear Monsieur Desgrez," Madame de la Fayette said, rising and dropping a deep curtsy before the lieutenant. "You know we will not tell any of your secrets."

"As you know, the case has been solved, ladies and gentlemen," Desgrez said, bowing to Madame de la Fayette. After a brief, thoughtful pause he added, "At least that is the opinion of my superior, Monsieur Michel de la Reynie."

"And yours also, Monsieur Desgrez?" Madame de la Fayette asked.

"To my mind the case requires further investigation."

"To my mind also," the duke remarked. "For example, what motive did Sainte-Croix have for causing the murders of the two brothers?"

"Revenge, possibly jealousy. We have learned that about ten years ago—in 1663, to be exact—Count Daubray the elder made use of a *lettre de cachet* to have the man thrown into the Bastille."

"Not really!" the duke exclaimed. "Why?"

Everyone looked at Desgrez in suspense. "Desgrez, stop tormenting us," Madame d'Argenteuil said sharply. "Go ahead and answer the duke's question."

"For repeatedly molesting a lady of rank," Desgrez said, winking.

"Well, that's certainly a spicy detail," the duke said. "What was the lady's name? Or don't you want to mention it?"

"I cannot say, Your Grace. The *lettre de cachet*, which I have examined, contains no name. It merely speaks of 'a lady of rank.' "

"Who can it have been?" the duke murmured pensively. "A mistress, do you think? I never would have thought the old fellow had one."

"We do not know. But it must have been a lady who was in some way connected with both Count Daubray and Sainte-Croix. And the connection must have been fairly intimate, to my mind. For the count was interested enough to swear out a *lettre de cachet*, which he probably would have done only after repeated warnings. And apparently Sainte-Croix disregarded the warnings and risked imprisonment for the lady's sake. Actually he was kept in prison only for ten weeks. But that stay in the Bastille seems to have had important results."

"What results? You'll be the death of me with your pauses, Desgrez." Madame d'Argenteuil cried out.

Desgrez sighed. "I have learned," he said, "that Sainte-Croix shared a cell in the northern tower of the Bastille with a certain Signor Exili, alias Eggidi. You won't recognize the name, mesdames. But I had the dubious pleasure of making his acquaintance at one time. In the course of my duties I accompanied him to Calais after he was released from the Bastille. He was banished from our country on the apparently well-founded suspicion that he had been concocting poisons. He went to England. Previously he had been in the service of Queen Christina of Sweden. It seems likely that Sainte-Croix owed his knowledge of poisons to this man Exili or Eggidi."

"All that throws new light on the crime," Mademoiselle de Scudéry said. "But it doesn't solve the mystery, does it?"

"No. Instead we have a whole series of unsolved problems. We know today that La Chaussée murdered the Daubray brothers. But

we do not know who killed their father. In fact we cannot even say
for certain that the father died by poisoning. Nevertheless, to me
these three deaths are three links in a chain; only the final link is
wanting."

"Could not La Chaussée also have killed the elder Daubray?"
Madame de la Fayette asked.

"Impossible," Desgrez said. "We have the best of proof that he
did not. From 1663 to 1668 La Chaussée was serving a term in the
galleys in Marseilles. Under the name of Jean Hamelin he had been
sentenced to the galleys for receiving stolen goods."

"Don't you have any leads for further investigation, Desgrez?" the
duke asked.

"We do, Your Grace. We still have that mysterious promissory
note and we still don't know who wrote it. It is, of course, possible—
Monsieur de la Reynie is inclined to think so—that the note has
nothing at all to do with the crime. Furthermore, the note may be a
forgery manufactured by Sainte-Croix in order to defraud the heirs.
Perhaps he thought it over and did not dare to put the strategem
into operation. But he hung on to the note for possible future use."

"Then this debt, real or fraudulent, was never paid, Lieutenant
Desgrez?"

"It does not seem likely, Your Grace, for then the note would no
longer be in the possession of the creditor, would it? It would have
been returned to the debtor. But then again, we must remember
that we are dealing with criminals. Possibly the debt was paid and
Sainte-Croix kept the note anyhow, on some pretext, intending to
blackmail the signer—who, if he were involved in the murders, would
not dare to use strong measures to get the note back. It seems to me
that there must be another person who directed Sainte-Croix's
activities as he directed La Chaussée's."

"Why, Desgrez, why?" the duke asked impatiently.

"In the first place, the motive of revenge ascribed to Sainte-Croix
doesn't satisfy me at all. I could understand that he might kill the
father to revenge an insult. But would he kill the sons, too?"

"There have been such cases, Desgrez. Is not the root of almost
all crimes passion—or money?"

"Money, Your Grace, that's it," Desgrez said with intensity. "Three
hundred livres for La Chaussée, thirty thousand livres for Sainte-

Croix. I can't get those sums out of my head. And then the tremendous fortune of the Daubrays."

Baron Leibnitz, who as a foreigner knew little about the crime in which everyone was so interested, had sat listening attentively all the while. Now he remarked with a smile, "From what you say, the Daubray fortune must amount to three million livres."

Desgrez started. "How did you arrive at that sum, Monsieur le Baron?" he asked in amazement. "Or did you know it beforehand. That is precisely the size of the Daubray fortune."

"No, I did not know," the baron replied. "But my mathematical sense of order—call it pedantry, if you will, Monsieur Desgrez—led me to conclude that it must be that amount. Three hundred livres is one per cent of thirty thousand livres, which would be one per cent of three million livres. Isn't that right?"

"Yes, damn it all!" Desgrez cried out, forgetting for a moment where he was. "You've heard the tale, Monsieur le Baron. Wouldn't you hazard, too, that both Sainte-Croix and La Chaussée were only the tools and that we have not yet laid hands on the real criminal?"

"Undoubtedly. And I should add that there is a ninety-nine per cent probability that the heir of the Daubrays is the real criminal behind the criminals."

"But why?" Madame d'Argenteuil exclaimed, shaking her corkscrew curls impatiently. "Since when does one arrive at a criminal by percentages?"

Desgrez paid no attention to her objection—if he heard it at all. He was momentarily lost in deep meditation. "The trouble is," he said softly after a while, "that we have not one but three heirs—all of them women."

"Can't you eliminate any of them?" the baron asked.

"I think I can discount the widow of the elder son. She did inherit a part of the fortune upon the death of her father-in-law and her husband. But La Chaussée confessed that Sainte-Croix had ordered him to dispose of her also."

"Very well. We ought to be getting close to the murderer. Who are the two that are left?"

"Old Daubray's daughters."

"Are they married, Monsieur Desgrez?" the baron asked.

"The older daughter is, the younger is not."

"One moment, Monsieur Desgrez. The note of indebtedness was

signed 'Daubray,' was it not? Was the older daughter already
married at the time that note was written?"

"She was, Monsieur le Baron. I see what you are getting at. You
suggest that the elder daughter would probably have signed her
married name and not her maiden name."

"Exactly, exactly, Monsieur Desgrez. What sort of person is the
younger daughter?"

"She lives in a convent, aloof from the world, and scarcely ever
appears in society. Very few people know her by sight. She is
friendly with nobody. But I have heard that formerly she used quite
frequently to attend theatrical performances in the Palais Petit
Bourbon and the Palais Royal."

"The convent and the theater?" the baron said pensively. "They
don't go together very well. Port-Royal refuses absolution to all come-
dians and even to all spectators of comedy unless they renounce their
former pleasures. Monsieur Desgrez, I hazard the guess that the lady
is embittered and envious of her brothers and sisters. Possibly she was
given only a token portion of the inheritance. In the loneliness of her
cell, which she seldom leaves for a look at society, although she longs
for the great world with every fiber of her being, she broods about
the injustice done to her. Hatred grows in her, overpowers her, and
she finally decides to eradicate this family which has treated her so
shabbily. She would be acting, then, not only for the sake of money,
but out of the passion of an outraged heart. It's all quite possible.
Even more than possible. How do you know that this demi-nun is not
the lady of rank whom Sainte-Croix paid court to, for whose sake the
father sent him to the Bastille? And perhaps at the moment she saw
her last hope of marriage vanish as a result of her father's intervention, perhaps at that very moment she decided to kill him. And her
brothers also, for she must have still feared that they would reject her
and suppress her chances for marriage after her father's death."

The baron broke off and looked at Desgrez, who was smiling. "You
don't seem to believe me, Monsieur Desgrez," he said with mock
dismay.

"But I do," Desgrez said quickly. "It is possible, quite possible,
as you say."

"Then why don't you arrest her, Lieutenant?"

"That wouldn't do at all. I might as well try to arrest the king.

Don't you see, Monsieur le Baron, I must have facts, not possibilities."

"You will never get them, Lieutenant. The crime took place too long ago."

"I believe I will."

"How, Lieutenant?"

"I don't know—yet, Monsieur le Baron. But facts have a way of cropping up in the most unexpected places—that is, if you do not hinder them. They are never completely suppressed. So I act accordingly—or rather, I do not act at all."

"I am afraid I do not understand your method, Lieutenant," the baron exclaimed.

The other guests had been listening attentively. Now Madame d'Argenteuil bent over to Madame de la Fayette and whispered loudly enough for everyone to hear, "Sometimes I believe the poor boy is out of his mind. Or do you think he is playing games with us?"

Desgrez's smile broadened. "Not at all, madame," he said. "What I mean is: I do not like to pull unripe fruit from the tree. When it is ripe, I just touch it and it drops softly into my palm."

"What fruit are you talking about?" Madame d'Argenteuil demanded crustily, and everyone laughed.

"The fruit of evil, madame." Desgrez was suddenly serious, and the deep furrow appeared between his brows.

There was a short silence. Then the baron said, "But to go on with our investigation: Who is the other sister, Lieutenant Desgrez?"

"A society lady. A woman renowned for her beauty all over Paris, as well as in Versailles. A special favorite of the king's—the relationship is altogether innocent, however—and of the queen's, too. A very wealthy woman and an excellent mother besides, so I have heard."

"A lady of society and a good mother. . . . That, too, sounds somehow contradictory," the baron observed.

"Alas," Madame de la Fayette sighed theatrically. "Who can be safe from your suspicions if the marquise is not—she who wins all hearts wherever she appears?"

"Yes, kindly let her be, for my sake, Baron," Madame d'Argenteuil said. "I played a few rounds with her in the Palais Royal a while back. And imagine, I even won."

"I shall certainly say nothing against a lady who enjoys such high patrons and splendid friends," the baron said, smiling. "Although all that glitters is not gold. But it seems to me that the signature 'Daubray' proves her innocence."

"So she might have thought, too—supposing she were the one who wrote the note," Desgrez murmured.

"Good heavens, my dear Desgrez, now you are starting," Madame d'Argenteuil said. "Before long you policemen will be saying that the Daubray case is the result of discord between all nobly born ladies and their fathers."

"Well, why not?" the duke said with a smirk. "After all, perhaps a father who interferes with his daughter's private life deserves to be murdered. I am happy to say I do not belong in this category, since I have spared myself the ungrateful task of begetting a daughter."

"The story of the sour grapes," Madame de la Fayette said smilingly.

"Ah yes, our good La Fontaine hit that off neatly," Mademoiselle de la Scudéry said roguishly.

"I surrender." The duke laughed. "Please forgive me for not considering that all you ladies are the daughters of extremely enviable fathers."

Madame de Sévigné, who had up to now taken no part in the conversation, suddenly spoke up: "Yet it is quite possible for a woman simply to forget her husband and her married name. It can happen when she is unhappy in her marriage and her heart—not her intellect, mind you—wishes to forget the existence of such a marriage."

All eyes turned toward her. Madame de Sévigné bowed her blond head and went on to explain: "Some years ago I had a friend whom I knew very, very well—almost as well as I know myself. One day in the Jardins du Luxembourg we saw her husband promenading around the fountain beneath the terrace. He caught sight of us and waved a greeting. 'Who is this stranger?' she said to me. Then she started in fright, turned pale, and whispered, 'Oh yes, it's my husband. I had quite forgotten him.' Their marriage was very unhappy and ended in separation."

"That certainly is remarkable," Madame d'Argenteuil said, with a searching look at Madame de Sévigné.

Madame de Sévigné flushed slightly and said, "It would also be possible for a daughter so to love her father as to forget the fact that she no longer bears his name."

"I beg your pardon," the duke said softly, as though he were afraid of waking a somnambulist. "Madame does not seem to realize that this daughter—if one of the daughters really wrote the promissory note—is suspected of having murdered her father. There is a contradiction there."

"Not at all," Madame de Sévigné replied. "Murder is another form of intimacy—or can be. Is it not true that murder is relatively frequent among blood relations as well as among married people? The tales and legends of all nations are full of such occurrences. Lieutenant Desgrez will tell you, I am sure, that these ancient horrors have not died out in our present day."

Desgrez nodded confirmation.

The gathering of well-bred people looked at one another in dismay, and for a moment the gaiety of the company was disturbed by one of those embarrassing, prolonged silences, the colloquial expression for which is that an angel is passing through the room. Outside they could hear the harsh gusts of wind and the soft slapping of snow against the windowpanes, snow that had long since placed a white hood upon the head of the solitary bronze horseman in the center of the Place Royale.

But then suddenly they all began to talk at once, and as though by prearrangement they shifted the conversation to other, more commonplace matters. All of them seemed to be trying to lay the ghost that Madame de Sévigné's words had abruptly conjured up in their midst. The door opened and two servant-maids in blue-and-white-striped dresses, with white caps on their dark hair, entered the room carrying trays heaped with cups, jugs, and plates. The fragrance of pastry spread through the room, and the sweeter aroma of steaming chocolate. The two pretty girls poured the chocolate into the delicate cups and smilingly passed the refreshments among the guests.

The gloom was forgotten, as though it had been chased out into the winter night, into the nocturnal city, where the only light was the dim, flickering glow of an occasional oil lamp swaying on the corner of some building and throwing an uncertain illumination into the chaotic gray drift of wind-whirled snowflakes.

ɤ XII ɤ

IT WAS with considerable reluctance that Michel de la Reynie, on the
following morning, in the Châtelet, gave Lieutenant Desgrez permission to visit the sisters of the murdered Daubray brothers and
question them. "Very well," he said after much demurring. "If you
consider it absolutely necessary, Desgrez, go ahead. But for heaven's
sake, be careful. The one sister is under the protection of the Church
and the other is married to a friend of the king. The slightest slip,
even just a breach of tact, can cost us all our necks."

"I shall try to outdo myself in courtesy," Desgrez replied with a
wry smile and left the room.

Accompanied by Cluet, he walked briskly through a snow-covered
Paris that looked amazingly clean. The Carmelite convent, a sprawl-
ing low building, was on the Rue d'Enfer in the Faubourg Saint
Marcel. Desgrez knocked on the closed gate. The half-veiled face
of the gatekeeper appeared behind a little barred window, and
Desgrez informed her that he wished to see Mademoiselle de Dreux
Daubray. He was extremely sorry, he said, to disturb the lady in her
pious retreat, but the police urgently needed information in a matter
of importance to her, information which Mademoiselle Daubray
might perhaps be able to supply.

The gatekeeper nodded without any sign of interest, and vanished.
After some time her pallid face reappeared behind the bars. To his
surprise Desgrez was informed that the lady did not wish to see him;
she greatly regretted that she had no information to give.

Desgrez turned this over in his mind while the sister at the gate
watched him, this time with some curiosity. Finally Desgrez took the
promissory note from his pocket. He handed it to the gatekeeper and
asked her to show it to Mademoiselle Daubray. He wished to have
the handwriting identified, he said. And he would also like to know
whether Mademoiselle Daubray knew anything about the debt mentioned in the note, and whether she was acquainted with anyone by
the name of Sainte-Croix.

The gatekeeper vanished. This time she was gone even longer.
When she returned, she gave Desgrez a reproachful look and handed
the note back to him. Mademoiselle Daubray, she said in a severe

voice, could only say that she had never seen the note before and had not known of its existence. This she would swear by her eternal salvation.

As he took the note, Desgrez noticed that it felt damp. He asked the gatekeeper, "Did Mademoiselle Daubray weep when she saw the note?"

The gatekeeper started. But she immediately recovered her composure and said with some acrimony, "I must say I consider it extremely unkind of you to remind the poor young lady of the unhappy fate of her family." Then she slammed the little window shut, and Desgrez and Cluet found themselves standing alone in the snow.

"Damn it all, we're no better off than we were before," Cluet growled, and gave Desgrez a look of perplexity.

Desgrez laughed. "Not quite," he said. "She shed tears. But why? From fear for herself, or from concern over the safety of someone else?" He considered for a moment. "You know, Cluet, there are a great many questions here, when you come to think of it. Why did she refuse to see us? You would think she would be eager to help us find her brothers' murderer, especially since the same person probably murdered her father also. Was she afraid of betraying her own guilt? Or is she covering up another person whom she knows to be guilty? But come, Cluet, we must bestir ourselves. We're dealing with a dangerous opponent. Any moment now we may find ourselves confronted with a new murder."

"Where to?" Cluet asked.

"The Rue Neuve Saint Paul, of course," Desgrez replied. "Let's see whether the other sister receives us."

They walked down the Seine to the Pont de la Tournelle and crossed the Ile Saint Louis by the Rue des Deux Ponts. At one point Desgrez stopped in the middle of the street and said, "You know, Cluet, I think our Carmelite nun knows who Sainte-Croix was. Did you notice that she didn't answer my question about him? The pointed neglect of that question rather convinces me that her conscience is very scrupulous and her statement true. Cluet, we are dealing with a most remarkable family."

They went on and crossed the northern arm of the river over the Pont Marie. They were now on the Quai Saint Paul. On their right was a small dockyard in which fishing smacks and ponderous cargo

boats were massed in apparently inextricable confusion. Here and
there on the Seine floated blocks of ice.

It was afternoon when they reached the Rue Neuve Saint Paul.
The Brinvilliers house was a large building with tall windows that
sparkled in the sunlight. It was well set in a moderate-sized garden
whose excellent design was apparent in spite of winter. The whole
was surrounded by a wall with a wrought-iron gate for entrance. A
servant appeared in answer to their ring. When they told him they
were from the police, he went to fetch his superior, the steward of
the household.

The steward, a white-haired man of dignified demeanor, but with
a good-natured round face, was considerably put out. "I am sorry that
I must disappoint you, gentlemen," he said. "Monsieur le Marquis
is still in Sains, his country estate in Picardy."

"What? Now, in the middle of winter?" Cluet exclaimed.

"Why certainly, the marquis is a very ardent huntsman," the steward said with an apologetic smile, as though asking their indul-
gence for this peculiarity on the part of his master.

"And Madame la Marquise? We especially wished to see the lady
of the house," Desgrez said.

"Oh, Madame is traveling." The steward again smiled apologeti-
cally as he added with servility, "We all miss her very much. The
house seems dead when she is not here."

"Hm," Desgrez said, "do you think Their Excellencies would mind
if we took a look around the house during their absence?"

"Certainly not, gentlemen," the steward replied. "Madame is very
proud of her house; she has chosen much of the furnishing herself.
Guests are always welcome."

"Even the police?" Cluet growled.

The steward laughed heartily, his face wrinkling as though Cluet
had cracked a first-rate joke. "Especially the police," he said. "They
are our protectors."

They entered the house through an impressive double door. Each
wing of the door was sheathed in bronze.

A second, high French door opened into a wide vestibule, which
was flanked by eight black marble columns. The floor was inlaid
with red and black marble, and the high, shell-shaped ceiling, which
extended up to the third story, was painted in fresco. The details
could not be made out in the dim light. But as soon as Desgrez's eyes

became accustomed to the dimness, he discovered that the subject of the painting was Cupid and Psyche. A dark-haired girl, the upper part of her body bare, was holding aloft a small oil lamp whose yellow light splashed into the surrounding darkness and showed the splendidly formed limbs of a sleeping youth.

Desgrez looked up at the painting with rapt interest. The steward busied himself changing the position of some chairs, muttering curses upon the negligence of his underlings. Desgrez took the opportunity to whisper to the sergeant, "Cluet—that painting on the ceiling—doesn't it strike you as peculiar?"

The sergeant stared at the painting for some time, then he looked uncomprehendingly at Desgrez. Desgrez sighed and said, "You know, Cluet, things have a way of speaking when men are silent."

The steward approached them and asked, "Did you say something, sirs?"

"We were admiring the painting on the ceiling."

"Yes, it is beautiful, most beautiful." The man sounded smugly pleased.

"Who painted it, steward?"

"Monsieur le Brune, a young artist with a great future, I dare say, sir. Madame la Marquise ordered it, of course, and I believe she suggested some of the details to the painter."

Desgrez nodded, and the three of them went on.

Both Cluet and Desgrez were also impressed by the large staircase, very wide at the bottom and narrowing in a fine curve as it mounted to the second story. The staircase, introduced, as it were, by two female statues at the bottom, had the effect of a silent invitation. It inevitably carried the visitor's gaze up along it and produced an irresistible desire to ascend. Cluet seemed to feel this unspoken allure, for, as if in a dream, he set his foot upon the first step. But the steward held him back. "Come, gentlemen," he said, speaking in a lower voice than he had used outside, "look at the ground floor first."

The vestibule was flanked on both sides by halls and salons. But there was little to see in them. The silken curtains on the windows were drawn, the chandeliers, covered with large cloth bags to protect them against dust, hung from the ceiling like huge wasp's nests. The furniture, too, was covered with white dustcloths, so that the three men were moving in the dimness among ghostly objects that seemed more like the suggestions of furniture than real furniture. Here and there the steward would lift the end of a linen swathing and say, "A sideboard by Boule. Note the inlay, gentlemen." Or he would point to the wall and whisper, as though he were telling a great secret, "That painting is by Poussin. It represents the fall of Icarus."

Desgrez took an eager interest in everything. Several times he stopped and let the other two men go ahead. He looked at the pictures, all of which represented mythological subjects, or he paused in front of one of the numerous mirrors which reflected his own face furrowed by thought.

"You have a great many mirrors here," he remarked to the steward.

"Mirrors are one of Madame's weaknesses," the steward said. Then he added, "It is quite understandable in a woman as beautiful as she."

They came to an oblong room which the steward called the gaming room. "Is Madame fond of gaming?" Desgrez asked.

"Very much so," the man said.

They went up the staircase and through a glass door and entered a room in which the most striking object was a huge bed, a veritable *letto matrimoniale,* of artistically inlaid wood, the high posts intricate with carvings, and the canopy richly embroidered. Above the bed hung a painting of the penitent Mary Magdalene—a distinctly second-rate work, Desgrez observed at once. The beautiful, long-haired penitent, large tears upon her rounded cheeks, was absorbed in contemplation of a skull which lay at her feet. She was in kneeling position. The effect of the whole was sentimental rather than moving. The steward noticed that Desgrez was attentively studying this piece of hack work, and said, "She is Madame's patron saint."

"Oh," Desgrez replied, smiling. "Then I suppose we are in the holy of holies here?"

"This is Madame's bedchamber," the steward said, and also permitted himself a discreet smile.

Desgrez looked around. Except for the splendid bed, all the furniture was extremely simple, almost provincial. There was a commode on which stood two silver candelabra; several round-backed, silk-upholstered armchairs; a small mirror; and, opposite the bed, a large fireplace framed in plain black marble. Desgrez sighed. The steward looked at him and shrugged. "It all seems lifeless, doesn't it?" he said. "But you can have no idea of what this house is like when Madame is here to animate it."

Desgrez gave a corroborating smile. Then, as the steward looked at him with ever-increasing interest, he said, "Well, my friend, there is no reason why we should take more of your valuable time. Our intention was to talk to a member of the family, but neither the master nor the mistress of the house seems to be home."

"No, neither," the man answered. "But perhaps I could be of help, sir, if you would care to tell me what the problem is."

Desgrez smiled. "It's only a minor matter," he said circumspectly. "There have been certain incidents in the neighborhood, nothing of importance, mind you—small thefts and the like—and some clues seem to point to the possibility that this house may also have been entered."

The steward's eyes grew wide with apprehension. "But nothing has been missing, not a thing!" he exclaimed.

"So I assume. This gang works with extreme caution. I did not want to alarm you, as they probably will never touch anything here, although the center of their activity seems to be right in the Marais. You see what I mean, don't you?"

"Yes, of course, sir," the man answered, obviously aghast at the news. "But I hope you don't think any of our household staff could be a member of that gang of criminals."

"That's just it. There is the possibility—and of course we would like to be sure. It's just a precaution, to protect the marquis and yourself."

"Monsieur le Marquis will be very grateful, sir. But I assure you that I watch the help closely, very closely. And I'm convinced that the servants are above suspicion. They are all honest folk, sir."

"I believe that you know your people well, steward. Nevertheless, you would do us—and your employer, too, I should say—a great service if you could tell me of anything strange that has ever happened in this house—anything out of the way."

"Anything?" the man exclaimed.

"Yes, my friend—for instance a quarrel, the sudden departure of a servant, a case of sickness, or the appearance of a stranger."

"But nothing of that kind has happened, nothing at all." Yet something like a doubt appeared on the steward's good-natured, rather empty face. "Yes," he mumbled, not quite sure of himself. "There was an incident which surprised us all very much . . . about five months ago, I should say. . . . But I don't know whether Monsieur le

Marquis would like me to talk about it. Perhaps you had better ask
Mademoiselle Julie—Mademoiselle de Grangemont, I mean."

"Who is she?"

"A relation of the marquis, sir."

"But steward, didn't you say that no member of the family was at
home?"

"Sorry, sir," the steward said, "but we hardly think of Mademoiselle
Julie as being one of the family. She is only second or third cousin to
Monsieur le Marquis. She acts as governess to the young ladies."

"Then why isn't she in Picardy with the children?"

The steward looked surprised. "I really could not say," he exclaimed. "I never considered the matter."

"Well, let us find out. That is an example of what I meant—a small
matter which seems a little out of the way."

"But, sir, you don't think that Mademoiselle Julie—"

"I don't think anything at all," Desgrez interrupted him with sudden impatience. "I make no assumptions. Come, let us go."

They left the marquise's bedchamber and went out into the corridor, which formed a gallery around the vestibule. The red and black
marble paving of the hall gleamed in the dim light. Above them on
the ceiling Cupid and Psyche could now be made out much more
distinctly. Again Desgrez examined the painting intently.

The steward knocked at one of the doors and then opened it. In
the center of the room stood a girl of about seventeen, a book in her
hand. She looked questioningly at the steward and then, with some
alarm, at the military figure of the sergeant. The girl was of a striking
blondness, and the look in her large blue eyes was one either of great
shyness or of anxiety. Desgrez saw that she was pretty and still something of a child—an altogether delightful young creature, whose
charm was not in the least diminished by her efforts to seem more
mature than she was.

The steward explained to her that the two gentlemen were from
the police and wished to speak to her.

"From the police!" she cried out, and looked at the towering Cluet.
"Oh, God, and I was just wondering again whether it wasn't my duty
to go to the police—" She broke off, but the apprehension in her eyes
seemed to increase.

Desgrez signed to the steward to go. The good man looked disappointed, but managed to mumble, "Please excuse me, mademoiselle.

I must see to the staff. Otherwise they'll just be idling downstairs."
He left the room, closing the door behind him. Desgrez listened to
his footsteps recede. Then he turned to the young woman, who stood
trembling, trying to steady herself by holding on to the edge of a
table.

"Please don't upset yourself, mademoiselle," Desgrez said in a gentle tone. "We really should not have bothered you. It is such a minor
matter."

"What is it, sir?" the girl cried out suddenly. "Is he dead? Please
don't try to break the news gradually. Tell me the truth." She put
her hand over her eyes and began to sob. Her slender body shook.

"Come now, little lady, take it easy," Cluet boomed, speaking
rather harshly in an attempt to cover up his emotion. "Nothing can
happen to you."

"To me?" the girl said, taking a handkerchief from her bodice and
wiping her eyes. "I am not concerned for myself. But he's disappeared—just vanished. Oh, I know he must be dead. That's why you
have come—to tell me." She was on the verge of tears again.

"No, mademoiselle, I assure you that we haven't come to bring you
any bad news," Desgrez said. "Indeed, we had no idea that anyone
had disappeared from this house. Whom are you referring to?"

"Nicolas—oh, I mean Monsieur Briancourt," the girl sobbed, blushing. With some effort she calmed herself and looked shyly at Desgrez.
She also glanced briefly at Cluet, who stood weightily by, stroking
his mustache in embarrassment. The sight of the sergeant seemed to
restore her composure somewhat, and something like the hint of a
smile appeared in her eyes.

"You take his disappearance very much to heart, mademoiselle,"
Desgrez said. "Was he a close friend of yours, this Monsieur
Briancourt?"

The girl blushed more deeply. She looked at Cluet again, who gave
her a good-natured, encouraging nod. "I loved him," she said almost
inaudibly. "But he—he loved someone else—I mean, until at the end
he found he cared for me."

"Who was the someone else?" Desgrez asked.

The girl did not answer at once. "I cannot tell," she whispered at
last. "That is his secret." She was again on the verge of tears.

"Very well," Desgrez said, smiling. "I will not ask you to be indiscreet, mademoiselle. But now tell me how and when Monsieur Briancourt disappeared."

Julie de Grangemont took a deep breath. She was obviously fighting back her tears, resolved not to break down again.

"I remember the day very well," she said. "It was the end of July and Marie-Madeleine—I mean Madame la Marquise—had gone out. It was quite late; I had already braided my hair for the night when suddenly Nicolas—Monsieur Briancourt—burst into my room without knocking. He had never done anything of the sort before. He fell to his knees before me, threw his arms around my waist and began kissing my dress again and again. I was shocked—but I must confess that it also made me glad." She paused and looked at Cluet. Then she went on, breathing heavily: "He said, 'Julie, I must run away. My life is not safe here. No, don't ask any questions, my darling. The less you know, the safer you are. I know that the net is drawing tighter around me. Today may be my last chance to get away. Goodbye, and forgive me—perhaps I shall see you again some time, when the danger is past and I have recovered myself.'" The girl dropped into silence, with a despairing shake of the head.

"And then?" Desgrez asked.

"I put on a mantle and implored him to take me with him. But he said, 'No, one sacrifice is enough. I cannot carry you away with me. I love you. Oh, Julie, how can you ever forgive me.' He pulled me close and kissed me on the mouth. But then he pushed me away and rushed out of the room. I went to the open window. It was a sultry night. Outside, flashes of heat lightning were illuminating the city, which lay below me. I saw him in the street. He was not walking, but running as though pursued by furies. And the wind preceding the thunderstorm that was rumbling off to the west whipped his hair back so it streamed out behind him." The girl's lips quivered and single large tears rolled down her young cheeks. She looked helplessly at Cluet.

"We'll find him, little lady," Cluet said reassuringly. "We'll find him if we have to turn all of Paris upside down."

"Oh, if I only knew that he is safe and well," the girl sobbed.

Desgrez looked at her in a friendly way, then cleared his throat and asked, "This disappearance of Monsieur Briancourt—was that the reason for your staying in Paris, mademoiselle?"

She looked a little startled. "Yes," she answered, blushing again.

"I thought it my duty to remain here, should he return. I thought he might need me. And my cousin, the marquis, consented to my remaining."

"I understand, mademoiselle. But tell me, did you know what your friend was referring to the night he left? Do you know of any danger which could have threatened him—or, for that matter, anybody else in this house?"

"No, monsieur, I have thought and thought but I really have not the slightest idea why he took flight. Sometimes I was afraid—" She interrupted herself and gazed helplessly at the lieutenant.

"Yes, mademoiselle?"

"I was afraid that he imagined things," the girl said with an effort. "You see, monsieur, he was of rather a high-strung disposition—easily suggestible, I mean. And he seemed to be in very low spirits for quite some time before he fled."

"Hm," Desgrez muttered to himself, " 'the less you know the safer you are . . .' " Then he addressed Julie again: "What steps did you take to locate him, mademoiselle?"

"I, Monsieur?" She seemed embarrassed again. "I just sat here and waited and prayed for his return. I did not dare to take any steps, as you put it—I thought I might endanger his life, for if it were true that he had enemies, they might be watching my movements."

Desgrez smiled. "Did you hear that, Cluet?" he said. "Mademoiselle is following my own method: sit tight and wait and don't disturb the flow of events—as the wise man says:

Not to go out of the house is to know the world of men,
Not to look out of the window is to know the ways of Heaven;
Hence we deem that inaction is the profitable course."

Desgrez chuckled, for both the girl and the sergeant were looking at him with amazement. "But to be honest about it," he continued with a sly glance, "I think the time has come to turn the rudder and sail for the open seas. After all, even Mohammed went to the mountain which refused to come to him. Can you tell us, mademoiselle, where Monsieur Briancourt came from? I mean, before he took a position in this house. And what was his work here?"

"He was the tutor," Julie volunteered eagerly. Her fear of Desgrez was gone, for she seemed to sense his determination to find her vanished sweetheart. "Oh, he was a very learned man," she went on naïvely. "He was a bachelor of theology and had studied law, too. That is why Madame's advocate, Monsieur Bocager, sent him here to help Madame la Marquise in some inheritance matter. Later he stayed because—because he liked it here. This was his first position, as far as I know. He was very young when he came here, you see, just nineteen."

"When was that, mademoiselle?"

"Two years ago in July, I think. Yes, it must have been then. It was shortly after Madame's elder brother, the Count of Offémont, died."

"Do you know whether he was a Parisian by birth, mademoiselle? Perhaps you know where his parents are to be found?"

"Oh, he was an orphan, just like myself. The Pious Fathers of the Oratorium of Notre Dame des Vertus in Aubervilliers brought him up. He used to visit them often, and once when I jokingly asked him whether he intended to become a monk he looked at me seriously and said, 'There is my true home, Julie, and I wish to God I had never left it.' I remember exactly how he said it because I was a little piqued. Oh, I'm so silly, monsieur."

"I don't think so," Cluet growled.

Desgrez smiled. "Hm," he said, grinning, "his true home? Well then, I must say my friend Cluet is right. You are a clever young lady, and I hope you will soon be happy as well."

Julie reddened. She gave an embarrassed smile. "I don't know, gentlemen," she said shyly. "It was such a short time . . . but I was really very fond of him . . ."

At this moment the steward reappeared. He seemed somewhat surprised to find everyone in such good spirits. Desgrez and Cluet bade goodbye to Julie and, accompanied by the steward, descended the splendid staircase. "Steward," Desgrez said, "the pretty child up there, Mademoiselle de Grangemont, told us about Monsieur Briancourt. Do you happen to know where he can be found?"

The steward said he did not know. He agreed, however, that Briancourt had been a pleasant and friendly young man, popular with masters and servants alike. His mysterious disappearance shortly before Madame's departure had surprised everyone and occasioned much talk among the servants, since they had observed that both master and mistress had treated the young man almost like a son. But since, as far as the steward knew, the marquis had taken no steps to locate Monsieur Briancourt, the steward himself had done nothing; he did not like, he said, to mix into affairs that were none of his concern. Then he asked whether Monsieur Briancourt could have been a member of that gang of criminals which Desgrez was investigating.

Desgrez glanced mockingly at the steward's round face. The man who did not like to mix in affairs that were none of his concern was quite obviously bursting with curiosity. They had reached the door by now. Desgrez gave the steward a vigorous slap on the back and said, "Au revoir, steward. Many thanks for your information. But you know it isn't right to mistrust your fellow men. Monsieur Briancourt is probably as innocent of any fault as a newborn lamb."

The steward gaped after the two of them as they set out down the snow-covered street.

After a while Desgrez asked his companion, "What do you think of that house, Cluet?"

"Very beautiful, Lieutenant. But I didn't like all those heathenish pictures of naked women and men on the walls."

Desgrez laughed heartily. "But Cluet," he said, feigning reproach, "they are the fashion of the day. The ceilings and walls of Versailles are full of them, too."

"I don't care," the sergeant growled. "I still think they are very immodest. Think of the children, Lieutenant, think of little Mademoiselle Julie looking at all that nakedness. They should have more pictures of saints—and decently dressed, mind you, not like that red-haired sinner with big tits they keep in Madame's bedchamber."

"You are quite a moralist, Cluet, aren't you? But you may have something there, though the pictures did not impress me so much as the countless mirrors, the gaming tables, and the sweep of that staircase."

They walked on in silence for some time. Desgrez seemed lost in thought, then he said, "That house is all hers. If we didn't know that there are a husband and children, too, I'd conclude that she lives there alone. It is built around her. I can even guess the color of her hair from the colors in the tapestries: it must be dark brown. Furthermore, she is self-centered, extremely proud of her beauty, dissatisfied with her life, sensuous, and probably impatiently waiting for an overpowering love to crown her existence."

"My God, Lieutenant," the sergeant exclaimed, "there you go again. How did you guess this time?"

"Well, Cluet, let's take the main picture on the ceiling of the entrance hall: Psyche with her lamp throwing its light on the sleeping god. What else is it but the soul of woman searching for a godlike love?"

"I don't understand this time, Lieutenant."

"It is not important at this point, Cluet. Soon we shall know more. But let me tell you, the lady has imagination and intelligence. She certainly isn't the childish dancing doll Madame Daubray described to us. And right there you have another of her characteristics: when she wants to make a certain impression, she is clever enough to make it to perfection. She is something of a riddle; there is a more substantial, a more primitive face behind this mask of a thoughtless, carefree lady of the world."

Cluet shook his head doubtfully, and Desgrez fell silent.

Desgrez and Cluet went on to the Quai de la Mégisserie to see Bocager, the advocate mentioned by Julie, whose address they had obtained from the steward. Bocager was a gray-haired man of about fifty. He appeared to be quite upset when Desgrez inquired about Briancourt. For a moment he leafed nervously through the papers on his desk, then looked up anxiously at Desgrez and said in a low voice, "I was afraid of something of the sort, Lieutenant."

"What were you afraid of, monsieur?" Desgrez asked.

"That things would turn out badly with Nicolas . . ."

"What do you mean? What makes you say that, Monsieur Bocager?"

The advocate riffled through his papers again. Then he looked searchingly at Desgrez and said, "He has been involved in a duel, hasn't he?"

"In a duel? Did he tell you that he intended to fight a duel?"

"Not exactly. But he came here in such a state—never in my life have I seen anyone so agitated—and borrowed my pistols. I warned him; I pointed out to him that duels are forbidden. But it was impossible to reason with him. He talked madly about murder, snatched the pistols from the drawer I had tentatively opened, and rushed off."

Desgrez whistled under his breath, then asked abruptly, "When did this happen?"

"Let me see, Lieutenant . . . it was in the summertime. Yes, it

must have been about the beginning or the middle of July. That was
the last time I saw Nicolas."

"What about the pistols?"

"The pistols? Oh, a servant brought them back a few days later.
Here they are." Monsieur Bocager opened a drawer of his desk and
handed Desgrez two huge old-fashioned pistols.

"Good Lord," Desgrez said, cocking the weapons and looking down
the barrels, "I've rarely seen a rustier pair of pistols in my life." He
handed them to Cluet, who also examined them.

"Those haven't been fired in ages," Cluet said, grinning.

"Probably the last time was St. Bartholomew's Night," Desgrez said
dryly. "Did the young man take powder and lead also?"

"No, he just rushed off with the pistols."

"That's lucky," Desgrez said. "The damned things probably would
have exploded in his hand. No, Monsieur Bocager, your friend
Briancourt did not duel with anyone or kill anyone—at least not with
your pistols. But tell me this, was there anything else about
Briancourt that struck you?"

Bocager reflected. "That is hard to say," he said after a while. "His
disposition had undergone some change during the last few years.
He'd become very pensive, absent-minded, sometimes quite depressed and, I might say, apprehensive, since he began working for
the Marquis de Brinvilliers."

"What did you think was the reason, Monsieur Bocager?"

The lawyer shrugged. "He did not confide in me," he said slowly.
"But when a nice young man behaves that way . . . it's usually that
he's in love, Monsieur—probably unhappily in love."

"Quite true. But then the question is, with whom?"

Monsieur Bocager paused. "As I've said, I do not know," he said at
last, obviously struggling with his conscience. "But the marquise is a
remarkably beautiful woman. I myself . . . but that isn't to the point.
I mean only that of course she was unreachable for him."

"Perhaps, Monsieur Bocager. But as you know, it has happened
that queens have become infatuated with their grooms. Why not a
marquise with her children's tutor? But against whom did the young
man want to use your pistols?" Desgrez reflected. "There's no point
to speculating," he said finally. "I must find Briancourt. Do you think
it possible, Monsieur Bocager, that he is in Aubervilliers?"

"Hardly likely. The Pious Fathers would surely have informed me. Yet . . . Lieutenant, perhaps . . ."

"Yes?"

Monsieur Bocager smiled. "You must understand, Lieutenant," he said, "that the Pious Fathers deserve their name. It occurs to me . . . in fact I think it would be quite possible that they might simply be holding Briancourt incommunicado and letting him spend his days in meditation—if he should happen to have confessed to them. . . ."

"But certainly not for six months!" Desgrez exclaimed.

"Oh yes, they might," the lawyer insisted. "They are indifferent to the claims of friends, business, or other worldly obligations. For them, the sole task men have on earth is to prepare the salvation of their souls; nothing else counts. They may not put it quite that way, but that is the principle by which they act."

"Well, we shall see," Desgrez said, and the two men took their leave.

"The best of luck!" Bocager called after them.

⚔ XIII ⚔

THE NEXT morning was fine and clear. Rarely had Cluet seen his friend Desgrez so cheerful. He kept humming melodies under his breath. Now and then he took his foot out of the stirrup and sat crosswise on his horse, as if he were using a lady's saddle. The horse was an aging gray which stepped along the snow-covered road at an even, careful pace, often shaking its head disapprovingly. It was rather cold, and Desgrez explained his peculiar mode of riding by saying that he was afraid his feet would freeze in the stirrup.

After about an hour's ride they reached Aubervilliers and soon found the settlement of the Pious Fathers of Notre Dame des Vertus. The place was half farm, half monastery. The low, straw-roofed buildings, grouped like chicks around a hen in a circle about the little chapel, were covered with deep pelts of snow. They rode under the stone arch of a gate, above which the Mother of God sat enthroned, surrounded by her Virtues, and entered a yard that smelled strongly of cattle. The doors to the barns were opened and they could catch glimpses of the steaming breath of the cows. A sharp-faced boy hurried up to them, took the horses' reins from their hands, and asked, "Do you wish to buy butter, sirs?"

"No, my boy," Desgrez replied. "Take the horses, water them and stable them," he said, giving the boy a copper coin. "We want to see Monsieur Nicolas Briancourt—that is, if he is in."

"He is in all right. But I don't think he will receive you, sir."

"Why not, my son?"

"Father Morel has imposed silence upon him until Christmas."

"Oh, wonderful," Desgrez laughed. "I must not forget to send Madame d'Argenteuil to Father Morel. But Monsieur Briancourt will see us anyway. Where does he live?"

"Over there," the boy said, pointing to a small house that stood somewhat off to one side of the other buildings. "He has been living there since he came back from Paris. He never goes out."

Desgrez and Cluet crossed the yard toward the house. The boy stood watching them, a dubious expression in his eyes. They found the door open. "Strange," Desgrez murmured, "there's always this rather sour smell in all religious buildings."

On their left was a very plain room, its furniture of unpainted pine wood; on their right was a kitchen with a large, smoke-blackened hearth. They ascended a creaking staircase and found themselves before another door. Cluet knocked. There was no answer. The sergeant looked questioningly at Desgrez. It was so quiet they could hear the cows outside munching at the hay in their racks. Cluet tried the latch. The door was barred.

"Open up, Briancourt," he called. "We know you're in there."

"I cannot. I am meditating," a young man's voice replied.

"In the name of the king, open up!" Cluet bellowed. "Or we'll break down the door!"

"One moment, one moment," the voice cried anxiously. They heard a chair scraping over the floor, then the sound of the bolt sliding. The door opened hesitantly. In the crack between door and jamb stood a young man with brown hair, large, frightened eyes, and a white, drawn face. He would have looked handsome were it not for the terrible strain written in both his bearing and features. Desgrez and Cluet saw that his lips were quivering. "Who are you? What do you want?" he whispered.

"We come from the Paris police," Desgrez said evenly. "May we come in?"

The young man's shoulders sagged. He moaned and leaned feebly
against the door for a moment. Then he recovered himself and said
tonelessly, "Come in, please."

The room, too, was furnished very simply; it resembled a monk's
cell rather than a room in a home. Above a cot covered with a rough
gray woolen blanket hung a picture of the Holy Mother. On the rude
table, before which stood a stool—the only chair in the room—lay an
open book, probably a religious work, to judge by the black leather
binding. Desgrez saw that the pages were covered with handwritten
marginal notes. Briancourt, whose eyes had been anxiously following
Desgrez's gaze, clapped the book shut and held his hands over it as
though to protect it from Desgrez.

"Hm," Desgrez said. "Are you still in love after all this time,
Briancourt?"

The young man stared at the lieutenant in surprise. "I? In love?
With whom?" he stammered.

"With Madame la Marquise, of course."

Briancourt cried out and raised his hands as though to push
Desgrez away. Desgrez watched him with a cold smile.

"Lieutenant Desgrez," Cluet exclaimed, "he's passing out on us."
He rushed up to Briancourt, who was collapsing across the table.
Cluet sat him on the stool and handed him a glass of water from a
carafe that stood nearby.

Briancourt drank. "I know," he said finally. "Julie—"

"She said nothing," Desgrez interrupted him. "Mademoiselle de
Grangemont has a very high opinion of you. Why, I cannot say. For
as far as I can see you're nothing but a coward."

Briancourt flushed hotly. He swallowed several times. Then he
looked up at Desgrez. "What I have been through is beyond human
strength," he said softly.

Desgrez gave the young man a somewhat friendlier look. He asked,
"Since you are staying here, Briancourt, why haven't you confessed?
To Abbé Morel, I mean. I hear he is your confessor."

"I have confessed," Briancourt exclaimed.

"Everything?" Desgrez asked.

"As far as it concerns me . . . yes," Briancourt said hesitantly.

"And what about the rest, Briancourt?"

There was a silence in the room. Outside, the squeaking and splashing of the pump could be heard as the stablehand rinsed out milk pails.

"You are quite right, Lieutenant," Briancourt said slowly. "I thought I could leave out that part of it. But I am entangled in it, caught like a bird in the hunter's net. And I can never, never go back. It is of no avail to me to read Saint Augustine's confessions when the lie remains in my heart . . . pious words upon my lips . . . hatred, fear, and lust in my heart . . ." Briancourt broke off and looked questioningly at Desgrez, but the lieutenant said nothing, only looked penetratingly at the young man. "You're quite right when you say I'm a coward," Briancourt went on at last. "I've struggled with myself. Ever since that night, and a thousand times before it—all the while I was in that house. But how can Father Morel understand this? He believes in man's goodness. I thought about going to the police. One night I was on the point of going to Paris. But I found the gate locked, and then I thought they couldn't possibly believe me. So I crept back to my room, without faith, without hope, my soul in despair, filled with unspeakable fear."

Desgrez, who had been listening with bowed head, looked up. "I don't precisely know what it is that lies so heavily on your conscience, Briancourt," he said in a not unfriendly tone. "But you are well aware that the witness to a crime becomes an accomplice if he conceals what he has seen. And believe me, your confession will help you find inner peace again."

"I know," Briancourt whispered. "And really I rejoice that you've come. But—how can I say it—it seems unbelievable even to myself. Often in the dead of night I suddenly start up from a restless sleep. Then I sit here on my cot and stare at these walls. It is so quiet, so utterly quiet that I sit waiting with pounding heart for some sound, for the creaking of a stair or the gentle soughing of the wind outside. Then it seems to me that I died long ago and am listening to the soft, soft sound, like the dripping water of a fountain, of time trickling into eternity. Then I remember it all again, and it's as though the whole burden of the world were shifted to my shoulders. Oh, my Father in Heaven, why dost Thou permit such things upon Thy earth?" Briancourt clapped his hands over his face. His shoulders twitched convulsively, but he made no sound.

They stood there as though under a spell—Desgrez thoughtful,

Cluet embarrassed and pitying—contemplating the young man who might have been the son of either of them.

"Briancourt," Desgrez said after a while in a soft but emphatic voice.

"Yes?" Briancourt started. Hesitantly he took his hands from his face. His eyelids were inflamed.

"Listen to me," Desgrez said, speaking slowly and laying stress on each word, as though he were talking to a deaf man, "both of us come from the police, Sergeant Cluet and I—my name is Lieutenant Desgrez, by the way—but that does not mean that we, too, have not made all sorts of mistakes, committed follies in our time. . . ."

Briancourt looked up at Desgrez in astonishment, the first faint intimation of a smile passing over his white face.

"Cluet and I are old soldiers," Desgrez went on, closing one eye briefly with the suggestion of a wink, "and we have seen all sorts of things, some of them highly unpleasant. You can well imagine, Briancourt, that in our profession we encounter mostly sorrow, misfortune, criminality, and baseness. Nevertheless, we also believe, like Father Morel, that there is goodness in all human beings. It's true, I'll admit, that sometimes it's damnably hard to find it. But if it were not so, Briancourt, and if I did not believe that, I would long ago have unbuckled this saber and thrown my spurs behind the stove. . . ."

"Me, too," Cluet growled.

"You can speak frankly to us, Briancourt. We know you are not a bad fellow. And, believe us, we do not feel called upon to preach morals to you. Our duty is simply and solely to find out what the facts are."

"Thank you for your confidence, gentlemen," Briancourt replied, glancing uncertainly from Cluet to Desgrez. "But it's so hard. I don't know where to begin."

Desgrez considered. "There are three things I want to know first of all," he said. "Why you left the marquise's home in such a hurry, why you fled, and why you borrowed Monsieur Bocager's pistols."

"That's just it," the young man exclaimed in despair. "There's a long story leading up to it, and you must know the whole story to understand. But to put it briefly, I knew that I was going to be killed and I borrowed the pistols to shoot the person who threatened my life."

"What kept you from carrying out your resolution?" Desgrez asked quickly.

Briancourt stared incredulously at Desgrez. But then almost immediately he said, "I discovered that he was not the murderer."

"Who?"

"Sainte-Croix!" Briancourt shouted.

"Ah!" Desgrez exclaimed. "The missing links in the chain are turning up." He looked at Cluet, who smiled foolishly and nodded. Then he turned back to the young man. "But Sainte-Croix was a murderer, Briancourt. You know that as well as we do, don't you?"

"A murderer, yes—but not my murderer."

"What a strange way to put it," Desgrez said. "You've not been murdered, after all."

"I haven't been. But Lieutenant, believe me, I don't exist any more . . . I'm not dead, yet I'm not alive either. It would have been better if those scoundrels had killed me."

"What scoundrels, Briancourt?"

"I don't know . . . I didn't know them. Two figures in the dark, two pistol shots, that was all," Briancourt said, anguish in his voice. He suddenly indicated the shoulder of his coat, where there was a patch. "You see, one bullet just grazed me. It wasn't something I dreamed."

Desgrez sighed softly. Then he asked, "Why should two unknowns have had designs on your life, Briancourt?"

"Because I came to my senses . . . because I refused to do it . . ." Briancourt sobbed. Suddenly he let his arms fall to the table, bent his head over the book, and began to sob aloud.

Cluet shook his head. He looked inquiringly at Desgrez, who went to the window and looked out upon the farmyard, waiting patiently until Briancourt grew calmer.

After a while Desgrez continued his interrogation. But Briancourt was so confused that he repeatedly became involved in contradictions; then he seemed to evade many of Desgrez's questions, and his replies became vaguer and vaguer.

Desgrez was experienced enough to realize that it was shame which inhibited Briancourt from speaking freely. And since he repeatedly declared that he wished to help Desgrez all he could and cast the burden of his sin from his soul, Desgrez tried his best to make the confession easier for him. But there were two difficulties: Briancourt obviously had no other witnesses to corroborate his incredible tale, and unfortunately he himself was hardly a reliable witness. He was tempestuous, overemotional, and superstitious.

It was getting dark when Desgrez informed him that he would have to lock him up for his own protection. "In any case, you will only be exchanging one cell for another," Desgrez said, indicating the simplicity of the room. "And I can assure you that we have some very comfortable rooms in the Conciergerie. There we can go over everything calmly. Besides, your testimony is so important to me that I cannot risk having you removed from this world by somebody who has an interest in the matter."

Briancourt, who had at first turned even paler, now nodded silently. He took his hat, his coat, and his book that lay on the table. At a moment when he thought his visitors were not watching him, Desgrez saw him surreptitiously take an oblong object wrapped in paper from one of the shelves and thrust it under his belt. But the lieutenant said nothing.

Desgrez had to take Father Morel partly into his confidence. The good abbé, a rather heavy-set, white-haired man, was at first so shocked he could scarcely speak. But Desgrez finally persuaded him that it would be best for the penitent to be taken to the safety of the stout Conciergerie walls.

The evening star was already sparkling in the sky above snow-covered Aubervilliers when Desgrez, Cluet, and Briancourt, the young man riding a borrowed horse, left the settlement of the Pious Fathers.

PART II

CONFESSIONS OF A YOUNG MAN

⌐ I ⌐

NEXT MORNING Desgrez went to see Briancourt in his detention chamber. He found the young man stretched out on the floor, peering under his bedstead. Desgrez smiled slyly, stood watching in silence for a while, and then said, "Good morning, Briancourt. Are you hunting mice—or looking for something else?"

Briancourt started. He looked up at his visitor in embarrassment. "Good morning, Lieutenant," he said, getting to his feet. "Yes, I have mislaid something. But . . . it isn't very important."

"So much the better," Desgrez said good-humoredly. He sat down on a stool. "Believe me, things do not easily get lost here. You will get it back—whatever it is."

Briancourt nodded and sat down, too, facing his visitor with a shy, questioning gaze. Desgrez took his time. He looked around the cell, feigning great interest in its furnishings. After a while he said evenly, almost casually, "Well, my dear friend, I thought a good deal about our problem last night, and I can not help feeling that my presence yesterday—and of course the presence of my good friend Cluet—upset you and kept you from speaking freely."

Briancourt made a gesture of dissent.

"Hear me out," Desgrez went on amiably. "I put myself in your situation and I could see that I would have behaved the same way. For unfortunately this crime, of which you are the sole witness, is involved with the kind of highly personal experiences that people generally keep to themselves. But, I'm sorry, Briancourt—silence, tact, consideration for yourself or anyone else are out of the question now. It isn't enough for you to name the guilty person; I must have the whole story from you, with all the details and in chronological order. I must know how, when, and where and as a result of what circumstances you learned all this. What we need is a complete picture. For any charge without a substructure of clarification would meet with incredulity, and that could have very unpleasant consequences —for me and for you, too."

Desgrez paused to let the significance of his words sink in. Briancourt shifted about nervously on his stool and whispered, "I'll co-operate—co-operate to my full extent, Lieutenant."

"Good," Desgrez said, looking hard at the young man. "I know it is not going to be easy for you. And so that my presence won't disturb and constrain you any more, I intend to leave you alone with your task."

Briancourt looked up at him quizzically. Desgrez explained:

"I have ordered the turnkey to supply you with pen, ink, and paper, so that you can write down your experiences right here, in complete solitude. What I want you to do is to write down more or less an accounting with yourself. People confess to themselves what they would not admit to their best friend, let alone a member of the police." He paused to smile reassurance. "So forget me. Bury yourself in your past. And good luck!" He got up and went to the door. There he stopped, turned back to Briancourt, and added, "One more thing. Stick to facts. When you've written down one fact, fix your eye on the next and aim for that one. That's the way to do it."

Briancourt had also got to his feet. Tormentedly, he said, "But I don't even know how to begin. There's so much—much too much— and it's all so difficult. . . ."

"Well, Briancourt," Desgrez replied, "begin with yourself. People always have a great deal to say about themselves. I'll look in on you from time to time to see how it's going." He nodded and left the cell. The door clanged shut behind him.

One evening about a week later, Desgrez walked swiftly up the stairs to his apartment on the Place Royale. Bending over the fireplace, he held a wooden spill in the embers until it caught, then lit a candle. He added several logs to the fire and took off his greatcoat.

There was a roll of paper in the pocket, which he carefully laid out on the table and pressed flat.

Without bothering to take off his tunic and don his brocade dressing-gown, as was his habit when he came home from work, he sat down in a chair, drew the candle closer, and began to read.

Gradually what he was reading took hold of him. After a while he was sitting motionless, his temple propped against his right hand, as still as if he had been transformed into a statue—like the bronze nymph which, now that the fire was burning brighter, emerged more distinctly from the shadow of the wall and with inquisitive, fishy eyes and a faintly mocking smile upon her pursed lips seemed to be listening to the silence. It was as though she, too, could hear the words which Desgrez, there at the table, was drinking in with greater and greater excitement:

"She was everything to me. Like the radiant sun, she had risen above my life, and it seemed to me that only in the light of her love did I truly appreciate the splendors of a world teeming with life, and the overwhelming abundance of created things. It seemed to me that hitherto I had wandered blind and insensitive over the earth.

"O my God, forgive me! Forgive me, O Lord, that I in my madness often compared her with that gentle Lady to whom I prayed in my childhood. And forgive me, especially, that even now I cannot tear her out of my heart. I know, yes, I know that you alone, O Lord, can forgive us for what we cannot forgive ourselves in all eternity.

"Lieutenant Desgrez would warn me that I must not go on writing in this manner. He insists on facts. Facts are what I am to reveal, and only facts. It is hard for me, I must say. For to me all true reality lies in my feeling. What are events and the sequences in which they appear to me? What are they but uncertain fantasms and fleeting dreams, if I do not raise them to the level of my feelings.

"But I must discipline myself.

"I never knew my parents, Parisians of poor circumstances who died in swift succession before I was one year old. Nevertheless, my childhood was a happy one. Kindly Providence saw to it that instead of a fleshly father I could call twenty spiritual fathers my own. And in place of an earthly mother the Queen of Heaven Herself spread Her beneficent hands protectively over my childhood and early youth.

"The regime of the Pious Fathers was a mild one. All their speech and all their acts were dedicated to the service of God. Yet life with them was by no means dismal. And the very first acts that could be performed by my still clumsy hands and my untrained reason were, for me also, a welcome service to the Mother of God, whether I drove the great-horned cows out to pasture or helped the children of Aubervilliers to bind sheaves.

"Often, in summer, when the warm wind swept across the broad and billowing wheat fields, I believed I saw the face of the Divine Mother herself, for the Holy Mother was painted in our little chapel wearing a dress richly embroidered with golden ears of wheat. But the Fathers taught me that this was a pagan belief, just as they put strictures against my believing that the silvery full moon or the peaceful evening star were the abodes of Our Lady.

"As I grew older, I devoted more and more time and effort to books. I was eager to discover for what purpose this world and I myself had been created. The Fathers looked with approval upon my zeal, and they instructed me in the languages of the ancient world.

"At the age of fourteen I was as learned as I was inexperienced in life. The Fathers then sent me to the Sorbonne, that I might have further training as a theologian. They thought, as I did myself, that I would spend all my life with them in Aubervilliers.

"I was seventeen years old and had already earned my baccalaureate in theology when I fell prey to a curious restlessness that grew stronger day by day. I knew very well what its source was. In the writings of the Fathers of the Church there is much talk about the ancient demons of the earth. Truly, the Fathers of our Church condemn them roundly, when they do not mock them. But I was struck when I read in my Augustine of the horde of spirits who, according to heathen belief, swarm busily around the marital bed of a young couple.

"I began dreaming about such matters, which are to be found over and over again in the writings of Tertullian, Origen, and the others. So feverish and enervating were these dreams that I spent my waking hours as if in a daze. Though I was more attentive than ever to the practice of my religion, a tiny crack seemed to have opened in the solid structure of faith. Through this crack, alluring and confusing, there entered a gentle, melancholy breath of that great dark other world which apparently has long since been buried, the world we call paganism.

"A terrible passion seized me to learn more and more about these demons. I read the writings of the ancients avidly. Strange fancies settled in my heart: Hesiod's tale that night-born Eros is the creator of the world; Plutarch's story of Osiris torn to pieces and Mother Isis wading, weeping, among the swaying reeds of the Nile. I read more and more of strange and weird figures, whose lineaments were unclear, but who were all closely tied to the Magna Mater, the Great Mother, whom the pagans believed to be the earth herself.

"To my good Fathers it seemed that I was reading all these books solely to deepen my theological learning. They could not suspect that the demons were already taking over my mind, that, if I may put it so, they shared my pillow at night. For I did not reveal my thoughts to the Fathers. On the other hand, I did speak to one of my fellow students. He laughed at me for attaching too much importance to these matters. There was nothing the least uncommon about such notions, he declared, and took me to the Jardins du Luxembourg. There, to my amazement, I saw white marble statues of the demons. But neither my friend nor anyone else in the park seemed to share my astonishment. People strolled quite indifferently past the statue of Diana, around whose slender legs the greyhounds gamboled; they scarcely noticed the full-bosomed Venus standing beneath the chestnuts, smiling, an apple in her delicate fingers. From the attitude of the passers-by, there was nothing which distinguished these figures from the figures of saints in our church.

"My amazement knew no bounds when one evening my friend took me to the theater in the Petit Bourbon. My friend and I stood high up in the gallery, jammed tight in the crowd. But it seemed to me that I was being raised into Heaven as soon as the violins, harps, and flutes began to speak in their many voices. The stage far below, with its long vistas of beautifully painted backdrop, simulated a forest, at the farther end of which was a white temple with many columns. I could scarcely believe my eyes, and in fact I uttered a low cry of incredulity, when suddenly from one side there appeared a band of goat-footed satyrs, with tails and horns, and from the other side a group of long-haired, half-naked nymphs came dancing toward them.

"Breathlessly, my mouth open, I watched the band of satyrs em-

brace the nymphs, apparently intending to perform before the whole
house the act for which the ancients excoriated them. But there was
an interruption. For now a crowd of agitated women appeared. Their
heads were adorned with ivy and they waved small staves. The
creatures of the forest fled before them. The women sang a song;
then they drank from laurel-wreathed goblets. Apparently they were
drinking very strong wine, for almost immediately they showed every
sign of being drunk. Then the hairy satyrs ventured forth again, and
the female river demons as well. This time the group of them was
reinforced by dryads, centaurs, lapiths, and other monsters, so that
the whole stage was crowded. Then the music swelled, became one
great cry of jubilation, joined in by the creatures on the stage and
all the spectators, who were standing now. Down the steps of the
temple descended a tall figure, a wreath of vine leaves twined about
his heavy brown curls, dressed in a brilliant red mantle with a spotted
panther hide thrown over one shoulder.

"My friend nudged me and whispered hoarsely into my ear, 'The
king!' 'The king?' I exclaimed. And then I grasped it—yes, it was he,
Louis, our king, the King of France. He was the Dionysus who moved
majestically, with radiant countenance, to the beat of the intoxicating
music, across the center of the stage. Before him men and demons
alike bowed down; around him rang out a paean of joy, of brother-
hood between men and the living forces of nature. And upon this
jubilant note the ballet ended, while in glowing red the royal mono-
gram appeared upon the pediment of the temple.

"I still remember my walk out to Aubervilliers that night. It was
already autumnal; diaphanous white mists, through which the gentle moonlight shone, floated whispering around the black trunks of
the trees. The woods now had taken on so mysterious a life for me
that I started when a withered leaf drifted to the ground. I inhaled
deeply the spicy fragrance of fallen leaves, red-cheeked apples, and
blue grapes, and deep within my lungs I felt the bracing vigor of
autumn. Oh life, life! I sang aloud, and once in an excess of joy I
embraced the great trunk of a tree and kissed its rough, cracked
bark while tears of joy streamed down my cheeks.

"My resolve was taken. I belonged to the world. I could not renounce the world, as I had once thought. It was not the music, not
the spectacle, not the red-mantled king as Dionysus that threw me
into such ecstasy and made me abandon the goal I had set myself

for so long. No, it was something different, something within me, a tempting voice which sang inaudibly in my ears, an allure I felt in my blood. And it was also something like a premonition of an overwhelming experience which I mysteriously felt to be approaching me from far away.

"But how was I to create a life in the world for myself? I was poor, without any means whatsoever, and could not expect the Fathers to continue to support me. To my unworldly mind, this question seemed extremely difficult. But it was solved for me on the following day. Today it seemed to me, as I reflected upon this, that I had been given demonic aid; it was as though the way was opened for me and my path smoothed as soon as I gave my heart to Eros.

"Staying with us in the settlement at the time was a Monsieur Bocager, a respected Parisian advocate, who made a retreat in Aubervilliers for a few weeks every year in order, as he said, to forget entirely the fret of business affairs and examine his inner world. We had become quite friendly, and next morning I informed him of my dilemma. He laughed at my embarrassed face and said, 'Nothing simpler, Nicolas, my boy. Come and work for me. I'll make a good lawyer out of you. Anyway, you ought to do well in Paris. With your scholarship and, above all, with your looks, you'll get far—especially if you don't too much play the monk with the ladies.' And he poked me in the ribs, chuckling.

"I felt enormously relieved. The Fathers agreed to my change of plan, although they were certainly not overjoyed.

"I began working for Monsieur Bocager, helping him write up his pleas and, in my spare time, studying law in the Quartier Latin. After the complexity of theological problems, law study seemed remarkably simple to me. When I remarked upon this to Monsieur Bocager, he said, 'Yes, in theory the laws are simple and clear enough. But not in practice—and it's practice that counts, Nicolas. Incidentally, I have a capital affair here for you.' He rummaged around his disorderly desk and handed me a tied bundle of papers. 'Madame la Marquise is waiting for these; they concern the estate of her brother, the Count of Offémont, who, as you know, did not forget her in his testament. The lady wants to leave Paris as soon as possible, so hurry along there. She lives in the Rue Neuve Saint Paul.'

"It was an extremely hot July day. The walls of the houses shim-

mered in the heat and harsh light of a merciless sun. I was covered
with perspiration by the time I reached the Rue Neuve Saint Paul.
At the house a liveried lackey opened the door for me and I stepped
into the spacious vestibule. A dim light filled this lofty room, and it
was pleasantly cool. The difference in temperature between the heat
outside and the coolness inside was so great that I began to shiver;
the perspiration on my forehead and shoulders felt icy.

" 'What is the matter, sir? Aren't you feeling well?' the lackey asked.

" 'It's just that I walked somewhat too fast,' I replied. 'I have come
from Monsieur Bocager, the advocate, and have some papers for the
lady of the house.'

" 'Oh, then your business is most important,' the lackey said. 'Come
right in.'

"He led me through several resplendent rooms. But I was so confused that I paid no attention to details. I noticed only that there
were large mirrors everywhere on the walls, reflecting one another
and seeming to increase the number of rooms infinitely. It seemed to
me that the lackey with golden epaulets who walked silently ahead
of me was leading me farther and farther into a labyrinth. Then,
with a strange negligence toward the necessary formalities, he silently pointed to a half-open silk hanging. Through the opening I
saw a small room in which sat a lady, at a harpsichord, her back to
me.

"The lackey left me. In my hopeless worldly inexperience, I stood
there like a statue, desperately wondering how I could approach the
lady without alarming her. In my heart I cursed the lackey who had
got me into this situation.

"I heard a soft chord, and then a singing voice whose slight huski-
ness gave it a touchingly tired quality, as though the larynx or lungs
were too languid to produce an entirely clear note. I could not tell
what the lady was singing, probably only a series of disconnected
syllables. I became more and more embarrassed at playing eaves-
dropper, but suddenly the harpsichordist drew a great full chord
from the strings. The crash of tinkling notes echoed through the high
rooms, and I started at the unexpected sound. She turned her head
slightly and asked in a teasing voice, 'Well, young man, how long do
you intend to stand there?'

"As she spoke, she raised her beautiful round arm, from which the
wide sleeve of her bright summer robe had fallen back almost to the

shoulder, and pointed to a mirror hanging at an angle over the harp-sichord. In the mirror I caught a glimpse of myself standing be-tween the silk curtains, my papers tucked under my arm. I started to move toward her, stammering something about Monsieur Bocager, and tripped over the edge of the rug so that I almost landed at her feet. As I recovered my balance I noticed that she was wearing very tiny silver slippers tied with large silk bows.

"She gave a clear, good-natured laugh. It seemed to me that there was not the slightest trace of mockery in that laugh. She was not making fun of my discomfiture, or of my clumsiness. That laugh delighted me beyond measure. It seemed to me—I know the com-parison is inappropriate—as though someone were gently dropping large pearls into a fragile silver bowl.

"I bowed low and handed her the papers. She took them from me, but seemed little interested, for without glancing at them she laid them down on the harpsichord. She kept looking at me, and of course I instantly lowered my gaze. 'What is your name, monsieur?' she asked softly, in a tone that seemed to imply a certain understanding between us.

" 'Briancourt,' I said, and foolishly added, 'That was my father's name, you see.'

"But she seemed not to have heard this idiotic remark. For, without laughing, she said, 'It is kind of Monsieur Bocager to send you to me, Monsieur Briancourt. I know so little about these matters. But tell me this right off, was there a will?'

" 'Yes, madame. Your brother remembered you in it.'

" 'How much?' she snapped out, so harshly, so sharply that I looked up in surprise and stared at her. I realized at once that I must have misjudged the sharpness of her tone. For her eyes, of a pure, gentle blueness that delighted me, were glowing at me in the friendliest way, and there was a kindly smile around the full red lips of her small mouth. But in that brief moment when I dared to look fully at her for the first time, I had the strange feeling that she had, so to say, two faces. The first, though it was by no means an artificial mask, did not quite conceal the second. Her high cheekbones, with just the faintest hint of something feline about them, and the small, round, energetic chin, did not quite suit the refined countenance of a spoiled lady of society. They seemed to hint at something underlying, a power, tension, and activity that made her delicacy all the more

moving to me. But any thoughts I might have had about the duality
of her nature were instantly swept aside by her femininity, which
for me was overwhelming. The chestnut curls which hung down over
her forehead and temples, her small breasts, slowly rising and falling
with her breathing and only half concealed by her gauzy summer
dress, brought to me the shattering realization that I was within
touching distance of a creature like those for whom I had longed
from far off.

"I pulled myself together as well as I could in my state of sweet
rapture and answered, 'The count has left you one hundred thousand
livres, madame.'

" 'One hundred thousand!' she exclaimed in a voice that seemed to
me to express disappointment rather than joy. But then she added
more calmly, 'It is a great deal of money, of course—but—but . . .'
And without finishing the sentence she looked thoughtfully, and at
the same time searchingly, at me, as though she were estimating me
or my possible skill as a lawyer. 'But let us drop that,' she said, suddenly gay again. 'I am quite hungry. And you must be, too, Monsieur
Briancourt, aren't you? Come, let us breakfast together.'

"I bowed silently and followed her into another room. In answer to
her ringing a tiny bell, the careless lackey who had brought me in
reappeared in his silent fashion and set the table. Our repast was
simple indeed. It consisted only of slices of a very white wheat bread,
and cheese and honey, with which we drank fragrant, creamy milk
from very tall glasses. But it delighted me; never had I eaten anything so wonderful. The servant, bending over my shoulders, served
me with a solicitude which contrasted strangely with the careless
indifference he had shown earlier.

"Awe before the great lady mingled oddly with an ecstatic feeling
such as I had never experienced before, so that the room and the
simple foods upon the table seemed to partake of divinity. She
seemed to observe the state I was in, for she said, 'But Monsieur
Briancourt, do eat.' And she bent forward so that I could see the
fine part between the waves of her glistening brown hair, took honey
from the comb with a silver spoon and spread it on the white bread
for me. I suddenly recalled what Homer sings of Calypso:

> Speaking thus, the goddess set a table before me,
> Laden with ambrosia, and she stirred up the amber nectar.

"As I consumed these simple foods, I was in a state of rapture, although my provinciality prevented me from expressing this except by the shiest of glances.

"The lackey had silently left us alone. Madame spoke of the papers I had brought to her from Monsieur Bocager, and said they were very important—though more important to her children than to herself. But unfortunately, she said, she had so little time to examine them; she would have to be leaving Paris in the evening.

"Then she gave me that meditative look of hers again and smiled with such friendliness and charm that I could feel my fearful, tightly locked heart open. 'Monsieur Briancourt,' she said, 'wouldn't it be possible for you to come out to me at Château Sains? That is our summer residence, and we could discuss everything there at ease.'

"A tremendous gladness took hold of me. I knew at once that I would go to Château Sains at no matter what cost, but I said modestly, 'I don't know, madame, whether Monsieur Bocager can spare me.'

"She laughed her high, clear laugh. 'Oh, he will let you go,' she said slyly. 'But what matters to me is that you go gladly, Briancourt. For my sake, understand?' And she fixed her blue eyes upon me with a look that was a curious compound of roguish plea and impetuous demand.

" 'Certainly I will go gladly,' I exclaimed. 'Very, very gladly.' Then, alarmed at my own boldness, I sagged in my chair.

"The lackey had appeared soundlessly again, like a phantom. He carried a silver bowl full of orange-red fruits which he set down on the table between us. They were, as I now know, pomegranates. At this time I had never tasted the fruit, which in our climate grows only in hothouses.

"The marquise picked out one particularly large and ripe fruit. Smilingly she held it up and looked questioningly at me, as though asking me to approve her choice. Then she divided the pomegranate and handed me one half.

"A sharp, aromatic scent, in which the fragrance of sunlit soil mingled with the moldy odor of damp tombs, rose to my nostrils as I thirstily touched my lips to the many-seeded fruit.

"That was how it all began.

"Monsieur Bocager readily gave me his approval and even went to

the Quai de la Mégisserie with me to buy me a pair of new shoes in
which, he jokingly said, I would worthily represent him before his
best client.

"It was the height of summer. Everything was new to me, and all
I saw pleased me: the stretches of woods to the north of Paris, the
highways lined with poplars, the small gray towns where we changed
horses. At night when the stars glistened moistly in the sky, I could
not sleep in my corner of the big, rumbling post-chaise. I remained
awake, while my fellow voyagers sat twisted in odd positions, snoring
all around me, and I thought of grand and poetic future glories for
myself.

"At last I reached Amiens. There, as had been agreed, I was to be
met by a servant who would drive me to nearby Sains. I had a few
hours to spare, which I used to visit the great cathedral of which
Father Morel had often told me, for he came from this vicinity. I
knelt on the cool stone before a deeply shaded picture representing
the Holy Virgin with her mother and her Child. After my eyes became accustomed to the dimness I made out details of the painting,
and these profoundly impressed me. Today, I know not why, these
details appear to stand in some close though obscure connection
with my experiences.

"The mother of the Holy Mother, Saint Anne, sat in a wide, half-
subterranean landscape of caves. Everywhere steep black cliffs towered up like columns. At her feet was a dark pond, rimmed by reeds
and fitfully reflecting her bent, meditative head. Her eyelids were
almost closed and there was a mysterious smile around the corners
of her mouth. The pool also reflected the face of her daughter, the
Holy Virgin, who, as is usual in this type of composition, was shown
sitting upon her mother's lap. The Christ Child was playing to one
side with a lamb.

"What made this painting so significant to me, I can scarcely say.
Not so much the concept of successive generations, it seemed to me,
although this was expressed here in a particularly felicitous manner.
No, it was something else. Probably it was the cave, the strange
towering cliffs, the dark, reflecting water. But above all it was the
face of the Virgin which merged with the landscape and, although
her veil was lifted, seemed to remain under an invisible veil. It
seemed to me that the Mother depicted there was no being of the
external world, but something within ourselves, a being out of our

dreams, out of the abysses of our souls—and having qualities of soul which, I believe, rise closer to the surface in women and girls than in us men.

"Since I still had time, I went down to the Somme and looked at the rich vegetable fields. For there, in the trenched overflow area of the river, everything flourishes. Of all the rivers of France the Somme spreads farthest into the surrounding meadows when it overflows its banks—almost like the Nile.

"Oh, how rich even a single day of our life is, what a superabundance of experiences it contains, if only our spirit is open to receive them. I was in a most happy state, for I was to see her again.

"The servant came. I mounted the horse which he had brought with him. He also was mounted. It pleased me to sit like a cavalier upon a steed of my own. We rode for somewhat more than an hour through a fruitful plain out of which rose low hills, their tops often crowned by fine groups of trees, so that the whole landscape resembled a park.

"It was early in the afternoon when we reached Sains. The château could scarcely be called that; it was, rather, a large, spreading country house. I dismounted and entered. A young girl, who introduced herself as Mademoiselle Julie de Grangemont, greeted me pleasantly and showed me to a simple, whitewashed chamber which was to be my room. Julie—I shall call her simply Julie, since we soon became friends—lingered at the door and asked with considerable concern whether the chamber was to my liking. At this I had to laugh and said: 'You would have to see my room in the Quartier Latin to understand why that question amuses me.'

"I soon became aware that little Julie had something on her mind. As she set the table with food and drink for me, I noticed that she kept glancing pensively at me out of the corners of her eyes. I told her that I had come, as a student of law, to advise the lady of the house in an estate matter. At that she looked stunned and her attitude toward me became perceptibly cooler. I shrugged inwardly and thought how right Father Morel was; he had always said that young girls are more full of humors than the weather in April.

"That evening I was invited to dine with the masters of the household. Only the marquis and Madame were present, since the children always ate separately. The marquis, a rather weak-looking, fair-haired man with a receding forehead that gave him something of the look of an overbred greyhound, barely regarded me. He spoke in a blasé voice of his social obligations in Paris and remarked that he intended to return there shortly.

" 'Do you mean little Dufa, my friend?' the marquise asked, and winked at me.

" 'Certainly, madame,' he replied smilingly, in a voice that sounded to me as though he were deliberately keeping it at a higher than natural pitch. 'You know how His Majesty dotes on the theatre. What is left for us, his obedient subjects, but to emulate his royal inclinations?'

"The marquise sighed. 'Especially when the theater appears to us in the form of so charming a person as Mademoiselle Dufa,' she said with almost imperceptible irony. 'When you return to Paris give her my regards and tell her that if I were a man I, too, would love her.'

"This was the kind of conversation that went on during the meal. I was embarrassed and taciturn, speaking only when the marquise addressed a question to me. I was relieved when the marquis rose, kissed his wife's hand, and left the room, without paying any attention to me. As I, too, was about to take my leave, the marquise asked me to stay and have a glass of wine with her. She asked me about my origin and my studies. A faint smile played across her beautiful face, and I could detect neither condescension nor irony in it. To my own amazement I found myself speaking freely of my past and my plans—although my voice, I soon realized, was growing more and more unsteady.

"After we had drunk two or three glasses of a sweetish wine, those blue eyes of hers turned, flashing, to mine and she asked me my first name. I told her.

" 'Well, well,' she said, apparently pleased. 'Nicolas—why, he is the patron saint of children, isn't he?'

" 'Yes, madame,' I replied, 'and of the shipwrecked.'

"Something strange happened. Her face became distorted, her mouth twisted, and her gaze suddenly became so icy that I started back. Confused, I wondered whether my remark had touched off some unpleasant memory of hers. But then I saw her features softening again. She raised the glass to her lips and drank. And as though the wine were some magic elixir, she became at once the pleasant, casually chatting lady of society that she had been a moment before.

But she must have noticed how taken aback I was, for she said in her husky, faintly weary voice, 'Forgive me, my dear Briancourt. Recently I have not had myself entirely under control. I have had all sorts of—all sorts of troubles.'

" 'I know, madame,' I said, and to my annoyance I found myself lowering my eyes. 'The death of your brother . . .'

"I broke off, feeling like a fool. Now, for fear of tactlessness, I had committed a real breach of tact. But she simply remained silent for a long time, so that at last I looked up at her. She smiled dreamily. 'That, too,' she said suddenly, sighing, 'that was a great disappointment.'

"How queer, I thought; most people would say 'sorrow' rather than 'disappointment.' But almost against my will I whispered, 'I can very well understand that, madame.'

" 'Can you, Briancourt?' she asked softly. I hardly dared to believe it, but I was almost certain that I saw something like affection for me in those lovely eyes of hers as she said, 'I feel we shall get along very well together, Briancourt.'

"That night I lay sleepless for a long time, listening to the soft night breeze that soughed through the heavy foliage of the trees in the garden. I had surrendered utterly to sensations of sweet longing. As I clasped my hands to pray to the Virgin, as had been my habit since my earliest childhood, I realized that I could no longer pray. An irresistible force that seemed to be operating close by me diverted me. An image of another woman appeared before my closed eyes in the darkness, the curve of her cheek, her curls, that tender look I thought I had observed. And the Holy Mother paled to a mere phantom among her Virtues—which now seemed to me even more unreal than she herself.

"In the following days I was busy arranging the papers I had brought with me, and making extracts from them to be used in a forthcoming conference with the marquise. This work did not take up too much of my time. I often chatted with Julie, whom I liked and who also seemed to like me, although she was very shy and always kept glancing around her, as though she felt that no member of the household ought to see us together or eavesdrop upon our completely trivial conversations.

"I also made the acquaintance of the marquise's three sons. I played ball with them, swam with them in the small river which, a

short distance from Sains, flowed into the broad Somme, and visited
the stables with them. These, it seemed to me, were not at all kept
up with the neatness and good order that had obtained at the farm
of the Pious Fathers at Aubervilliers.

"One aspect of the household struck me as strange. The marquise
always kept her two small daughters strictly separated from the sons.
They were not allowed to play with us, and when the four of us
went down to the river I frequently saw the blond heads of the two
girls at one of the windows. They would be gazing longingly after us.

"I had been only a few days at Sains when the marquis left for
Paris. His departure was a relief to me. But the marquise appeared to
me to be rather downcast. At table she scarcely spoke, although
there was no uncordiality in her bearing. Once I heard her sigh
deeply in the adjoining room, and another time, when I met her in
the hall, it seemed to me that she had been weeping; her eyes were
inflamed.

"As everyone remembers, the summer of 1670 was unusually lovely
and warm. Several times the marquise invited me to go for walks
with her; she was fond of walking in the vicinity of Sains in the late
afternoons. At such times she was much more cheerful and open
than when we were at home, and I, too, felt much more at ease when
we had left the servants and children behind us.

"One day, as we were walking over the meadow, which shim-
mered in the heat of the sun, we passed a patch of ground thick with
the open flowers of red poppy. 'Look, Briancourt,' she said, touching
my arm, 'see how passionately their redness stands among all these
useful plants—almost like a great love among the ordinary sensible
affairs of everyday life.'

"I started. It seemed to me as though she had read my mind. 'Yes,'
I answered with embarrassment, and to say something I added, 'but
the flower has another significance also. The ancients called it the
bringer of dreams—the flower of death.'

"Her hand on my arm contracted so convulsively that I looked at
her in amazement. But I saw only her beautiful chestnut hair; her
head was turned away from me. For some time she walked along
silently beside me. I realized that my casual remark had greatly
agitated her. There was something weary about her ordinarily proud
and springy gait, as though she were stepping over an invisible ob-

stacle. And I myself felt faintly disturbed, although I could not have said why.

"We came to a ravine which abruptly and unexpectedly cut into the flat mowings. We had often visited it on our walks, for even on the hottest day it was pleasantly cool by this dusky, narrow gorge which was always filled with the soft murmur of flowing water. Following the narrow path, we descended down to the brook, which at one point, where the ravine widened out, formed a small pond rimmed by reeds. On the other end of the pond there was an old dam. Here stood the half-crumbled walls of a mill and a large black wheel coated with green moss. Although the water slapped incessantly against the dam, the motionless wheel lent to the hidden pond a quality of dedicated peacefulness.

"Here amid juicy green plants, which were kept so wet that they always emanated a faint but not unpleasant odor of decay, we sat down on a small bench. For a while we listened in silence to the purling waters that moved in a thin, transparent stream over the black dam. A solitary ray of sunlight fell through the tops of the trees and painted a gleaming spot upon the surface of the still pond, whose blackness gave the impression of unfathomable depths.

"The marquise looked at me and her eyes smiled. 'Briancourt,' she said, taking my hand and stroking it, 'forgive me for my silly behavior a moment ago. You are the only person in the world with whom I can speak frankly. I believe Providence has sent you to me. For I can sense that you do care somewhat for me.'

"My heart gave such a leap I thought it would burst from my breast. I blushed and stammered something about eternal devotion.

"That amused her. 'But of course it's quite possible that I'm mistaken,' she said, laughing, but looked searchingly at me. 'Perhaps you have given your heart to little Julie. She is really so nice, just the sort men go after, I think.' And she laughed even harder, an oddly discordant laugh.

" 'No,' I stammered, 'how could I possibly . . .'

" 'What's that?' she asked, laughing still, and slightly mocking.

" 'When the sun has risen, who can still see the stars,' I exclaimed hoarsely.

" 'A compliment!' she cried, clapping her hands softly; and her surprise was only half pretense. 'Why, Briancourt, I never would have thought it of you.'

"I threw myself upon my knees and covered her hands with ardent kisses, stammering disconnected phrases, everything my heart poured out, without my reason's taking the time or trouble to sift it. I remember only that I called her the meaning of the world and the goddess and light of my life, and that I really believed everything I said—just as I had believed it all before as I lay sleepless in my white room and my chaotic emotions invented all sorts of endearments for her.

"For a long time she let me kiss her small, firm hands. Then she stroked my head and said softly, 'We must be reasonable, my young one. You are a nice boy, but good heavens, I could be your mother.' And then, with that frightful concern for the humdrum and normal that seldom deserts women, she added, 'Now get up, Briancourt, or you'll ruin your clothes on the wet ground here.'

"I stumbled to my feet, collapsed upon the bench, and clapped my hands over my face, sobbing. 'I am lost,' I moaned, 'lost forever . . .'

" 'Why? Good Lord, why?' I heard her ask in amazement.

" 'Because—because I cannot tear this love out of my heart, because I am nothing and you all, madame. The whole world lies at your feet.'

" 'What has that to do with it?' she exclaimed. Then, softly and pensively, she added, 'Briancourt, you underestimate yourself. You are young, charming, and innocent. I feel . . . I feel I could love you . . . if there were not the difference in age . . .'

"I sprang to my feet again. 'No, it is utterly impossible,' I cried, throwing my arms wide apart to express my despair.

"She looked silently at me. Gradually, under the gaze of those great eyes, so pure and clear, cool and estimating, I became calmer. 'Listen to me, Briancourt,' she said in an unemotional voice, 'tomorrow two gentlemen are coming to Sains, and I must inform you of certain matters so that you will understand what it is all about.'

" 'I will do everything for you, madame, everything in my power. You may be sure of that,' I whispered. But I felt disappointed and ashamed.

" 'I know I can rely on you, Briancourt. I knew it when I first saw your face in the mirror—in my Paris home. You will say nothing of this to anyone, will you, Briancourt. You see, my dear, I am poor, poor as a beggar.'

For a moment I thought she was joking. But her seriousness and air of gloom convinced me otherwise.

" 'That can hardly be, madame,' I said dubiously. 'You own this estate, your house in Paris, and now in addition you are receiving an inheritance of a hundred thousand livres. I cannot understand.'

" 'I cannot understand myself,' she cried plaintively. 'But Sains and my house on the Rue Neuve Saint Paul are heavily overmortgaged. The same is true of my husband's estate in Morainvilliers. When I married, my father gave me a dowry of a hundred and fifty thousand livres. Some time afterward I inherited fifty thousand livres from my grandmother. I inherited from my father also. My husband had a large fortune—over six hundred thousand livres. . . . But it's all gone, all of it. The creditors with their usurer's interest are driving me mad. Briancourt, you must help me, if you have any feeling for me at all.'

"I was stunned, but I still doubted that her predicament was real. She must be temporarily embarrassed, I thought, nothing worse. 'But the inheritance is still forthcoming,' I urged.

" 'What difference will it make!' she cried. 'Don't you understand that the creditors lie in wait for it like foxes ready to spring upon a fat goose. Those demons once actually attached my carriage; they stole my estate of Nouars from me. But I saw to it that it was nothing but a ruin when they laid their filthy hands on it. Now—I know it— they are eying my horses, my furniture, my pictures, my mirrors— even my bed—they would even take my own bed from me. But I don't intend to be robbed any more. I will fight—for myself—for my children. And when I fight, I use any means . . .' She paused, breathing hard, almost sobbing with emotion. Her large eyes sparkled with rage; her slender fingers were crooked, and the tender, rather too white skin of her face was drawn tight over her high cheekbones. Never before had I seen such an exhibit of unrestrained feminine wrath. I could scarcely believe that this was the same woman who a moment ago had stroked my hair with such kindness. 'I hate them,' she cried, losing control of herself completely. 'I hate them all, the bloodsuckers.' Her scream rang piercingly through the narrow wooded vale; an echo answered mockingly from the wall of foliage.

"I must have looked utterly stunned. For as soon as she looked at me she started and immediately calmed herself. I had already noticed this characteristic of hers, to change her moods so suddenly. I

had the impression that the gentleness she now showed was just as
genuine, just as unaffected, as the hatred which a moment before
seemed to be consuming her. Again and again I was to be surprised
at these abrupt metamorphoses. It would have seemed hardly less
incredible to me if, as happens in old fables, she had suddenly been
transformed into a raging beast.

"As we walked slowly home she discussed with me the details of
her difficult situation. Thus I became her confidant, and along with
the love that now filled my heart I felt for her also the confused
stirrings of pity—while at the same time I asked myself what she
possibly could have done with all her fortune, a sum of more than a
million livres.

"The following morning she sent for me. I found her in the company of the two men of whose arrival Julie had earlier informed me.

"She introduced one of them to me as Monsieur de Sainte-Croix.
He was tall and quite prepossessing in appearance, but I took a
dislike to him at once. That energetic Roman nose, that imperious
and ironic look in his gray eyes, and the hard line of his chin did not
suit the semiclerical garb he wore. My distaste was considerably
augmented by his familiarity with the marquise—overfamiliarity, it
seemed to me.

"The other gentleman, Monsieur de Laune, was a solicitor. In contrast to Sainte-Croix, who was not a person you could overlook, De
Laune was a colorless little man with a sharp, mousy face, whitish-
blond hair, and the bare suggestion of eyebrows. He had the unpleasant habit of licking the palm of his hand, then rubbing it dry
against his cheek. His look of sly cunning, his obviously hypocritical
humility, which went ill with the impertinent tone of his voice, instantly made me think of the classical type of the crooked lawyer.

" 'Monsieur de Sainte-Croix is an old friend and brother-in-arms of
my husband's,' the marquise said to me. 'And my friend as well, I
believe I may say. Monsieur de Laune has managed many business
affairs for me and possesses my full confidence. I've told the gentlemen that you are devoted to my interests, my dear Briancourt.' She
gave me a fleeting smile. 'So we can speak quite candidly with one
another.'

"De Laune, his hand rubbing his cheek, now explained in detail
what I already knew—that the inheritance of one hundred thousand

livres would just cover the demands of the creditors, but that not a sou of it would be left for Madame unless some measure was taken. To think of something to do was the reason for their presence here.

" 'There is only one way,' Sainte-Croix said in a voice that involuntarily reminded me of a saw-toothed knife. 'Madame must make out a note of indebtedness to me—say for fifty thousand livres. I will then claim the sum from the inheritance and repay it to Madame as soon as I have received it.'

" 'What do you say to that, Briancourt?' the marquise asked, with a searching look at me.

" 'I beg pardon,' I said, bowing to Sainte-Croix, who was sitting with crossed legs, head raised imperiously, in his armchair, 'but your proposal seems to me unfeasible, Monsieur de Sainte-Croix. According to the law the older creditors must be satisfied first. A promissory note made out today would be worthless.'

" 'That's correct,' De Laune murmured.

" 'Certainly,' Sainte-Croix said mockingly, 'but how would the matter look if we dated the note back?'

" 'That would be cheating!' I exclaimed, and instantly regretted having expressed myself so bluntly.

" 'Come now, young man,' Sainte-Croix said, his eyes flashing at me, 'it's just a business device, no more.'

" 'A business device,' I said. 'Very well. But how will it look if the Probate Court demands a sworn corroboration of the date? Would you be willing to take the oath, Monsieur de Sainte-Croix?'

"Sainte-Croix looked haughtily at me.

" 'There's hardly any point to such a question,' De Laune whispered, licking his paw.

" 'Not so, not so, De Laune,' Sainte-Croix said. 'Monsieur Briancourt is quite right to call our attention to the danger of being forced to commit perjury. But how about this, my young friend: I have in my possession a note that Madame made out to me four months ago.'

"I was taken aback. It was inconceivable to me that the marquise could have borrowed money from a person such as he. My dislike for him was growing with every passing minute. But I tried to dissemble my feelings and only asked, though in a rather cold voice, 'For fifty thousand livres, Monsieur de Sainte-Croix?'

" 'No,' he said, the scorn in his voice stronger than before, 'for thirty thousand, to be precise.'

"I looked at her as she sat there, so fragile and beautiful in her sweeping silk morning gown. Her lovely head was tilted to one side, but it seemed to me that she threw a swift look at Sainte-Croix—a look of fear and perhaps of hatred as well. Then she turned to me and said, in a voice that seemed to me wearier than usual, 'The note does not come due until January, Briancourt.'

" 'That is true, madame,' Sainte-Croix said. 'I have mentioned it not to remind you, but to find out whether it could be of any use to us in the present predicament.'

" 'Unfortunately not,' De Laune sighed, rubbing his cheek. 'Unless we decide to change the due date of this note back to April or May of this year—'

" 'And slip into perjury again? No, De Laune,' Sainte-Croix interrupted mockingly.

"We talked on back and forth for a while. Madame was very quiet. Since the mention of that damnable note, she seemed to have lost her previous good spirits. Her hands kept fussing with her hair, although her coiffure was perfectly in order. Now and then she closed her eyes and would open them only to look sadly out to the garden, from which the voices of the children at play could be heard.

"I felt very uncomfortable. I was bothered by that promissory note, and the talk and proposals of these two visitors were not calculated to relieve my feelings. Everything they proposed was unclean and bordered on the criminal—until at the end, faced with the insolubility of the problem, their proposals became utterly fantastic. Looking at me, De Laune proposed that someone should persuade the dead man's widow, Madame Daubray of Villequoy, to pay the money to the marquise directly, circumventing the court, so that it would escape the greedy hands of the creditors. I was more amazed than horrified—amazed that a man supposedly familiar with the law could seriously voice so childish a proposal. But my amazement increased when Sainte-Croix, that repulsive fellow in semiclerical garb, suggested—I did not know whether in jest or in earnest—that perhaps the messenger carrying the money could be attacked and robbed in some lonely place.

"At this point the absurdity of it all became too much for me. I stood up and said, 'Madame, I believe there is really nothing to do but to satisfy the creditors. At best, a few of them may perhaps be persuaded to defer collection of the debt, or part of it.'

"To my surprise Sainte-Croix agreed with me—so that apparently his former preposterous proposals had only been intended as mockery. 'You are right again, young man,' he said in his arrogant, patronizing tone. 'There is nothing for us to do but wait.'

" 'Wait? Wait for what, my dear sir?' I asked, trying to make my own voice sound ironic—although I am afraid I only half succeeded.

"He was amazed and I had to restrain myself from flinging some insult into his face. 'Until the next inheritance, of course,' he laughed.

"This incredible piece of tactlessness in the presence of the marquise, who had only recently lost her brother, threw me completely off balance. I looked at her, and she returned my glance with embarrassment, her lower lip quivering. But almost at once she composed herself and she smiled questioningly at me as I bowed to her. Then, with head held high, I left the room, not deigning to give Madame's peculiar guests another glance or bid them goodbye.

"I stayed in my room the rest of the day in order to avoid meeting the two men.

"That afternoon, as I was looking out of my window, I saw her walking in the garden with Sainte-Croix. They were talking agitatedly together, and in his tense face I could not discover a trace of mockery. Once they paused for a moment under a tree. He took her hand, raised it and kissed it—and she allowed it, without surprise or anger.

"The blood rushed to my face. I stamped my feet. Damned idiot! I cried inwardly. Filthy charlatan! Then I felt ashamed of this outburst of helpless jealousy. For a long time I sat on my bed and thought over my relationship to her.

"Julie came, bringing me my supper. I saw that she was upset; her hands shook so that she almost spilled the glass of milk she was placing on the table. I thanked her. She did not reply, but stood hesitantly in the doorway, with lowered eyes, lingering there as though she could not tear herself away. Then she looked cautiously out into the hall and came back into my room, softly closing the door behind her. 'Monsieur Briancourt,' she whispered without looking at me, 'I feel it is my duty to warn you.'

" 'About what, Julie?' I asked, involuntarily falling into a whisper, as she had done.

"Her lips moved without making a sound. Then it came. 'I warn you, Briancourt,' she said, her voice suddenly firm and almost harsh. 'Be on your guard. More is at stake here than you suspect.'

" 'What is at stake, Julie . . . what?' I asked.

"Again she hesitated a long time before she spoke, as she had been doing all through the conversation, 'I don't know,' she said at last, 'and if I did know I would not say. You know that I am related to the marquis and that he has kindly taken me into his house.'

" 'But if you want to warn me—and, believe me, I am grateful to you, Julie—you must tell me what you are warning me against.'

"She came up so close to me that I felt her warm breath in my face. 'Such peculiar people come here!' she cried out.

"I was shaken. Her strange and apparently unfounded apprehension had seized me also. But then, as though from some deep abyss in my soul, there arose the ugly thought that she was speaking out of jealousy. I could feel a wry, sly smile creeping over my face.

"She saw the smile, and I realized that she understood its significance.

"She stepped back, half turning away from me, so that I saw her fine features in profile, and with head bent she said tonelessly, 'As you wish, Briancourt.' Then she left the room. Ever so quietly, she closed the door behind her.

"I was left alone. And a vague anxiety filled my heart.

"The air in my little room was stale. I felt as though I were inside a whitewashed grave and threw the window open. It was already growing dark in the garden; the soft, warm rain drizzled steadily down from a sky that could not be seen.

"I could stand it no longer. I swung myself over the window sill into the damp garden, which from moment to moment was filling with a deeper darkness. As I walked on I had the sensation that this darkness was a damp, heavy substance which I could feel with my hands, a substance that smelled of dying and moldering plants.

"Beside the moldy earth I smelled the cemetery odor of the hepatica and birch and the harsh autumnal fragrance of the asters. Then I started. Close beside me, in the deeper gloom beneath the foliage of a huge ash that towered up from the invisible ground to the invisible sky, a small white figure stood like a phantom, like the embodiment of my fear.

"I no longer knew whether I went up to her or stood still. But suddenly she had taken hold of me and a pair of firm lips clung to my mouth. Will-lessly, I moaned aloud. There was a wild chaos in my heart, a weird mixture of terror, voluptuousness, and sorrow. I felt her hands in my hair and responded to her kisses, with which the warm rain mingled. I felt as if I were under some incredible enchantment, as though the warm earth herself held me in her embrace. Her thick, dark hair, hanging loosened like a mane to both sides of her white face, had a sharp fragrance like that of the asters.

"She was dressed only in a diaphanous white nightdress. I felt her graceful body beneath the tulle. My lips sought the erect tips of her firm breasts, wet from the warm rain.

"Suddenly she laughed softly. 'This is my thanks, Nicolas,' she whispered, half tender, half mocking, 'but this is one of those days when I must deny myself to you. You know, now. So be sensible, my poor boy.'

"I stood numbed. I had been on fire and was now suddenly frozen.

"She rearranged her dress and closed it over her breasts. 'That is the way I am,' she said, as though she noticed what was going on inside me. Then she added in a perfectly matter-of-fact way, 'I am always on fire when I am in this condition.'

"I was speechless. This first revelation of the secrets of femininity was so prosaic, so utterly different from what I had dreamed of and expected. Yet I felt that I could not go on standing there silent as a post. I pulled myself together and said in a shaking voice, 'I love you so much, madame.'

" 'If you do, call me Marie-Madeleine . . .'

" 'Forever,' I whispered. 'Forever.' I took her small hand and kissed it fervently. 'Mad— Marie-Madeleine, how did you know I would come to the garden?' Never had I spoken a name with such pleasure, such a sense of overwhelming sweetness.

" 'I wanted you to come. And you came,' she said, shrugging, as though that were self-evident. 'You were right, Nicolas, altogether and utterly right.'

" 'Right about what?'

" 'This morning. You alone, Nicolas, were devoted to my interests; neither of the others was. They were only trying to trap me. Especially that rogue Sainte-Croix with his thirty thousand livres. I could see how his tongue was hanging out for my money.' The wrath in her voice, which was still slightly husky, turned to sorrow. 'I really don't know what to do or where to turn, Nicolas. Stay with me, my darling. I feel that together we will find a way—for our mutual happiness.'

"'How much I want to,' I sighed, laying my hand lightly on her shoulder, which felt cool and soft beneath the thin nightgown. 'But you know, Marie-Madeleine, that I must return to Paris—to Monsieur Bocager.'

"She did not answer at once. The rain was falling harder now; it pattered harshly in the foliage of the ash trees, and I saw with concern that her nightgown was soaked through and clung closely to her slight body. But this incidental discomfort did not appear to trouble her; she was like a person completely absorbed in some difficult enterprise. 'I, too, must go to Paris,' she said thoughtfully. 'We could ride together.'

"The rain was now coming down hard. I threw my coat around her shoulders and accompanied her back to the house. Her bedroom, I noticed, was in the wing of the house opposite mine. She gave me a brief, hard kiss and then agilely, without making a sound, clambered to the sill of her open window.

"It was pitch-dark, and the sighing and splashing of the heavy rain drowned out all smaller noises. Nevertheless, as a precaution against discovery, before venturing toward my own window I turned back to the depths of the garden from which we had come together.

"When I looked around, I saw that she had drawn the curtains of her window and had lit a candle. The dim light painted the silhouette of that delicate, slim and yet strong body against the curtain. She must have thrown off her wet nightdress, and was drying herself, as the movements of the shadows showed—drying first her hair and then, bending forward slightly, her breasts, abdomen, and legs.

"I did not look away. She is mine, I thought.

"Three days later I sat beside her in her carriage. It was now the beginning of September, and a cool wind blew across the stubble of the harvested fields. She sat shivering and taciturn in the corner of the coach. I realized that something was troubling her. Often she closed her eyes, as though the light of day bothered her; but she

would soon open them again and twitch the folds of her skirt with
nervous hands.

"I did not dare to ask the reason for her uneasiness; I felt a distinct
aloofness between us. But suddenly she broke the uncomfortable
silence to tell me that her brother Jacques was sick and that the
doctors doubted he would recover. I took her hands in mine and
expressed my sympathy, but to my amazement I saw a crooked smile
spreading over her beautiful face, distorting it to a mask of scorn.

"She noticed my amazement. The smile vanished as though it had
never been, and she said wearily, 'My brother and I have not been on
good terms. He had not behaved very nicely toward me.' Then she
closed her eyes and relapsed into her silence again.

"These words and her peculiar behavior disturbed me. It seemed
to me that life's moral fundaments, which are its natural bases as
well, were being overthrown. For the first time in my life I rejoiced
that I was an orphan and that the men I called my fathers were my
fathers only in the spirit and not in the flesh.

"A feeling of happiness and warmth poured through my soul as I
thought of Notre Dame des Vertus and of our learned and devout
conversations. It seemed to me I could hear again, as I had all
through my childhood, the silvery voice of the bell of our small
chapel. But I was wrenched out of these pleasant thoughts by her
voice. She had turned toward me, her ill humor had utterly vanished,
and her eyes shone tenderly at me as she said, 'Forgive me what I
said before, Nicolas. I know it must have sounded harsh and loveless
to you, for you cannot possibly know all I have suffered at the hands
of my family, darling.'

"Like a tidal wave, my passion for her returned. I seized her hand
and covered it with kisses. I stammered that there was no need for
anything to be forgiven but my own foolish behavior.

"Smilingly, she pointed to the coachman, whose tasseled coat could
be seen through the front window of the carriage, to remind me to
behave with greater restraint. But her eyes were full of the promise
of love and her hand rested familiarly on my knee as she said that
she could not do without me, that I must stay with her. I made her
feel like a woman, again, loved and desired, whereas before my
arrival she had felt herself almost like a sexless thing. Not to love,
she said, was as good as being dead—while on the other hand, she
added with a pensive smile, all love had to be paid for by death.

"She often expressed herself somewhat mysteriously. I did not always understand what she meant, but I could sometimes sense a vague threat emanating from her words. The more affectionately she spoke, the more distinct that threat would become.

"She persuaded me that I would be wholly happy in her house, and I quickly agreed to be the tutor of her three boys, if only Monsieur Bocager were willing to discharge me from his service.

"When we reached Paris, I went to see Monsieur Bocager at once. He not only did not object to my change of plans, but congratulated me upon making such swift progress. Father Morel, however, whom I saw that same evening in Aubervilliers, took a far more skeptical attitude. He looked long and searchingly at me and remarked that I ought not to bind myself too firmly or for too long a time.

"But, driven by a wild lust which I did not hesitate to call love, I disregarded Father Morel's warning just as I had my own better judgment. I was jubilant when, a week later, I sat with her once more in the coach that was to take us back to Sains.

"During that week, as Monsieur Bocager had informed me, the marquise's younger brother had died a very painful death. I found the marquise wearing mourning. Her wide mantle, edged with a great deal of black lace, emphasized the pallor of her face. I saw at once that she was, as I had expected, terribly upset. Her behavior was hectic and disjointed. She scolded the coachman for failing to buckle a bundle properly on the back of the coach, and her attitude toward me alternated between cool aloofness and superficial cordiality. Moments when she sat mournful, her face expressing doubt and scorn, would alternate with sudden fits of wild and unwarranted merriment. It seemed to me that she was on the verge of one of those nervous collapses to which women sometimes fall prey, usually, so I have heard, as a result of some crisis in their sexual life.

"That evening we reached Louvres-en-Parisis. We stopped there at The Sign of the Big Stag. Since the dining room was filled with a noisy and high-spirited company of hunters, the marquise ordered supper brought to her room and invited me to dine with her. I had been assigned the room next to hers.

"I can still see her room, a simple, whitewashed, rather large chamber, the walls adorned with pairs of stags' horns. In the large and colorful tile stove a fire was burning; on the sideboard and the table, candles in simple candlesticks made of white stoneware were already lit. By their dim light I discerned a curtain embroidered with large flowers. Behind this curtain was the marquise's bed.

"We sat down. The innkeeper himself served us. He was a small, bearded man with powerful, broad shoulders and a strikingly large head which rather gave him the appearance of a gnome. He served us with roast wild boar and filled our glasses with a heavy, earthy, sweetish wine which I think must have been white Burgundy. He behaved very respectfully toward the marquise and addressed her only in whispers, as though out of sheer awe he were unable to raise his voice. On the other hand he was offensively familiar toward me, and kept filling my glass, each time giving me, it seemed to me, a wink with one of those small, black eyes of his.

"Finally he cleared away the dishes and brought in another bottle of wine, from which he poured me a full glass.

"She had risen from the table and was in a corner of the room, before the mirror, arranging her hair. The innkeeper bent down so close to me that I could smell the onions on his breath and whispered, 'It is a double bed, monsieur.'

"I sat petrified, my hand gripping the fluted base of the glass as I tried to think how I could call the fellow to account for his impertinence. But before I could make up my mind, he had left the room. I heard him busying himself outside putting fresh wood into the tile stove, which was fired from the corridor.

"It was very warm. I had drunk several glasses of wine, and I was little accustomed to strong drink. The effects made themselves felt in an inward relaxation. What I felt was not really a sense of joy, but rather of excited anticipation.

"I looked at her. She was still standing in front of the mirror, completely absorbed in her own appearance. Abruptly she turned and looked thoughtfully at me. She tossed her head back so that her mane of hair fell in long, beautiful waves down over her shoulders. Never had I seen a woman like this. I half rose from my chair in surprise and desire.

"Without smiling, resolution and darkness in her ordinarily clear eyes, she stepped up to me and pressed me back into the chair. Then her right hand took my chin in a firm grasp and she bent down and kissed me hard on the mouth. I shivered, and sat wordless.

" 'Well, Nicolas,' she said—and there was a note of harshness in her voice—'how do you like me tonight?' There was a peculiar earnestness in her penetrating glance.

"I stared at her, spellbound. The oval of her face, the high cheek-bones, the flowing hair—it was like a phantom sprung from the sweet mists of the wine. Behind her the white wall with the stag horns swayed slowly.

" 'You're so different tonight, Marie-Madeleine,' I whispered. 'You are beautiful. . . but. . .'

" 'But,' she demanded insistently, her eyes fixed unflinchingly upon me.

" 'I love you,' I cried.

" 'You wanted to say something else, Nicolas. Say it. I must know.' She bent closer to me again and touched my ear lightly with her tongue.

" 'It's nothing,' I stammered, confused. 'It's only your hair. I didn't think it would be like that.'

" 'Does it disappoint you, Nicolas?' she asked with soft mockery. And then added naïvely, 'You know, as a child I was a golden blonde —but now it has all grown dark—all. . . .'

" 'You could not be more beautiful—oh, my darling,' I exclaimed, and put my arms out to her. But she drew back. 'No,' she whispered. 'I want more than that—I want all of you. You must tell me everything —everything, Nicolas, so that I can tell you everything. Oh, you—you child, haven't you realized how I need you—how I hunger for some-one?'

" 'What is the matter?' I asked her anxiously, for I saw tears in her eyes.

" 'You first,' she whispered tensely. 'Tell me what you have seen in me. Be honest—even if you offend me—because I want to be honest too.'

"Confused, I took another drink. Thoughts, fragments, shards of thoughts like single clots of ice floating upon the raging waters of an obscure feeling, went whirling through my brain. 'It was only a momentary impression,' I said, my tongue thick, 'but as you stepped up to me with your hair down and kissed me, it seemed to me—I thought of someone else. . .'

" 'Of whom?' she snapped. And I saw that she was so excited that her eyes had become faintly crossed.

"I staggered to my feet. 'I don't know exactly,' I mumbled. 'It isn't any human being—just an image, a vision of a great figure, figments of whose features I have seen scattered here and there in the world. The look in the eyes and the roundness of face of a pregnant woman, the summer wind over the ripe ears of grain, the full light of the moon among glistening trunks of trees. But also the long-haired bacchantes on the stage of the Palais Petit Bourbon and the head of St. Anne in the cave looking down into the black waters of a reed-lined pool. . . . All that—and much much more. . . . It is there in the faces of all women. One would have to be a great poet to describe it. She is magnificient—and terrifying at the same time. But above all she is ancient as the world, for all her radiant youth, of sacred origin!' I fell silent, shaken, knowing that I would never be able to describe it. In my own ears everything I had said sounded wholly inadequate and foolish.

"But she seemed to have understood what I meant. She seized my hand and kissed it. 'Her!' she whispered. 'You compare me to her!' And suddenly she added resolutely, 'You do not know whom you are speaking to. But now you will learn.'

"I gaped at her. Her voice was hoarser than usual and sounded rough and jagged. 'I am a murderess,' she said without emphasis, as though she were simply making a statement of fact about something of which she was sure I must have known long since.

"I stood before her. I wanted to say something, but I could only feel the quivering of my lips and was unable to utter a sound. With so tremendous an effort that my forehead broke into perspiration, I finally cried hoarsely, 'That isn't true. You are a mother.'

"'Yes,' she said, 'I am a mother, but a murderess, too.' She fell silent. Then suddenly she screamed, 'It's too much, Nicolas. I can't go on this way.'

"I stood there stunned. But still I did not believe her. I had vaguely heard that women are sometimes seized by delusions whose origin is connected with their sexual life. 'Marie-Madeleine,' I said, trying to calm her, 'believe me, you have done everything you could do. For your brother, I mean. You must not torment yourself with these self-reproaches.'

"She laughed scornfully, then regained control of herself with an effort and said suddenly in an altogether factual tone, 'You refuse to understand me, Nicolas. I have killed my brother Jacques. And be-

fore him my brother Antoine. I had both of them poisoned, one after
the other.'

"I looked at her. I saw that she was speaking the truth, or thought
she was. Still I could not grasp fully the monstrous thing she had
told me. This woman I thought I loved, this delicate woman with
her large eyes, her sweet, frail white temples, the murderess of her
brothers? It was impossible. And yet as I thought about it, it seemed
no longer quite so impossible. There was something cruel, wild,
primeval, something hard to put into words, something about her
tonight as there had been that rainy night in the garden. The elegant
lady with the charming, somewhat absent smile, the clear, rather
tired voice, the lady of court in her stiff gown, was only a disguise
behind which lay a tremendous force of femininity and amorality, a
primeval creature who had revealed herself to me now and then in
brief passionate phrases. This other person, the woman behind the
society lady, might be anything—and therefore might well be a murderess.

"I had remained silent for a long time, deep in thought. The crack-
ling of a piece of wood in the stove brought me back to the present.
She, too, had been silent. Now, as I looked at her without speaking,
I saw that her mood had shifted completely once more. Where a
moment ago her face had bespoken despair, now there was a look of
great sanity, back of which I seemed to read something like affection
for me. It seemed as though my knowing had relieved her; as though
she felt a stronger fondness for me now that I knew her secret. And
to my shame I must confess that in spite of my confusion and dismay,
in fact my terror, this feeling was far from unpleasant. It seemed to
me that my heart reached out invisible hands to her, eager to embrace her warmly, to possess her. But I came to my senses and, with
a faint doubt still in my voice, I asked, 'What kind of poison was it,
Marie-Madeleine?'

" 'How do I know,' she said. 'It was a white powder and a colorless
water. Sainte-Croix made it.'

" 'The blackguard!' I exclaimed, and I must confess that my hatred
and indignation were based upon jealousy of this rival, not horror for
the crime. 'Did he himself give it to your brothers?'

" 'Oh no, my dear,' she said lightly. 'One of his lackeys took care of
that. A very capable man.'

" 'My God, Marie-Madeleine,' I cried out, 'have you no heart at all to be able to talk this way? And why was it done? For heaven's sake, tell me why.'

" 'My brothers behaved very badly toward me, Nicolas. That is all I as a woman can say to you,' she murmured. Her face was distorted with hatred as she spoke.

" 'Do you feel no repentence? No remorse? Your own brothers!' I moaned, looking uncomprehendingly at her. She did not answer at once. She sat with her face bent forward, so that it was illuminated with a reddish light from the fading embers beneath the stove grate. Her splendid hair flowed to one side in a dark, living mass. The crown of her head had a wonderfully fine, yielding look. 'No,' she said softly at last, 'I regret nothing. I would do it today if I had not already done it.'

"I was still feeling the aftereffects of that sweetish, heavy wine, of which I had taken far too much, and it all seemed like a bad dream. Her face, the white room, the stags' horns—in my half-intoxicated state there was a tremendous attraction, a peculiar stimulus about it all, in addition to the horror.

"Noiselessly, she moved through the room, putting out the few candles, so that only the reddish glow from the stove dimly illuminated the chamber, casting a ghostly web of light upon the walls. She moved about as though floating. With both hands she reached up to her shoulders, and her heavy gown fell to the floor at her feet. She stepped out of the dress and bent down to untie the ribbons of her shoes. Now she was wearing only a thin undergarment. Her face was half turned toward me, and I saw the line of her bent neck and the gleaming nakedness of her shoulders between the dense masses of her hair.

"I stood in the middle of the room, supporting myself against the table with one trembling hand. There was a sourish taste in my mouth. My heart pounded with fierce anticipation, and yet I was frozen to the spot. I could no longer move and my tongue lay leaden in my mouth.

"Slowly, without haste, but with a kind of seriousness and devotion, she completed her preparations. She removed her garters, rolled her silken stockings down to her ankles, and drew them off. Smilingly, she studied her small feet and briefly touched them tenderly with her fingers. The relaxed pleasure she took in the beauty and warmth of her own body, and the lovely movement with which she tossed her hair lightly back from her temples and bound the dark waves of it with a ribbon, reminded me of the animal contentedness and proud delight of a cat cleaning itself.

"She was so absorbed with herself that she paid no attention to me. I was still standing wordless, like a statue. But now, as though she suddenly recalled my presence, she turned her gaze toward me and called out impatiently, 'Well, get undressed, darling.'

"Awkwardly, with an embarrassment that my angular clumsiness only increased, I removed my shoes, hose, and upper garments. I immediately felt even more out of place and altogether preposterous. I was glad for the almost total darkness which prevented her from seeing me, for I felt myself infinitely ugly and ridiculous—I with my long, bony limbs, my wretched inexperience, my theological ideas— to find myself in the bedroom of a beautiful, half-naked lady of the world. . . . I, a Christian, though a sinful and lost apostate of a Christian, at the bosom of Aphrodite. . . .

"My agitation, my fear of this first mingling with the feminine principle, was accompanied by a painful longing, so that in the confusion of overwhelming emotions I almost forgot the horrible story she had told me. But far in the background, so that I was hardly conscious of it, gnawed the horror—death. And—must I say it again? —it was death itself, standing like a pale phantom in the distance, that whipped up my lust to sheer madness and gave meaning and depth to this mingling of man and woman—as though both of us, frail and helpless creatures separately, could together, becoming one, successfully defy the everlasting threat of extinction, of no longer being.

"She had gone over to the curtain of the bed and jerked it vigorously open. Now she sat on the edge of the bed, leaning back slightly, resting on her arms. Behind her in the semidarkness the white sheets gleamed. 'Come,' she said hoarsely, tenderly—and again she reminded me of a cat. 'Come to me, my darling.'

"I knelt before her. My palms felt the coolness, the firmness and wonder of her thighs and the curve of her hipbones beneath the thin silk undergarment. Madly I kissed her feet, her toes, her slender calves; I kissed her knees, her thighs.

" 'Oh, you like me. That feels good,' she sighed hoarsely, and ran her hands through my hair. Then she held me back and jumped up. With a single movement she slipped off her undergarment and threw herself back on the bed. Shaking herself, she dug her dark head into the pillows. But suddenly she started up again. I saw the fine outline of her shoulders and her pointed breasts, with a soft reddish glow upon them. She laughed. 'Listen, my sweet,' she said, laughing, 'keep my secret. Oh, my little one, keep my precious secret.'

" 'I will, dearest, I will,' I moaned. She gripped my shoulders hard and with her strong, small hands drew me down to her."

Desgrez looked up and thoughtfully regarded the candle, which had burned down to a stump. He rose and paced slowly back and forth in the room. Then he stopped before the bronze statue, but almost immediately turned away and threw several sticks of wood on the fire. Drawing the chair up to the fireplace, he sat down and looked into the flames, which crackled and snapped for a while and then began to burn with a bluish fire.

For a long time he sat without moving. He looked up at last when the bells of the nearby Church of St. Paul's struck midnight. With a sigh he went over to the table and picked up a quill-pen lying there. Absently, he dipped it into the inkwell, slid a sheet of paper across the tabletop, and began scribbling on it.

First he made a rather clumsy drawing of a female figure which bore a remote resemblance to the bronze nymph. Then he stopped, smiling, and made the following notes:

Motive: money. Investigate the marquis's finances. But even so, something is wrong here.

Her relationship with Sainte-Croix. Is she the lady of rank mentioned in the *lettre de cachet*?

Get Le Mesnil working on the Versailles gossips.

Her relation to Briancourt. Sensuality alone? Hardly. She must have wanted something from him. Call Briancourt's attention to this.

Briancourt's reliability: witnesses for the surrounding circumstances: De Laune, Julie, innkeeper of the Big Stag in Louvres-en-Parisis. Question them.

Desgrez read through what he had written and then, yawning contentedly, removed his tunic and boots. He slipped into his tattered dressing-gown, dropped onto his bed, and closed his eyes.

⊁ II ⊁

IN MID-AFTERNOON, two days later, someone knocked shyly at the door of the attic apartment on the Place Royale. In response to Desgrez's cheerful "Come on in," the door opened. In the doorway, a timid expression on her pretty face, stood little Julie de Grangemont.

"Good day, Mademoiselle Julie," Desgrez said good-humoredly. "It's nice of you to come all the way over here. Forgive me for not having called on you instead—but please sit down." He removed a book from one of the chairs and carelessly wiped the seat of the chair with his hand.

Julie sat down gingerly and looked timidly around the room. Then, her eyes fixed anxiously on Desgrez's face, she said softly, "Sergeant Cluet slipped your letter into my hand. . . . Oh, Monsieur Desgrez, is it really true? Have you really found Nicolas?"

"We certainly have, mademoiselle. And he is in good health, although still somewhat troubled mentally. But I must ask you to tell nobody—nobody at all."

"I will not if you don't wish me to," she said firmly. "Is his life still in danger?"

"That I do not know, Mademoiselle Julie," Desgrez replied. "But I do not dare take any chances. That is why I have him in the Conciergerie." He paused, then added, "Monsieur Briancourt knows of certain matters, and this knowledge could cost him his life if I do not guard him carefully. One person—and possibly several—would undoubtedly wish very much to silence him."

"Oh," Julie whispered, aghast. "I won't say anything. You can depend on that, Lieutenant Desgrez."

"Good," Desgrez said, smiling at her. "And you must tell no one of our meeting, either, mademoiselle."

"Yes, Lieutenant," she said, with a childish nod of the head.

"And now, mademoiselle," Desgrez said, sitting down opposite her. "I want to ask you for a piece of information which is very important to me. Is it true that in August 1670, at Sains, you warned Monsieur Briancourt against the marquise?"

Her cheeks turned pink and she looked down at the floor. But almost immediately she recovered and said, "Yes, it is true."

"Why did you do so, mademoiselle?"

The blush deepened and she appeared to be on the point of tears. "I was jealous," the girl forced herself to say.

"Was that all?" Desgrez asked, with an overtone of disappointment in his voice. "How did you happen to say to Monsieur Briancourt, 'More is at stake here than you suspect'?"

"Must I answer that question?"

"As you wish, mademoiselle. But you did say it, did you not?" Julie stared indecisively into space. "Yes," she said abruptly, stamping her foot, "I did say it—or something like it—it's so long ago I no longer remember exactly how I put it. But I can tell you why. By chance, as I was passing the drawing room that day, I heard someone say, 'We'll have to involve that young jackanapes Briancourt in the affair somehow; we must have him eating out of our hand.' Then I heard her laugh and say, 'Kindly leave the boy to me.' "

"She? Whom do you mean?" Desgrez asked quickly.

Julie started. "I must not say," she exclaimed anxiously.

"It isn't necessary, mademoiselle. But the someone you heard speaking first was named Sainte-Croix. Isn't that so?"

Julie remained silent. She had obviously made up her mind not to answer the question. Desgrez saw that she was trembling. "I understand very well, mademoiselle," he said mildly, "that you wish to protect the honor of the family that has taken you in. I will not trouble you with any more questions. Thank you very much. You have helped Monsieur Briancourt, and me as well."

"How so?" she asked in surprise.

"Ah," Desgrez said, wagging his finger at her, "the police ask questions but do not answer them."

She rose. "Mayn't I see Nicolas for a moment?" she asked.

"Quite impossible, Mademoiselle Julie. I will send him to you when all this is over."

"And suppose he does not want to come, Lieutenant Desgrez?"

"Then I will drag him by the hair with these hands of mine." Desgrez smiled and showed her his fists.

He opened the door for her, and they stepped out into the hall together. "Do you know, Monsieur Desgrez, I feel myself getting older every day," she sighed.

Desgrez pretended amazement. "Indeed?" he drawled. "How old are you, mademoiselle?"

"Seventeen," she said very earnestly. She shook hands with him cordially and tripped down the stairs.

He watched her until the door closed behind her. "An extraordinary age," he murmured, shaking his head. "To think that one was once that young oneself—it's quite incredible."

Still smiling, he re-entered his room, where the bronze nymph's eyes gazed into space with an air of cunning.

The following day Desgrez learned to his regret that the lawyer De Laune had gone off on a long trip to the northern provinces and therefore was not available for questioning. However, Desgrez then called on Monsieur Bocager and succeeded in getting him to say, though with many reservations, that Monsieur de Laune did not enjoy the best of reputations in the legal profession. He had some very wealthy and high-born clients, Bocager said, and had been involved in a good many shady, though never quite illegal, financial transactions.

This information, which substantiated Briancourt's testimony, gave Desgrez a welcome opportunity to inquire about the financial status of the Marquis de Brinvilliers. But now Bocager made difficulties. As was his habit, he fumbled with nervous hands among the heaps of papers, documents, and accounts that were scattered all over his desk, as though to hint to his visitor that his time was valuable and that he was being detained from his urgent task of making order in this chaos. But Desgrez sat unmoved. At last the lawyer sighed deeply and said, "You see, Lieutenant, my services are wholly confidential as, for instance, a physician's. I would at once lose all my clients and might just as well go begging if anyone found out that I talked loosely about their private affairs." He weighed his next words for a long time before he finally spoke. "Of course if you could show me an order from the Châtelet, that would be another matter entirely. I would then have to obey, whether I wanted to or not."

"That's just it," Desgrez replied, the deep furrow between his brows appearing again. "We cannot give you any such order—not yet."

"Why not, Lieutenant?"

It was Desgrez's turn to sigh. "My dear Monsieur Bocager," he said with a melancholy that was half pretense, "the Brinvilliers are among the first families of France, enjoying the very highest protection. And as you know, the Paris police are subordinate to authorities who would never permit a criminal investigation of that family unless we could provide proofs which we can obtain only by investigation. Under the circumstances there is nothing for us to do but to sound out the terrain on, so to speak, a private basis, and to hope for the lucky accident which will supply us with the necessary proofs and give us the mandate to make official and public charges. I believe I have hit on this lucky accident—in the person of Nicolas Briancourt!"

"Aha," Bocager said, suddenly intensely interested. "Then why do you not proceed with the official investigation, Lieutenant?"

"Because I must convince myself of the truth of Briancourt's testimony before I can present the evidence to my chief."

"Nicolas is absolutely honest," the lawyer said with conviction. "I would put my hand in the fire on that score."

Desgrez smiled at Bocager's unexpected warmth. "I think so, too," he declared. "But doesn't the young man possess a somewhat overheated imagination?"

"Well," Monsieur Bocager admitted, "he is simple, idealistic, fiery, easily carried away—like all young people who are worth anything."

"Exactly," Desgrez said dryly. "There you have my difficulty."

"I see," Bocager said slowly. "Tell me, Lieutenant, is this case really of such immense importance that it is worth all the trouble you are going to?"

"The crime in question is a frightful one," Desgrez said seriously, "and of course every crime must be punished. Moreover, acts have taken place which endanger the public safety, morality—the very existence of society itself. I know that this is a phrase often bandied about—but you would be serving the cause of justice and your fellow men, Monsieur Bocager, if you would permit yourself a little indiscretion toward me."

Bocager was impressed by Desgrez's earnestness. He gave his visitor a candid look and asked, "Can you assure me that my name will not be mentioned until the investigation has become official?"

"I certainly can, Monsieur Bocager. Anything you tell me will remain our secret."

Bocager reflected. Then he said resolutely, "Ask your questions, . Lieutenant."

Desgrez smiled briefly and asked, "Is it true, Monsieur Bocager,

that the Marquis's house on the Rue Neuve Saint Paul and his estate
in Sains are heavily overmortgaged?"

"Mortgaged up to the chimneys, Lieutenant—far beyond their
value, in fact; recently I had to decline to help the marquis obtain
further loans."

"Is it true that the marquis's personal possessions have been attached?"

"Several times. Even the carriage, which by the way has not been
paid for, was taken from him. But up to now I have always succeeded in recovering his property. I borrowed from Peter to pay
Paul, as the saying is."

"Which have been the most difficult years for the marquis—finan-
cially speaking?"

"Let me see now, Lieutenant." Bocager reflected. "In the summer
of 1670 I was asked to secure a large loan for him—to my extreme
surprise, since the marquise had just inherited a considerable sum as
the result of her elder brother's death. Yes—and then the younger
brother died, leaving almost his entire fortune to the marquise and
her children. I paid the loan back—with outrageous interest, by the
way. I thought then that the family ought to be back on a sound
footing, but in the fall of 1671 and the spring of 1672 I had to raise
large sums which as yet have not been paid back."

"Then you would say that the marquis's financial situation is unsound?"

"Unsound!" Bocager exclaimed, and again he riffled through his
papers. "He is on the verge of bankruptcy, my friend. That is," he
added more softly, "unless the marquise's sister or Madame Daubray,
her elder brother's widow, do not come to her aid again—or unless the
marquis receives a special gift from the king."

"How do you explain this state of affairs, Monsieur Bocager?"

"Well, Lieutenant, that is another question entirely," the lawyer
replied. "A question I have often asked myself, without ever finding
a plain and simple answer. But a life in Versailles—so many servants,
magnificent clothing, costly presents, select wines—such a life con-
sumes a great deal of money. . . . In fact, Versailles, which has transformed independent landowners into mere courtiers, is ruining the
French nobility. The Brinvilliers aren't the only ones. And our peasants are being ruined, too. After all, they have to support all this
splendor and wastefulness by the work of their hands, and their

reward is that they starve to death in their mud hovels." Bocager stopped short, looked with embarrassment at Desgrez, and shrugged his shoulders. But when Desgrez nodded solemnly in agreement, the lawyer went on in less excited tones, "And then the marquis, like all these court gentlemen, keeps a mistress—a creature of the theater, so far as I know—and that sort of whore is usually expensive."

Desgrez grinned; he liked the advocate's bluntness. "And what about the marquise?" he asked slyly.

"A perfectly charming woman!" Monsieur Bocager exclaimed with conviction. "Pleasant, always friendly, and simple—and for a lady of her rank she possesses a really overwhelming candor."

"Do you really think so?" Desgrez could not refrain from saying.

Monsieur Bocager was surprised at his visitor's skepticism. "You just don't know her," he declared. "If you did you would agree with me. Of course," he added after a pause, "it is said that she gambles—for very high stakes, in fact—she's rumored to have lost ten thousand livres in one night. But I . . . I believe the envy behind such malicious calumny is all too obvious."

Desgrez did not contradict him. "That is all I wanted to know," he said, getting up. As he thanked Bocager he could see from the advocate's disappointed expression that he would have liked to continue the conversation—probably to discuss Briancourt's testimony. But Desgrez bowed and left.

Desgrez went to see Briancourt in the Conciergerie. He found the young man busy writing.

"I've come to thank you for the information you've given me so far," the lieutenant said.

Briancourt, pen in hand, turned on his stool and asked in a quavering voice, "Do you believe me, Lieutenant?"

"Yes, Briancourt. I haven't wasted time and I have already obtained confirmation of some of your statements from other sources. I'll explain all that to you some other time; right now it would only confuse you. Of course there are several details that require explanation, but probably these explanations will be forthcoming as you go on with your story. But meanwhile, as I considered the whole thing, one element has struck me as psychologically mysterious: why did the marquise keep her daughters so strictly segregated from her sons?"

Briancourt looked at him in such amazement that Desgrez smiled
and added, "Yes, I know that seems altogether beside the point to
you. But in my experience it is just such incidental details which a
criminal does not consider it necessary to conceal that most clearly
unmask his motives and designs. I'd be grateful to you if just by the
by you could tell me something about the children."

"Gladly," Briancourt said, still rather surprised. "The two daughters, Marguerite and Thérèse, were respectively fourteen and thir-
teen when I first saw them at Sains. The marquise treated the little
girls coldly, almost with hostility, and I was much surprised when
she remarked to me quite early in our acquaintanceship that it would
probably be best for the girls if they became nuns. I did not understand her reasons. The girls were charming, well brought up, and
quite pretty, though not—I mean, though they were not as beautiful
as their mother. They were almost completely under the care of Julie,
who did her best to compensate for their mother's lack of love for
them. But I'm afraid she herself was only a child then."

"And what about the boys, Briancourt?"

"The oldest, Antoine, who was twelve years old at the time, resembles her very strongly. He has her high cheekbones, her blue
eyes, and even her look of resoluteness. In the family he was often
jokingly called Master Police Chief. It was hoped, the marquise told
me, that in later life he would be appointed to this post, which his
uncle and his grandfather had held. The two other boys, Jules and
Henri, were twins and quite unlike the eldest; in fact they resembled
neither their mother nor the marquis. They were merry and wide-
awake boys, much given to silly pranks, and occasionally subject to
violent tantrums, which I, of course, was very stern about." Briancourt flushed. "I'm afraid I was not always just and that I spoiled
Antoine, who was the idol of the entire household."

"How do you explain the separation of the girls and boys, Briancourt?" Desgrez asked after a long, reflective pause.

"I suppose it's not so unusual, Lieutenant. . . . That's done in
many wealthy houses, even in bourgeois houses."

"Yet it must have struck you as strange. Otherwise you would not
have mentioned it so expressly."

"That's true. But I've never really thought about it, Lieutenant.
Don't mothers frequently love their sons more than their daughters?"

"Hm . . . yes, that does happen." The explanation did not seem to satisfy Desgrez fully. "But now let's turn to something else entirely, Briancourt. You remember I asked you to keep steering from one fact to the next. I know that is hard for you—we prefer to tack around experiences that have shaken us too deeply. But I absolutely must know what the marquise asked you to do."

Briancourt started. He stared aghast at Desgrez. "How do you know that?" he stammered. "I . . . I mean . . . that she . . . wanted something of me?"

Desgrez did not answer the question. "You understand what I mean, don't you, Briancourt," he said.

"Yes . . . certainly . . . I only mean, it's as if you could read my thoughts, Lieutenant Desgrez," the young man said, still confused. With an effort he composed himself. "That's just what I've written down this past week—not without a struggle with myself, as you say. . . . Here it is, on this paper." And he pointed to the closely written pages on the table.

"So much the better. Give them to me now. Then I won't have to bother you any more."

Briancourt gave Desgrez a sheaf of loose pages, and the lieutenant leafed hastily through them. "I can see already you know what I want," he said amiably and took his leave of Briancourt, who sat still on his stool as the lieutenant went out.

Desgrez hurried home and began to read the next portion of Briancourt's tale:

"The next several weeks in Sains passed as in a dream for me. Almost every night I crept to her room, and she devised ever-new variations upon amorousness, so that all day I went about quite stupefied, only to awaken again to real life at night, for life had become more and more my cohabitation with her.

"There were times as I lay beside her, numbed as though by a deadly poison, or as I touched her body with trembling hands, when she would suddenly begin to talk about her brothers. Then it was as if the dead clustered softly around our bed and demanded our attention.

"She did not speak with anxiety or repentance, but in a wholly objective and matter-of-fact way. In her faintly husky voice she would describe to me their appearance, their habits, their characters, and especially the manner in which she had brought about their passage from this life to the other.

"Dulled by the continual excesses, inwardly corrupted by my association with her, I was nevertheless filled with a panicky horror every time I heard her speak with such coolness and calm about them. She could not have spoken with less emotion if she had been telling me that two chickens had had their necks twisted at her orders. These talks would throw me into a cold sweat; I shivered and shuddered and was often on the point of springing out of her bed and leaving her forever.

"That first night in Louvres-en-Parisis I believed I had sensed that the murders were on her conscience. Why otherwise should she have informed me? It seemed to me that she wanted to find relief from her burden by confessing, by having me to share her knowledge of the crime.

"But now that I did know and she could be sure that I was wholly under her spell, she seemed to be enjoying the triumph of a victory over her conscience. If her conscience had ever troubled her, it had now successfully been silenced.

"She was not only unfeeling, she was scornful, and sometimes the flame of hatred for the dead men burst through her icy exterior. It seemed that what she wanted from me was not forgiveness for her act, but rather a full sanction for the double murder.

"I did not fully understand her. To this day I do not understand her. I realized that the death of her brothers, especially of her younger brother, had been of great financial help to her. But the obvious motive of gain, which she candidly acknowledged, was not the sole motive for the murders. Indeed, I doubt whether it was the principal motivation for these terrible crimes.

"Or, was her hatred for these two brothers, which she reiterated again and again, possibly only an excuse? Was she pretending, trying to persuade herself of this hatred, since the most horrible crime seems forgivable if it is committed out of the chaos of passion rather than from cold calculation?

"On the surface she seemed cold and calculating enough, almost a Cartesian spirit; but back of this clarity, which was expressed by that deceptively sane look of her eyes, there raged, in illogical confusion, wild and sinister passions which no one would ever have suspected could inhabit this fine and fragile vessel.

"What was the origin of her hatred for the dead men? From what had it sprung? I asked myself this question again and again as I lay beside her in bed and listened with fearful heart to her furious outbursts. Was it only transferred hatred for her own misdeeds, as symbols of which her dead brothers rose like phantoms in her conscience? Was it repentance, still unrecognized, furiously rejected, that proclaimed itself as hatred? That too is possible—I know it well.

"Again and again, whenever I asked her the reason for her hatred, she became confused and answered my question in an oddly dry, sterile tone, in the same sterotyped phrase: 'They did not behave decently toward me.' When I asked her what she meant, she remained stubbornly silent, or with a sigh of sudden lust drew me to her soft body.

"One night both of us had drunk a great deal. Outside, a storm howled, tossing splatters of rain against the window. Now and then the unearthly light of isolated flashes of lightning pulsed through the room, revealing to me the ghostly white mask of her face upon the pillows, surrounded by the dark frame of her hair. The face lay there as though separated from her body, like the head of Medusa with the snakes frozen in death. I saw that an absent smile hovered around the corners of her mouth—as though frozen there, it seemed to me. Her eyelids were shut. She lay perfectly still, like a dead woman on the bier, with the ascetic, ultimate smile of the dead.

"I listened to the gurgle and sigh of water outside, the noises of this nocturnal world which does not concern us and which we do not understand. I was overcome by fright and felt an immeasurable melancholy. 'Marie-Madeleine,' I whispered, 'are you asleep?' I asked although I knew she was not.

" 'You ask questions and ask questions,' she murmured almost inaudibly, so close to my ear that I felt her breath. 'You want to know everything. It does not occur to you that if I conceal a great deal, it is only out of kindness to you. . . .'

"Soundlessly the light filled the room, then vanished like a fan snapping shut; but the moment of brightness was sufficient for me to see that her eyes were still closed. I had raised myself on my elbow and was staring down at her face—like a white phantom beneath me on the pillow. 'Tell me just this,' I whispered. 'What grievance had you against your brothers?'

"She did not answer me. I sat thus for some time, leaning on my elbow. My arm began to hurt and my shoulders were cold as if they had been transformed into lumps of ice. I did not dare to move, and stared into the darkness, which seemed to be full of flickering shadows.

"Again the bluish light flashed weirdly through the room, which seemed to me to have changed into an endless subterranean cavern. The light went out, but I had seen enough. The archaic smile around the corners of her mouth had relaxed. After a while, during which I listened anxiously to the howling of the storm and the wild splash of rain outside, her quiet, level breathing indicated to me that she had fallen fast asleep.

"But I myself could not sleep. I stretched out full length beside her and looked up into the darkness above my head. Now and then would come a soundless flash and I would see the ceiling. It seemed like a white tablet from which sinister powers had wiped away all laws, all the commandments governing the human order.

"Like an avalanche thundering down into the valley and gathering all before it as it plunges into the depths—so my guilt seemed to me. With awe and terror I felt that I, too, was involved in the dark fate of the house of Daubray. And yet, though I had a premonition of it on that tempestous night, I still did not comprehend how dangerously far I had already ventured into the web. I did not know that the road I had taken must lead to a place from which there were but two paths, one to crime and one to death.

"At the beginning of November, the weather turned cold and rainy and we moved back to the city house. All winter long I saw her rarely. She was often away, at Saint Germain, at Versailles, in the Palais Royal. With silent bitterness I became ever more keenly aware of the tremendous difference in station between us. She was after all the noble great lady and I was an insignificant tutor of lowly origins.

"Sometimes we met at table. The marquis was almost always absent; probably he spent most of his time with his dancer, for whom, Marie-Madeleine had told me, he had furnished a luxurious little apartment in the Rue Royale. While Marie-Madeleine never showed me any ill will, her amiability was such that it was more offensive to me than rudeness. At times, when she entered the room in which I sat, she looked at me with obvious amazement, as though surprised to find me in her house.

"I began to think that those confidences of hers had been bogus, that she had only told me all those horrors in order to test my presence of mind and to make fun of my inexperience.

"There she was, radiantly beautiful, almost always in formal attire, wearing precious gems in her hair—a lady of the court with whom, as I heard, the king himself often danced.

"In her house she was hostess to the noblest and richest men and women of France. Dukes and duchesses, counts, ministers, cardinals, and archbishops, generals and the ambassadors of foreign powers came to her soirées. The house would be brilliant with innumerable candles, the yard and the entire street lined with splendid carriages.

"On such occasions I always fled to my top-floor room and sat brooding over a closed book. I felt myself thrown aside. Now and then I opened the door of my room and listened to the sounds from the ground floor, where the guests thronged. I heard their voices, the scurrying of the lackeys and the singing of the violins playing dinner or dance music. Sometimes she sang for some particularly honored guest. On these occasions I was shaken to the core; my eyes filled with tears, and more than once I vowed to leave this house, where I was suffering so terribly. But never did I have the strength of will to carry out any such decision.

"Could this celebrated beauty who enjoyed the affection and admiration of her brilliant world possibly be the murderess of her brothers? Impossible, I decided, and whenever I reached that conclusion I felt relieved of some of my burden, although doubts still shook me deep within my heart. When the guests had gone and I lay sleepless in my room, which was dimly illuminated by the lantern above the outside portal, it would seem possible to me again. Then I hated her, but at the same time I longed to have her with me again and I dreamed of lying in her arms and feeling the tips of her breasts against my skin. Her guilt had not made me indifferent to her as a woman; it had mysteriously augmented her attractiveness.

"Then I would often get up softly, push back the bolt on my door in the hope that she would come to me. Sometimes I crept out into the hall and listened for sounds from the silent, deserted stairwell. So great was my longing for her that my imagination deceived me and I thought I heard the soft step of her bare feet on the stair carpet.

"But she never came. Immeasurably disappointed and yet feeling a certain relief, I would return to my room. Then it would be long

before I could fall asleep. I would lie brooding in the agonizing twilight stage between sleep and waking. Everything would appear in
an aspect unsure and uncanny. Outside lay the nocturnal streets of
Paris, which has been called one of the most beautiful cities in the
world. But at such times it seemed to me a place of crime and death,
though also of sweet temptation and dark lust that were constantly
creating new lives and making new deaths. Space, time, even the
course of the constellations, were filled with weirdness. Bits and
fragments of old myths, in which I had perhaps been too much
absorbed, passed through my overwrought mind and I could not
cast them out.

"But at bottom I knew very well that it was not the world, but my
own life, myself, from which these obsessions stemmed. Often in
my depravity I longed to lose the faith which, so I thought, was
causing my moods. But the Christianity within me could no more be
extinguished than the paganism that, in my simplicity, I had thought-
lessly conjured up out of its grave.

"My days I devoted to my pupils. Often, when the weather permitted, I took them to the Jardins du Luxembourg, and this association with children restored my soul. In my leisure hours I frequently
visited my fathers in Aubervilliers, and I also confessed to Father
Morel—but not everything. I confessed only that I had fallen in love
with a married woman, but said I was trying to root this passion out
of my heart. Although this did not correspond to the truth, I myself
believed it at the time.

"It was during this winter that I became fond of Julie. At first she
avoided me, as she had done at Sains. But after a while she changed
in her conduct toward me. She must have noticed that the marquise
and I were no longer on the same footing as before, and perhaps she
told herself that I had broken with the marquise. And so she began
to nod to me in a more friendly way, and I soon discovered that she
sought chances to meet me.

"She was an orphan like myself and had been raised in a convent.
There were many things in common between us, and soon we were
able to talk easily and cheerfully with one another.

"It became our habit to take our afternoon chocolate together in
her room. Outside, the snow lay deep and the wind shook the shutters.
But inside the room the stove cast a pleasant warmth. We sipped
the hot chocolate. On the sofa the two daughters of the marquise

would be sitting, busy with knitting or other girl's handiwork. But it was Julie's presence, her expressive voice and her gay laugh, which made these hours meaningful to me.

"I knew very well that I loved her and that she loved me. I knew that she was the woman for me. Yet I could not free my heart of that unhappy passion for the other woman. Sometimes I persuaded myself that this passion had died, but I still felt it raging deep underground within me, dull as a half-suppressed pain, tenacious as the glowing heart of an apparently dead volcano.

"The one love had nothing to do with the other. They scarcely touched one another; as emotions they seemed to coexist without affecting each other. For my love of Julie was human, it was domestic and kindly. But my passion for the marquise was inhuman, it was destructive and dangerous. Never, even had it been within the realm of possibility, would I have dreamed of marrying the marquise and founding a family with her—but in Julie's presence I frequently dreamed of marriage.

"One evening Marguerite, the marquise's eldest daughter, fell ill very suddenly. Julie called me to help her. The child lay on the chaise longue on Julie's room. Her face was a chalky white, her forehead beaded with perspiration, her blue eyes staring, filled with horror, and unnaturally large. Now and then she writhed in terrible convulsions.

"I felt her forehead. She was icy cold. I offered to call a doctor.

"'There's no time for that, Nicolas,' Julie cried. 'Bring milk—much milk.'

"I rushed down to the cellar and returned with two pitchers of milk. The sick girl drank one whole pitcher, but refused to take any more.

"'She must take it, Nicolas,' Julie whispered to me. She was so agitated she could barely speak.

"She bent the child's head back and held her nose. I pressed against her jaws to force her mouth open and poured the milk into her, almost the entire pitcher. But suddenly, with an access of tremendous strength—from fear of suffocation, no doubt—Marguerite tore loose from us and sprang up from the chaise longue. In the middle of the room she stopped and vomited violently. Then she collapsed, her strength all gone, and we put her back to bed on the chaise longue. She fell asleep at once; the convulsions were over. She breathed quite peacefully, and gradually the flush of health returned to her white cheeks.

" 'Don't you think I ought to call a doctor now anyhow?' I asked softly.

"Julie did not answer me. To my amazement I saw that she was angry and that her lips were quivering with rage. Her fists were clenched and she screamed, 'The monster, the beast!'

" 'What do you mean?' I cried out with surprise. Then I came closer to her and asked, 'Ought we not rather thank God that the child is better?'

"She started, staring incredulously at me. Then, weeping, she threw herself into my arms.

"I felt her warm body shaking, pressed against mine. And I bent her head back and kissed her cheeks, which were wet with tears, and then her lips, which were parted as though in amazement.

"And she returned my kiss.

"In May, Julie and I returned to Sains with the children. The marquise was held up in Paris by some business, and, to my sorrow, I was soon to learn of what nature it was.

"In that lovely time of the year, the earth renewed and the park smelling so sweetly of lilac, Julie and I took long walks, usually accompanied by the children.

"With all my waking senses and my rational mind I had decided for Julie; but underground, on the verge of wakefulness, I still felt myself under the spell of the other woman. When the sun went down and the night spread over the earth, she was the stronger. But when the morning dawned serenely, with the cheerful voices of the children and the songs of birds in the garden, her image faded and Julie resumed her gentle dominion over my feelings.

"There were not only two women, there were two worlds struggling with one another within my heart. Yet this is not put quite right, for in actuality there was no conflict, no struggle within myself. The two women were like two stars to me, each of which rose and set in perfectly natural ways according to definite laws. And the one commanded the day, the other the night.

"In the midst of a quiet conversation Julie would often grow thoughtful. She would look at me, just for a moment, but searchingly, as though trying to read something from my expression. But with a cunning that I myself felt to be dishonest and ugly, I avoided speaking of the marquise. If I did mention her, it would always be in a casual, deliberately dry tone of voice. For it was one of the peculiarities of my so different relationships with these two women that my love for Julie was clear and unequivocal, and that I openly showed it, whereas my dark passion for the marquise was something about which I had to keep silent, like an evil, shameful secret.

"With the clairvoyance of someone in love, Julie probably suspected that my passion continued to work within me; but the suddenness with which I fell under the marquise's spell again must have come as a terrible surprise to her, as it did to me.

"Early in July the marquise came to Sains, and the very night of her arrival I crept through the garden to the window of her room, and found it open. She had expected me, and accepted my caresses. But I felt an opposition. She did not make love to me with that ardent, almost morbid rage of the previous autumn; rather, she gave herself as a gift.

" 'You are different, Marie-Madeleine,' I said. 'Is something troubling you?'

" 'Yes, something is,' she said in her husky voice. 'I'll tell you what it is in a moment. But first tell me this: You've kept my little secret, haven't you?' She laughed, but I could sense the seriousness in her intonation.

"I felt sorry that I had come. For already I realized that I was wholly caught up in her net again—that net woven of voluptuousness and crime. 'I have kept it,' I said, 'and always will.'

" 'I hope so, Nicolas,' she said harshly and threateningly. 'I have a way of treating traitors that isn't a bit pleasant.—But,' she added more mildly, 'what's this between you and Julie?'

"I started. The speed with which she had discovered our relationship frightened me. 'I like Julie very much,' I said shyly.

"She laughed. 'You don't have to be bashful with me, Nicolas,' she said scornfully. 'Do you imagine I'm jealous because that little blond goose makes eyes at you, or you at her? Have you slept with her?'

" 'But Marie-Madeleine, consider that—'

" 'So you haven't,' she interrupted me. 'Just as I thought. Disgusting, these women that get all hot and never come to the point of opening their legs.' She laughed loudly.

"I was repelled by her. Blood rushed to my face. I was hot with

indignation, and I gathered my resolution to answer her. 'You have
no right, Marie-Madeleine . . .'

" 'Very well, my boy,' she interrupted me, almost good-naturedly.
'I will refrain from touching upon emotions that seem to be sacred to
you. I don't want to offend you. I need you, Nicolas.'

" 'Do you?' I said dryly.

" 'You don't sound very enthusiastic,' she said, with an edge to her
voice.

" 'I don't know what it is about.'

" 'It's simple enough, Nicolas,' she said, and now her voice was
pleasant, with a note of tenderness. 'I have your happiness in mind—
you must believe that, even if I'm occasionally hard on you. What
do you say, would you like to earn five thousand livres?'

" 'Five thousand livres?' I uttered a low cry.

" 'With that you can buy yourself a practice as an advocate and
set up a household—with Julie, for all I care, if you don't become
bored with her.'

" 'Five thousand livres!' I still could not grasp it. 'For what, Marie-
Madeleine?'

" 'There isn't much work attached to it. . . .'

" 'What is it?' I asked in great suspense.

" 'Listen, my darling. As you know, my financial situation is anything but good. I scarcely know where I am going to get money for
the next few months. After all, you have enjoyed me, and I will not
keep myself from you in the future—even if you love this little
girl . . .'

" 'I love you,' I stammered hoarsely; the sensuality in her voice
had taken hold of me again.

" 'Don't interrupt me, darling. What I want to say is this: You must
do something for your little mistress for once. It's relatively simple.'

" 'But what is it, Marie-Madeleine?'

" 'There is my sister-in-law in Villequoy. She is very rich, Nicolas.
Almost the entire Daubray fortune is in her hands—that fortune
which really belongs to me and my children. My sister-in-law is a
thin, straw-blond woman, a melancholic with no real interest in life.
The devil only knows why my brother married her. Now that he is
dead, she sits there all alone, forever dressed in her widow's weeds,
mourning her fate. In short, Nicolas, the woman is getting nothing

out of her money and her life. It would actually be an act of mercy to free her from her misery.'

"Several times I opened my mouth and closed it again; I could not utter a word. I knew what she wanted, and yet I could not believe my own conclusion.

" 'You see what the situation is,' she went on softly, unemotionally. 'Sooner or later she will undoubtedly die of melancholia, but I, of course, am interested in having this event take place as soon as possible.'

" 'Oh, my God,' I whispered.

" 'Did you say anything, Nicolas? No? Well, then, listen. I knew as soon as I first saw you that you were the right man for this task. You are good-looking and modest. You inspire trust. Moreover, you are learned, and I believe she has studied Latin and even Greek. She loves to talk about those things—about God and so on—you know what I mean. You two will get along splendidly—maybe you'll even get her to go to bed with you, who knows? If you agree, I'll try to get you a post as secretary with her. There won't be anything to worry about. We will put a trustworthy man to work for her as gardener, and he'll help you with the operation. His name is La Chaussée—'

" 'La Chaussée? Is that the same man . . . I mean . . . with your brothers?' I asked, my voice hoarse.

" 'He has demonstrated his practical value,' she said cryptically, with a low laugh. Then she brushed her soft hand lightly over my cheek. 'I will supply you with the stuff,' she went on. 'It leaves no traces. You may not even have to mix it into her drinks or food yourself, if that goes against your grain. La Chaussée can probably attend to that. But you will have to be present to see that she takes it. As far as the details go, there is no sense in discussing them tonight; the actual circumstances will pretty well determine them. But I must know whether you will do me this favor, Nicolas?'

"I swear by all that is holy that I did not think for a moment of helping her with this crime. But—to my shame I must confess it—I feared her. I did not dare to reject her request out of hand, as I should have done. She had spoken so urgently, so persuasively, that I saw I could not possibly talk her out of her plan then. But I still hoped that I might be able to do so in the future.

"I saw that she was getting restless. I could feel her eyes upon me as she asked, 'Why don't you answer, Nicolas?'

" 'I . . . I must . . . think it over . . .' I stammered.

" 'Think it over?' she cried out scornfully, a quiver of repressed wrath in her voice. 'What is there to think over? Is this your great love for me—that you refuse me a little service like that, and when I am so concerned about your future? Or don't you love me any more, Nicolas?' She pressed her body against mine. The fragrance of her hair, beside me on the pillow, intoxicated me. 'I do,' I moaned. 'Oh, Marie-Madeleine . . .' And my hand groped down to her waist.

"She freed herself, and I was surprised, as I had been so often before, by the unexpected strength in her little hands. 'Not now,' she said, harshly and yet tenderly, 'I am not the woman to give myself to a man when I am not convinced of his love. That I don't stoop to.'

"I was silent, the diabolical brew of lust, repugnance, and fear churning bitterly within me.

" 'Is it so hard to decide?' she whispered close to my ear, so that I felt her warm breath. 'Say yes, darling—and we'll celebrate the victory in advance. . . .'

"I felt the terrible force of temptation. I was dizzy. I could feel my resistance ebbing away, yielding to this beautiful, vital woman's body which she was offering to me as payment for murder. But I managed to stammer, 'I . . . cannot . . . I want . . . I must . . . think it out.'

"Furiously, she drew away from me. 'Go,' she snapped icily. 'Leave my room and don't try to come again until you've come to your senses.'

"I staggered up. 'Good night, Marie-Madeleine,' I said. She did not answer. Hesitantly, I left her room and went to my own.

"There I lay for a long time without sleep. I considered whether I ought not to leave Sains at once, in the middle of the night. But I felt that the bonds which fettered me to her in spite of my horror were not yet broken. And I also feared her vindictive nature. Finally it occurred to me that I must save Madame Daubray, her sister-in-law. In the beginning that was, I suppose, an excuse I made to myself for remaining in her presence. But gradually it developed into a real resolution. I guessed that she would not carry out the murder as long as I, with my knowledge of her plan, was there to watch developments. I even played with the thought of warning Madame Daubray.

But that was hard to accomplish, since on the other hand I did not want to abandon to the penalties of the law this woman who was my mistress.

"A few days later I saw her in the garden. It was a hot day. Butterflies fluttered as though stunned by the powerful rays of the sun over the freshly mowed lawn. She was wearing a thin, low-cut dress. In one hand she held a large pair of garden shears, in the other a bouquet of freshly cut roses. 'I am expecting a guest,' she said, smiling at me. 'Sainte-Croix. These roses are to remind him of the days of our friendship.'

"I could feel jealousy rising hotly within me. She looked at me searchingly. 'Have you decided, Nicolas?' she asked.

" 'I don't want anything to be done to Madame Daubray,' I said. 'I will protect her with all my might, Marie-Madeleine.'

"She looked at me in such a way that I thought she would grow angry again, but she only shook her head and said, 'You quite misunderstand the real situation, Nicolas. You have gone much too far to turn back now. It makes me sad that I have been so deceived in my estimate of you. But I am certain that in the end you will recognize the inevitable. Or do you really intend to stand in the way of the future and the welfare of my children?'

" 'No,' I replied, amazed at her giving such a reason for her intended crime. 'But you can hardly think of building the future of your family upon—upon the death of Madame Daubray.'

"How otherwise was she to do it, she remarked equably, shrugging her shoulders as though she could not comprehend my objection. She stood pensive, her lovely face, turned half to one side, resting against the roses in her hand. 'It's true,' she said unemotionally, 'I've also considered my husband's mother, who is quite wealthy and stingy as well. Does the old woman want to live forever, instead of doing something for her children for a change? And then my sister Thérèse. You see, Nicolas, I'm afraid she will bequeath her money to the Church if I don't take the necessary steps in time.' She sighed heavily. 'But,' she went on thoughtfully, 'there's little sense in attempting too many enterprises at once. Things may get out of hand when you do. One after the other, I always say. That is why I'm concentrating on my sister-in-law for the present.'

"It all seemed quite incredible to me. It was incredible how this dainty, lovely creature with the shears and roses in her hand, in the midst of this fragrant, summery world, could so conjure up death by her words that one almost felt its physical presence.

" 'You're not human,' I cried out. 'You're a monster!'

" 'A monster?' she said, and the stereotyped, archaic smile I knew so well spread over her face. 'Oh no, I'm only me.'

" 'Without a trace of pity you condemn to death the people who should be the dearest in the world to you!' I cried, and my voice resounded so loudly across the lawn and among the trees that I myself started in fright.

" 'What do you mean, shouting at me here!' she snapped. Her eyes were dark with fury and her cheekbones showed prominently through the tautened skin of her face. 'You miserable bookish creature, you Godseeker—shouting at me, your employer—here in my garden, beneath my trees, upon my ground! Haven't you had the pleasure of me! And now you wriggle like a crushed worm—now that you are asked to pay for your pleasure . . .' She raised the hand that held the shears, the point toward me. For a second I thought she would strike me, but she let it fall clanging to the ground. 'There, bend down and pick it up for me, you flunky. Perhaps I will kill you after all.'

"As though her words had numbed my will, I actually bent down, and she kicked me hard in the side with the sharp heels of her little shoes. It did not hurt very much, but it made me angry. The shears shook in my hand. 'I am going now,' I cried. 'I am going forever.'

"She stepped up close to me. 'That would just suit you, wouldn't it, you little cad,' she whispered. 'Clearing out now after having misused my body and pumped all the information you could out of me. But watch out, I warn you. I won't waste any time. One step out of my house and—' She broke off and took a deep breath. 'I am not joking,' she said. 'What I did to my own daughter I would also be able to do to you. . . .'

"That robbed me of the last remnants of my composure. 'What?' I whispered, involuntarily falling into her tone. 'You yourself tried . . . your daughter . . . Marguerite . . . that time last winter? No, no!' I shuddered. 'I beg you, Marie-Madeleine, say it isn't true.'

" 'I didn't give her much—just a little to punish her,' she whispered. Afterward I was sorry. She's my own child, my eldest. I love her deeply—more, much more than you can possibly understand. That's just why. Oh, it's all so hard!' She had tears in her eyes and suddenly looked much older.

" 'Why did you, why?' I moaned.

" 'It isn't easy for a woman like I am to have a growing daughter. Everything about her—her youth, her budding breasts—reminds me that soon I must step down from the stage,' she sobbed. 'And now you, too. You want to abandon me. . . .'

'Then send her out of the house!' I shouted. 'Oh, I don't understand you! I don't understand myself any longer.'

" 'But you love me, Nicolas,' she wept. 'I know you do, even though you deny it. You must stay with me always, my darling! Forgive me all the mean and nasty things I said. I hate myself for saying them. Can you forgive me . . . your love? Or do you want me to kneel before you . . . ?'

"She made a motion to fall to the ground at my feet, but I caught her in my arms and kissed her on the mouth. 'You see, my darling,' she whispered, 'you do still love me. It's just been a little lover's quarrel. How terribly barren the world would be were it not for our love. . . .'

"I could hear the note of triumph in her voice, but alas, I was no match for her. She spoke soft endearments to me, she reveled in recollections of our nights, she touched my hands, my cheeks, with her tongue. And it seemed to me that her hatred, her rage of before, and even this new cause for guilt, multiplied my lust a thousand times. Senselessly I stammered protestations of love again and promised to stay with her. I even agreed (though with inward reservations) to play my part in the planned murder of Madame Daubray, although my blood ran cold when I heard that Sainte-Croix knew all about it and that the rogue was coming to Sains to deliver the instrument of murder, the poison, to us.

"I know that my position was shameful for a man who had even a spark of honor. I know that never in all my life shall I be able to do sufficient penance for it.

"Sainte-Croix came that night. He treated me with less condescension than he had the previous summer, and even seemed to hold a rather guarded admiration for me. Apparently he thought he recognized in me a scoundrel of his own ilk, although I occasionally caught him glancing skeptically at me out of the corners of his eyes. And he avoided speaking openly to me about the planned murder;

he confined himself to obscure hints, usually accompanied by a mocking grin.

"I soon noticed that between him and her there was a physical intimacy which suggested that he had once been her lover, or still was. In my presence, to be sure, they took care and preserved all the forms of social aloofness; but when they thought they were unobserved by me, as sometimes when they were walking in the garden, they dropped the pretense and spoke to one another like people who are very close. In my jealousy I so humiliated myself as to spy upon them, and one morning I actually crept behind a thicket, expecting they would pass by and betray themselves by actions or words.

"Once I saw him kiss her. He did so with a repulsive voluptuousness, licking her arm like a dog and actually touching her shoulders and breasts. While he did so, she smiled her sweetest smile. I broke out into a sweat and it took a tremendous effort on my part not to rush out of my hiding place and knock him down.

"That evening I confronted her. So pressed, she did not deny that he had touched her, but said it meant nothing at all. In her heart she cared for me alone, she said, and Sainte-Croix's familiarities were painful to her; but she did not dare to offend him outright because it was he who supplied the means that could provide her and her family with an untroubled future. In my folly and drunkenness of soul I believed her, all the more so because she accompanied these words with caresses that robbed me of all ability to think.

"What a state I was in! I was torn between the most contradictory emotions. Hatred, jealousy, and fear mingled in my heart with the terrible lust to possess her. Quite aside from all the commandments of morality, which I daily violated, my reason should have told me that she did not love me and only offered her body to me in order to make me a willing tool for her crimes. But I lived under an enchantment, like those characters of legend who are said to have vanished for years and decades in the caves of Astarte or the mountain of Venus.

"Only at twilight, when the setting sun gilded the western windows of the house and the vesper bell from the nearby village of Sains tolled its soft admonishment across the fields to me, did I think back upon my childhood, when at that sacred hour I would always kneel down in my cell to thank the Mother of God for the fullness of the day just spent. But these brief moments when my conscience spoke to me passed without effecting any change in my life, although my days and nights were filled with a gentle sorrow, like a memory of lost paradise.

"When Sainte-Croix left Sains I agreed to ride along with him as far as Amiens. It was already evening by the time we arrived at the city, which lay peacefully in the last rays of the sun, overhung by a thin bluish smoke from the evening fires on the hearths. Sainte-Croix dismounted and said goodbye to me. 'Briancourt,' he told me, 'you must get to the business soon. The marquise is growing impatient. And between ourselves, my dear fellow, impatience on the part of beautiful and highly placed ladies is sometimes dangerous.'

" 'I am ready,' I said. 'I am ready to serve her.'

"He looked dubiously at me, then shrugged his shoulders. 'What have you got to lose, Briancourt?' he said. 'Sometimes I envy you. You're so young. When it's all over, go to Italy. Take my advice. The courtesans in Venice and Rome surpass anything that France has to offer.'

"I felt myself blushing, although I desperately fought against that feeling of shame. I wanted so much to be as worldly as he, for all that I despised the man. 'Women don't mean anything to me,' I exclaimed vehemently, and I myself could hear how insincere I sounded.

"He smiled gently, not even with mockery; in fact he was rather friendly, as though he were touched by this clumsy proof of my inexperience. 'Well, we will see,' he said mysteriously, and went on his way, while I turned back toward Sains.

"During the following weeks the marquise kept urging me to come to the point. 'The thing cannot be postponed any longer, Nicolas,' she said to me more than once. 'I can already see the bottom of my strongbox. Marguerite needs an outfit for the convent school. And Antoine, too, must be equipped as befits his station when he goes to the military academy. If you won't do it for my sake, at least do it for my children.'

"The monstrousness of the idea of committing murder on behalf of her children's welfare never seemed to occur to her. She spoke of the plotted crime quite coldly as the 'Villequoy enterprise,' or 'that transaction with my sister-in-law,' as though it were a perfectly honest business venture.

"But I talked back and forth. There were days when I flatly refused to help and days when I asked for more time. She grew visibly cooler toward me. The window to her room remained closed to me. But we also stopped having passionate quarrels. Soon she spoke more and more rarely about the plan and finally stopped mentioning it entirely.

"In secret I congratulated myself. I hoped that time would help. Winter was approaching, and with it the distractions of court, balls, and the theater. Perhaps she would forget all about it, and I had made up my mind that in the spring of the following year I would return to Monsieur Bocager. But although I took this resolution, I made the reservation that I would visit her occasionally. My ties to her had loosened, but they were by no means broken.

"The day she set out for Paris I accompanied her to the carriage, which stood in the yard in front of the white château. One of the lackeys had already opened the carriage door for her when she turned toward me again. She looked charming in the heavy furs that framed her small face. The brown gleam of the fur set off the fineness of her cheeks, which were flushed from the cold, fresh air, and the delicacy of her face, with its radiant blue eyes. Over her mass of hair she had tied a dark silken scarf, the way peasant women wear their simple woolen shawls.

"I felt a deep tenderness and would have liked to take her in my arms and kiss her. The thought that I had possessed this beautiful, fragile creature, whom even the lackey standing at the carriage door could not refrain from giving a glance of admiration, filled me with such ardor that my cheeks burned.

" 'Bon voyage, madame,' I said.

" 'Say that you will do it,' she whispered to me. 'Say it as a farewell gift to me, and I will love you forever.'

" 'I will, I will,' I stammered in my infatuation. 'I will do everything you command, Marie-Madeleine.'

"She smiled at me. But then I saw, or thought I saw, that beneath that superficial expression there was the hint of something else, something resembling doubt, or hatred. It lasted only for a moment and vanished immediately. For a second her eyes had been icy; now they smiled at me with kindness again.

" 'Well, we will see,' she said, just as Sainte-Croix had done, and she lightly stepped up on the running board, leaning on my arm.

"The lackey closed the carriage door behind her. The four horses stepped forward. I looked after her. The boys, whom she had just embraced tempestuously and promised a hundred different presents, rushed all around the carriage as it slowly rolled away and called in their strong, clear voices through the cold winter morning, 'Oh, Mama! Best, sweetest Mama!' Her little hand in its white glove waved from the carriage window like the fluttering wing of a white dove.

"Julie, the children, and I spent the next few weeks in great peace and harmony. Shortly before Christmas we, too, went to Paris and established ourselves in the house on the Rue Neuve Saint Paul.

"Again, as in the past winter, I seldom saw her. Once more she was wholly the grand lady, present at every one of the court functions, of which there were an unusually large number this year— since, as I heard from Monsieur Bocager, the Marquise de Montespan, who loved amusements of all sorts, had once more taken full possession of the king's heart.

"Whenever Marie-Madeleine was at home, as of course she could not entirely avoid being, she was pensive and depressed. The reason for her low spirits was quite apparent to me and the other members of the household. Neither I nor the lackeys and maids had been paid for months. The food merchants complained bitterly to the steward and threatened to cut off deliveries. Jewelry and silverware were pawned, and once even the carriage. Marguerite could not be sent off to convent school because there was no money for her out- fit—until at last the marquise's sister, who lived in the Carmelite convent, sent the necessary funds. I felt much easier when the charm- ing, rather shy child was out of the house.

"Only once did the marquise speak to me about her plan during this period. The conversation took place in the gallery, where we met by chance. She was coming out of her room in full court regalia, her brown hair crowned by a diamond-studded diadem that glis- tened coldly. She was wearing a sweeping skirt of red silk, with a broad hem of gold lace. In her hand she carried a small painted ivory fan. I knew she was on her way to court. The marquis was already waiting below in the carriage.

" 'Nicolas,' she said hastily, 'do you remember your promise in Sains?'

Then a change took place within me. I could see that she was as beautiful as ever. But her beauty did not touch me. The pallor of her face and her restless eyes suddenly inspired in me such disgust that I involuntarily shook myself.

"She noticed it at once. She was always able to read my face like a book. 'You're a miserable wretch, Nicolas,' she whispered.

"I thought she would fly into rage, as she had that time in the garden. But her expression remained cold. Then she half shut her eyes. Her forehead became slightly furrowed with thought.

"I found this unexpected calm more disturbing than if she had sprung at my throat. I stood there trembling, unable to speak, unable to think. I was like an empty bellows. But then life returned to me in a great surge. 'I won't,' I cried in a low voice. 'I will not kill.'

"She quivered and threw a quick glance over the banister of the gallery to the vestibule, where the footman stood waiting for her. Then she smiled to herself, that strange smile of hers, without menace or mockery. A primordial smile which did not seem meant for me at all, but was perhaps a tribute to those mysterious substructures upon which our existence is founded. She sighed deeply and said calmly, as though stating a fact, 'That is your final resolve?'

" 'Yes,' I said, 'that is my unalterable determination.'

" 'Good,' she said reflectively. 'Then things must take their course.' Silently she stood there for a while. Then she walked past me and descended the stairs. I heard the door open and close again.

"All this happened very quickly, in much less time than it has taken me to tell it.

"A few days later I noticed that a new lackey had been taken into the household, a haggard man who smiled in a peculiar fashion whenever he caught sight of me. And he saw me often; he seemed to seek me out. He gave his name as Basil. Whether that was his real name, I do not know.

"At that time I had a young gray cat which Monsieur Bocager had given me. She was a very affectionate little thing and she had taken to spending the evenings with me, lying with her small head on my thigh, or sitting in my lap when I was reading.

"One afternoon I did not feel well. I felt slightly sick to my stomach.

I started downstairs to the kitchen, but on encountering Basil, I asked him to bring me a glass of milk. 'Certainly, certainly, monsieur,' he said. He sped away and soon reappeared with the milk. I took the glass into my room in order to drink it there and then lie down. As I re-entered the room my cat brushed affectionately, tail raised, against my legs and meowed softly, slyly eying the milk.

"I poured a little of the warm milk into the bowl that stood by the fireplace, and watched with a smile as the animal, purring contentedly, thrust her neck forward and began lapping the milk.

"I was just about to put the glass to my mouth when I was startled by the cat. She meowed loudly, in an angry, complaining tone I had never heard before. With two leaps she rushed upon me and dug her claws right through my trousers and painfully deep into my leg. I tried to shake her off. Then I noticed that her soft little body had become stiff and tense. I lifted her up. She did not resist, and when I looked closer at her I saw that she was dead.

"Stunned, the dead animal on my knees, I sat there a while staring into space. It took some time before I recovered sufficiently to raise my glass and smell it. It seemed to me I could detect a faint, peculiar odor. I staggered to my feet and went to the window. There I laid my forehead against the icy windowpane and tried to think.

"With pounding heart I considered what I ought to do. I could confront the scoundrel, but of course he would deny everything. I decided to go to the police, but immediately rejected the thought. I was undoubtedly being watched and if I now left the house I would be exposing myself to a dagger in the back or a pistol shot. And would the police believe me, even if I brought them the milk as proof of my suspicion? Would not Basil be able to represent the whole thing as a mistake? For many households keep arsenic and other poisons to exterminate vermin.

"Or should I reveal her guilt to the police? The possibility of my doing so was probably the reason for this attempt to eliminate me. Perhaps I had an exaggerated concept of her power, but I had the clear conviction that I would not be allowed to get as far as a police station. And even if I did, it was still her word against mine. In fact she could turn everything about and claim that I had proposed the poisoning of Madame Daubray. What then? Oppressive images rose to my mind; I saw myself in prison, under torture, on the executioner's block.

"The thought came to me that I might send Julie to the police. But perhaps she, too, was being watched. Moreover, I was ashamed to drag this innocent girl into such filth.

"In the end I did nothing at all. Faced with the difficult decision, I relied upon time and chance, which, I somehow thought—I don't myself know quite how—would set things right. I decided to play the innocent, but to observe everything that was going on about me with the utmost keenness.

"I began by taking soundings of my situation. First I reported the death of the cat to the steward, without letting him know the manner of her death. It became evident to me that the steward and the regular lackeys and maids knew nothing about what was taking place in this house and were in no way involved. Only the marquise herself and Basil were aware of the game that was being played.

"It was an uncanny house. Rich and elegant, filled with outstanding works of art, inhabited by innocent children and presided over by a strikingly gracious and beautiful woman, for me it had become the abode of criminal phantoms. The danger to my life was always on my mind. The phantom seemed to listen ironically when I tutored the boys or read them the naïve fables of La Fontaine. The phantom walked silently beside me over the inlaid floors, sat down at table beside me, and lay down with me in my bed at night. The contradiction between the fine semblance and the terrible reality was so great that I sometimes feared I would go mad. There were moments when this dichotomy seemed to cut not only through me and through this house, but through the whole world, through all of existence. Everything was infected for me. Death dwelt in all things.

"It was worst at table. Eating, which among all peoples who have gone beyond a state of sheer barbarism is considered not only a necessity and pleasure, but something of a fine art, was for me a curse and a torment. If I did not watch closely, if I relaxed my vigilance only for a moment, I might very well find myself ingesting not the food for new energy, but the bane of a painful death.

"Basil was one of the table attendants. He placed the most alluring foods and drinks before me. Their odor rose to my nostrils, and back of my chair I heard the scoundrel murmuring recommendations for this food or that drink. Often I clutched the arms of my chair convulsively in order to keep myself from seizing a knife and stabbing the fellow. And all the while I had to put on a pleasant expression and chat amiably in order to maintain the pretense that I knew nothing.

"The marquis was served by his own valet, and I soon noticed that he made a point of not taking anything that Basil put on the table. I came to the horrifying realization that the marquis knew or suspected what was going on in his house. He never said a revealing word, but his attitude was enough for me. From then on I made a point of asking for some food or wine that he was being given, pretending to be attracted by just these particular things. "We seem to have the same tastes, Monsieur Briancourt," he said, throwing a smile at the marquise.

"There we sat, the three of us. The blond Marquis, blasé and spindly, she, splendidly dressed, and I in my dark, clerical garb. In polished tones we talked about this and that. The fragrance of the wine mingled with the honey smell of the candles, and the prisms of the crystal chandelier reflected our vacant faces. It made a fine picture. The fear which surrounded all of us like a ring was unseen.

"It was more difficult for me when the Marquis was not at home. Then I ate only the courses which the mistress of the house was eating, or I excused myself for not coming to table by pretending that I was ill. At night I would secretly steal down to the cellar and take eggs, fruit, and bread from the cupboards. I would eat these foods in my room, after carefully examining them and wiping them off with a cloth.

"This state of affairs lasted for several months, until the spring of 1672. I had lost considerable weight, less because of my stringent diet than because of my constant anxiety, an anxiety which plagued me even in sleep with terrible dreams.

"One day, at the beginning of April, I had taken my young charges to the Quartier Latin to show them the colleges and other institutions of learning. By the time I came back to the Rue Neuve Saint Paul I was feeling very hot. In the hallway Basil met me. He had a large glass of ice-cold lemonade in his hand and tried to press it upon me. 'There, Your Grace,' the rogue said. 'Drink this, Monsieur Briancourt; it will cool you off. I carefully prepared it for you myself.'

"The memory of my cat rose vividly to my mind. 'No,' I replied. 'I don't want anything to drink.'

" 'But you must,' he said impudently. 'Just taste it and see how good it is.' And the scoundrel came up to me, gripped my shoulder, and forced the rim of the glass against my tightly closed lips.

" 'You villain!' I screamed. 'You want to poison me!' I pushed him away, snatched the glass out of his hand, and hurled it to the floor, where it was shattered to bits.

" 'But Monsieur Briancourt, what's the matter with you?' he whined. 'It was only for your good—such a warm day.'

"The marquise came hurrying down the stairs, her face white and distraught. 'What is going on here?' she asked, looking at me.

"I was trembling with rage. 'Madame,' I shouted, 'this scoundrel— I will leave the house at once if you don't throw the rascal out instantly. He wanted to force me—'

" 'Very well, Monsieur Briancourt,' she hastily interrupted me, 'the man is dismissed.'

"Attracted by the noise, lackeys and pages came running out to the hall. They looked at me in amazement and asked in whispers what had happened.

" 'Basil has been guilty of impertinence to Monsieur Briancourt,' she answered quickly, and turned to the steward. 'See that the man leaves the house instantly.'

"But Basil had already vanished silently as a ghost. I never saw him again."

After finishing reading this latest installment of Briancourt's confession, Desgrez closed his eyes and sat still for a while. He appeared to be sleeping. But suddenly he got up, went to the window, and looked out upon the quiet square.

It was one of those mild nights that anticipate spring before spring has really arrived. There was a nearly full moon in the sky, with white clouds passing slowly over its face so that the lawn below, with the bronze horseman in the center of it, would be alternately illuminated and shadowed, the monument itself first blazing forth, then almost blotted out and remaining only a suggestion of a dark object of uncertain outlines. The effect of the shifts of darkness and light fascinated Desgrez. He looked down eagerly and even bent forward to lean a little out of the window.

Then he stepped back and, as he had done the last time, made a few rapid notes on a sheet of paper. He wrote:

Task: to convert a subjective testimony to objective statement of facts.
Briancourt: what did he actually experience of all that he believes he
experienced?
Witnesses: Julie, the marquis, Basil.

He read through what he had written and then, after a moment of
hesitation, crossed out the first two names. Then he wrote underneath:

In spite of all appearances it seems as though after the death of Sainte-
Croix only one person exists who can convict the murderess of her crimes:
the murderess herself. But perhaps [he added after a moment's reflection]
even she cannot provide legally conclusive proof of her crimes.

ꞏ III ꞏ

THE STEWARD at the Brinvilliers' house in the Rue Neuve Saint Paul,
whom Desgrez visited the following morning, received his visitor
with an air of depression. "Alas, Lieutenant," he sighed when Desgrez
asked him why he looked so downcast. "I don't know what is happening with our masters. A few days ago Mademoiselle de Grangemont,
whom you met here, left us. Yesterday I received a letter from
Monsieur le Marquis, who is at Sains, ordering me to dismiss all the
servants. And now," he added reproachfully, "you have come."
Desgrez smiled and reassured him: "My visit will cause you no
further dislocation, steward. The police are only interested in one of
your lackeys, a man who called himself Basil, although his real name
is probably something else."
The steward, Desgrez saw, was of such an inquisitive disposition
that he forgot his melancholic humor and said eagerly, "Basil? Yes,
I employed a man by that name, but only for a short time. Just for
two months, about a year ago, if I remember rightly."
"Right, that's the man," Desgrez said. "Where did you hire him
from, steward?"
"Let me see—yes, that's right, I didn't hire him. Madame la Marquise personally engaged the man. It surprised me at the time because Madame has never bothered about such matters. He was,
incidentally, a very quiet and well-conducted fellow who held aloof
from the other servants and never attracted attention. That was why

I was so surprised to hear that he had been impertinent to Monsieur Briancourt, which was the reason for his sudden discharge."

"What was the nature of the impertinence?"

"Well, I don't really know, sir. Madame ordered me to dismiss him —but he had already left of his own accord, so that I was not even able to pay him his back wages."

"Hm. . . . Tell me, steward, wasn't there a loud dispute at that time, so that all the inhabitants of the household came running?"

"Why, no, Lieutenant, not at all," the steward replied. He was visibly offended. "Such incidents do not occur in houses where I am in charge. Moreover, Basil was not the sort of person who would have participated in a loud dispute—he was meekness itself. What crime is he charged with?"

"One moment—I'll tell you in just a minute. But first, please answer this question for me: During the time Basil was employed here, did any of the inmates of the house suffer from stomach trouble or serious nausea or vomiting?"

The steward stared at Desgrez in amazement. "Well, I can't really say," he murmured, perplexed. "I suppose someone felt ill now and then, as people always will, but we had no real sickness, except for Sophie who had it in the lungs. But yes, Mademoiselle Marguerite once was sick to her stomach—but that was long before Basil's time. The young lady is much too fond of sweets."

Desgrez stood thinking, so long that the steward glanced uneasily at him. At last he said with a faintly ironic smile, "Thank you very much, steward. I believe I should be committing no indiscretion if I tell you that we are interested in Basil because he very probably attempted to poison someone."

"For heaven's sake!" the steward exclaimed. "And to think I had him here in the house! If Monsieur le Marquis knew of that!"

"Why don't you tell him?" Desgrez said after a brief pause. "I believe Monsieur le Marquis ought to be kept informed of such matters."

"Certainly, sir," the steward agreed. "But at the same time it's terribly embarrassing—even though I was not the person who engaged such a rogue."

"Exactly," Desgrez said equably, with a suppressed smile, "if I were you I would call the Marquis' attention to that fact also. Ladies ought not to interfere in affairs that are really not their concern."

The steward nodded eagerly, and from the rather foolish look of self-importance on the man's face Desgrez concluded that he felt that for once in his life his merits were fully appreciated.

A few hours later Desgrez entered Briancourt's cell. The young man was sitting on his bed, a picture of inconsolable gloom, his arms dangling slackly, and the look in his eyes one of hopeless sadness. He looked up wearily. "I have written nothing more," he said. "I cannot go on."

Desgrez sat down. If he was disappointed, he gave no sign of it. "Perhaps together we can remove the obstacle, Briancourt," he said.

"No," the young man replied with stubborn conviction. "It stands before me like a huge wall of rock, absolutely immovable. I cannot get beyond it." He looked down at the floor, his eyes sightless, filled with anxiety.

Desgrez considered. "Do you find yourself still unable to tear this unfortunate passion out of your heart?" he asked at last.

"No, it is not that."

"Then what is it, Briancourt?"

"Something else, something entirely different," Briancourt whispered agonizedly.

"What?" Desgrez insisted.

Briancourt sat silent for a long time, head bowed, obviously struggling with himself. Finally he looked up. "God!" he cried out. "It is God!" He looked questioningly at Desgrez.

Desgrez had started involuntarily at the outcry. "Isn't it strange," he asked softly, "that it should be God who is an obstacle in the way of truth? Hasn't that struck you as odd, Briancourt?"

"Yes, of course . . . I mean . . . I've expressed myself wrongly," Briancourt stammered. "It isn't . . . it is the guilt . . . my sin. In spite of everything that happened before, this is the most frightful, the most unforgivable part of it. . . . Everything within me . . . everything . . . fights against my confessing it."

"And yet," Desgrez interrupted him in a stern but not unfriendly tone, "you have already confessed it to yourself. And that was the real difficulty, Briancourt. What restrains you from communicating your fault now is only a residue of weakness, of self-love."

"Oh, if you only knew, Lieutenant Desgrez," the young man cried passionately. "I have blasphemed against all that is holy. I have

polluted our Lord's prayer with murder, lust, and poison." He
stopped, horrified, and stared open-mouthed at Desgrez.

"Now you have even said it," Desgrez said soothingly. In an even-
tempered, sensible tone he added, "The fact is established. What is
lacking are only the details and the logical succession of events which
led you to this spiritual confusion—which, I believe I can sense, has
been the most painful of all your torments."

Briancourt nodded. "But it is just the details that are so terrible,
so blasphemous," he said miserably.

"Nevertheless, Briancourt, they must be spoken, they must be laid
bare. I was tempted to say: 'the more terrible the better.' Have you
never had the experience that harsh and utterly pitiless exposure of
truth is in itself almost a banishment of the lie in which we have
hitherto lived?"

"Yes, I have," Briancourt said, visibly surprised. He looked hard
at Desgrez. "I have had that experience during the past few weeks—
and I have just had it again, just this minute. I feel encouraged—and
my existence seems meaningful to me again. But . . ." He paused.

"What is it, Briancourt?"

"You sometimes do not speak at all like a policeman, Lieutenant
Desgrez," Briancourt exclaimed.

"Don't I? What do I sound like?"

"Like a priest."

Desgrez smiled. "Perhaps that is because my best friend is one,"
he said. "On the other hand, whenever I have examined deeply
enough, I have encountered spiritual roots beneath all deeds and
misdeeds, and perhaps it takes theological insight to appreciate their
full significance. Man is, after all, a creature bound to God—and
especially when he is most unwilling to admit it." He sat still for a
while, smiling thoughtfully. Then he stood up, sighing, and said, "But
I believe I can leave you alone now, Briancourt. Au revoir."

"Many thanks, Lieutenant," Briancourt said. "I will try to finish
the account."

The young man did in fact succeed in overcoming the residue of
his inner resistance, and a scant week afterward Desgrez again had a
considerable sheaf of papers from Briancourt's pen. Their significance
seemed to the Lieutenant this time to go beyond the purely criminological angle; as he noted during his first hasty reading, these latest
pages were so thoroughly and unrestrainedly subjective, had so much

the character of a confession, that no reader could doubt that their author spoke the truth—or thought he was speaking the truth.

The new section read:

"The murderess who had now tried to take my life, through the instrumentality of Basil, was still a woman to whom I could not be indifferent. It was not really her beauty that exercised so desperate an attraction for me, but her cruelty, her corruption, her cunning— all those very traits which she employed in trying to put a swift end to my life.

"Her will to destruction, which was perhaps directed principally against herself, although it resulted in her ruthlessly annihilating those closest to her, lured me irresistibly. It seemed to me that I had to solve the riddle embodied in her personality. Dimly I sensed that it had acquired for me a far greater significance than that of any mere mystery. It sounds like incredible mockery, but in fact my inability to escape from her was due less to my erotic drive than to my theological instincts.

"That spring only Antoine and the marquise and I remained in Paris. The marquis had gone to Sains and had taken the twins with him. Marie-Madeleine did not go out as much as she had used to, and was aloofly friendly toward me. I assumed that the planned attempt on her sister-in-law's life had been abandoned and congratulated myself on having acted just the way I had done.

"One day I got up the courage to ask her for my release from her service. 'Madame,' I said, timidly enough, 'I believe that my usefulness in your house has come to an end. Antoine has made sufficient progress so that he can attend the military academy in the fall. And I should also like to go back to Monsieur Bocager, who urgently needs me.'

"That was a lie. But she pretended not to understand the real reason for my request. 'I certainly will not stand in the way of your career,' she replied evenly. Then she smiled.

"And then the devil took hold of me. Without considering that I was once again entangling myself in the old net, I cried out, 'I can never stop caring for you, madame.'

"A look of animal satisfaction spread over her face, which was at that moment more catlike than ever before. But she reveled in the triumph of her femininity only for a moment; then her expression became one of profound thoughtfulness. 'That is true,' she murmured. 'We must love one another—or hate one another.' It seemed to me as though she were catching a ball I had thrown her. With her slender fingers she brushed the brown locks back from her temples. Her face was so bared that I imagined I could see the fine bones shimmering through her skin. With a shamelessness so great it was almost innocence, her large eyes turned upon me and she whispered tenderly, meaningfully, 'Nicolas, I have a new bed in my room, with rich inlays of precious woods, woods that are fragrant. It's supposed to be old—ancient. Wouldn't you like to see it, darling?'

"'Yes,' I said hoarsely. 'I—I should like to see it.'

"The radiance in her eyes intensified. She smiled more warmly at me. 'Then come tonight—but softly, softly, when the bells of Saint Paul's strike midnight. Then I will show you the bed as it must be shown. . . .'

"'I'll come,' I whispered, quivering. 'Oh, my dearest mistress, if only everything between us could be good again.'

"'Yes, everything will be good,' she murmured, her eyes wide, still fixed upon me. 'You will come back to me . . . and soon there will be peace, calm . . . deep sleep.'

"All afternoon I waited for the night. When darkness began to fall and the thrushes outside in the garden began their evening songs, I was seized by a strange uneasiness, which soon became intense anxiety. For a long time I stood at the open window looking out into the mild, dark spring night. A chestnut tree in the garden wafted to me the tart scent of its blossoms, which had just opened.

"I heard the bells of Saint Paul's from a distance that seemed to have increased with the fall of night. I counted the slow strokes, which went on reverberating within me long after they had died down outside. Ten o'clock. I stood thinking. It seemed to me as though something were approaching me from out there, from the outspread nocturnal city. Something vague, but which concerned me intimately and had something to do with the smell of the chestnut blossoms.

"Of course, that was it. Fragrant woods, she had said. And she had spoken of peace, of deep sleep. Where before had I smelled this scent. I remembered: in the cemetery at Aubervilliers. Every spring.

"I smiled to myself. But suddenly, like a bolt of lightning, the thought flashed terrifyingly through me: Suppose she had meant that kind of sleep. Sleep under a covering of earth!

"My knees turned weak and I leaned my weight against the window sill. Once more the bells of Saint Paul's sounded. They struck a single dark, solemn note that rang in my ears like a caesura, dividing all my past from all my future.

"Half past ten. I still had one and a half hours. Quietly I left my room, closing the door silently behind me. I leaned over the balustrade and listened for sounds from below. It was so still that the house itself seemed to have fallen asleep. Only in the cellar, far below, someone was still busy with dishes and I could make out the almost inaudible singsong of a maid's voice.

"From her room, whose door was opposite the big marble staircase, a stream of candlelight fell through the thin tulle curtain drawn over the transom above the door. From my position I could see through the transom only the corner of her bed, the area before her big fireplace, and the fireplace itself, which on such a warm night as this was closed. Now she herself moved from the other side of the room into my line of vision. She was wearing her wide, white silken nightgown and, her head tilted slightly to one side, was negligently combing her hair, which flowed in a dark, heavy stream around the sides of her face and almost down to her waist. As she moved back and forth, combing the hair, disappearing and reappearing, she seemed like a creature out of the sea. Her face, seen from diagonally above, looked broader, her forehead lower and rounder, than I knew them to be, and the long waves of her hair intensified the impression of a water nymph.

"I stood observing her for about half an hour and could discover nothing extraordinary in her behavior. But then she went up to the fireplace and opened the panel which covered it when it was not in use. Out of the fireplace stepped the tall figure of a man. I could not recognize him; a narrow mask, with slits through which his eyes glistened, covered the middle part of his face. But his bearing and his size reminded me of Sainte-Croix.

"The man stretched several times. He must have had to crouch inside the fireplace. Then he went up closer to her and embraced her. I stood motionless, watching, my hands resting on the balustrade for support. It seemed to me that I was watching a theatrical performance from a poor position in the gallery. As on a stage, the two figures and their movements seemed detached from reality. They were talking to one another, as I could tell by the movement of their lips and the expression of their faces, but I could not hear a word, and this soundlessness intensified the impression of artificiality, as though the two were not even actors, merely marionettes.

"But terror ran like a paralysis through my limbs as I thought of the significance of this puppet play I was observing. What should I do? The simplest thing, undoubtedly, would have been not to go to her at all and to lock myself in my room. But my indignation at the trap she had planned for me, and unfortunately also my jealousy, were both so great that I resolved to risk all and confront her.

"I went back to my room and desperately searched for a weapon. For a long time I hesitated between the fireplace poker and a sharp bread knife, but finally chose the latter because I could conceal it beneath my jacket. When I went back out into the hall I saw that she was alone again and the panel to the fireplace had been re-placed. I waited a while longer, then softly descended the stairs and knocked on her door.

"She opened it at once. She was somewhat surprised and uneasy when she saw me. 'Is it already midnight?' she asked.

" 'Not quite yet,' I replied; 'but the house is so quiet that I decided to come now.' I felt no fear. I even felt strangely detached, like an actor, and the thought flashed through my mind that I ought to play the part assigned to me as well as possible.

"She had recovered her composure. 'There is my bed,' she said smilingly, closing the door. 'How do you like it, darling?'

"I went up to the bed and managed to praise it. I even knelt down as though I were particularly interested in inspecting the inlay more closely, and while I did so I threw a rapid, surreptitious glance at the fireplace. The door did not fit tightly at the bottom, and through the crack I glimpsed a pair of shoes and the hem of a coat.

" 'The bed is very wide,' I said matter-of-factly. 'Wider than French beds.'

" 'It's Italian—what they call a *letto matrimoniale*,' she replied, passing her hand nervously over her mass of hair. 'A great queen is supposed to have owned it in olden days.' She smiled meaningfully. I found her more beautiful than ever. Her barely suppressed excite-ment lent to her eyes a special gleam which I had hitherto seen only in moments of sexual ecstasy. Apparently murder was for her another form of lust.

" 'But now get undressed, darling,' she whispered coaxingly in her hoarse voice. 'You'll stay with me all night, won't you?'

"Never before had I felt her tremendous power in so naked a form. For a moment an overwhelming longing seized me like Satan himself and almost blacked out my mind: the longing to die in her arms. I actually took off my jacket, but then I dropped heavily into the chair. With dangling arms I sat staring senselessly at the floor.

" 'What's the matter, my darling?' she whispered close to my ear. 'Hurry . . . hurry . . .'

"Beneath this show of tenderness I imagined, deep inside, I could hear mockery and menace in her hoarse voice. That gave me the courage to pull myself together. I sprang to my feet and cried out, trembling with rage, 'What you haven't told me is that your bed is to be my coffin!'

" 'Your coffin?' she exclaimed, and stammered in a whisper, 'What . . . what do you mean?'

" 'That you've hidden the scoundrel who is supposed to murder me —in the fireplace there,' I cried. And I drew out the knife and started toward the fireplace. But she threw herself upon me suddenly, with the strength and agility of a panther, so that I fell back upon the bed, the knife raised high in my right hand. She held me down, her knee on my chest. Her face, distorted by fury, was so close to mine that her wide-open eyes seemed enormous to me. Her hands scratched at my throat, trying to choke me. But I summoned up all my strength and threw her off. I threw her down hard on the floor. She clasped my legs in her arms and sank her teeth painfully into my left hand.

"At that moment the door to the fireplace flew open. The man sprang out and stood there for a moment, in a long, flowing coat, the mask over his face. 'Sainte-Croix,' I shouted. 'Murderer! I recognize you!'

"He hesitated for a moment. Then he sprang to the window, which was half open, and vanished. I heard him land heavily in the garden and then I heard the snapping of twigs as he made off through the bushes.

"I groaned aloud. She was breathing heavily. She lay at my feet in a heap, still holding my left hand, but now she was kissing it

again and again. At the same time she was whispering words which
at first I did not understand. 'Do it,' she whispered, 'do it anyhow. . . .'

"Then she crawled, feeling her way with her hands like a blind
creature along my legs until she was kneeling before me on the side
of the bed. There was a deep rent in her nightgown; one of her
shoulders and her breasts were bared. Her hair hung in disorder
over her forehead and down her back. It seemed to me that she was
rising up before me out of limitless depths of water.

"'Kill me with the knife,' she whispered. 'It's better if you kill
me—for me too. . . .' And again she bent over my left hand and
kissed it. 'See my throat,' she went on whispering. 'Cut it through
here. It doesn't take long. If you don't do it—someone else will.'

"'I don't want to kill,' I whispered in horror. 'Not you—nor anyone
else.'

"'But you must. You must. Don't you understand that it must be—
if you still love me,' she whispered, and gestured at her breasts. 'I
will not make a sound. I'll lie perfectly still—perfectly obedient and
naked. . . . Oh, death is sweet. . . . If you cannot be without me,
then kill yourself afterward—with the knife there—then we will always be together.' She went on whispering in this way for a while
longer, dissolved in sensuality, as though the death by my hand for
which she lusted were the most intoxicating of raptures, the most
festive of nuptial beds, the meaning of the world.

"Filled with horror, I could feel the monstrous temptation stirring
within me and I hurled the knife far away from me. 'I cannot,' I
groaned. 'I am not a murderer.'

"'Oh, too bad,' she whispered. 'Now when the opportunity is here
. . . Do you want to live forever?'

"'Oh, Marie-Madeleine,' I sobbed, 'how can you do this to me? I
never . . . never . . . would have said a syllable of what I know. Do
you hate me so very much?'

"She stared pensively at me, as though she were pondering hard
whether she loved me or hated me. With a very feminine, graceful
movement she brushed the hair back from her forehead and ran her
small hands down along its waves, over her temples and her shoulders, which were now gloriously covered by it.

"'No,' she said softly, still looking at me, 'it was the same as with
my father. . . .'

" 'With your father?' I was horror-struck.

" 'Him, too. I had to—don't you understand? There was no other way. I was terribly sorry for him. He loved me so much and often kissed me, even when he lay stretched on his deathbed. *"Ma petite fille,"* he used to call me. "What would all the world mean to me if I didn't have you, my daughter?" He said that when he was lying with his whole body wasted, the white skin stretched tight over his poor bones. . .'

" 'Marie-Madeleine,' I cried out, 'stop it!'

" 'No, no, you must know everything. Don't you understand that I loved him more than anything else in the world, that he was my idol as I was his—father and daughter—don't you understand that?'

" 'Stop it, you monster.'

" 'A monster? Me? You're so unjust to me, Nicolas!' To my amazement she began to weep. Sobbing still, she went on, 'I'm not a monster—that isn't true. How often I prayed to God to show me another way. How painfully I struggled with myself before I gave him the poison—again and again—every time it was a struggle.'

" 'What! You did it yourself! You. . . !'

" 'Who else? I told you I loved him madly—he was my father after all, so do you think I would have left him to the hands of others, to a La Chaussée, for example?'

" 'You yourself—you!' I was close to tears, but suddenly I was overpowered by rage. I gripped her by the shoulders and shook her back and forth so that her head wagged like that of a doll stuffed with straw. 'At least do not speak of love,' I snarled at her. 'Say you did it for money—for his money . . .' I was so furious that I became choked and could not go on.

"She wiped her eyes and looked at me in uncomprehending amazement. 'Of course I did it for money. For what else? Have I denied it?' she whispered. She took a deep breath. 'He had lived his life and enjoyed it. Now it was my turn, mine and my children's. Can I help it that the world is—is arranged that way?'

" 'What's that? What do you mean, arranged that way?' I asked, and I felt a sudden overwhelming fear.

" 'Why, the way it is,' she replied impudently, and gave me a wide-eyed, challenging look. 'What is here and breathing today is fertilizer for what comes tomorrow, and that again is fertilizer for

what is to be the next day—like the leaves of the forest. Everything
has its day in the sun—and everything has its death.'

" 'No,' I cried out. 'I won't believe that of you.'

" 'Of me?' she whimpered, and she pulled herself up higher. She
embraced my waist and laid her head tenderly against my thighs,
looking up at me with a cunning expression. 'Look around in the
world, Nicolas. Or are you really so miserably weak—such a lamb?'

" 'Say what you will,' I exclaimed, 'you cannot get around this one
thing: you did it for money. Only for accursed money.'

" 'For money. Of course. Why does that seem so especially repre-
hensible?' she asked in amazement, and after a while she added
reproachfully, 'You don't even ask me about my feelings.'

" 'Your feelings!' I thought I could not possibly have heard aright.

"She protruded her full red lips in a pout and said in an offended
tone, 'My father was always interfering in my life. That was not nice
of him. . . . I was a grown woman—thirty years old. I needed men—
that's the way I am. And then he took my lover from me and threw
him into the Bastille. Right in the middle of the Pont Neuf he had
his police snatch my lover out of my carriage—from my side. Can a
woman of honor forgive a thing like that?'

" 'Then you did it out of hatred—in revenge,' I said, and I was
almost glad to find this motive where I had seen only cold calculation.

"She raised her head, but with lowered eyes, as though she were
considering my question. 'I did not hate him,' she whispered tenta-
tively. 'I loved him. I loved him very much. That is true, Nicolas.
You must believe me. I simply had to do it. Otherwise I would have
died. I could not eat, could not sleep, could not think or make love.
I was on the point of killing myself. It was he or me—I had to decide.
. . . When he was dead I knelt beside his bed and kissed his cold
hands and temples—and there was a great peace within me, such as
I had not felt for a long, long time. And I thought, it is done now. . . .'
She still knelt, thinking, her lips moving soundlessly. Suddenly she
sprang to her feet. 'But now,' she wailed, 'now I know that I was
mistaken—it was not meant to be him, but me!' In a fearful state of
excitement she ran to her dresser, pulled open the drawer, and began furiously rummaging through her clothes. Stockings, pieces of
underlinen, perfume bottles and powder boxes were tossed to the
floor. She searched, searched. . . .

"A bolt of terror ran through me. I rushed to her side. 'What is it? What do you want to do, Marie-Madeleine?'

" 'Make up for what I failed to do. Here—here it is!' she exclaimed triumphantly. In her hand she held a powder box. She tore off the cover.

"I threw myself upon her, struck at her hands. The box fell, and a white powder spilled over the floor. 'Are you out of your mind!' I panted. 'Do you think that through this—through the greatest sin— you can make amends?'

" 'I cannot go on,' she wailed, wringing her hands. 'I don't want to go on living.'

" 'Poison,' I moaned, shaking with disgust. 'Do you never think of anything but poison . . . poison . . . and more poison!'

" 'You want to abandon me,' she wept. 'There's no longer anyone in this world who loves me. Am I all alone?'

"I was moved by the sight of her standing there, wringing her hands desparingly, weeping. Black shadows in the hollows of her cheeks made her eyes seem larger. She seemed to me like a wide-eyed creature of the night. But yet she was a woman, a delicate and beautiful woman with tender, yielding temples and a rounded, womanly forehead.

"She perceived my weakness immediately. Coaxingly she embraced me and pressed her body close against mine, so that I felt her breasts against my shirt. 'You've saved me, darling,' she whispered tenderly. 'Save me entirely now. Come . . . do it with me . . . there on my bed . . . so that I can again feel myself a human.'

" 'Not that way,' I cried out. I freed myself and gripped her shoulders, forcing her down on her knees.

"She looked at me uncomprehendingly. I clasped my hands on the bed, bowed my head and began murmuring a prayer. Beside me I heard her whispering hoarsely. She knelt in the same posture as mine and repeated my words.

"We recited the Lord's Prayer. 'Forgive us our trespasses as we forgive those who have trespassed against us,' I heard her saying, and for the first time in my life I realized the meaning of those words that can so lightly be repeated.

" 'For Thine is the kingdom and the power and the glory in eternity. Amen.' I felt that my existence, which a moment before had hovered confusedly above abysses of uncertainty, suddenly had a meaning again, a goal, a central core. I felt easier at heart.

" 'Marie-Madeleine,' I said softly but firmly, 'the first step has been taken. But it is still insufficient.'

" 'What do you mean, darling?' she asked, looking penetratingly at me while she brushed her hair back from her forehead.

" 'Now you must confess everything before all men. You must take the punishment upon yourself. Then—and only then—all will be well again.'

"She turned pale. Her eyes filled with terror. 'Are you going to inform against me?' she whispered.

" 'I? No. You—you must do it yourself, out of your own free will. Don't you understand that, Marie-Madeleine?'

" 'Yes, I understand.' She sighed, relieved. 'Ah, how good you are, my darling.'

" 'Come, get dressed. I'll go with you to the police.'

" 'Now?' she cried out in horror, her arms raised and palms turned as if to fend me off. 'In the middle of the night? No, no, it would create a stir. . . . I must see my children once more. . . . I must consider what to say. . . . No, tomorrow . . . the day after . . . next week—yes, next week, certainly. . . .'

" 'It mustn't be I who makes you do it,' I said sadly. 'The decision must come from yourself alone, Marie-Madeleine. Otherwise it is worthless.'

" 'From myself alone, my darling! That's it, don't you see, that's why I must think it all out carefully. So that I will not make any mistakes.' She came up to me, took my chin and kissed my closed lips. 'You're so cold,' she whispered, with disappointment and a tender sadness. 'Kiss me, my darling, to show that you're not angry with your little girl—even if she's behaved so badly tonight.' And she pressed closer to me.

" 'No, I'm not angry with you,' I said.

" 'But do you love me?' she persisted.

" 'Yes, I love you,' I gasped out. 'I love you more than my life.'

"She laughed softly with satisfaction. That low laugh cut like a knife into my mood, which was still one of solemnity. It outraged me, but in another area of my soul, which had only developed through my life with her, it enraptured me—against all my better judgment.

"She had got onto her bed. Wide-eyed, she crouched there, still studying me with an attentive tenderness that made me shiver. Now she stretched out, with her hands clasped behind her head. She was enjoying the sensation of her own body. With utter lack of shame, she drew off her ample nightgown. 'It's torn anyway,' she murmured. I saw her slender thighs, which glistened in the candlelight, the soft muscles of her abdomen, and her gleaming, pointed breasts.

" 'Come, my darling,' she whispered, and laughed again—a laugh full of promise. With a low, contended purr, the purring of a preda-tory beast, she locked me in her arms and, with that sudden access of strength so characteristic of her, pressed me against her body. I cov-ered her with kisses—her half-parted lips, her breasts, her loins, her thighs.

" 'Now,' she cried hoarsely, triumphantly. 'I'll never let you go again.'

"And so I made love to my murderess. I plunged into lust and pleasure as into a black, warm, bottomless pool.

"When I left her bed at dawn she called to me, 'Don't forget the knife, darling.'

" 'What knife?' I asked sleepily.

" 'The knife with which you refused to kill me. It's lying there under the dresser.'

"I groped my way to the dresser, took the knife, and left her room. With a feeling of utter dizziness I closed the door behind me and slowly and quietly climbed the stairs to my room.

"I felt hollow, utterly empty. I despised myself as I had never despised another human being.

"My sense of inner annihilation was so frightful, all seemed to me such a waste and void, that I felt a sense of aversion for my very existence. I hated myself. Everything about me seemed bathed in despair. The thought of destroying myself came to me and would probably have overwhelmed me if I had been sure that death would have been the final termination of my torment. But I had the feeling that what I was now experiencing was only a foretaste of the hell that awaited me in the twilight of the hereafter.

"Of one thing I felt sure. The state in which I now was, was un-tenable. I had to do something to get myself out of it. And so, on the afternoon of the third day following that fateful night, I set out for Aubervilliers, intending to confess everything to Father Morel. But

on the way there I began to waver again. The vastness of my sin, not
lust alone but blasphemy, suddenly became apparent to me. I realized to what depths I had fallen. The monstrousness of the crime I
had so long concealed would be a heavy blow to Father Morel. I
even doubted that he would believe me. Would he not think I had
gone out of my mind—precisely because he knew me, or thought he
knew me? It seemed incredible, even to myself, that I should be
involved in such frightful events.

"And so I turned back and for a long time walked about indecisively in the vicinity of the Place Royale. The sinister towers of the
Bastille which rose up against the darkening sky of evening seemed
to me a warning to my conscience that I must at last do something to
restore justice. I resolved to confess everything to an unknown priest
in the nearby Church of St. Paul's. I would be able to speak more
freely to a stranger.

"I was approaching the church from the Avenue de Saint Paul
and had already entered the small walled-in cemetery behind the
sacristy when suddenly two shots were fired at me. One bullet whistled close by my ear; the other grazed my coat above my shoulder. I
saw two figures swinging their legs over the wall of the cemetery.
Instantly I was overcome by a savage rage, which was partly rage at
my own hopeless predicament. I felt like a lamb being led to the
slaughter.

"I rushed after the assassins, leaping over the gravestones, and
swung myself over the wall after them. I saw them some distance
away in the Rue Beautreillis. Shouting, I ran after them. This vicinity
at this time of day was quite deserted, but from the balcony of a
house a maidservant looked after me with gaping mouth. I ran with
all my might, hands clenched. But they were faster than I. Soon
they vanished among the trees of the park around the arsenal. It
was hopeless to pursue them into the gardens, where they could
easily lie in ambush for me. And it was at this point that I suddenly
realized that I was weaponless.

"I hurried on to Monsieur Bocager and asked him to lend me two
pistols. He was upset by my appearance and behavior, and my request for weapons threw him utterly off balance. 'For heaven's sake,
my boy,' he said, 'don't do anything foolish. You know that dueling is
punishable by the galleys.'

" 'It's not a question of a duel, but of murder,' I exclaimed, and I tried to explain to him. But I could read in his eyes that he did not believe me, and finally I virtually snatched the pistols from him and rushed out, paying no attention to his warnings. I stuck them into my belt on the left and right side, without even thinking that they were not loaded and that I had neither lead nor powder.

"The attack and my own senseless activity had made me feel somewhat better. At last things were beginning to happen. I wanted to shoot the criminal who undoubtedly stood behind those two hired assassins; to be shot myself. It did not matter to me which the outcome would be.

"I was firmly convinced that none other than Sainte-Croix had sent the two assassins after me. For I thought that, since that night, I was certain of her and that she, in turn, must be completely convinced of my unconditional devotion.

"At Sainte-Croix's house in the Rue des Bernardins, a servant opened the door. He uttered a low cry when I drew the unloaded pistols from my belt, waved the barrels under his nose and ordered him to lead me to his master. But then he shrugged and obeyed.

"Sainte-Croix was sitting in a *fauteuil*, propped between white pillows. He was pale, his temples were sunken and his eyes wide and filled with anxiety. It was the greatest disappointment of my life to find him in this state. I had expected to confront the bold, sardonic man of the world I had always seen, but he was quite obviously a dying man. He glanced indifferently at the pistols in my hands, smiled somberly, and said in a voice in which even the note of scorn had grown weary, 'If you've come to shoot me, Monsieur Briancourt, you will not shorten my life by many days.'

"Endlessly disappointed, I stood there feeling like a fool with my pistols and my heroic resolve. Sainte-Croix signaled to the servant to leave the room.

" 'Sit down, Monsieur Briancourt,' he said without mockery, gesturing toward a chair. 'I am glad you have come—even with pistols. I had been wanting to ask you something.'

" 'If you please,' I said in embarrassment, and I sat down. I glanced at my pistols and put them back in my belt.

"He had closed his eyes and was apparently thinking. I felt a wave of bitterness rise in me. It would all have been so simple. But now the path of violence was closed to me. 'Why did you send assassins to kill me?' I asked, trying to recover my hatred. 'Because I know everything?'

" 'I did not send anyone to kill you, Monsieur Briancourt,' he said— and to my amazement I felt that he was speaking the truth. 'And you do not know everything—no, not everything. Otherwise you would—I won't say pity me, but understand me.'

"I swallowed hard and said nothing.

" 'No, I don't want to excuse myself,' he sighed. 'Neither myself nor her. We should have had the strength, but we did not. Step by step the Evil One led us from crime to crime.' He brooded for a long while. 'Briancourt,' he went on at last, 'I do not want to speak of her, although she, too, is a part of my guilt, perhaps the greatest part. But what does anyone know of his fellow men, even those closest to him? I know you despise me—justifiably, I might say. Can you imagine that I, too, was once pure-hearted and innocent, that I, too, believed in love?'

"I stared at him in astonishment. What is he up to? I wondered. Is he trying to soften me?

" 'It all began in the most innocuous way,' he went on softly. 'Or with the sort of thing that is customarily called harmless among the nobility and at court. Do you know, by the way, that I am not a nobleman? My name is simply Godin—I added the Sainte-Croix myself. But to keep to the point: It began with a wager between two young men concerning a young woman. We wagered five hundred livres, which I would not have been able to pay if I had lost—'

" 'I don't care to hear about it,' I interrupted, my heart pounding with jealousy.

"He smiled sadly. 'You're quite right, Briancourt,' he said, 'but that's the worst of it, that no one wants to listen to us. Here I've been sitting all through the long nights. Often I can scarcely take a breath; it is as though a mailed fist were clenched around my heart. It's probably something to do with the muscles of my heart, the doctors say, but it also seems to me as though it is the numbing weight of my evil memories which is slowly crushing me. This last night I tried to pray. I went over everything just as it happened. Fact after fact, without extenuation, without making excuses. And what do you think happened, Briancourt?' He looked at me, an anxious, questioning look.

" 'Nothing!' I said.

"He started and in amazement half rose from his chair. 'How do you know that, Briancourt?' he asked.

" 'Since I have been in the marquise's house I know about such things,' I said defiantly.

" 'You, too, Briancourt! I thought it happened only to me,' he muttered, staring into space.

" 'Why?' I asked. 'Do you think yourself so unique that even God has to invent a special treatment when—when He punishes you?'

"He looked exhausted, but now his features became somewhat animated. 'That's just what I wanted to know, Briancourt,' he said, and looked at me in suspense. But then he became confused and said, 'You must ask Briancourt, I thought last night when I sat here unable to sleep. He's a theologian, after all.' He fell silent, staring vacantly again.

" 'Go ahead and ask,' I said harshly.

" 'Well, you see,' he stammered, 'you see   I've written some treatises . . . certain treatises, I mean . . . on the inner essence of Heaven and Hell, and on the Holy Trinity also. Possibly you don't know, but I sent these books into many houses—many elegant houses —and mostly to ladies. But that was only a pretext, you see, to introduce myself. What I really wanted to sell was—the poison I was making.' He took a deep breath and added softly, 'Was that a sin against the Holy Ghost?'

" 'What else was it?' I cried out. 'You've mocked what is holiest. You have poisoned not only bodies but the souls of men.'

"He covered his face with his hands. I was amazed. But when he removed his hands, there was a crooked grin on that sunken face, that face marked by death. Scornfully he asked, 'You think this sin cannot be forgiven?'

" 'Never! Not in all eternity!' I exclaimed. And I myself could hear the pleased malice in my voice.

" 'A fine Christian you are!' he said with a cutting contempt. 'How complacently you cling to your dogmas.'

" 'It's true there is such a dogma,' I said more calmly. 'But that this sin cannot be forgiven is something I have learned by personal experience, just as you have.'

" 'You, Briancourt? Why, that's hardly possible.'

" 'I prayed with her, understand? I thought I could convert her. I rejoiced. I felt perfectly sure of Heaven's aid. I assumed that Heaven spoke through me to her—but in the very midst of this imaginary security she pulled herself up and destroyed me—forever.'

" 'Yes, it was like that,' he said pensively, and he looked down at his wasted hands. 'Is there no way at all?'

"He addressed this question more to himself than to me, but it infuriated me because I had asked it of myself a thousand times. 'Yes, there is,' I snarled at him. 'Go to the police station on the Place Maubert and tell them all about it. You will find people to listen to you there.'

"He looked at me searchingly, his lower lip quivering like an old man's, and I saw the fear in his eyes—the fear that I would carry out what I had proposed that he should do.

"I felt myself growing weary, weary unto death of this hopelessness, this circle of obstacles which I could not break through only because of my contemptible weakness. I even think I yawned. And I felt a great temptation to close my eyes. But then disgust rose bitterly to my tongue. I stood up slowly, watched closely by those fear-filled eyes of his. 'Don't be afraid of my doing anything, Sainte-Croix,' I said wearily. 'I, too, have reached the end of my rope.'

" 'But that is just it,' he said softly, and I realized that he feared my weakness more than he did my strength of will. His looking at me in that way, the knowledge that he despised me, made me angry again—or perhaps I was only pretending rage to myself so that I could face myself. 'The devil with you!' I exclaimed. 'Why am I speaking to you? Go on and die. Reap in death the harvest you have sowed all your life!'

"With this theological invective I left him sitting there and went out. In the hallway I encountered the servant, who had apparently been listening at the door. He was holding an iron poker in his hand, but he did nothing but glare wickedly.

"I slammed the door of the house behind me. It sounded to me like stage thunder before the Last Judgment, so that in spite of the darkness within me I smiled.

"That summer she did not go to Sains. She stayed with friends in Versailles and came only occasionally to Paris. It was her almost continual absence which made it possible for me to go on living in her house.

"It was an oppressively sultry day toward the end of July. The hot, moist air weighed like lead upon me, and all day long I felt a heavy discontent that made it impossible for me to do anything. I rummaged among my books and some theological essays that I had brought with me from Aubervilliers. Here and there I read a sentence, without quite grasping what I was reading and forgetting it again at once. I threw myself down on my bed, but there it was even hotter and more uncomfortable. Wearily, I looked around and saw on the floor a slip of paper that must have fallen out of one of my old books. I picked it up and unfolded it. It was already quite yellowed.

"It contained notes written in my own hand on Ptolemy the Gnostic's æon system. I had made a rather confusing, though schematic sketch of that intricate world view which held that Bythos, the abyss, and Sige, silence, are father and mother of the vast multiplicity of intellectual, spiritual, and material substances which compose our world and presumably determine its destiny.

"I smiled dejectedly and thought of the dim lecture hall of the Sorbonne where, probably taking notes from some teacher, I had committed these gnostic ideas to paper. Under it, probably also from dictation, I had written in a bold, boyish hand, 'But whosoever is of this world (this meaning the psychists) and is overpowered by woman will not attain to truth simply because he has yielded to the lust for woman. We therefore, the psychists, who are of this world, require continence so that through it we shall reach the place of the middle.'

"It seemed to me as though someone had suddenly struck me a hard blow on the forehead, and suddenly all my thoughts and experiences became ordered around one central point.

"Sitting on my bed, my perspiring brow resting on my hand, I recognized clearly for the first time that I was a psychist, that is to say a person whose being revolves around his soul, his emotions. Although I could not imagine myself as a different kind of being, I knew that such beings existed, and I condemned myself harshly for having—as I have mentioned at the beginning of these notes—always viewed the ultimate basis of reality as founded in my feelings. For this bent of my nature with its vague premonitions, its excesses, its unrestraint, its inclination to find divinity in woman—this bent was what had led me to the position I was now in.

"Out of the blue there came to me as I sat there on my bed that hymn to the psyche which Hippolytus has passed on to us. Years

ago, when I first heard it, it had made a great impression upon me
and I remembered almost exactly how it went. Softly I hummed it to
myself:

> My soul has put on a temporary form
> And is tormented by its conduct, which death dominates.
> Now it rules on high, looking upon the light;
> Now it weeps, hurled into darkest misery;
> Now it is wept for and rejoices;
> Now it weeps and is judged;
> Now it is judged and dies,
> Now knows no longer escape. Unhappy at evil,
> Wandering, lost, it stumbles into the labyrinth.

"I felt deeply moved. For the poem spoke to me, of myself. I was
surprised at how much time had passed. Evening was already falling.
The heat had not abated. In fact it seemed to me hotter than ever.
The city, unreal as a mirage in the desert, lay bathed in a sulfurous
yellow light. Heavy cloud banks loomed on the western horizon, beneath which the sun was hesitantly dropping. The leaves of the
trees were perfectly still, as though they were carved out of stone.
Motionless, too, were the vanes of the windmills near the great black
cross of Montmartre, to which I raised my eyes.

"A fearful sense of expectancy, a weary, desperate waiting, hovered over the roofs and gardens from the blunt double towers of
Notre Dame far off to the southwest, where the newly erected dome
of the Invalides stood, like the navel of the city, darkly marked
against the last dimmed gleams of light.

"Voices reached me. I looked down. There, in the yard, stood the
carriage, the team of four hitched to it, all of glass and gold, as
magical as a carriage in a fairytale. One of the festooned lackeys was
holding the door open. Then she came out of the house. Delicate,
light-footed, with soft bare shoulders and arms which appeared, in
the strange yellowish light, as if carved out of old ivory. Her dress
glistened like silver. She had thrown the train lightly over her right
arm. In her mass of hair a diadem glittered, and a heavy necklace of
pearls caught the light just above the base of her breasts. There
was an archaic splendor about her—the magnificence of an Astarte
overladen with symbols and adornments.

" 'Palais Royal,' I heard her say to the lackey, who with a low bow
handed her a silvery-gray mantle. Then the carriage door closed

behind her, and after a while I heard the ringing, lively hoofbeat of the horses moving off toward the west.

"Suddenly I was seized by horror. That was it. It was my death I had seen in charming disguise, in gala dress.

"I stood motionless, spellbound, at the window, resting my head in my hands and gazing inward, where she still sat enthroned, as woman, as goddess, as murderess. The city faded out, but I did not notice. Only the distant rumbling of an approaching nocturnal thunderstorm brought me back to a realization of where I was.

" 'Now or never!' I cried the words as a command to my half-paralyzed brain. Something within me still refused, preferring death near her to life without her. But I overpowered it, I thrust it away from me, choked it back. Insanely afraid that I might weaken again, I turned away from the window and ran out to the hall. Taking two and three steps at a time, I leaped down the stairs. On the last flight, my coat caught in the fretwork balustrade and I tripped. I fell down in front of Julie's room, and I saw a gentle light coming through the crack under the door.

"I stumbled to my feet again, pulled the door open, and fell to my knees before Julie, who cried out in fear. With trembling hands I embraced her waist, covered her dress and her feet with kisses. What I said I no longer remember. I believe I asked her forgiveness and her blessing.

"She, too, was a woman. But what a difference! She wept and wanted to go with me. Much as I would have liked to take her, I refused. I did not dare to involve her in the vengeance which, I felt, would follow in my footsteps.

"Then I was out in the street. The warm wind preceding the thunderstorm whipped through my hair. I ran until there was a sour taste in my mouth and I had to stop, groaning for breath. For a few steps I walked and then I began running again, but more slowly.

"It was pitch-dark, except for the occasional bluish light from lightning flashes, which for moments revealed an uncanny landscape. Trees along the sides of the street raised their rustling branches aloft like despairing arms. Sometimes they seemed to me like the hairy heads of vengeful goddesses which the earth, rumbling, had released from her womb. Then dense night would fall again and I stumbled on with outstretched arms through the darkness until the flickers of lightning again illuminated the streets.

"Then long shadows sprang out at me and dissolved. It seemed to me then that they were waiting for me in the shrubbery of gardens along the street, lurking there to strangle me. I did not become any calmer until I reached the convent of the Daughters of the Holy Virgin. The instant that the lofty dome emerged for a moment from the night, the rain began to pour down, as though the heavens themselves wished to wash me clean.

"Like a haunted castle with unassailable walls and towering turrets, the Bastille flashed whitely at me out of the night, stood still for a moment, and then faded. I groped my way along the Rue des Tournelles and crossed the Jardin des Arquebusiers, where I had often spent the afternoon with the children. There I climbed over the wall and squeezed through the palisade which guards it from the outside.

"Slowly I waded through the city moat and climbed back to land. I stumbled over swampy ground, past the gnarled willows with their gnomelike heads, until I reached a meadow. Cows were standing silently about or plucking and chewing the wet grass. I threw myself down on the grass. The rain slacked; it fell mildly, almost consolingly upon me, and the flashes of lightning had become noiseless, like great will-o-the-wisps lighting above the marshes.

"It seemed as though I were saved."

Every day for the next week Desgrez went over the notes with Briancourt. He questioned the young man about the details of every incident, in the hope that his answers would reveal other possible witnesses. But obviously the only one was the servant Basil, for whom the police were already scouring the city.

Briancourt continued to maintain that the marquis must have known, or at least have suspected, what was going on in his home. But under existing law the marquis could not be forced to testify against his wife. And, in addition, interrogating him was a highly delicate matter, since the police had no jurisdiction over the high nobility. Only the king or the Parliament of Paris or a special court could subject him to questioning. And to the chief of police it still seemed premature to call the matter to the king's attention.

With some difficulty Desgrez succeeded in persuading his superior to let him call upon the marquis and have a "preparatory conference" with De Brinvilliers in which he would sound him out as circumspectly as possible about the events in his household.

The marquis was temporarily in Paris, trying, Desgrez learned from Bocager, to raise a new loan. Desgrez found him—a spindly blond man with a receding forehead—in his home, where everything indicated that the household was to be moved. Several lackeys were at work under the direction of the steward, wrapping pictures and mirrors in sheets. The marquis himself, very elegantly dressed, was standing with an abstracted expression in front of a richly gilded harpsichord that stood unsuitably in the middle of the splendid entrance hall.

Desgrez introduced himself. The marquis started slightly, but immediately recovered his composure and said, indicating the lackeys with a glance, that he unfortunately had little time; he would have to be leaving Paris within the hour.

"I am sorry to come at so inconvenient a time, Monsieur le Marquis," Desgrez said with a humility that he did not try to make sound convincing. "But unfortunately things have happened in this house which have attracted our attention—if I may permit myself the phrase."

The marquis gave him a haughty stare. "Things that concern the police? What sort of things?"

Desgrez sighed. "You must have heard, Monsieur le Marquis," he said, "that one of your former servants, Basil, is under grave suspicion of having attempted to commit murder?"

"Yes, to be sure, my steward spoke of it. But—but with the best will in the world I do not see why I should be molested in regard to a servant, monsieur."

"Do not forget, Monsieur le Marquis, that we are responsible for your safety, too, as long as you remain in Paris."

"What does that mean? What are you getting at?" the marquis exclaimed.

"We believe we have reason to assume that this man Basil—and another person—planned to poison you, too."

Desgrez saw that the marquis's beringed hand, almost a girl's hand in its fineness, was quivering slightly as it lay on the keyboard of the harpsichord. With difficulty he retained his composure. "That is really outrageous," he said softly, and added in a blasé tone, "I must say that the police seem to have rather remarkable conceptions about our private life. This is a noble household, monsieur!"

"Quite right, Monsieur le Marquis. But may I recall to your mind that your own brothers-in-law were killed by poison, and in an equally noble household, so that the conclusion is all too obvious that in the person of this man Basil we may have another La Chaussée, who is just as likely, and perhaps more likely, to be seeking to take your life, Monsieur le Marquis, than the life of an unimportant household tutor."

"Briancourt!" the marquis cried out. "Did Basil try to kill Briancourt?"

"He certainly did," Desgrez said, coolly regarding the marquis, who was staring at him, baffled. "But what is alarming is that behind the hired murderer—here as well as in Villequoy—stood someone else."

"Sainte-Croix! the marquis exclaimed, and he placed his shaking hand imploringly on Desgrez's arm. "I know it can have been none other than Sainte-Croix."

"It is someone else," Desgrez said firmly.

"Who then? By all the saints, who is it?"

"I may not give the name," Desgrez said calmly, and he looked hard at the marquis. Under that searching gaze the marquis suddenly lowered his eyes, and to Desgrez it was plain that he knew who was meant.

The marquis swallowed several times. He kept vainly wiping his eyes, which repeatedly filled with tears. "Ah, Lieutenant," he moaned, "what a tragedy, what a collapse! My name, my position at court, the king's favor, my fortune, and even this house here—all gone. . . ."

Desgrez looked at him, a quiver of contempt at the corners of his mouth. "You forget one thing, Monsieur le Marquis," he said icily.

"What? What else?" the marquis whispered. He drew a strongly perfumed lace handkerchief out of his cuff.

"The children, Monsieur le Marquis," Desgrez said.

The marquis looked at him in surprise, uncomprehendingly. Desgrez bowed, murmured an apology, and took his leave.

Outside he breathed deeply of the fresh air.

PART III

THE FRIENDLY ABBÉ

〈 I 〉

"CRIMES DO NOT take place in a vacuum. Like everything that happens among men, they are conditioned by their environment and therefore, like customs and art, have a particular style. There are fashions in murder, too." It was Desgrez speaking to the police chief of Paris, Michel de la Reynie, in the prefect's office at the Châtelet. Between them, on the top of the huge desk, lay a blue folder containing the confession of Nicolas Briancourt.

La Reynie was distinctly ill-humored. He growled, "I don't know what you're getting at with these speculations, Desgrez." And his round eyes stared crossly at Desgrez.

Desgrez smiled, but his smile vanished almost immediately. "No, sir," he said, "but I should venture to say that the Daubray case will not remain the only one of its kind for very long. You know very well, sir, that a whole series of lucky coincidences rather than our efforts have led us to the murderess. But we cannot always count on such coincidences and—"

"Let us stick to the Daubray case," La Reynie interrupted impatiently. "Have you questioned this fellow Briancourt thoroughly?"

"Several times, sir. I could not get much more out of him than he had already written down. The one additional fact of importance is that her plans included the elimination of the Marquis de Nadaillac also."

"Good Lord, what for?" La Reynie sighed.

"Always the same reason. The marquis is a cousin of her husband's, and years ago was her lover. According to her own statement her younger daughter is presumably the child of this relationship. When they broke off he promised to remember the child in his will. The marquise sent Briancourt to him to remind him of the promise. But Nadaillac had changed his mind, and his sister, Madame d'Artefeuille, backed him in his refusal. Very probably that saved his life, since under the circumstances there would have been no gain for Madame de Brinvilliers in having him killed."

"What a charming woman!" La Reynie exclaimed. "The perfect little spider female—murdering every man she ever loved. What surprises me is that she hasn't yet taken care of her husband."

"Me, too," Desgrez said, smiling. "All the more so since this is one case where you could not help sympathizing with her a little."

"Don't be so frivolous, Desgrez." La Reynie grinned. "Tell me what else Briancourt had to say."

Desgrez considered. "Oh, yes," he said, "Briancourt knew, though only from hearsay, that there was a connection between Sainte-Croix and Farmer-General Pennautier."

"What bearing has that on this case?" La Reynie asked uneasily.

"A rival for Pennautier's office, a Monsieur Saint Laurent, died very suddenly. So did Pennautier's father-in-law, who left a fortune to him. . . ."

"For God's sake," La Reynie exclaimed with distaste, "not every sudden death has to be a murder."

"Certainly not," Desgrez said coldly. "But in this case it is not without interest that after her father's death Pennautier's wife separated from her husband."

La Reynie studied his fingernails. Finally he shook his head. "Have Pennautier arrested," he said. "It will cause a tremendous scandal, but we have no choice. What else?"

"Briancourt also knew about the relationship between Canon Dulong of Notre Dame and Sainte-Croix," Desgrez said, throwing a challenging look at his superior.

"Well, and?" La Reynie asked.

"From Canon Dulong one thread leads to the Bishop of Mans, whose predecessor in office also died with surprising suddenness."

"Enough!" La Reynie exclaimed angrily, springing to his feet. "I forbid you to implicate the Church, too. Do you wish to defame everyone in France who is distinguished by wealth, nobility, or piety?"

Desgrez shrugged. "I am not defaming anyone," he murmured sadly. "I am just as surprised and shocked as you are, sir. And I am afraid—I am very much afraid that we will not succeed in exterminating the ultimate roots of the evil."

"What does that mean?" La Reynie asked, his excitement ebbing away very slowly.

Desgrez fell silent. Then he took a deep breath and said softly, "Don't you see, sir, that all these crimes derive from the conditions in which we live? That these murders have come out of the extravagance, the degeneracy, and the emptiness of the life of the upper classes?"

La Reynie's round eyes gazed anxiously at Desgrez. Desgrez saw that his superior wanted to say something but could not find the words or the courage to say it. Now La Reynie bowed his head, hastily opened the cover of the blue folder, and immediately clapped it shut again. Then he sat down. "Desgrez," he said, "that is a task for statesmen, educators, and the clergy. As far as we are concerned, we can only convict criminals of their crimes and bring them to court within the framework of existing conditions. We cannot change society—" He broke off as though he had already said too much. Then, suddenly, he began speaking much more easily of something else. It was as though he were relieved to drop this involved and delicate subject. "Incidentally," he said, "His Majesty the King wishes to see you. Tonight, in Versailles."

"To see me?" Desgrez asked in amazement.

"His Majesty remembers you. In connection with the Orléans affair. As you know, I was in Versailles yesterday. It was extremely unpleasant at first. His Majesty called Madame de Brinvilliers a Megaera and said that I, as chief of his police forces, should have prevented his dancing with her at his birthday celebration! I—and at the time I knew nothing whatsoever about all this. But His Majesty said I should have known. Poison is the dagger of women, he said, and then he was so pleased at having coined this *bon mot* that his temper became much better. He repeated it afterward to the young Duchess of Orléans, the German princess, who was extremely indignant—and that pleased His Majesty even more. From then on he was very gracious to me, and I was even invited to sit at the queen's

table. I sat beside Madame Scarron, the widow. Oh, I meant to say
beside Madame de Maintenon, who is in charge of the education of
Madame de Montespan's children—a rather full-bodied lady, but with
very beautiful eyes, I must say. She battered me with questions about
details of the murders and the amours of this ridiculous fellow Briancourt. And I soon noticed that not only her pretty eyes, but the eyes
of half the company at table were fixed on me. They were hanging
on my every word. Yes, it was for a change—the first in a long time—
a thoroughly enjoyable evening. . . ." The usually short-spoken police chief went on for quite a while. Desgrez, who at first had been
surprised at his superior's unwonted cheerful loquacity, grew more
and more thoughtful. His face took on an expression of melancholy
distress. But the police chief, enjoying his social triumph perhaps
more consciously in memory than he had in the reality, did not
notice the lieutenant's depression. In any case he considered Desgrez
something of an eccentric and a rather difficult subordinate.

Early that evening Desgrez left for Versailles in La Reynie's carriage, which his superior, with a surprising access of generosity, had
placed at his disposal. His feet in their high riding boots propped up
against the front seat, he sat leaning back comfortably, meditating
and glancing now and then at the landscape which for so long had
been deeply familiar to him. On his left, flanked by still leafless
poplars and elms, flowed the Seine, swollen with the waters of spring-
time. Beyond, on the other bank, the Champ de Mars stretched out
in the soft, misty air. The many-windowed structure of the Invalides
formed a fine architectural terminus to the field.

As the heavy carriage bobbed around the hill of Chaillot, Desgrez
was startled out of his thoughts by loud calls. A hollow-cheeked
man of indefinite age, dressed in rags, was hobbling along beside the
carriage crying out in a pitiable voice, "Give me a sou, monsieur. I
am terribly hungry. Just one sou!"

Desgrez fumbled in his pocket for a copper coin. But when the
beggar noticed the buttons and braid on Desgrez's tunic and realized that he had been begging from a police officer, he uttered a low
cry of horror and hobbled off. In vain Desgrez called to him to come
back. The man paused for a moment some distance away, looked
around anxiously, and then crawled off into a group of bushes like a
whipped dog.

The little incident made Desgrez even more thoughtful. For a long while he held the copper coin in his hand, studying its inscription. There was the head of the king, that fleshy face with its hooked nose, surmounted by the curled wig and crowned with a laurel wreath. It was the laurel that bothered Desgrez most, this symbol of fame, glory, and victory. He pondered upon the event which had first drawn the attention of the great king to himself, an unimportant member of the Paris police force.

That had been almost three years ago. In midsummer of 1670, to be precise. The Duchess of Orléans, the king's sister-in-law, who was a daughter of unlucky Charles I of England and therefore called by the French people Henriette d'Angleterre, had just returned from a highly important mission in England. There she had convinced her brother, Charles II, of the wisdom of an alliance between England and France against Holland. This clever, charming young woman who liked being surrounded by poets and philosophers was a favorite of both the court and the people for her charity and kindness. But a few days after her arrival in Saint Germain she had died suddenly. There were whispers of poison and talk about a glass of lemonade which she had taken just before she was seized by those attacks of agonizing pain that had ended in her death. Moreover, rumor whispered the name of the murderer—none other than her husband, and the king's brother, the Duke of Orléans.

It was a scandal that imperiled the reputation of the royal house and the whole foreign policy of France. The English ambassador made representations in Saint Germain; dispatches from his king, he said, demanded an immediate investigation by the police. There was all the more reason for investigation since the doctors could not agree on the cause of the duchess' death. Maréchal, the king's personal physician, believed the death was due to a perforation of the stomach caused by a neglected ulcer, but the other doctors shook their heads dubiously.

For good or ill, His Majesty the King of France had to take the bitter pill and invite the police into his own house. The task of investigation, of questioning the various persons of the royal household, from the Duke of Orléans down to the dead duchess' tiring-woman and the kitchenmaids, was assigned to Desgrez. It was a rather ticklish job and he would gladly have been spared it if that had been possible. For only with the greatest discretion was he able to inquire into these people's past, their relationships to one another, and the peculiarities of their characters. His Majesty wanted a confidential report on the findings. But at the same time he wished all the gentlemen and servants of his court to be represented in the end as pure as angels. And the report had to sound objective as well.

As far as purity went—and this Desgrez had observed at once—there was none to be found. Quite the contrary. Desgrez's familiarity with the underworld had toughened him, and he was not easily shocked, but he was appalled at the abysses he was forced to uncover. Behind the veil of courtly ceremonials, back of the beauty, grandeur, splendor, and charm, he encountered a veritable viper's nest. And he did not have to dig very deep to find it.

For the men and women of the court, all of whom claimed to be themselves as pure as the driven snow, were only too willing to go into detail about the evil traits and actions of their fellow courtiers. Undoubtedly, many of the tales Desgrez heard were untrue, prompted by envy. But when he had sifted through them all, enough damaging evidence remained.

There was extravagant egotism, which shrank from no crime so long as it could be kept secret. Ambition and vanity were expressed in a childish preoccupation with who doffed his hat to whom, or who had precedence at the Grande Levée. Such matters occupied the minds of these people who imagined that they were the flower of France. Almost all of them hypocritically put on a sticky piety, since the king considered himself devout; but at bottom all were atheists. Their religion consisted in observing the rituals; for the rest they had faith only in themselves and their own careers, which they endeavored to further by any and all means. God was like France to them—the source from which their money and positions flowed if they had acted rightly, which meant unscrupulously.

Desgrez in the carriage smiled bitterly to himself. He thought of the women who as long as their looks lasted sold themselves for money and empty honors and who when they had grown old devoted themselves to a kind of moldy superstition that reeked to high heaven even more repulsively than had their previous prostitution. Against this picturesque background he suddenly saw the crimes of the Marquise de Brinvilliers as understandable. The devil knows, he told himself, the Countess of Soissons, Olympia Mancini, with whom the king himself was infatuated when he was young, isn't much better. I'm almost certain that that scoundrel Exili sold her the poison that time. And people frankly reported concerning her sister, Marie Anne, the Duchess of Bouillon, that she was interested in having her husband killed so that she could marry the Duke of Vendome—she was his mistress at the time anyway. . . . Nice women—full-bosomed, eyes like black cherries, all right—but with the devil in them, too.

And then the man to whom suspicion pointed. Philip of Orléans, small, toadying, forced always to play second fiddle to his self-assured mighty brother, whom he resembled as an ape resembles a man. The Italian blood of the grandmother, Maria de Medici, had come out again in Philip—that Maria of whom Henry IV had said, "I would prize her as a mistress if I did not have the misfortune to be her husband."

Philip's waist was feminine, his chest rounded, and even his small, plump fingers, decked out with diamond rings, had something infamously female about them—as had his coquettish movements and his saccharine loquacity. It was generally known that the Chevalier de Lorraine and the Marquis d'Effiat were his lovers; and it was whispered that the chevalier, whom Henriette had banished from her presence, had poisoned her with the consent of her husband.

Desgrez interrogated the chevalier. He put his questions carefully, matter-of-factly; it would not do to forget that he was speaking to a member of the house of Guise. It was quite possible that the chevalier might have committed murder not out of offended ambition, but out of the ancient hatred for the Bourbons.

But the chevalier had a perfect alibi—at Henriette's orders, he had no longer had entry to Saint Germain and had been far away in the north of France at the time of her death. Nor had any of his henchmen been anywhere near the lady at the time. The only person close to him who had been on the scene was the duke, his "friend." The tiring-maid who had brought the lemonade to the princess and the chef who had prepared it were unquestionably honest. And they asserted that no one besides themselves had touched the lemonade. The princess, overheated on that hot summer day, had very quickly drunk three glasses in succession, the entire contents of the pitcher.

With great satisfaction Desgrez composed a report clearing not only the duke and the chevalier, but the entire court, of all suspicion.

Then the king had sent for Desgrez. In his mirrored private room,

with the stern, puritanical Colbert standing by his side, he had posed
majestically, his right foot somewhat forward—he was very fond of
this particular pose—and in his resonant, imperious voice he had
said amiably, "We have read your report with attention, Lieutenant
Desgrez. We knew what you would discover, for we have not for a
moment doubted that Madame died a natural death. But we would
not neglect to thank you for your conscientious completion of a painful task. Were you not previously, if our memory does not deceive
us, an officer in our Argenteuil Regiment?"

"I was, sire," Desgrez had replied, bowing.

"Do you know Madame d'Argenteuil?"

"Very well, sire. I live in Madame's house."

"Give Madame our greetings and tell her we wish to see her in our
presence more often." At his last words a fleeting smile passed across
the king's complacent face and vanished again. Desgrez bowed once
more and was dismissed with a gesture of the hand as regal as it
was gracious.

Now Desgrez started up out of his memories and noticed that
the carriage had already crossed the Seine. Slowly the horses drew
the carriage up a hilly road, between dense pine trees. Beyond the
branches, big and bright, hung the full moon.

In a few minutes he would be in Versailles.

⨍ II ⨍

THE MOONLIGHT embellished the castle that the king, out of a strange
whim, had started to build here a few years before in the marshy,
unhealthy region. It was not quite finished. There was still the astrin-
gent smell of lime everywhere, and Desgrez could discern workmen
busy on one wing even now, at night.

In the spacious yard which mounted the low hill there was a
swarm of carriages, thickest in front of the main portal of the building. Servants with torches, grooms leading horses, ladies and gentlemen guided by lackeys increased the confusion, so that Desgrez's
vehicle soon had to come to a halt. He ordered his coachman to
drive up to the stables and wait for him there. Then he left the
carriage and walked.

Although the lieutenant was not easily impressed by sheer expansiveness and splendor—he was in the habit of calling such things the delights of fools—and although he thought that, at bottom, the huge castle was tasteless, he nevertheless shared in the feeling of almost everyone who visited it: the breathtaking sensation of being in the heart of the world. Which was precisely the feeling that the king, one of the vainest men who ever lived, had intended to arouse in his subjects, allies, and enemies by the erection of such a wastefully expensive, pointlessly huge structure. The French people were by nature economical, and therefore nothing impressed them so much as official grandeur that cost huge sums.

Versailles, the cynosure of the world. It certainly was that now. And the feeling of belonging to a people that could make such a display of power and glory inadvertently lent to Desgrez a heightened self-assurance. His own experiences in Saint Germain were forgotten.

He entered the palace through a side portal after exchanging a few words with one of the guards. He strode down a long corridor intersected by other corridors, and soon realized that he was lost. Stopping one of the numerous lackeys who went rushing by him, he asked for the apartment of Le Mesnil, the king's *valet de chambre*. The lackey immediately breathed respect; Le Mesnil was, among the servants, what the king was among the courtiers. He led Desgrez directly to Le Mesnil's room.

Le Mesnil was a man of about forty who had adopted many of the king's mannerisms of speech and behavior. He was virtually bursting with elegance and self-esteem. However, he greeted Desgrez with what residues of cordiality he had left, for, some years before, Desgrez had by silence done him a great service in an unpleasant affair that might have cost him his position.

Desgrez told the *valet de chambre* that the king had sent for him, but that he had preferred letting Le Mesnil announce him rather than the marshal of the court, since if he appeared publicly he might attract unwelcome curiosity.

"How tactful! How charming!" Le Mesnil whispered, bowing repeatedly. "I shall announce you at once. His Majesty is at supper at the moment." He glanced quickly at his watch, a heavy silver sphere hanging from his waistcoat.

They mounted to the second story. On the way they encountered ladies and gentlemen who stared at Desgrez's uniform in surprise.

Then Le Mesnil asked him to wait in an anteroom. But he returned immediately and invited Desgrez into the main room.

This was, as Desgrez immediately saw, a bedroom. A table had been moved up to the fireplace, in which a small fire was burning. But it was rather cold in the room anyhow, for the windows were half open. At the table sat the king. Opposite him, toward the side of the room in which the bed stood, sat the Marquise de Montespan. At the moment the king was rinsing his hands in a silver bowl that a servant was holding out for him.

Desgrez remained in the doorway and bowed so low that the slouched hat in his right hand touched the floor. "Approach, Lieutenant Desgrez," the king said. Everything he did was dignified; the movement with which he now dried his hand could not have been done with more polished majesty by the most skillful actor.

The marquise started to rise, probably in order to leave the king alone with his visitor, but the king gestured amiably to her to remain. She was, Desgrez saw, even more beautiful than he remembered. The ample golden-blond hair, twisted into curls at the sides, framed a rather long, almost Spanish face of great purity. There was nothing sweet, nothing insipidly charming about her; what was amazing was the classical simplicity of her beauty. You did not notice it at all at first glance, and at the second glance it overwhelmed you. Desgrez saw that her violet-blue eyes flickered toward him in a look in which, to his surprise, he thought he discerned fear.

"It is the ladies who make life hard for us," the king said, smiling. But the smile vanished as he dramatically threw his arm forward, pointing at Desgrez, and asked imperiously, "Desgrez, do you believe in the guilt of the Marquise de Brinvilliers?"

"Absolutely, sire."

"That amazes me, Desgrez. You used to be a cautious man," the king said, measuring him with a glance. "And you have nothing but the report of this young fool, who possibly has imagined it all out of unrequited passion."

"It is ungrateful . . ." the marquise began, but at a glance from the king she broke off and fell silent.

"I require clear, unambiguous proof," the king continued, "and you, Desgrez, must provide it."

"We have the promissory note, sire," Desgrez replied.

"The promissory note? But that can be interpreted in various ways."

"Certainly, sire. But then why has the marquise fled to England? Why does she not surrender to Parliament in order to clear her name?"

The king was struck by this. "I had not thought of that," he murmured.

"I should think it would have been the duty of your police, sire, to have prevented her flight," Madame de Montespan interposed, and her sweet lips smiled mockingly.

"No one is alert." The king sighed. "All the burdens rest on our shoulders. But in this affair we are not willing to content ourselves with a mere suspicion. Have you any conception, Desgrez, of what these murders mean for us, for France—if they have really taken place?"

Desgrez bowed silently.

"We have become a laughingstock in the world," the king said bitterly. "My agents report that the people in Paris are cynically whispering that the marquise is not the only one, and that we had intended to appoint that poison-maker Sainte-Croix to the office of our cupbearer. . . . And it is true. We ask ourselves: if this has really happened, are we, is our family in Versailles, still safe? Is it not possible that in our own house there may be another Ravaillac— a poisoning Ravaillac?"

"Oh my God," the marquise whispered. She had turned white; her lower lip was quivering. Desgrez saw that he had not been mistaken. The fear in her violet eyes was perfectly plain now.

Desgrez, too, was shocked, for he knew that the king shunned any reference to Ravaillac, the assassin who had stabbed his grandfather in the open street. And it was rare that the king raised his voice in anger as he had just done.

But Louis regained his composure at once. "In short," he said quietly though no less imperiously, "I insist upon clarity. And you, Desgrez, must provide it—as you did before in Saint Germain. I entrust this task to you alone. Take care of it any way you please, but I want you to arrest the marquise and provide me with un- equivocal proof of her guilt. I intend to bring to bear all the force of the law and make an example of her for all to see, a warning that France will not tolerate poison and murder, no matter what the station of the criminal. Bring me the proof, Lieutenant Desgrez!"

"Certainly, sire," Desgrez replied, again bowing low.

The king smiled, in a sudden shift of mood. With the same winning but imperious gesture that Desgrez knew well, he dismissed the lieutenant, who backed out of the door. The king raised his wine glass. But Desgrez noticed that the marquise's eyes continued to follow his movements anxiously until Le Mesnil softly closed the door behind him.

As Desgrez passed through Chaillot again on his ride back to Paris, he peered out of the window of his carriage at the moonlit landscape, through which wisps of mist floated. Some distance away, in front of a dark mass of shrubbery, he thought he recognized the gaunt figure of the beggar who had accosted him earlier in the evening. He ordered the driver to stop, and got out of the carriage. But when he approached the shrubs he realized that he must have been mistaken. There was no one there.

As he stood, from beyond the Seine there rose up out of the moonlit expanses of countryside a long-drawn-out howl. Desgrez listened attentively; it sounded to him like a wolf. But the howl was not repeated. He heard nothing but the soft sigh of the night breeze among the underbrush and the snorting of the horses.

Hesitantly, looking back several times, he got into the carriage again and the drive home continued.

⚊ III ⚊

AT THIS period there existed a kind of secret postal service among the monasteries and convents of France, and this system of communication sometimes extended beyond the frontiers. Desgrez now concentrated his attention upon this mail. His agents had already drawn an invisible cordon around the house in the Rue Neuve Saint Paul, Sains, and even around Villequoy, and had established that no letters were going to England from any of these places. But he felt it a safe assumption that the marquise was getting money from France somehow. The most probable person to send it would be Mademoiselle de Dreux Daubray, the marquise's sister, in the Carmelite convent on the Rue de l'Enfer.

It was a ticklish matter to check on the convent's mail. For the

Church formed a sacrosanct state within the secular state, and Desgrez saw no way to suspend its prerogatives. But to circumvent this
immunity was another thing and caused Desgrez no great pangs of
conscience. Clericals leaving the Carmelite convent in the stagecoach
were addressed by friendly gentlemen and found themselves invited to dinner or a glass of wine at the halting station, without their
ever suspecting that their baggage was being searched by Desgrez's
agents while they sat with their cordial companions.

This patient procedure bore fruit. A bill of exchange for four
hundred livres was found, made out to the marquise and addressed
to a certain house in London. Under the circumstances, of course,
Desgrez's men had to permit the letter to go on to its destination.

At this juncture, diplomatic machinery was set into motion. Minister Colbert wrote to his brother, the French Ambassador in London,
requesting him to demand the extradition of the marquise. But for
inexplicable reasons the English government made difficulties. Finally, after much tugging back and forth, the British yielded to the
point of declaring that the marquise could be arrested on English
soil by the French police—but the British police would take no part
in the proceedings.

Obviously the marquise had highly placed friends in England.
When Desgrez arrived in London he found that the bird had flown.
The marquise had departed for the Netherlands.

That made the situation virtually hopeless. Now the marquise was
under the protection of France's enemies, and the war had blocked
up all diplomatic channels to Holland. Still Desgrez did not abandon
the pursuit. By means of the letters to and from the Carmelite convent he followed the marquise's trail from Rotterdam and Antwerp
to Ghent. She was approaching the theater of war and the borders
of France. The scent was getting stronger.

But at this point the agent in Sains slipped up. Desgrez learned
too late that the marquise had moved boldly to Cambrai by way of
Valenciennes, and had asked her husband to meet her there. But in
spite of the urgency of her request the marquis had refused. When
Desgrez learned of her presence in France and made ready to strike,
she was gone from Cambrai.

Almost three years had been consumed by this exciting pursuit.
All Desgrez's efforts, the work of all the agents he had employed,
the huge cost of maintaining a virtual cordon around France, the

diplomatic difficulties—all seemed to have been in vain. To all appearances, letters and money were no longer being sent from the Carmelite sister to foreign parts. The marquise seemed to have vanished for good, as though the earth had swallowed her. Desgrez had to admit to himself that his opponent was extremely cunning.

But he refused to accept defeat. He conjectured that the marquise was probably hiding out somewhere just across the border, thinking that money could be smuggled to her easily there from Sains or Paris. So he alerted the French secret agents, many of whom were in the vicinity because of the war with Holland.

One of these men was a certain Descarrières in Liége—a somewhat unsavory person who, like many of his kind, found it necessary to change his name occasionally and sometimes went by the name of Bruant. In the past, Descarrières had been an agent of Fouquet, Louis XIV's first Minister of Finance. Fouquet's lavishness with the public funds—a lavishness principally directed toward himself—and his fondness for Mademoiselle de la Vallières, who had also attracted the king's eye, cost him his position and his liberty. Fouquet was convicted in a sensational trial, and with him all his underlings fell.

Descarrières's purse was ever shrinking and he was anxious to get back into high governmental favor that would assure him the juicier assignments. Informed by Desgrez of the king's interest in the Daubray case, he set to work feverishly and soon learned—to his immense delight—that the much-sought Marquise de Brinvilliers was close by. She was staying in Liége, in the Convent of Noble Ladies.

Descarrières immediately sent a message to Desgrez suggesting that he come to Liége to arrest the marquise. In his joy over the impending improvement in his financial situation, Descarrières overlooked the fact that the marquise was in a convent which the police could no more enter than they could the Carmelite convent in the Rue de l'Enfer in Paris. Liége was, to be sure, occupied by French troops advancing toward the Netherlands; but no French general would dare to batter down the doors of a religious institution.

Quoi faire? Descarrières was aghast at this complicity between crime and religion. He sat at a table in conference with Lieutenant Desgrez, Sergeant Cluet, and six policemen who had come from Paris with them. In anticipation of future prosperity, Descarrières had generously brought out the last bottle of wine in his cellar. But the rich, heavy wine provided no solution; if anything it produced

greater confusion of mind. Descarrières grandiloquently talked of
the prince bishop, and of the mayor of Liége, although he knew quite
well that neither of these gentlemen could force the Convent of the
Noble Ladies to yield anything it was unwilling to yield. Cluet, undoubtedly under the influence of the wine, suggested that they
should disguise themselves as Dutchmen, clamber over the walls of
the convent by night, and take the marquise by force. But Desgrez
shook his head. There was no use in attempting a disguise, since
everybody knew that none but the French police was interested in
laying hands on the marquise.

Desgrez frowned. Then, his forefinger rubbing against the tip of
his nose, he looked at Cluet with a sardonic grin.

"I don't know whether my idea is due to the wine," he said, "but I
think I've found the way. If only I were as good an actor as Monsieur
Poquelin."

"What do you mean?" several of the men asked.

"Tell you later, boys," Desgrez said. "Let me sleep on it. If my little
idea seems as good to me by the sober light of morning as it does
now over the wine, why then—yes, then I think we've found something to try."

IV

THE MAIN street of Liége, which descends sharply to the Meuse
River, was jammed with soldiers. For Liége was one of the Marshal
d'Estrade's principal rear bases. The marshal and his army were
some thirty miles north of the city, near Maastricht.

Through the throng of infantrymen, cavalry, rumbling gun carriages, and requisitioned peasant carts pressed a large carriage.
Seated within, leaning indolently against one corner of the seat, sat
an elegantly dressed abbé whose court dress and generally well-
groomed appearance seemed wholly out of place amid the crude
tumult and the mustached martial faces in the street. A good many
disapproving glances were cast at him. But the clerical gentleman in
his short black-silk cassock, with its narrow collar and cuffs of the
finest snow-white batiste, merely smiled contemptuously and with a
condescending gesture raised the gold-rimmed glasses of a lorgnette
to his eyes.

His dark, slightly wavy hair fell down to powerful, though not particularly broad, shoulders. His longish, finely chiseled face might have seemed handsome had it not been for the powder which he had applied far too heavily, with what seemed to be a distinctly feminine vanity. He seemed also to have rouged his lips.

People in the street who noticed the abbé—and he made so striking a sight that it was scarcely possible not to notice him—deduced from his appearance that he could not be a genuine religious. Probably he was a titular abbé, that is to say a courtier—possibly a prince's tutor or even from Versailles.

Luckily appearances could deceive. The spoiled and elegant looking abbé in the carriage was none other than Lieutenant François Desgrez. With distinct repugnance, but with a determination to carry the thing through, he had chosen the disguise of a particular type of abbé, a type well known in French society, whose temperament was far more secular than spiritual. In the great noble houses such abbés frequently played the part of confidential advisors and entertaining companions. Good social manners, wit, gaiety, and a certain breadth of philosophy which enabled them to reconcile the requirements of religion with the habits of worldliness were expected of these men. Frequently they were themselves of noble origin. Their personal piety was quite acceptable to amoral society, so long as they restricted the exercise of it to themselves and did not trouble their environment with moral adjurations.

In his role as an abbé, Desgrez had paid a visit to the convent the previous day—and now hoped to be able to win the confidence of the marquise.

The nun at the gate of the Convent of Noble Ladies, which rose high above the river just outside the gates of the city, received him with a low curtsy and an air of respect. When he asked to see Madame de Brinvilliers, she led him inside.

Now Desgrez found himself in a rather large room, where the chill and damp of the winter still lingered. It was furnished impersonally and tastelessly: Wooden chairs and benches; a large table on which lay books bound in black leather. There were a few paintings on the otherwise bare walls, apparently painted by the inmates of the convent themselves and indicating good will but little talent.

The paintings were all of female saints. Catherine of Siena, a pot of lilies by her side, looked languidly into space. Saint Agnes caressed a lamb that looked dreadfully like a poodle. And a coal-black, wild-haired creature apparently represented Saint Mary of Egypt.

Desgrez felt uncomfortably tense. The paintings, bad as they were, made him aware of the fact that he had penetrated into a wholly female world. To distract himself, he went to the only window and looked out. But he saw little there to reassure him. The trees in the garden were still bare. Their black branches lowered above the still unplanted rectangular vegetable beds. Behind these, leaning gently askew, stood the crosses above the mounds, where former inmates of the convent slept their eternal sleep.

Desgrez started and looked around. The figure of a woman stood beneath the painting of Saint Mary of Egypt. It was the marquise. Her build was as delicate as Briancourt had described it. Her look was thoughtful and penetrating. At the sight of those eyes, mournful and unnaturally large, and of her complexion, he unvoluntarily lowered his own gaze.

"I beg your pardon, madame," he said, confused. "I did not hear you come in. My name is Dubois. I was on a mission to Marshal d'Estrades at his headquarters. Now official affairs will keep me in Liége for a few weeks. Yesterday I paid a visit to this convent in the course of my duties. The abbess told me that a lady of the high nobility is in retreat here. I felt that I ought not to miss the opportunity of paying my respect to my countrywoman and to inquire whether I could be of service to Madame."

"Your visit is a great surprise," the marquise said softly. "Have you heard nothing about my—my misfortune?"

"Certainly," he replied, sighing, "but slander is common in Paris. Scarcely anyone escapes it."

"You don't believe it?"

"No, of course not," he said, and he felt that his voice sounded honest because at the moment he actually believed in her innocence.

"Oh," she breathed. She put her right hand to her breast. "But do sit down, Monsieur l'Abbé. I'm sorry—this room is not very comfortable."

"No, I would not say it was, madame." He glanced around the walls once more and shrugged. Then he quickly drew up a chair and stood holding the back of it until, with an easy, graceful movement, she had sat down. He took a seat facing her. "Why do you not return to Paris, madame? It must be dreary, vegetating in this provincial environment—without friends, without your children, without everything that makes life bearable."

"It is out of the question," she said darkly, tilting her head so that he saw the fine line of the part between the mass of hair. She fixed her eyes wide upon him, and he saw that tears were sparkling in them.

"But there is no point in complaining," she said, shaking her head. "Tell me about Paris."

"That is rather a large order, madame." He smiled.

"I no longer get any news at all. Nobody writes me. But tell me this: Is Madame de Montespan still as close to the king as she used to be?" She looked at him with a feminine curiosity that drew an understanding smile from him.

"She still is, madame," he said. "But there is also talk of others. Of Mademoiselle Fontanges, who is said to be as naïve as she is beautiful. And the Duchess of Soubisse, who, it is said, madly loves her husband and consented only when the king promised him a more lucrative post. And finally there is Madame de Maintenon."

"Who is she?" the marquise asked eagerly. "I have never heard the name."

"No wonder, madame, since it is new. It is the name of a small estate which the king has graciously presented to the deserving governess of his natural children—"

"What's that?" she interrupted him. "She cannot be that plump little widow of the author who wrote the *Roman Comique?*"

"The same, madame. The widow Scarron, née d'Aubigné, if I am not mistaken."

The marquise clapped her hands, laughing, and exclaimed, "The widow Scarron. Who ever would have thought it!"

Looking at her, he realized now for the first time that she was beautiful—of an extremely feminine beauty with her pure rounded forehead, her dark hair and prominent cheekbones which broadened the upper part of her face and gave it the faintest hint of a deep animal quality. She looked at him, and the little outburst of frivolity vanished abruptly. She smiled cunningly to herself and her cheeks, a moment before an almost sickly white, became delicately tinged with a pastel flush. Then her eyes began to shine at him, serene and imperious, with the confidence of her female power, and she said in a husky voice, "Tell me more, my dear abbé."

He might have been mistaken, but it seemed to him that her request contained more than an invitation to retail gossip. Suppose she knows who I am, he thought confusedly. She seemed to notice his uncertainty, but she apparently ascribed it to a cause more flattering to herself. In any case she dropped her glowing eyes and waited patiently, with the equanimity of a creature for whom time does not exist, for him to go on.

"What I was going to say," he stammered, with difficulty getting a grip on himself, "is that in spite of these rivals Madame de Montespan is still dominant. She remains the first. And in fact—if it is permissible to speak to one beautiful woman of another's beauty—she is very good-looking indeed. I saw her in Versailles—"

"You have been in Versailles recently!" she exclaimed, leaning forward tensely.

"Yes, madame. Did I not tell you that I had a mission from the king to Marshal d'Estrades?"

"Yes, though you did not mention that it was from the king, monsieur."

She is sharp, Desgrez thought. I shall have to take care. Aloud, he said, "Madame ought to see Versailles now."

She sighed. "Has it been greatly changed?" she asked melancholically.

"You would hardly recognize it, madame. What our good Le Nôtre, the landscape architect, has done with that unpromising area borders on wizardry. You ought to see the little ballet theater in the open air! And the murals, the decorations—Lebrun and Girardon have surpassed themselves."

He saw that she was listening with yearning in her eyes. That was her world. And although it was not his, although at bottom he despised it, he made an effort to describe it as more splendid, dignified, beautiful, and amusing than it was in reality. He painted for her a tender utopia, a gallant idyll. He knew very well that it was not the real Versailles—and she knew it, too. But she was delighted by the ideal, which stood in such a glorious and at the same time depressing contrast to her present existence in this desolate convent. She was greedy to hear more—more and more.

He spoke to her about the theater and the ballet, about Lully's and Couperin's music. He touched on fashions, on Paris gossip, and even mentioned the famous clerical orators. One of these, Bossuet,

had recently delivered an address for the funeral of Marshal
Turennes which surpassed in solemn pomp anything he had ever
done before. He spoke of Marly, of the grand fountains which were
being created, and which would be fed by diverting a river from its
natural bed.

He sensed that he was speaking well. A strange enthusiasm had
taken hold of him and loosened his tongue. Its origin lay not in the
subjects he was discussing, nor in his desire to overcome the obstacles
to his plan by talking. His sense of soaring eloquence, of unfailing
inspiration, which was amazing to Desgrez himself, came from this
woman, from the enamel-blue gleam of her eyes, which rested upon
him with a yielding tenderness.

He knew very well that this tenderness in her eyes was directed not
so much toward himself as toward the subjects he was talking about.
Yet he could not help feeling a warm and by no means unpleasant
sensation as her eyes rested upon him.

At last he fell silent, feeling that although he had spoken for a long
time he had left unspoken what was most important.

The plan, he suddenly remembered. Oh yes, the plan—he had
almost forgotten it.

She had risen and now she came up to him. She drew a lace handkerchief from her bosom. He looked up at her in some alarm as she
stood beside his chair, seeming much taller and slenderer. A faint
fragrance of attar of roses emanated from her, and the scent of this
became stronger as she touched his upturned face with the handkerchief.

He stared at her uncomprehendingly. She gave a bright, silvery
laugh and said, "You have used much too much powder, my dear
abbé." And she again brushed the handkerchief over his face.

"Powder?" he stammered. "Why—yes—it was quite dark in my room
this morning."

"Was it?" she said softly, studying him. She took a small, round
silver-framed mirror that hung from a chain from her left arm and
held it in front of his face. In the mirror he saw his own startled look.
"There," she said, "that is your true face. Do you recognize yourself,
my dear abbé?"

"I suppose I looked as if I were wearing a mask?" he exclaimed,
and felt a start of dismay at what he had said.

"Like an abbé on the stage," she replied, smiling. "The powder does not suit you at all. Nor, for that matter, does the cassock. Are you aware, monsieur l'abbé, that you have a—a rather military quality about you?"

It took all his self-control not to betray his alarm. "Perhaps that is because I was once an army officer," he said.

"You see, I guessed it right away."

"How did you, madame?"

"Oh, I don't know. . . . Perhaps by your carriage. And sometimes you use words that only army people use."

"One can hide nothing from women." He sighed with mock sadness.

"You need hide nothing from me, my friend. I like officers much better than courtiers—Oh, forgive me, that was tactless of me."

"Not at all, madame, I feel the same way," Desgrez managed to say.

Several elderly ladies, boarders at the convent, entered the dreary salon. They sat down and began chatting softly with one another. But their keen interest in the abbé was all too obvious. They kept throwing shy glances at him, and one lady, who was apparently hard of hearing, held her ear trumpet in his direction, as though she did not wish to miss a word of the conversation between the marquise and the abbé.

Desgrez welcomed the interruption. His nerves were still quivering, and he found difficulty in speaking with as much facility as before. He took his leave of the marquise.

"You will come again, won't you?" the marquise said urgently.

"Tomorrow—if you like, madame."

"Yes, by all means, come," she said happily. "I feel as if I am alive again for the first time in ages." The look in her eyes as she fixed her gaze upon him contained, it seemed to him, a hint of a promise.

He bowed and left, followed by the keen glances of the old ladies.

That evening at Descarrières's house he could read in the eyes of his subordinates their eagerness to hear what had happened at the convent. But they did not question him, and he did not volunteer to tell them anything. Later, when he was alone with Cluet in his bedroom, Cluet told him that he had spoken to the mayor of Liége. That dignitary had set aside a room in the citadel as a prison cell for the marquise—if Desgrez succeeded in capturing her.

Desgrez sat, half undressed, on the edge of his bed and stared at the candle which dimly illuminated the room. At last he said with a sigh, "Cluet, there is a tremendous difference between our ideas and reality, especially where the idea concerns a human being. There is a gap there that we never imagine beforehand. In our minds, everything is as simple and well-ordered as a proposition in geometry. But in reality . . ." He broke off and relapsed into his brooding.

"I don't quite understand what you mean, Lieutenant Desgrez," Cluet said after a while.

"It seems"—Desgrez sighed again—"that I have begun something I shall find hard to finish. An unexpected obstacle has cropped up." He dropped into silence again and then, as though he needed to take a running start each time he wanted to speak, said at last, "Let's go to sleep, Cluet. I feel certain the morrow will bring new surprises."

⚹ V ⚹

THE FOLLOWING morning he called at the convent at the same hour as on the day before, and was again shown to the gloomy salon. The marquise was apparently expecting him, for she came at once, entering the room with her light step. Smiling a response to his greeting, which he tried to make as unforced as possible, she brushed her right hand over her hair and stepped beneath the painting of Saint Mary of Egypt, a composition of brown and black out of which the eyes of the penitent saint glowed whitely.

The marquise was wearing the same simple dove-gray dress as the day before, the same black shoes, and the same coiffure, whose curls and ringlets contrasted rather sharply with her otherwise nunlike appearance. But Desgrez noticed at once that something had changed about her. He quickly realized that today she was wearing under her left eye a mouche, that is, a beauty patch, also called an *assassin,* because of its presumably "killing"effect. The little artificial spot on the milk-white skin gave her face an altogether different expression. The dejected little woman of yesterday had transformed herself into a *femme fatale.*

He felt touched that this woman who had once had gala dresses, jewels, and a splendid house at her disposal when she wished to make an impression on a man was now reduced to this single tiny patch of sticking-plaster. But at the same time he had to admit that

none of the women he knew could, with all their arts, have achieved
the desired transformation as perfectly as the marquise had done by
means of this small black patch.

His conclusion, he soon realized, was mistaken. If the marquise was
interested in making a conquest of him, she was behaving in a strange
fashion.

"Let us sit down," she said. "I have given orders for no one to disturb us. I must talk with you, my dear abbé."

"So we did yesterday, madame," he said, smiling.

"Oh no. Yesterday you talked—Oh, you will never know what that
meant to me—But today I have resolved to speak." Her nervous fingers began arranging her hair. "I spent half the night thinking about
us. . . ."

"About us?" he exclaimed.

"This place is very well suited for meditation. Ever since I have
been here I have been meditating. The most trivial incident, which
in Paris would never have struck me, becomes here an overwhelming experience."

"I understand, madame."

She looked sharply at him. "I believe you do understand," she said.
"Although when I first saw you I rather doubted. Don't take that
amiss, my dear abbé."

He made a gesture of dismissal and forgiveness, although he was
quite uncertain what she was getting at.

"It isn't easy to know how to begin," she said after a pause. "We
know each other only a few hours. But you have a male mind, and
I have always been able to discuss things only with men. And so during the night I decided to tell you everything."

"Everything?" he cried out in surprise.

"You said yesterday, monsieur l'abbé, that you had heard of my
misfortune. And now I must confess to you that I am not altogether
innocent of the deaths of my father and my brothers."

Desgrez was thoroughly perplexed. It was a cheap trick to obtain
her secrets in such a fashion. But almost immediately his detective's
instincts triumphed over his hesitation, and he leaned eagerly toward
her, wholly the policeman.

His confusion did not escape her. She looked at him searchingly
before she went on in a low voice, "No, my dear abbé, I am no mur-

deress—and yet I am not innocent. She stopped and then, with resolution said, "Sainte-Croix was my friend."

"You loved him?" he asked almost inaudibly, solely to have something to say, for she had expected something from him.

"He is the only man I ever loved—aside from my father, of
course. . . ."

The case is very different, Desgrez thought promptly. But he said
nothing and listened tensely. It was as though he had an inner ear
capable of hearing a concealed meaning behind the obvious sense of
her words.

"I was very young when I married," she said, becoming more and
more absorbed in inward contemplation of her life. "Not even seventeen. As a child I was lonesome and not very happy—there were all
sorts of things, but they are not part of this story . . ." She broke off
once more, then continued: "I needed a support—orderly conditions,
a backbone, so to speak. I was passionate, easily impressed, incon-
stant. But I felt within myself a powerful will, only it had not yet
taken shape. No one had ever troubled about my upbringing. But
now, in my marriage, I thought I had found the firm foundation and
at the same time the goal of my life.

"I loved my husband and my children and thought I always would.
But then my husband turned away from me—that was during my
third pregnancy—and I learned from gossip that he was keeping a
dancer as a mistress. I raged, I wept, I made scenes—with the result
that my husband avoided me more and more, though he did not
break with me entirely.

"Then one day he brought one of his old regimental comrades into
my house. It was Sainte-Croix. He was tall, witty, a Gascon by birth,
and he paid court to me. I liked him at once, and he liked me, too.
Soon we were living in a *ménage à trois*, which I suppose is what my
husband had planned from the beginning so that he would be free of
me and able to go on pursuing other women. But I thought I had
found the lover that my husband could no longer be to me. I was
happy, although I often suffered from fearful premonitions that this
happiness could not last.

"In order to overcome these premonitions, in order to prove my
happiness to myself, I did not make a secret of my relationship with
Sainte-Croix; I showed myself openly with him. That was a fatal
error. For my family intervened. My father and my brothers forbade

my creating a 'scandal,' as they called it. Previously they had only shrugged their shoulders at my husband's infidelity. That was something else again. He was a man and I a woman.

"But I insisted upon my 'rights,' and the result was that my father had my friend thrown into the Bastille. For my father was a man of powerful character who permitted no emotions to stop him from undertaking anything he recognized as necessary. And yet he loved me—as I did him. Perhaps that sounds strange, my dear abbé, but it was not so much injured pride as jealousy of me, his daughter, that made him take such an action. For although he was ordinarily as hard and unbending as the great cardinal is supposed to have been, he always treated me as tenderly as an inamorata. So he was deeply moved and, with tears in his eyes, promised to have Sainte-Croix released when I, overcome by sorrow, threw myself at his feet and promised never to see Sainte-Croix again." She fell silent and stared blankly, absorbed in her memories, at the pale spots of light cast upon the floor by the spring sun.

Desgrez cleared his throat and said carefully, "Certainly, there is a great fault there, madame, but perhaps the fault is more your husband's and Sainte-Croix's than your own. I still do not see a connection between what you have told me and what people are saying about you in Paris. But—I am afraid you broke your promise and saw Sainte-Croix again?"

"I had to see him again," she said passionately. "But, oh my God, how he had changed. Physically he was the same, though he had become thinner, but his soul had been wrecked. He had thought he was going to be sitting in the Bastille for years, decades, and that I—that I had forgotten him. My dear brothers had told him so. She is dancing and amusing herself, they had said, and she already has a new lover, the Marquis de Nadaillac, and laughs with him about you, Sainte-Croix, when she hasn't anything better to do with him.

"Now he must have seen that this wasn't so. But still he could not forget it. The wound to his pride went on festering. He was gloomy, distrustful, scornful, full of resentments—he who before this had always been open-hearted, gay, trustful, and so candid as to be almost naïve.

"One day he began to tell me about a certain Sieur Exili, an Italian with whom he had shared a cell. The Italian had spoken to him about poison as the most effective and at the same time most discreet

means for getting rid of enemies. And Sainte-Croix reminded me that
in former days we often used to visit the Swiss apothecary Christo-
pher Glaser, on the Ile Saint Louis, and for amusement had tried all
sorts of chemical experiments under his direction. 'At that time,' he
said, 'I was unknowingly forging the weapons for the future.'

"I was frightened. I knew very well what he meant. But I believed he was only talking in order to relieve his tormented heart. I
did nothing—and it is just in my doing nothing, in my silence, that I
now see the terrible guilt I have incurred." She gave Desgrez a
frightened look and asked anxiously, flushing, "Do you believe me,
monsieur l'abbé?"

Desgrez nodded.

"You see, that was how it was—that was it," she exclaimed, and
Desgrez could hear a faint note of triumph in her voice. "On the one
side he stood, alone, poor, humiliated. On the other side my family,
one of the most powerful families in France, rich, tremendously
proud. But I only did what all of us women do when our heart im-
pels us—I stood by the man I loved. And today, out of that fact, they
are trying to convict me and are calling me a poisoner and a
murderess."

"I see the connection," Desgrez said dryly.

"I pointed out to him how kind my father was, how he loved me
and I loved him. I implored him not to take revenge. And he—he
promised me that he would not carry out the intention he had hinted
at. He lulled me into a sense of security, deceived me—"

"I beg your pardon, madame," Desgrez interrupted, leaning forward stiffly. "May I point out a contradiction. You just said that you
stood by idle—and now you say you begged Sainte-Croix to spare your
father's life."

She started and he saw her cheeks flush again. "Oh," she said,
quickly composing herself, "it is hard for a woman to express herself
logically. I only wanted to say that I neglected to denounce Sainte-
Croix to the police or to warn my father. And in that I now see my
guilt, and it gives me no peace. For as you know, monsieur, Sainte-
Croix broke his promise to me—that is, if my father and my brothers
really did die of poisoning. For to the last Sainte-Croix denied that
he had had any hand in their deaths."

"There can no longer be any doubt on that score, madame. That fellow La Chaussée—I believe that was the knave's name—confessed everything before his execution."

"Yes, indeed," she said quickly. "Sainte-Croix lied to me—and I hate him for that now. . . . Oh, how could I have been so trusting."

"There is another point," Desgrez said hesitantly. "But forgive me, madame, you owe no accounting to me. . . ."

"Please ask any questions you like, my dear abbé," she said, looking trustfully at him. I am grateful for your interest. For what I want to establish is the truth—the whole truth."

"The point I have in mind has to do with a promissory note. It is said in Paris that this note first made the police suspicious of you."

"Oh, I am glad you mentioned that!" she cried, looking at him with eager eyes.

"Is it true, madame, that you made out such a note? Or is that, too, mere slander?"

"No, no, it's true."

Desgrez swallowed and sat speechless, groping for words. Without effort, like a ripe plum, this vital confession had fallen into his lap. "But in Paris," he went on hesitantly, "they say that it was a payment to the murderer."

To his amazement she laughed lightly. "There, now you can see how people imagine all sorts of things. Oh yes, they have a wonderful imagination when it comes to slandering their betters. But my dear abbé, I never paid that note. Otherwise I would have asked for it back, wouldn't I?"

"Why, yes, certainly—but I don't understand . . ."

She gloated over his confusion, chuckling under her breath. Then she grew serious. "My financial situation was such that I had to do something," she said gravely. "I saved those thirty thousand livres from the hands of my creditors, saved them for my children, by assigning them as a debt to Sainte-Croix. That is the whole secret of the promissory note which has led people to such horrible conclusions."

Desgrez saw the piece of evidence upon which he had founded his case slipping away. But he reached out for it once more and said, "As far as I know, madame, what excited the suspicions of the police was the fact that the note was not signed with your married name, but signed Daubray."

He started in alarm. She had sprung to her feet, breathing convulsively, her whole body quivering with passion. She was squinting as if she had lost control of her eye muscles. "I am a Daubray!" she screamed furiously, the crooked, quivering fingers of her right hand clawing at her breast. "I, the daughter, my father's favorite, the heiress, the only true Daubray after him on this earth." He saw her catch his alarmed look and make an effort to calm herself. She only half succeeded. She sat down, but her breath still came and went in a series of sobs and her hands, resting now in her lap, still trembled.

"I beg your pardon, madame, I did not know . . ."

"There was no way for you to know," she said, slowly growing calmer. "I—I myself did not know. But just as you said that, I suddenly realized why I always sign my name Daubray. How could I call myself by the name of that unfaithful straw-haired fool I was given to, turned over to? Gobelin—haha—or Brinvilliers—those degenerate petit bourgeois carpet-makers!" She stared into space for a moment. "But, my dear abbé," she went on in a lower, confidential tone, "that is what eats at my heart. That a loving daughter who has the force and the will to carry on the great traditions of the family should have been pushed out, pushed into a filthy marriage, solely because she is a woman. And that was not enough. When she finally has succeeded in finding some sort of happiness, her father and brothers come to her with long sermons and moral preachments and snatch away her one consolation—again because she is a woman.

"I will say nothing of my father. He was after all the head of my family and probably thought it his duty to do what he did—although it was most unjust to me. But my brothers! Who gave them the right to tell me how to behave and to condemn me? No, monsieur l'abbé, my brothers were worthless. They were unworthy of my name. Oh, I know they are dead, and hypocritical convention demands that we say nothing but good of the dead—even if they were killers, killers of the souls of others. And I want to forgive them. But what can there be worse than killing the soul of a twelve-year-old girl. . . . Why did they not remember then that I was only a woman—a woman?" She fell silent, and her eyes wandered restively along the walls, from which the figures of female saints in their impossibly stiff garments looked woodenly down upon her like dolls on top of a child's toy box. It seemed to Desgrez as though she were having difficulty breathing, as though she felt oppressed by the atmosphere of this rarely aired room. And her next words confirmed this feeling.

"Come, monsieur l'abbé," she said, getting up, "let us walk in the garden so that at least we can see the sky above us."

Outside it was cool, so that until they emerged from the shadow of the building she shivered. There was a spicy, strong smell of black earth, from which the first bright-green tips of narcissus were just beginning to shoot. The buds on the fruit trees were swollen already and a first starling hopped over the garden plots.

Silently they walked side by side until they reached the iron gate that separated the garden from the graveyard. There was a small arbor with the black vines of grape winding over the lattices. They sat down beneath it on the bench.

"I know I have no right to burden you with all these things, my dear abbé," she said. "But I have no one to talk to, not a soul. The good ladies would never understand me."

"Oh, not at all," Desgrez replied. "I am only sorry that I can do so little to relieve you, madame, of all these undoubtedly needless self-reproaches. For—may I speak frankly?"

"Please do, monsieur l'abbé," she said, looking at him with tense expectation.

"There is only one authority, madame, which can clarify everything and which has the power and the good will also to restore your reputation. That is the Parliament of Paris. Therefore I would advise you, madame, to go to Paris of your own free will and surrender to its court."

"Impossible," she exclaimed. "I will never do that!"

"And why not, madame? Do you have so little confidence in your own cause? You have just explained everything to me."

She reddened and said confusedly, "What can I—a solitary woman —do to fight all these prejudices? Perhaps you do not know, monsieur l'abbé, that my father was a valiant defender, all his life, of the monarchy and a determined foe of Parliament. In Paris they have not forgiven my family for that."

"But your brother, the baron, was himself a member of Parliament —if my memory does not deceive me, madame."

"You are right, my dear abbé. But still and all, still and all—I don't trust the lot of them. If they can get back at the Daubrays in any way, they will certainly do so." She fell into a brooding silence for a moment. Then she looked up at him as though there were a silent understanding between them and said meaningfully, "I don't care about the Parliament at all. Let them believe whatever they like. What I've said I've said only for your sake. Because I don't want to appear in your eyes as a—a murderess."

"Why does that matter so much to you, madame? My opinion is of no great moment."

"Oh yes it is."

"How so, madame?"

"Because—because I feel a friendliness toward you."

Confused, he met the radiant look in her eyes. "I can say the same for myself," he replied after a moment. "I feel a great liking for you, madame."

She held out her right hand, and he brought it gently to his lips and kissed it. As he did so, he noticed that she was not wearing a wedding ring.

She smiled gratefully at him. But her expression was pensive as she said, "But . . . what must you think of me, after all this, my dear abbé. How foolish, frivolous, irresponsible, and defiant I have always been. The situation in which I find myself now—what else is it but the consequence of my character."

"Yesterday you called it a misfortune, madame," he pointed out.

"That is true," she said quickly. "Much of it is due to misfortune. Do you think that men are the nemesis of all unfortunate women, my dear abbé? They were mine, at any rate. All failed me when I needed them most. Their understanding, their aid, their love—or what is called love. But above all my father—and my brothers. They were the roots of my misfortune. Never, even though I stand again free, rich, and respected, will I forget the fact that it was they who— never . . ." She went on moving her lips soundlessly, as though she were telling herself what she could not tell him. But then her expression changed, her bearing stiffened, and she gave him a searching, challenging look. "But I shall not give up hope," she said with sudden resolution. "If I myself . . . if I could find and love a man who was worthy of my love—ah yes, then, then nothing in this world would matter to me. I would follow him to Canada, to the wilderness, if his way led there."

Desgrez, abashed, had risen. She, too, stood up, and he saw the disappointment in her eyes. "I beg your pardon, madame," he said uncertainly. "I had quite forgotten that one of my superiors is expecting me for an important conference. In your company time flies by so quickly."

"Indeed," she said dryly, with a haggard look. Then she raised her eyes to his. "Why, my dear man," she said softly, "was what I just said so irksome to you?"

He gathered his forces. "It was not irksome to me," he heard himself saying. "It is only that it came as such a surprise—" He broke off. She looked questioningly at him. Her disappointment had vanished, he saw. "Because, I, too . . . because I feel the same," he heard himself going on. Discomfiture and deliberate cunning struggled indecisively within him. "Because I have a great liking for you."

"Ah," she sighed, relieved, her eyes probing his face.

"I did not expect anything of the kind in Liége. It came to me so unexpectedly—this feeling. You see the state I am in. I must think it all over, order things in my mind—by myself, alone."

"You are a strange man, my dear abbé," she said, laughing, but still attentively watching him. "Do you know how you look now?"

"No, madame."

"As though your conscience were bothering you."

"No, certainly not," he said quickly, and gave a forced laugh. "But I really must be going."

"Come," she said with emphatic gaiety, taking his arm gently. "Here is a gate in the garden wall. You don't have to pass through the convent."

He opened the gate, which was shut only by a wooden bolt, and kissed her hand once more in farewell, promising to return the next day.

⁊ VI ⁊

THAT NIGHT Desgrez sat at the table in his room and by the light of an oil lamp wrote down all that the marquise had told him. When he was finished, he carefully reread the closely written pages. Then he sat for a long time with head in hand.

All the while Cluet, in the back of the room, had been sleeping deeply, as his heavy breathing indicated. Now he started up abruptly from the pillows and said sleepily, "Are you still working, Lieutenant Desgrez? It must be past midnight."

Desgrez turned around to face Cluet, who with his peaked night-cap and the dangling ends of his big mustache, looked like the kindly father of a family of ten. "I have been thinking, Cluet," he said slowly, "and the fact stares me in the face, that we have no evidence against the marquise that cannot be interpreted more than one way." He picked up his notes and read them aloud to the sergeant.

With hairy hand Cluet rubbed the sleep from his eyes and listened with concentration. When Desgrez had finished, the sergeant reached under the bed and took out a bottle of brown cider. He took a long, gurgling drink and then offered the bottle to Desgrez, who gestured refusal. Cluet wiped his lips and replaced the bottle under the bed. Then Cluet said, "You forget one thing. We have Briancourt's confession."

"I have not forgotten that, Cluet," Desgrez replied. "But Briancourt never saw anything; he only heard what the marquise thought necessary to tell him—if she said it at all."

"Do you doubt it?" Cluet asked in alarm.

"No, I don't. But Parliament has a perfect right to doubt Briancourt's testimony. For why should the marquise have put the rope around her own neck by telling Briancourt about all these murders?"

"In order to persuade him to murder Madame Daubray."

"That is what he says, Cluet, but does it sound credible? Don't forget, my friend, that Briancourt is a poor devil and the marquise a lady of high rank. Suppose she testifies to Parliament that she only told him horror stories in order to enjoy his gullibility and his terror. Women sometimes do that, you know."

Cluet pondered. "Then there is nothing else to do but to put the two of them to torture," he suggested.

"That is what I fear most, Cluet."

"Why so?"

"Because the marquise has an iron will and even under the greatest torment will insist upon her innocence. But Briancourt will break down at the first degree and recant everything. In fact I am afraid he will take back everything he has said the moment he sees her again."

"You sound very sure, Lieutenant Desgrez."

"Because I now know the two of them, Cluet. She is a strong woman who knows exactly what she wants. But Briancourt is a weakling who can be led one way or the other without much trouble."

"And yet he did not do what she wanted him to do."

"His fear was greater than his sensuality; that is all he deserves credit for," Desgrez said with a bitterness that Cluet had never before seen him show. He brooded gloomily, then sighed and added, "But the case must be carried to its conclusion. Do you know the little grove of poplars by the Ourthe, near the convent, Cluet?"

"Yes. Is that the place?"

"Have Descarrières be there tomorrow."

"Certainly, Lieutenant Desgrez," Cluet replied.

Desgrez put out the light, undressed, and lay down. Cluet's even breathing showed that he had promptly fallen asleep again. Desgrez himself stared into the darkness and fell into a restive half-sleep only when the first hesitant gray of morning began to light the room.

⚓ VII ⚓

THE DAY was lovelier and more springlike than the preceding day had been, and they once again sat side by side on the bench in the little arbor. The marquise had laid her hand lightly on his and asked him to tell her about his past. He spoke to her of the time he had served in the Argenteuil cavalry regiment. As frequently happens to old soldiers, his own military experiences began to fascinate him. He forgot for what purpose he had come here and became completely absorbed in the varied adventures of his youth. He knew he was telling the story well and conjuring up the past so distinctly that he imagined he could smell its special atmosphere of horses, leather, and tenting.

She was a good listener. She did not interrupt him and showed by her looks that she was following his words with an attentiveness which was far more than a polite interest.

After he had told her about how he got his wound, he abruptly fell silent. "Go on," she said impatiently, giving him a little poke.

"There is nothing more to tell about that, madame. One life was past and another began. The wound fever, the interminable lying in sickbed, the sleepless nights were, if I may put it that way, the midwives that raised me to a new existence."

"May I ask you a question, my dear?"

"Please, madame."

"As you were lying under the horse and the battle raged all around you—what did you think then, François?"

He started. "You know my first name?" he asked, worried.

"You mentioned it several times in the course of your story," she replied, laughing. "Please call me by my Christian name also: Marie-Madeleine. But now answer my question."

"I thought nothing at all, madame. I was unconscious and did not come to until my friend Cluet began dragging me from under the horse."

"And then?"

"Then I cursed—at the enemy, at the bullets that had struck me, at myself, at everything. Probably I did so because I did not want to have to think. For I was actually not annoyed, and probably more in a mood to bless than to curse the world which was being given back to me."

"And later, François?" she asked eagerly.

"Later? Why, later, of course, I had to think everything over. And lo and behold, the fact stared me in the face that I knew nothing."

"Nothing?" she repeated anxiously.

"Nothing at all," he said, shaking his head. "I lay in Madame d'Argenteuil's house—her husband had fallen in battle shortly after I received my wound, and she was glad to have me to take care of—and everything struck me as mysterious. The leaves of the chestnut tree in front of my window, the sunlight, my own body—everything that I had previously never given a thought to was now all strange. For before, you understand, Marie-Madeleine, I had been right in the midst of things, like an actor in his play; but now I was sitting on the outside, a spectator, though one who understood neither the scene nor the plot.

"A tremendous curiosity took hold of me. There was a fine library in the house. I read through it. Montaigne, Pascal, Descartes, Plato, Dante, and hundreds of others—I crammed them into my mind. Madame d'Argenteuil borrowed books from her neighbors. I read through the whole Place Royale, so to speak. And after I had read all that, I was then acquainted with the views and opinions of all those excellent men—but I did not know myself." He fell silent and smiled to himself.

"And then?" she asked softly.

"Then I set about the rather tough job of finding out something about myself—which is where I should have begun if I had not been such a fool—But what is the matter, Marie-Madeleine?" he exclaimed, for her eyes had filled with tears. "Do you find me so pitiable?" he asked.

She swallowed. "Don't joke, François," she said reproachfully. "Can't you see that I am in exactly your situation—that we are as alike as two twins?"

"We? Alike?" Desgrez said in amazement.

"I, too, was an actress on the stage you speak of, François. The scenes: Saint Germain, Versailles, Le Marais. I played the lady of rank, powdered, bejeweled, splendid—at the formal dances at court, in the candlelight of the gaming tables, in my own house, in my carriage. More than that, I played life—and I also played death." She paused. "But then came my misfortune. I fled from one foreign land to the next and the world showed its other side to me—irreconcilable, pitiless. The game was over, although at first I went on hoping it would begin again. I found that I was cast back upon myself. I had no books, still less the mind to read them; I meditated upon my past simply because I had nothing else left. Oh, François, looking back, with the new insight into things that my misfortune has given to me, I saw everything as a harder, grimmer, more terrible. . . . In my cell I could not help asking myself the question: Why did you do that? And who are you that you were able to do that?"

She dropped into silence. Desgrez gazed shamefacedly into the garden, at the black earth warming itself in the sharp sunlight. Doves moved gravely about with iridescent plumage, and with slapping wings a pair of lovers flashed upward in a short flight to the wall of the garden. "It will be Easter soon," he said.

"François," he heard her saying, and felt her hands clasp his firmly, "I knew at once that you had come to save me. You must stay with me always—forever." She brought his hand to her lips and kissed it.

He was so stunned that it did not even occur to him to withdraw his hand. His mouth slightly open, he looked at her, studied this creature whom he had come to destroy. Her cheeks, their whiteness emphasized by the contrast with her dark hair, had the look of one just come from a cell, just recovered from illness.

"Why are you staring at me like that?" she asked, and then she began to laugh. She laughed with reckless high spirits, like a small girl. "Do you like me?" she asked with naïve curiosity. "Do you think you could love me—as I do you?"

He rose. The movement, like a twinge in his old wound, restored his composure. You must, you must, he commanded himself; it is now or never. In his mind's eye he briefly saw the figure of the king ordering him, with that impressive motion of his hand, to arrest her. If I do it, he thought, I will not be killing her. We have no real proof. But she—she will hate me then.

"What is the matter, François?" he heard her ask in a concerned voice. "You're so strange. You've become mute."

"Forgive me, Marie-Madeleine," he said, and once again he fell wholly into the part which not so long ago he had decided to play, never suspecting how difficult it would become. "It is these surroundings, this gray convent, that oppresses me. How can one speak freely of feeling here?"

"It oppresses me, too," she sighed, also standing. "Just think—for more than a year now I have been living within these walls."

"Then let us go. It is such a fine day, and I know a lovely spot down there by the river. You will like it."

"Oh, is there a river there?" she exclaimed longingly. "I love running water. . . ."

"Only a small stream, really," he said. "But now, with the melting snows, it has grown to be almost a river." He took her arm.

"I don't know, I really don't know whether I should go," she said hesitantly, looking at the wooden gate in the garden wall.

"But why not?"

"Yes," she said, stamping her foot gently as if impatient with her own qualms. "I will go. Formerly, when I saw that gate, I always thought: It leads to death. But now, with you, François, I know it leads to liberty—to love."

With averted face he busied himself at the gate, taking longer than necessary to open it. It screeched harshly on its hinges as it swung wide. Before them the earth lay green, a faint spring mist, radiant with sunlight, hovering over all. "Oh, how beautiful, how lovely," she exclaimed, raising her arms ecstatically.

As he closed the gate behind them, she placed her hands on his shoulders and pressed her head softly against his chest. "François," she whispered, "I am alive again." And she pulled his head down to her face and gave him a long, intimate kiss on the mouth.

⁊ VIII ⁊

SLOWLY THEY STROLLED along the edge of a deeply rutted road that
led across the fields. The ground was still soft from the spring rains.
She leaned on his arm as they walked, and sometimes she stood still
to take in deep breaths of the tart air. Then he would stand silently
beside her, watching with bitter emotion the look in her eyes as she
gazed joyously over the meadowlands. After her long confinement
behind gray walls, everything seemed new and wonderful to her;
while in every blade of grass, in every sapling, he saw only a silent
reminder of the inevitable moment of betrayal which he was nearing
with each step. Involuntarily he walked more slowly. The sense of
the irrevocability of time numbed his will as it slowed his steps.

But she noticed nothing, neither his hesitancy nor his shamefaced
silence. They came at last to the Ourthe. The elemental waters, concerned only with themselves, flowed swiftly along beneath crooked
willows whose gnomelike heads with long, dangling green hair bent
down over the dark surface of the stream. From last year's gray
reeds, broken by the snow of the preceding winter, frogs cried their
high-pitched, trilling love calls like strange birds. As they approached, the frogs fell silent and dived into the water with a low
plop and splash.

"The old song," she said, smiling and pressing his arm. "They sing
in the spring. Even as a child I always felt that they were not little
creatures calling, but she—she herself."

"Who?" he asked, standing still in surprise.

"The earth, my friend."

He regarded her, thinking that Briancourt had at times seen in
her a personification of the earth itself. It seemed strange to him; he
saw only a very feminine creature with rounded forehead, brown
locks, and remarkably large and beautiful eyes.

"Why are you looking at me so strangely, François?" she asked
tenderly. "It is almost as though you had just discovered me." Then
she started back and pointed a frightened hand at a tree.

"What is the matter?" he asked.

"There! don't you see? There, behind that tree—a man lurking.

And there is another. And there. François, we are surrounded by robbers! And you—you have no weapons, François."

He looked up the small slope, covered with poplar trees, and saw Descarrières, who gave him an admiring grin. Looking around, he saw Cluet also, his mustached face deadly serious. Here and there his men emerged from behind the trees. But they did not come any closer. They were waiting for his orders.

"Perhaps we can buy ourselves off," she whispered excitedly. "Have you any money with you, François?"

"No."

"Well, do something, for heaven's sake, François."

This was the bitter crowning of years of work, the moment he had so long wished for and now cursed. He cleared his throat. "Madame," he said calmly, "these men are not robbers. They will not harm you."

"Then who are they?" she cried out in terror. "And what are you?" She gave him a look of fright and doubt.

"I am Lieutenant Desgrez of the Châtelet in Paris."

She cried out, one single piercing cry that immediately stopped, cut off short. He saw that she had set her teeth firmly. Her cheekbones protruded from under the taut skin of her face; the blue of her eyes had darkened. "You will pay for this, pay for it horribly," she cried out, her voice quivering with hatred. "Do not forget that I am a Daubray."

"The king himself has ordered me to arrest you, madame."

"You have toyed with me—as no one ever did before," she moaned, breathing heavily. "You despicable murderer of women—worming your way into my confidence, into my heart. You're not a man, you're a low villain—a scoundrel—a spy. . . ."

"Madame, there is little sense . . ."

"Whatever happens to me, Desgrez, you will be ashamed of this moment all your life. . . . If you knew. Oh, if you only knew . . ." And she burst into tears.

"I know, madame," he murmured.

"You can drop the hypocrisy now, Desgrez!" she sobbed. "Go ahead and laugh at me. Gloat over your triumph. Perhaps the king will promote you to captain. And I will be dragged in chains to Paris and my head cut off—to amuse the mob. . . ."

"Madame, I will do everything—"

"You have done everything," she interrupted him. "What else do you want of me? Do you want to enjoy my humiliation? Or do you expect me to love you, too, and perhaps thank you?"

"Madame, believe me—"

"Go away, I can't stand the sight of you," she cried out, and then she laughed scornfully. "Oh, I forgot. You cannot even do that. Then turn me over to one of your decent, honest hangmen—it will be a relief to see his face."

His own face turned a fiery red. She looked at him as if he were her lackey, and he himself felt like a crawling worm. His voice was hollow as he called out, "Cluet, take Madame to the carriage and accompany her to the citadel."

"Aha, so there really is a Cluet. At least that was no lie," she said, looking at the sergeant who with embarrassed face came closer, hat in hand. "Will Madame please follow me," Cluet said.

"I have no choice, Sergeant," she said, abruptly quite calm. "Kindly let me lean on your arm. I do not feel well."

"If you please, madame."

Leaning on Cluet's arm, she walked up the slope between the poplars without giving Desgrez another glance. Descarrières signed to the guards to follow. Then he stepped up to Desgrez, who stood lost in thought. "By Jove, Desgrez," he said, "you certainly turned that trick neatly. My respects, my friend."

"Do you think so?" Desgrez said wearily.

"Congratulations, Lieutenant. You're a famous man now—don't you realize that?"

"Unfortunately I do, Descarrières. But what now?" Desgrez looked utterly lost. But Descarrières, if he noticed anything at all, apparently ascribed Desgrez's state to a reaction after the excitement of the past hour. "I have obtained permission from the mayor to remove her baggage from the convent," he said zealously. "That is very important, Desgrez. Perhaps we'll find something."

"What do you think to find, Descarrières?"

"Why, poison, of course; poison, Lieutenant. Then we would have the final proof which is still lacking."

Desgrez looked thoughtfully at the man. "Descarrières," he said, "I should like to examine her cell in the convent by myself tomorrow morning. Will that be all right with you?"

"Of course, Desgrez. Only I would like to ask one thing of you."

"What is that?"

"That you will inform His Excellency the Minister that I have
done my very best in this affair. That's very important to me."

"You can depend on that, Descarrières."

ꜰ IX ꜰ

DESGREZ WAS RELIEVED that the gatekeeper did not recognize him
as the clerical visitor of the previous day. For he was wearing his
uniform. She said, "We have already heard from the mayor that
Madame has obtained a military escort to accompany her to Paris."

"That is correct, sister," Desgrez replied. "Madame has instructed
me to pack her things. Men will come this afternoon to take the bags
to the post station. May I be shown to Madame's room now?"

The gatekeeper nodded and asked him to follow her. They went
down a long, low arched corridor with whitewashed walls and a
floor of large paving stones. The gatekeeper stopped in front of a
door, opened it with one of the keys in her large bunch, and said,
"This is Madame's room." She glanced briefly in and then went away.

Desgrez entered the room and closed the door behind him. The
dim chamber vividly reminded him of the cells in the Conciergerie.
The small window high up in the wall looked out over the garden,
and the sun cast the shadows of the iron bars embedded in the
window-opening upon the narrow bed that stood against one long
wall of the room. Otherwise there was nothing in the room but a
small, rickety table and a three-legged stool. Under the table stood
a worn traveling trunk with brittle leather straps, and at the foot of
the bed several dresses hung from nails in the wall.

In many places the whitewash had flaked off the walls, and these
were without ornamentation except for a small copper engraving
which hung over the head of the bed. It seemed to have been torn
carelessly out of a book and represented, Desgrez saw, Saint Mary
Magdalene weeping over a skull—a composition similar to the painting he had seen hanging over the marquise's bed in her home on the
Rue Neuve Saint Paul.

The poverty of the room, and even more the picture, which bore
the inscription "Une grande Pécheresse" (A Great Sinner), startled
Desgrez. For a long time he stood before the bed with an expression
of perplexity. Then, with a sigh, he set to work.

He unbuckled the leather straps of the trunk and opened it with the key that Cluet had taken from the marquise. One by one he took each article out of the trunk and laid it carefully on the bed. There were clothes, underclothes, linen, all worn and repeatedly patched unskillfully with large stitches, but cleanly washed and faintly fragrant with attar of roses. He found a pair of shoes with worn heels, and another pair of silvered leather with large ribbons, carefully wrapped in paper and obviously the fugitive's most precious possession. Desgrez held the shoes in his hand for a long time, wondering at their small size.

At the bottom of the chest he found a cake of soap, a vial containing only a few drops of attar of roses, and several papers, which he quickly looked through. They were bills from artisans of Ghent and Antwerp, a letter from her sister, Mademoiselle Thérèse de Dreux Daubray, promising to send money soon, and another letter signed Henri. This was a passionate epistle in which the writer, in cliché phrases, assured her of his love and expressed the hope that he would soon be holding her in his arms again.

Piece by piece Desgrez put all these articles back again in the order in which they had been. Then he carefully searched the room. In the drawer of the desk he found only a used quill-pen and a bottle of half-dried-up ink. He pulled the drawer out entirely, but there was nothing concealed behind it. He loosened the tabletop with his knife, tapped the legs of the table and of the stool to make sure they were not hollow. He went through the pockets of the dresses hanging on the wall.

His examination of the bed took him a long time. He inspected the mattress seam and even cut it open in several places—but found nothing but horsehair. He also examined the pillows, the bedposts, the slats. He ran his hands along the walls, crawled along the floor and convinced himself that all the paving stones were firmly mortared down. He climbed up on the chair and examined the iron bars of the window. Nowhere did he find a package or any trace of powder. If the marquise had possessed poison—and he strongly doubted that—she must have concealed it somewhere else, in the building or in the garden. Possibly she had buried it or hidden it in the hollow of a tree, the thought came to him. But such an extensive search could only be conducted officially, and that was impossible on

Church property. He had not found the conclusive piece of evidence
that the king had demanded of him.

He sat down on the bed and pondered. Suddenly it occurred to him
that something might be hidden behind the rather large nails in the
wall. He took down the clothes and, with an effort, pulled out the
nails. But there was nothing, nothing but a trace of reddish sand from
the bricks.

As he folded the dresses into the trunk, his gaze fell upon the engraving over the head of the bed. Inwardly convinced that it was
hopeless, he nevertheless took the engraving down, tossed it on the
bed, and also drew out the tiny nail from which it had hung. He had
to smile at himself. The hole it left was as small as a needle prick.

With the handle of his knife he drove the nail back in, and was
about to hang up the engraving when he noticed that the back of it
was covered with writing. He went over to the window, where the
light was better, and instantly recognized the strong handwriting,
the large letters, of the promissory note. Leaning against the wall, he
read, and the longer he read the more the amazement in his eyes
grew and the more the sheet of paper in his hand shook.

On the back of the engraving was written:

I accuse myself before God and before you, my father. I accuse myself
of having trafficked in sinful wise with my brothers. I was twelve years old.

I accuse myself of having lived in adultery for fourteen years with a
married man. I gave this man a great deal of money; he ruined me. Two
of my children are his. I love them dearly. I wished my father dead many
times, and my brothers perhaps three hundred times.

I accuse myself of having killed my father. I did it for his money,
although I loved him. My brothers I had killed by the hand of a lackey.
I have tried to kill myself because I was seized by horror of myself.

I accuse myself of having given poison to my husband five or six times
and to my oldest daughter twice. But I repented and gave them antidotes.

Seven years ago this Easter I confessed and took the Eucharist without
intention of bettering myself. I have continued the same life, in the same
disorder of soul, and since then I have not confessed.

                                                        Daubray.

Desgrez sat down on the bed again, the engraving beside him, on
its face. He picked it up and read it again and again until he knew
the confession by heart. Then he slowly rose, folded the paper, and

put it into his pocket. With a hesitant backward glance, he left the room.

The sister at the gate wondered what had happened to the officer. He did not respond when she bade him goodbye, and walked with head hunched between his shoulders, feeling his way as though he could not see. She imagined he had had a sudden attack of illness.

PART IV

THE TRIAL

⋌ I ⋋

DESGREZ STOOD on the gallery near one of the great white pillars that supported the huge dome of the roof and looked attentively down into the round hall. It was an impressive spectacle, such as the baroque age loved not only in the theater, but upon the greater stage of life as well.

The Parliament of Paris, once one of the legislative organs of the kingdom, was even now, under the absolute monarchy, the highest court in the land. And this Parliament was well aware that all of France was following the trial with feverish interest, and that almost every hour messengers left for Versailles to apprise the king of the course of the proceedings.

Upon the platform sat the president, Monsieur de Lamoignon, in a high-backed chair carved with the golden crown and the silver lilies of the Bourbons. The president guided the assembly like a conductor handling a well-trained orchestra. He was about sixty, with a longish, thin face which must have been handsome in his youth and which now, refined by age, bespoke so much experience, wisdom, and kindliness that Desgrez could not conceive of a man better suited to the difficult task of finding justice in this case.

Like all members of the Parliament, Monsieur de Lamoignon wore the sweeping scarlet mantle trimmed with ermine and, upon his head, the heavy powdered white wig of waves and curls which did not quite suit the fineness of his features. A golden chain dangling

ponderously from his narrow shoulders and a golden gavel lying on
the table before him, next to his red cap, were the signs of his
special dignity. Beside him, two on his right and two on his left,
sat the judges: Potier de Novion, Le Coigneux, Le Bailleul, and De
Mandat. Below him, filling several rows, were the councilors of
Parliament. The president's dais rose out of their midst like the
throne of justice.

To the left of the semicircle of councilors, on the black-and-white
paving stones, stood two chairs with reed seats for the defendant and
her attendant, Madame Duruche. Neither of the two were present at
the moment. Back of these chairs was a bench for Maître Nivelle, the
defendant's lawyer, who sat in a black mantle and with unpowdered
wig. At the moment he was agitatedly scratching his forehead, for the
crown prosecutor Palluau, was introducing to the court a witness
Nivelle had known nothing about.

She was a young girl who wore a striped dress, a white pleated
coif on her dark hair. Her name, Palluau informed the assemblage,
was Marthe Biguet, former tiring-maid of the marquise. As Desgrez
watched, the girl curtsied so low that she seemed about to collapse
into a heap of skirt and petticoats.

"Well, my child," Palluau said soothingly, standing behind the
girl like a huge raven, "tell the gentlemen about the poison."

"Madame—" the girl burst out, "Madame sent me one day to get
her powder."

"When was that, my child?" Palluau croaked. Desgrez sensed that
he was trying to make his voice sound gentle.

The girl turned to face him. "It was in the summer, six years ago,
as I've already said, Monsieur Palluau."

"Yes, fine, my child. But you must tell the court, not me."

The girl repeated her statement bashfully. Then she went on, "I
went to Madame's bedroom and took a box—I thought there was
powder in it. But when I came to Madame—she was in the gaming
room, at her harp—she said, 'What have you brought me here, you
silly goose; why that's arsenic.' "

Desgrez saw a fleeting smile upon the president's face; it vanished
instantly.

The girl turned again toward Palluau with an inquiring look. "What
did Madame do then?" he asked her.

"She took the box, put it into the pocket of her gown, and said, 'I'll exterminate a good deal of vermin with this yet.' "

"That is all. You may sit down," Palluau croaked quickly, touching the girl's shoulder. "Unless the honorable attorney for the defense has any questions?" And he peered nearsightedly in the direction of Maître Nivelle.

Nivelle stood up. Desgrez was struck, as he had been on the preceding days of the trial, by how sad the man looked. The ends of his large mustache dangled moistly, and his brown eyes were filled with melancholy. "I have no questions to ask the witness," he said softly, as though speaking to himself. "But I should like to ask the prosecutor what the witness' testimony has to do with the indictment."

"It is conclusive proof of the possession of poison," Palluau croaked, and he hopped several steps toward the melancholy defense attorney.

"Well . . . and?"

"Poison was the instrument of murder."

"That is the unproved charge against my client," Maître Nivelle said, gazing into space. "But, my dear sir, the fact that Madame possessed poison in the year 1670 does not prove that she gave it to her brothers. On the contrary. She did not conceal the fact, but said quite frankly: 'This is arsenic for vermin.' I myself keep arsenic in the house—as do almost all home-owners in Paris—for use against rats. Does that make me a poisoner?"

"Maître Nivelle wishes to jest," Palluau croaked. "I base my indictment upon three facts. Upon the promissory note, the testimony of Briancourt, and Madame's own confession. The testimony of Marthe Biguet merely establishes that Madame had poison in her possession. Nothing more."

"That I concede," Nivelle said, and mournfully resumed his seat.

Palluau blinked inquiringly at the president, who nodded. Bowing to the judges, then, the little man in black began his summing up:

"Your Excellency, honorable judges and councilors of the Parliament of Paris: No forensic gifts are required to prove indisputably the guilt of the defendant. The facts speak for themselves; there can be no doubt. On this and the preceding days you have heard my witnesses: Monsieur de la Reynie, the chief of police; Maître Briancourt; and Lieutenant Desgrez, who succeeded in locating that remarkable document in which the defendant accuses herself of parricide and fratricide. I cannot advance more convincing evidence than the very accusation which the defendant, without coercion, of her own free will, has leveled against herself."

He paused for a moment to let this sink into the minds of his audience, then continued, "Indeed, I venture to say that my principal witness against the Marquise de Brinvilliers is none other than the Marquise de Brinvilliers. Before our turn came, my honorable and excellent gentlemen, another sat in judgment upon the marquise —and there remains nothing for us, the Parliament of Paris, to do but to sustain the verdict of that Supreme Judge.

"It is true that the marquise now audaciously denies having committed the murders. She had already begun her denials in Mézières, where I first interrogated her. You yourselves, gentlemen, have had the opportunity to hear her interpretation of the circumstances and her assertions of innocence. For everything she had explanations that sounded plausible enough when taken one by one, but which taken together can never in all eternity overcome the accumulation of damning facts.

"Gentlemen, in life you will often have noticed that false interpretations of an event are almost always complicated, while the true story is quite simple. Thus the marquise insisted that she wrote the promissory note in order to deceive her creditors into the belief that she had an older debt, intending by this trick to save thirty thousand livres for herself. Yet the fact stares us in the face that this was a real debt, payment for work performed. Lieutenant Desgrez, who knew of the mysterious deaths in rapid succession of the three Daubrays—deaths which medicine could not explain—immediately suspected that this work performed consisted of the murder of the three men—and that, gentlemen, was a conclusion he came to before he even knew about the poison which was found in the same chest as the promissory note. So clear were the connections to his criminologically trained mind that he instantly set about the task which ended temporarily with the confession of La Chaussée and his execution.

"Temporarily, I say. Because La Chaussée's confession still did not explain the presence of the promissory note. The true significance of that note came to light only with Briancourt's revelations and the marquise's own confession.

"But I am anticipating. Let us linger a while over the promissory note. If that note, as the marquise asserts, was never paid, what was Sainte-Croix living on? We have determined that neither he nor his wife possessed any wealth. The treatises he wrote produced little income. And yet he lived on a fairly high scale, with a household steward and several servants. How could he afford all that? By the sale of poison, gentlemen, and by hiring out his henchmen, whom he paid three hundred livres, while he received thirty thousand livres for the murders they committed on his orders.

"One more point, gentlemen. If that promissory note had really been intended to frustrate creditors, as the marquise now asserts, then I wish to ask: how is it that no court, no lawyer, no creditor ever saw it? How is it that it was never used for the purpose for which, according to the marquise, it was written, but instead moldered idly away in a chest?"

Palluau went on piling one bit of circumstantial evidence upon the next. He carefully examined every incident and with strict logic added it, brick by brick, as it were, until his indictment stood like a solid building upon a firm foundation.

Desgrez, still leaning against the pillar, closed his eyes. It was very hot in the gallery; outside the July sun was burning fiercely down upon the dome. The facts the little prosecuting attorney down below was using had mostly been gathered by Desgrez himself. The prosecutor's interpretation was logical and just. And yet something about it troubled Desgrez. Palluau's portrait of the marquise was inaccurate. It was not the woman he had known in Liége; the prosecutor was depicting a far more superficial person, who had committed murder solely for the sake of money.

For the State's purposes such a picture might well do. It was a transparent motive, one even the biggest fool could understand.

The long afternoon hours wore away infinitely slowly for Desgrez —hours during which he listened to that croaking voice which apparently was explaining everything inexorably, strictly in accordance with the truth, and which nevertheless circled haplessly around the truth without ever coming to grips with it. He thought wearily of the years he had devoted to solving this case. And now that his own solution was being objectively presented to him, it did not satisfy him.

It seemed to Desgrez, for whom Palluau's speech was now only a series of meaningless noises, a croaking accompaniment to his thoughts, that the marquise's guilt was composed of many layers. And Palluau in his summing up was considering only the topmost and obvious layer: avarice, which had led her to disregard all moral laws.

But avarice, strangely linked with the impulse to squander money senselessly, to throw away hundreds of thousands of livres, was understandable only in the light of the society to which the marquise belonged. As Desgrez had once hinted to the chief of police, this crime was not an individual failing.

Desgrez opened his eyes and looked at the semicircle of benches, which were filled with eagerly listening spectators. They were almost exclusively members of the high nobility who came daily from Versailles, Saint Germain, and Le Marais to this overheated gallery in order not to miss a single moment of the sensational trial of one of their own.

The two front rows had been gallantly reserved for the ladies. These ladies wore black masks over the upper halves of their faces in order to avoid recognition. It was as if they felt a touch of shame, as if they were conscious of the unseemliness of their insatiable curiosity. They were resplendently dressed in flowing garments, so low cut in front that their white powdered breasts were often revealed as far as the nipples. Their fingers, and their hair, artfully twisted into long curls, glittered with jewelry. Many of them wore the value of a large estate set into a single small ring. In their hands they held fans of ivory and painted white silk, and as they sat they kept fanning themselves. Their eyes, peering obliquely out of the black velvet masks, glowed with cunning, coquetry, and an avid interest. Around them was a cloud of fragrance from their perfumes.

They behaved with dignity, out of respect for the Parliament, and spoke to one another in stage whispers. As attentive as if they were sitting in a theater, they watched the spectacle of the trial, unaware that below them the tragicomedy of their own lives was being enacted. For they, too, were spoiled by luxury and sensuality. They, too, were given to squandering and pleasure-seeking. But perhaps they obscurely sensed that the croaking indictment of Monsieur Palluau, whose preposterous figure they joked about among themselves, was also an indictment of themselves. For more than one little white hand that rested gently upon the red velvet of the balustrade had at one time or another dropped a pinch of white powder into the wine of some rich relative or some faithless lover.

At frequent intervals lackeys appeared and distributed glasses of cool lemonade, daintily carved portions of roast chicken and white bread. And lips painted blood-red opened greedily beneath the black masks, like the mouths of harpies.

Desgrez recognized many of them in spite of their disguises. There was the Princess of Tingry, one of the queen's ladies in waiting, who was said to have tried to do away with her own children. He recognized her by her high forehead and withered breasts. She was over sixty, tried to act twenty, and still slept without distinction with princes and lackeys, in the belief—Desgrez smilingly recalled having heard this—that sexual activity was the best preservative of a youthful appearance.

There, sitting close together although they now hated one another, sat the Mancini sisters, of Italian origin and of low birth as well. Now, by the favor of their deceased uncle, Cardinal Mazarin, they were respectively the Countess of Soissons and the Duchess of Bouillon. Both of them were still tolerably good-looking—and both had probably murdered their husbands.

And there were the Marquise de Fouquières, the Duchess of La Ferte, the Countess of Roure, Madame de Charpentier. And all these high-born or highly placed ladies had, as Desgrez well knew, been connected with the underworld of Paris, with counterfeiters, thugs, magicians, and alchemists. And with Sainte-Croix. That was a public secret that Versailles refused to admit. After all, anything can be forgiven to pretty and complaisant women, the flower of society— even if they are a wee bit poisonous.

But who was that? The lady had half turned and was looking at him in an impudent, challenging way. She must be very sure of herself. Desgrez well knew that most of these women were afraid of him. But this one was not. Who could she be? He had seen that clear gaze, that narrow, rather longish face, that mass of golden-blond hair before.

Then he recognized her. She was Diane Athenais, the Marquise de Montespan, the true queen of France. And those mocking eyes and the defiantly pouting lips of that small, sweet mouth seemed to be saying: "Now try to do to me what you have done to the marquise." It was the challenge of an enemy—a very powerful enemy. But

Desgrez did not think of the power which in a moment could have him thrown into the dungeons of the Bastille forever. He felt that this beautiful, arrogant woman, this courtesan who had placed her numerous bastards among the princes of the royal house, was a symbol of all the misery of France. She was the symbol of all the wasteful luxury, the pomp, the immorality of the court, and the helpless starvation of the poor, who ate the grass of the fields to fill their stomachs. All the other women around her had individual faults; in her all the faults, the guilt of all, were joined in one person. She was the ruin of the country. She was the true criminal. Suddenly Desgrez saw that the Marquise de Montespan was the second layer in the guilt of the Marquise de Brinvilliers.

He felt the blood rush to his face. And quivering with indignation, he accepted the gauntlet that had been thrown before him with that impudent look. At the moment he could do nothing but return her look with equal impudence, with as much challenge, and this he did. He stared steadily at her, the furrow deep between his brows. And he had the satisfaction of seeing her hesitantly lower her eyes. She shook her head slightly and turned away to one of her ladies in waiting.

The fury that had seized him so suddenly continued to vibrate for a long time, like the string of a harp. An inner voice told him that he must keep this woman in mind. But who could ever get at her, he thought. The chronicle of her sins was long enough, but her position was far too high for an insignificant lieutenant of the Paris police force to do anything about them. Yet his inner voice insisted. Who knows, it whispered to him; perhaps she has some skeleton in the closet which will help you to trip her up one of these days.

Down below, Palluau was croaking something about God and conscience. His skinny arms waved imploringly at the platform, and Desgrez's thoughts returned hesitantly to the complicated motivations for the crimes of the Marquise de Brinvilliers. Palluau wanted the defendant to be convicted by the court; that was his duty as prosecutor, and he was doing a splendid job. But Desgrez wanted more. He wanted to be able to see the psychological processes that had led to the crimes.

Had the marquise committed murder because of her sex, because she was mistreated and scorned as a woman? Was the money she had so desperately desired only her cheap substitute for the love and respect she had been unable to find in the spoiled, superficial society of the day—in spite of her beauty and high position?

Such explanations seemed valid to Desgrez. But even they did not satisfy him. He saw the gears meshing, but something was still missing: the leaden weight which, in falling, set these gears in motion and transformed evil feelings and thoughts into evil deeds.

Down below, a liveried parliamentary attendant, a sly and stupid-looking fellow with straw-blond hair, came into the room carrying a pole with a tiny flame burning at its tip. On tiptoe he moved silently around the hall lighting the candles clustered in the chandeliers. Palluau paused in his summing up and looked at the man as though not quite grasping what he was. Then he went on in his monotonous, croaking voice.

The sneaking movements of the attendant had reminded Desgrez of a silent incendiary. Now he leaned his head back against the pillar. A thought suddenly flashed into his mind. Was there an author of evil, he wondered, a father of sins? Did the devil exist?

⌐ II ⌐

EARLY THE FOLLOWING morning, Desgrez stood once more at his observation post in the gallery.

The president, De Lamoignon, struck his gavel three times upon the table, and all conversation ceased. Councilors, judges, and spectators rose while a priest stepped to the platform and prayed with folded hands.

After all had taken their seats again, De Lamoignon spoke. "It is the decision of Parliament," he declared in his resonant, well-modulated voice, "to hear today the honorable counsel for the defendant, Maître Nivelle—likewise in the absence of the defendant, since she is not entitled to knowledge of the procedures of Parliament. I request the attention of judges and councilors for the defense."

Maître Nivelle, with his large, drooping mustaches and melancholic brown eyes, stepped to the center of the rotunda, where yesterday Monsieur Palluau had stood. He bowed low to the president and began in a gentle voice:

"Honorable president, judges and councilors of the Parliament of Paris: Permit me to confine my attention to the three points which

my learned opponent, Monsieur Palluau, cited yesterday as the principal bases for the charge against my client. These are the promissory
note, the testimony of Briancourt, and the marquise's confession."

He paused, his head bowed in thought. Then, with a resolute
gesture, he threw his head back, looked squarely at the councilors,
and said:

"Gentlemen, the defendant is of very high birth, and she is accused
of a frightfully unnatural crime: parricide, the murder of her father.
Under circumstances of such weight the proofs of the crime must be
unequivocal. Parliament cannot rely upon half-probabilities, second-
hand testimonies, and the morbid self-recriminations of a confused,
persecuted soul.

"My learned opponent asserts that truth is simple. But is it truly
so? If we wish to be honest, must we not confess that there are many
things in this world we do not understand, and that frequently we
do not understand ourselves? Is the highest truth of all, the truth of
our Christian religion, easy to understand? No, gentlemen, it is not.
For if it were, the best minds of mankind would not for a millennium
and a half have been engaged in the interpretation of the Gospels.

"A mystery as great as God, however, is man, His creature. I venture to assert that, except for our Lord Jesus Christ, no one has
penetrated the essence of man's nature. Life and the handling of
men are complicated, because man himself is so complex. Only lazy
minds which deal in easy abstractions remote from reality find everything easily understandable. Montaigne pondered the question of his
nature all his life, and ended in skepticism. Descartes searched for
reality and hit upon untenable axioms. But Pascal, our clearest
thinker, bowed to the inexplicable and believed in the 'hidden God,'
the 'Deo abscondito.'

"Homo absconditus, gentlemen! Let us keep remembering that we
are dealing with a human being, not with a mathematical figure or a
mechanical doll.

"But enough of this. Let me say first of all that I, too, her defending
counsel, find the Marquise de Brinvilliers guilty!"

A rustle and whispering of excited voices passed through the hall.
The president started up, staring incredulously at Maître Nivelle.
Desgrez could scarcely believe his ears.

"Yes, I find her guilty," Maître Nivelle cried triumphantly. "But
guilty of what, gentlemen? There lies the difference between Mon-

sieur Palluau and myself. I find Madame guilty of swindling, of
frivolity, of adultery, and of despair—but not of murder. Yet murder,
of her nearest kin, is charged in the indictment, and the president
could well call me to order and command me to limit myself to the
subject of this trial—murder. But then I would have to reply: 'I cannot expose the insubstantiality of the evidence against Madame without considering her guilt, and in particular her feeling of guilt.'

"The promissory note that was found is proof of a fraud, or rather
of an attempt to defraud, on the part of my client. For if that debt
had not been a sham debt, if it had indeed been paid, then either the
note would no longer exist, or at least it would have been receipted
by the pretended creditor, Sainte-Croix. Briancourt reports in his
confession that in the late summer of 1670 he attended a conference
at Sains at which this very swindle was discussed in his presence by
Sainte-Croix and De Laune. He mentions a promissory note of fifty
thousand livres and another of thirty thousand livres; the latter was
supposed at the time to have been in the possession of Sainte-Croix.
At this point I should like to stress that Briancourt continually confuses things which he actually experienced with matters which became general knowledge as a result of the trial of La Chaussée. For
De Laune, whom we have questioned, knows only of a promissory
note for thirty thousand livres, which was made out in order to deceive the marquise's creditors.

"This note is without doubt the promissory note which has been
placed in evidence. It was, as my learned opponent has observed,
never used, either because my client's financial situation improved
as a result of the death of her younger brother, Baron Jacques de
Nouars, or because Sainte-Croix drew back from the swindle for
fear of perjury—the danger that Briancourt had pointed out to him.
The note was forgotten—or perhaps saved by Sainte-Croix to be used
for future blackmail.

"In any case, the existence of the promissory note by no means
proves that my client paid thirty thousand livres to Sainte-Croix for
the murder of her brothers.

"Gentlemen, La Chaussée, Sainte-Croix's hired murderer, declared repeatedly under torture that his master had again and again
warned him not to let Madame know anything about the planned
murder of her brothers. Why? Because Sainte-Croix was inwardly
convinced that Madame would do all within her power to prevent

him and his hired killer from carrying out this frightful crime. Far
from there having been a criminal agreement between the marquise
and Sainte-Croix, Sainte-Croix instead considered her attitude to be
the principal obstacle to his crime and warned his henchman accordingly.

"I am firmly convinced that La Chaussée, confessing under terrible
torments, spoke the truth. What could he gain by lying? The testimony of this man who knew that he was close to death is a thousand
times sounder as evidence than a scrap of paper which can be interpreted one way or another."

Maître Nivelle fell silent. He was silent so long, thoughtfully
scratching his forehead, that the councilors grew restive and the
president looked at him in questioning surprise. But at last he bowed
to the platform and continued: "Gentlemen, I come now to Briancourt's testimony. In the beginning I said that I would not neglect
the human element, and so now I ask myself, with your permission:
What kind of person is this Briancourt who has leveled such grave
charges against my client?

"You yourselves have seen him in court. He was unsure of himself.
He trembled all over. His voice was so low that the president repeatedly had to order him to speak louder. He groaned, he sobbed,
he clapped his hands over his face, and once, to the amazement of
all of us, he suddenly knelt down and cried out despairingly: 'I am
guilty, guilty before the Mother of God, whom I have murdered in
my soul.'

"On the whole I felt sorry for him. Often I was on the point of
jumping up and coming to his aid. I could see clearly that he believed
he was speaking the truth. But at the same time I realized during the
first few minutes I listened to him that he is a person altogether
incapable of recounting his experiences as they actually took place.

"Gentlemen, Briancourt is a creature of emotions, a dreamer, almost a madman. What a character! A ballet in which our king appeared throws him into such an ecstasy that he reels drunkenly
through the woods, kisses trees, and suddenly decides to change the
whole course of his life.

"Even as a young boy he filled his susceptible mind with heathen
nonsense which he eagerly dug out of the Church Fathers and the
classics. He confuses the marble statues in the Luxembourg Gardens
with saints; His Majesty with Dionysus; and the marquise—to whom,

unfortunately for him and for her, he was sent on business—with the
nymph Calypso from the Odyssey. But these were by no means the
limits of his incredible fantasies. Everyone knows that, at puberty,
boys frequently go through a crisis. Briancourt has never emerged
from that crisis—and this, I may say, frequently happens with shy,
well-brought-up boys. Hating his own impulses, and therefore hating
the object of his sensual longings, he confounds her with the great
nature goddesses of mythology. He calls her Venus, Isis, Astarte.
He compares her to the Mother Anne. He speaks of her metamor-
phosis' from a woman to a raging beast. He ascribes to her the stereotyped smile of archaic statues. He makes her speak of 'her earth'—
this boy who even as a child had, by his own confession, thought that
the earth was the Mother of God. Finally he even places her in a
landscape which must be called mythical!

"You will remember, gentlemen, the dark ravine in which he first
confessed to her his love. But I have discovered that no such ravine
exists anywhere near Sains, or in fact in all of Picardy. It exists only
in the fantasies of that unfortunate young man."

Several councilors leaned toward one another; their voices came
like a hissing to Desgrez, high up under the roof of the rotunda. The
masked ladies fanned themselves vivaciously.

"But," Nivelle continued, "the dangerous concept in these dreams
and fantasies of Briancourt, which might otherwise be harmless, was
his knowledge that the heathens considered the Mother of Life as
being also the Mother of Death. This doctrine made a tremendous
impression upon him; it fitted in with his fear of his own sexual impulses. The dogma, if I may call it that, is, by the way, not only
purely pagan. We find it also in Genesis, where the curse of death is
the consequence of copulation by the first human couple. We find it
in the Gospels in the passage that speaks of the children of Heaven
who do not marry and do not beget. And finally we find it in Christian philosophy: Saint Thomas says in his *Summa contra Gentiles*,
Book III, chapter 71: '*Non esset unius generatio, nisi esset alterius
corruptio.*'

"Briancourt ascribes the same train of thought, put in different
words, to my client when he makes her say: 'What exists today is
tomorrow fertilizer for what is to come.'

"Is it not clear, gentlemen, that this is not the marquise speaking,
but Briancourt himself? For it is he who has never outgrown his

puberty—and, permit me to add, it is he as a theologian—who is literally obsessed by this connection between sexuality and death.

"But even that would have remained harmless, merely the notions of an eccentric, if certain real events had not come along to stimulate Briancourt's fantasies and to convert the gloomy inspirations of his sick mind into what seemed to him absolute certainties. In September 1670 he hears of the death of the marquise's elder brother, and this is swiftly followed by the death of the younger brother. This untimely death of a foremost member of this august assembly created a great sensation in Paris and Versailles. Monsieur Bocager, the lawyer who employed Briancourt, discussed the case with him in detail. Thereupon Briancourt became very thoughtful and to Monsieur Bocager's surprise left the office without bidding him goodbye, although he was ordinarily an extremely polite young man.

"What passed through Briancourt's mind at that moment? We do not know. But I venture to assert that even then his vague dreams of life and death were beginning to crystallize into the figure of the goddess of death. For immediately after the conversation with Monsieur Bocager came what Briancourt called the 'unveiling' of my client.

"Gentlemen, the Marquise de Brinvilliers has, of course, never been Briancourt's mistress. His erotic dreams painted those scenes in bed, those naked thighs and pointed breasts of which he speaks again and again in his confessions. The great lady, the famous beauty of Versailles, stood unattainably high above him; only in his fantasies could he bring her down to his level.

"How do I know that, gentlemen? I have questioned the proprietor of the Big Stag in Louvres-en-Parisis. He was stunned when I asked him whether he had ever whispered to Briancourt, 'It is a double bed, monsieur.' Never, he declared, would he have permitted himself such a remark in the presence of a lady. Not the proprietor of the inn but Briancourt himself, in his desperate infatuation, whispered this phrase.

"In fact Briancourt slept in another room, which was not adjoining the marquise's room but was situated at the far end of the corridor. That nocturnal confession, therefore, by the testimony of an unimpeachable witness, can never have taken place.

"To anticipate later events at this point, I have questioned the Marquis de Brinvilliers himself, Mademoiselle de Grangemont, the

steward, and all the lackeys and maids in the Rue Neuve Saint Paul
and in Sains. I have asked them whether they knew anything of an
affair between the marquise and the tutor. None of these persons
could report to me even the slightest suspicious circumstance. Yet
Briancourt claims that for a while in Sains he shared the marquise's
bed every night—a circumstance that could not possibly have been
kept secret. Everyone of us knows the incurable prying habits of our
lackeys.

"And yet I cannot pronounce the marquise entirely guiltless. She
was friendly, too friendly, toward the young man. She treated him
like a member of the family and informed him of intimate matters
which she would have been wiser to keep silent about. She has told
me that she was well aware that Briancourt had fallen in love with
her and was becoming more and more infatuated—infatuated to the
point of madness. It should have been her duty to put an end to all
familiarity. But, gentlemen, let us not forget that the marquise is a
woman—and that women have from time immemorial taken an understandable pleasure in playing such a game with a devoted young
man.

"I can, moreover, suggest an extenuating circumstance for my
client's frivolity. Aside from Briancourt she had not a single person to
whom she could speak her heart. Her marriage was unhappy; she
had no women friends whom she could trust; Mademoiselle de
Grangemont and the children were too young. And she had to air
her oppressed soul somehow, to someone. Her choice fell upon Briancourt, who appeared to be to her, what he must also appear to be to
you, gentlemen, an irreproachable and well-disposed young man.

"Now at last I come to the crucial point, a point which requires all
your attention from a psychological point of view, gentlemen. If this
point is clearly understood, the whole structure of the indictment
collapses like a house of cards. I have said that she had to speak her
heart. But what was it, gentlemen, that she had to speak about if
she were not to go wholly to pieces psychologically?"

Maître Nivelle looked questioningly at the councilors, turning his
head around the full semicircle. The councilors, for their part, stared
at him, and the splendidly coiffured heads of the ladies up in the
gallery leaned forward over the red velvet of the parapet.

"It was her consciousness of guilt!" Maître Nivelle said, raising his
right hand and pointing toward the center of the dome. His hand

dropped slowly down again. "Her own sense of guilt led my client into this terrible situation and will now, I hope, lead her back to her children and to a better life.

"Gentlemen, it is evidence of the grandeur of the human mystery, and of the fact that the soul is engaged continually in a dialogue with its Creator as well as with its society, that no one can in the long run keep the burden of a terrible secret to himself without the greatest suffering. Our Mother, the Church, has recognized this fact clearly and has created the sacrament of confession to provide for this aspect of our inner life. This sacrament plays a crucial role in my plea, as you will see later on.

"For the present, let me say only this: that the marquise, as we have it from her own lips, last confessed to a priest in the year 1669— and that she did so with the sinful intention of not changing her life. The Church could not give her absolution because she was not repentant—and yet she still felt the need for confession. And so she confessed to an underling, who, since he was a student of theology, seemed to her a good substitute for a priest. She confessed to Briancourt!

"But what did she confess? We cannot, as I must stress again and again, give any credence to the fantasies of Briancourt. But our task is considerably simplified because we have here the written account of an altogether rational and intelligent person, Lieutenant Desgrez, to whom the marquise likewise confessed her guilt in the spring of 1676 in the Convent of the Noble Ladies in Liége. Moreover—how poignantly this demonstrates her oppression of soul, her urgent need —she made this confession at their second meeting, after she had known Lieutenant Desgrez only a few hours. She has informed me that in the year 1670 she told Briancourt exactly what she told Lieutenant Desgrez six years later, when she thought him an abbé attached to the court.

"This unhappy woman's emotions pronounced her guilty—and with a certain validity—of the death of her father and her brothers. Not that she gave her father poison or paid the murderer of her brothers thirty thousand livres for accomplishing their deaths, as my learned opponent, Monsieur Palluau, maintains. But, gentlemen, the murderer, Sainte-Croix, was her lover. She sensed, when he was freed from the Bastille and spoke to her about Exili, that he intended to revenge himself upon her father and brothers for having imprisoned him—and yet she did nothing to warn her father or her brothers. She went on living with Sainte-Croix in an adulterous relationship.

"Under the heavy burden of this guilt her heart gave way, and I can well imagine her saying to Briancourt in her excitement: 'I . . . I am the one who killed my father and my brothers.'

"But that her guilt consisted in her silence and in her immoral relationship with Sainte-Croix—which actually led to the murders of her kin—this, gentlemen, was something Briancourt did not understand. He took her words literally and at once believed that she had killed her father and used a henchman to have her brothers killed.

"Woman has always been suspect to theologians; instinctively they see her as the aide and comfort of Satan. And this is what Briancourt did—Briancourt, who was full of fear of his own eroticism, who ardently desired this beautiful and unattainable woman, and who knew, or at least guessed, that she was the mistress of Sainte-Croix.

"In the oppression of his heart he felt, nevertheless, a great jubilation. The temptress whose sight, whose presence aroused in him a veritable inferno of contradictory passions must of course be evil. And now he heard her calling herself a murderess.

"This was the final touch to the image of the ancient goddess offering life or death with either hand. Again and again Briancourt emphasized that she was both the tenderest of mothers and lovers and a merciless killer. But he was not cohabiting with the marquise, not with any real woman at all: in his dreams he possessed a pagan phantom which arose menacingly out of a frightful laceration in his own soul. It was with this nightmare that he spent those wild nights during which, as he significantly states, the constant presence of death conferred a special sweetness upon ardent embraces.

"But, gentlemen, you will rightly say: If my account is correct, how is it that Briancourt was able to write that he knew as early as 1670 that the marquise's brothers had been killed by a hired assassin named La Chaussée?

"The answer I give you is: He did not know. For do not forget, gentlemen, that Briancourt's story was first written down in the winter of 1673. By that time the facts had become public knowledge as a result of La Chaussée's trial. And Briancourt, who took an understandable interest in everything connected with the Daubrays, skillfully incorporated the known facts into this memorial to his fantasies.

"Let me say once more, gentlemen, that I do not believe Brian-court has consciously lied. I consider it quite possible that his unre-quited passion stimulated him to write this tale of his. But on the whole I would say that his confused mind is simply incapable of distinguishing between fantasy and reality.

"Briancourt himself was very conscious of the confusion of his mind and has mentioned it in several places—as for example when he quotes:

> 'My soul has put on a temporary form
> And is tormented by its conduct, which death dominates.
> . . . .
> Now knows no longer escape. Unhappy at evil,
> Wandering, lost, it stumbles in the labyrinth.'

"Gentlemen, it is utterly impossible for this illustrious assembly to accept the testimony of a mentally ill, or at least very unstable, person as evidence of incredible, unnatural deeds.

"Is it not strange, gentlemen, that Briancourt cannot provide a corroborating witness for a single one of his charges?

"Let me give you a few examples. The eldest daughter of the marquise falls ill. Mademoiselle de Grangemont is supposed to have exclaimed, 'The monster, the beast,' meaning, of course, none other than the marquise, who allegedly gave poison to her own daughter. But unfortunately Mademoiselle firmly denies ever having said any-thing of the kind. And moreover this daughter, who is very fond of sweets, suffers from frequent stomach aches. The poison in this case, gentlemen, was not arsenic but—let us put it bluntly—a whole pound of bonbons."

Several of the councilors smiled agreement. And one of the masked ladies in the gallery sighed longingly.

"And it is the same everywhere, at every point that I have in-vestigated," Nivelle continued. "For example, Briancourt maintains that the marquis was aware of the possibility of poison and ate only foods especially prepared for him. The truth is that the marquis, on his doctor's advice, avoided all heavy dishes and ate mostly omelettes, which were prepared by his valet.

"Then Briancourt describes a grand scene in which the servant Basil allegedly tried to poison him with a glass of lemonade and was then dismissed by the marquise in the presence of many members of the household. But none of the lackeys can recall any such incident.

"Futhermore: two shots were fired at Briancourt. No one but himself heard them. He betakes himself to Sainte-Croix to confront the man. So he claims—but neither Madame de Sainte-Croix nor any servant of the household ever saw Briancourt.

"Then there is the matter of the incident in Madame's bedroom in the Rue Neuve Saint Paul. Loud shouts, struggles, calls—but nobody in the household heard a sound. Apparently all of them were stone-deaf.

"According to Briancourt's story, a murderer hid in the fireplace—probably Sainte-Croix, so he says. However, at this time Sainte-Croix lay in bed, in his home in the Rue des Bernardins, suffering from a severe heart attack. But the murderer, when exposed by Briancourt, leaps out of a window that is situated no less than twenty feet above the garden. An amazing performance for a man with a severe heart condition!

"I think these examples suffice. But, gentlemen, consider the altogether irrational behavior of this strange witness. He claims that the milk which killed his cat would have provided irrefutable proof that an attempt had been made to poison him. But he does not take this proof to the police. He keeps his peace. He remains in the house where death supposedly may strike him at any moment. Why, gentlemen? Because at a level of his mind which even he is not aware of he is convinced that his sick mind is only producing imaginary terrors that have no basis in reality.

"And then, finally, his flight! Gentlemen, he might have gone off quite easily to Monsieur Bocager, who certainly would have received him kindly. But not he! Not Briancourt! He runs off as though pursued by furies. Who are these furies? They are the terrible visions, the nightmares of his sick brain. He is running away not from the marquise, but from himself, from his own madness.

"It is this madness, this breakdown of his reason, which drives him to climb over the city wall and wade through the city moat instead of walking out through the Porte Saint Antoine as any sensible person would have done—if any sensible person would have walked out to Aubervilliers in such a thunderstorm.

"The picture is clear. I will no longer try the patience of this illustrious assembly with examples which all point to the same conclusion: that the witness Briancourt is not of sound judgment and is not aware of the responsibility that he has taken upon himself in indulging in his fantasies.

"I herewith make the motion that this house dismiss the testimony of Briancourt as the fantasies of an insane, or at any rate mentally disturbed, person and that this testimony be given no further consideration as evidence against my client, the Marquise de Brinvilliers."

Maître Nivelle stopped, exhausted. His voice had grown hoarse, and he looked more melancholy than ever. Monsieur de Lamoignon rose. "I wish to thank the counsel for the defense for his efforts," he pronounced resonantly. "We shall take the motion that has been made under careful consideration." He raised his gavel and struck it three times. "I herewith declare this Parliament in recess until the second hour of the afternoon, at which time I shall request the worthy counsel for the defense to continue his interpretation of the case." The president donned his red mortarboard and, accompanied by the judges, left the platform.

The ladies in the gallery were also standing, and now they talked loudly among one another. "I am starving for a grilled grouse," a lady called to a gentleman in the back rows. "In a moment, in a moment," the man called back. "Let's drive over to the estaminet by the Royal Palace."

Cluet came up the stairs with drooping mustaches, an expression of amazement in his kindly eyes. He turned to Desgrez, who was still leaning against the pillar observing the masked ladies. "By the Lord," he said, "if I listen to that man any longer I myself will believe that black is white. But I wonder how he's going to explain away the marquise's own confession."

"Oh, he will try," Desgrez replied, smiling at Cluet. "I already have a suspicion of how he will do it—the melancholy fox."

⌐ III ⌐

IT WAS even hotter than it had been that morning. After Lamoignon opened the session, Nivelle took the floor again. The crowd listened tensely. It seemed to everyone that the defense counsel was faced with an impossible task. It was so still in the hall that, when Nivelle paused, the beating wings of the pigeons could be heard as, now and then, they rose up suddenly to flutter around the dome, their fleeting shadows passing across the marble flagstones.

"Honorable president, judges and councilors of the Parliament of Paris," Nivelle resumed. "My learned opponent, Monsieur Palluau, said yesterday that his principal witness against the Marquise de Brinvilliers is none other than the Marquise de Brinvilliers herself. This seems in fact to be the case, for aside from her own statement there is not, as I have shown, any other evidence that will hold water. But I am surprised that Monsieur Palluau has forgotten one of the fundamental principles of Roman law: *Non auditur perire volens.* Which is to say, he who wishes to destroy himself may not be heard by the judges; his testimony is by law null and void.

"Yet let me first discuss this document, this so-called confession by the marquise. With it the indictment against my client stands or falls.

"The document is an engraving of Saint Mary Magdalene, my client's patron saint. On the back of it is her statement, which begins thus: 'I accuse myself before God and before you, my father.'

"Gentlemen, how would it be possible to express more clearly the fact that this document is a confession—a confession addressed to God and the marquise's deceased father, but not to any human court, even the highest. For there is a vast difference between a religious confession which by divine grace leads to absolution from sin, and the criminal confession which through the machinery of justice leads to the punishment of the criminal. It is our duty to see this distinction clearly and to keep apart these two disparate types of confession. For anyone but an ordained priest to interfere in the dialogue between God and the sinner is a violation of the Mystery of God and the human soul and constitutes one of the most terrible sacrileges that any man or any assemblage can commit.

"The absolute secrecy of the confessional has been emphasized at the Councils of Mainz, of the Lateran, of Trent, and at many other Church Councils. His Holiness Pope Clement VIII has expressly stated in a pastoral letter that the secrecy of the confessional extends to letters to an absent confessor and even to loose sheets of paper upon which a person makes notes of his faults in preparation for confession. If a layman finds such a sheet of paper, he is bound to maintain the strictest silence upon its contents and to give the sheet to a priest as soon as possible.

"It is deeply to be regretted that Lieutenant Desgrez did not do this and—"

De Lamoignon struck the table with his gavel, interrupting Nivelle, and said, "Counsel for the Defendant, I must state that Lieutenant Desgrez delivered the document under seal to Parliament. If, therefore, there is any fault to be found it is the fault of Parliament, not of Lieutenant Desgrez."

Nivelle bowed, and after a short silence continued:

"The fact that the document is a confession of a religious nature is evidenced by my client's reference, at the conclusion of the document, to a previous confession. Such words could only be directed toward a father confessor.

"I myself, being a layman, have consulted for instruction the *Treatise for Confessors* by Rodericus Acugua, Archbishop of Portugal. In this book an incident is related which clearly shows the inviolability of secrets of the confessional. The story is as follows:

"To Thomas de Villanova, Archbishop of Valencia, a prisoner was brought from the local prison. The man was a murderer who refused to go to confession. Questioned by the archbishop, he testified that he had confessed a murder to a priest, not knowing that the man he had killed had been this priest's brother. The priest had promptly denounced the murderer of his brother to the police, and the man had been condemned to imprisonment for life.

"At the urging of the archbishop, the verdict was reviewed and the murderer pronounced not guilty for lack of evidence. But the priest who had violated the secret of the confessional was burned alive!

"I could adduce many similar cases. But all of them point to the same principle: a priest may not reveal what he has learned in confession—not even under the threat of death. The confession, whether spoken or written, is a sacrament and can never serve in a court as legal proof of the guilt of the person who has confessed.

"I therefore move that the confession of the Marquise de Brinvilliers be stricken from the evidence and that all information contained in it be treated as if it had never been read and were unknown. But if the illustrious house should reject this motion, I further move that the document be submitted to the Sorbonne for a decision by the learned members of the clergy as to the religious or nonreligious character of my client's confession."

For some time the president, hand covering his mouth, had been whispering with the judges and then writing on a sheet of paper. Now he whispered something to one of the two halberdiers who were standing motionless behind his chair all the while, like plaster casts of men in armor. The halberdier tiptoed toward Nivelle, who looked up at him, took the paper, and read it swiftly. "Thank you for your consideration, Your Excellency," he said, bowing to the platform, "but I am quite prepared to continue my plea and to finish it today."

The president nodded, with a gracious smile. Nivelle was silent for a while. Then he said: "His Excellency was so kind as to point out to me that words once spoken cannot with the best will in the world be made unspoken. What that means is that my client's confession, whether or not it is considered a religious confession, must necessarily influence the judges in their verdict, no matter how honestly they endeavor to erase it from their memories—in fact, perhaps, precisely because of that endeavor.

"The fact that the document is a confession, as I have explained, makes the matter all the more difficult. Like the mythical seafarer, we find ourselves between two monsters. For either a confession speaks the truth—or else it is no confession."

Someone in the hall sighed aloud. It was a token of the terrible tension under which everyone was laboring. At the sound, even the stern, furrowed faces of the judges relaxed into fleeting smiles.

It seemed as though Nivelle, having apparently driven himself into a corner, considered this smile an encouraging sign. For he continued in a voice that had suddenly become fresh and energetic:

"What is truth? That, gentlemen, was the question of the skeptical Roman in that greatest of all trials in the history of mankind—a trial which against the will of this judge ended with the condemnation and painful death of the one absolutely innocent Man who ever walked this earth.

"What is truth? I also ask myself, not skeptically, like Pilate, nor with the self-assurance of my learned opponent who yesterday declared that truth is simple.

"Gentlemen, there have been times in which thinkers were convinced of the dichotomous, the dual, the divided nature of truth, in which they spoke of a natural and a theological truth. Not the worst of our thinkers have assumed that the truth of the heart can contradict the truth of reason. Jurisprudence, however, has to do only with reason, only with natural truth.

"But we have here before us a religious document. That alone, gentlemen, should make us cautious, for here a soul in a state of shock is struggling to reach the subjective truth of the heart, not the objective truth of external circumstance which can alone be of importance in a court of law.

"My client is struggling to attain the sense of her guilt, the repentance, the self-abasement which alone can restore peace to her harrowed soul.

"At the beginning I said that my client is not without guilt. Wherein, then, does her guilt consist? Here, in this document, we can read her opinion of it. She committed adultery which resulted ultimately in the death of her father and her brothers. More than that she had, as she herself writes, wished several times that her father were dead, and wished her brothers dead some three hundred times.

"Gentlemen, malicious wishes are not within the province of human courts; they are subject only to the judgment of God, for whom wishes are acts. For as it is said in the Gospels: 'Whosoever looketh upon a woman to lust after her hath committed adultery with her already.'

"But how can this be? you will ask. For she says quite plainly: I have killed my father and had my brothers killed by the hand of a lackey.

"That seems to be, as my learned opponent claims it is, an unequivocal confession, indubitable proof. But can it really be taken as such?

"Gentlemen, it cannot. For here we are once more confronted with a great mystery. It is this: that to the human conscience, when it examines itself, evil wishes are the same as evil deeds, because the conscience is the voice of God within us. Indeed, the evil wish, the corruption of the soul, appears egocentrically to the conscience as worse and more important than a crime that is actually committed, in which others are actually struck down.

"It is a well-known psychological fact that death wishes against anyone at all arouse in us a sense of guilt. In the worst cases this feeling of guilt can lead to a *pseudologica phantastica*, in which a person confesses to crimes which he has never committed. The honorable Prefect of the Police has informed me that when sensational

murders take place, individuals frequently give themselves up to
the police, claiming to be the murderer—individuals who, it can be
conclusively demonstrated, could not possibly have been at the scene
of the murder or have had any connection whatever with the crime.

"If such cases are hard to understand, how easy to understand is
the guilt feeling, the self-accusation on the part of my unhappy client
who wished her father and her brothers dead and who actually committed the adultery which stood in a direct causal connection with
their deaths.

"My client is far from being the sort of wildly imaginative person
that the witness Briancourt undoubtedly is. You yourselves have
heard her in this hall, you have heard her deny, definitely and digni-
fiedly, with all due respect to the president and members of this
august assembly, the crime of which she is here accused.

"And yet, gentlemen—my client is a woman. The sudden death of
her lover, Sainte-Croix, released the sense of guilt which had long
been burning within her. It flared up. Beside herself with terror, feeling that from now on she must bear alone all the sinfulness of her
past, she fled to England. My learned opponent has attempted to
find express proof of her guilt in this flight of hers. Yet it is proof only
that she felt herself guilty—quite a different matter, gentlemen.

"Fathers of the Church Saint Athanasius and Saint John Chrysos-
tom withdrew from the slanders of their enemies by flight. Were
they thereby admitting that the slanders were true?

"But in the case of my client, we have before us no saint but only
a weak woman cradled in luxury and attention from birth, who was
altogether unable to confront the storms of public persecution which
now roared down upon her as a result of the exposure of Saint-Croix's
murders and the fantastic revelations of Briancourt. Horrified, she
recognized that what she had feared was true: Sainte-Croix had
murdered her brothers and probably her father.

"And so she fled, leaving her home, her children behind, wander-
ing almost penniless from country to country. No one welcomed her,
she had no one to whom she could speak her heart. Not the police
was pursuing her, but her own conscience, the feeling of the grave
weight of guilt she had incurred. This is what drove her from Am-
sterdam to Antwerp to Ghent to Cambrai, and finally to Liége.

"There at last, in the stillness of the convent cell, she faced the invisible, inexorable pursuer whom she could not shake off though she

A LADY AT BAY

went to the farthest ends of the earth: her own conscience. She fought for the truth, for the existence of her soul. And the testimony to that terrible struggle—in which in the agitation of her self-indictment she confused the subjective feelings within her with the dark events in the outer world—the testimony to that terrible struggle within her soul, I say, is this very confession which my learned opponent wishes to make out a legal document containing objective facts.

"My client confesses a further grave sin. Several times in her despair she attempted to commit suicide. Horror of her wrongdoing was greater even than her love of life.

"Yes, gentlemen: does not the crown prosecutor see that behind this confession there remains the lingering idea of self-destruction; that here, too, she is making an attempt to take herself out of this world. And so I once more call upon the basic principle of our law: *Non auditur perire volens.*

"The other matters that the marquise confesses in this document do not concern us. For the charge which I am answering here is an indictment of murder of father and brothers—not of incest, not of alleged attempts to poison husband and daughter.

"But I will not neglect to say that neither the marquis nor Mademoiselle de Brinvilliers are aware of anyone's ever having attempted to poison them. In regard to her daughter, as I mentioned this morning, we have been able to prove by the testimony of Mademoiselle de Grangemont that her stomach aches were not due to poison, as Briancourt so boldly asserts, but to an overindulgence in sweets.

"I have now removed the three points upon which the prosecutor by his own statement has based the indictment. I have shown that as objective evidence they are legally without validity. The fancies of a mentally ill man and the pangs of conscience of a confused soul cannot be made the basis of a sentence of death. What the prosecutor needs are facts—nothing but facts—confirmed by unobjectionable, credible witnesses.

"Such witnesses my learned opponent has been unable to bring before this illustrious assembly, and so I am left with the duty, Your Excellency and honorable judges and councilors of the Parliament of Paris, of requesting you to dismiss the indictment against my client for lack of proof.

"Gentlemen, restore the good reputation of the Marquisate of Brinvilliers and give the mother back to her children. And as for the true guilt which has so troubled the conscience of my client, leave it to the judgment of Him who said that a repentant sinner is more welcome in heaven than ninety-nine righteous men."

Nivelle stopped and bowed low to the president. As though this were a sign that they could give way to their painfully restrained agitation, the female listeners in the gallery began talking loudly among themselves, and even the judges and councilors began whispering.

Monsieur de Lamoignon rose. "Silence!" he cried out, raising his right hand and holding it out commandingly toward the spectators. When the hall had quieted down, he turned to Nivelle, who still stood before him in the center of the rotunda, head bowed. "The Parliament of Paris thanks you, Maître Nivelle," he said. "I propose that tomorrow we confront the defendant with the principal witness for the crown so that we may determine which of them speaks the truth. Have you any objection to this procedure, in the interests of your client, Maître Nivelle?"

Nivelle reflected a moment. "No, Your Excellency," he said firmly.

"Then I herewith recess the session of the Parliament of Paris to the eighth hour of the morning of the fifteenth day of July, 1676," the president declared, and with three blows of his gavel he dismissed the meeting.

Desgrez saw Nivelle slowly return to his seat, where he gathered up some papers, and then, his face melancholy as ever, leave the hall through a side door. The councilors, too, had risen and followed the president in solemn procession, walking in pairs, out through the main doors, which the two halberdiers held open for them. The masked ladies, accompanied by well-dressed escorts, chatting and jesting, thronged toward the steps as if they were coming from a masked ball. The fragrance of their perfumes lingered above the gallery long after they were gone.

Desgrez stood alone, leaning against the pillar. Then he slowly descended the steps into the hall, which was now empty, and after a moment's hesitation sat down on the defendant's chair.

It was very still. The pigeons were no longer flying; they had roosted for the night. Suddenly there sounded a brassy thunder. The bell of Notre Dame nearby announced that the hour was seven.

Slowly the clanging faded out. It seemed to Desgrez that the whole chamber was one great ear now, listening attentively to the silence.

A last golden ray of the setting sun came through one of the windows and fell upon the gavel, which lay solitary upon the table up on the platform. Then that light, too, went out, and the bluish shadows of approaching night settled upon all the objects in the hall. The building, the dome, the pillars, the bold curve of the gallery, built so firmly of marble and granite, seemed with the fading light to become dematerialized, to be reduced to phantom insubstantiality.

Desgrez thought of the woman who tomorrow would be here, once again struggling for her life as she had done for so many days already. He thought of the duality of truth of which Nivelle had spoken, and he felt again the helplessness that had overcome him that time he lay wounded under the weight of his fallen horse.

I have done nothing but my duty, his weary brain repeated for the hundredth time, a monotonous and not very convincing chant. But suddenly he started and peered at the platform, trying to catch a glimpse of the gavel which had vanished in the darkness. There had been a sound like the low blow of a hammer—and like a voice from the platform where the president had been sitting.

Desgrez sat for a moment longer. Then he stood up, smiling. He knew well, from the long, slow years when he had been recovering his health, that this voice, which he heard rarely, only in solitude and at moments when there were difficult decisions to make, was a voice within himself. And suddenly he saw what he must do to solve the Daubray case for all time. He set about it at once.

ſ IV ſ

IT HAD GROWN somewhat cooler. The summer night was mild, and an almost full moon bathed the steep roofs of the old houses on the Pont Saint Michel as Desgrez crossed the river and turned down the long Rue de la Harpe.

Striding vigorously along, he soon reached the extensive gardens of the Sorbonne and went up to the door of a two-story house. The concierge, an old man who sat at the open door with a cat on his lap, had fallen asleep on his stool. Desgrez passed by him and into a dark corridor. He groped his way along the wall and knocked at a door.

"Come in," a gentle voice called.

Desgrez opened the door and entered a room furnished with the utmost simplicity. At the window opposite sat a narrow-shouldered man in a cassock who turned to confront his visitor. His pallid, sickly face seemed to consist, like those portraits of the dead found at the Fayum, only of eyes, with large, black pupils, whose expression was at once kindly and austere.

"So it is you, François," the man said. "Sit down." He gestured toward a battered leather armchair.

"You don't seem very surprised to see me, Edmond," Desgrez said, sitting down.

"I have been expecting you for the past quarter of an hour."

"Oh, have you?" Desgrez said. "Then I suppose you also know why I have come?"

"I have been thinking about that." The man smiled shyly at Desgrez, then lowered his eyes and gazed thoughtfully at a bunch of white roses in full flower which stood in a porcelain pitcher on a small table near him.

"And?" Desgrez asked softly.

"She is lying, François, she is lying. I am certain of it."

Desgrez did not ask how Edmond Pirot knew this; years of experience with his friend had taught him that he would receive no answer.

"Do you know her?" he asked instead.

"I have seen her only once. That was in June 1666 in Senlis. She was looking out of the window of a tavern called Trois Pots d'Etain. She gave me a friendly nod, and I returned her greeting and went by. But, François, I was never able to forget that face. It pursued me. . . ."

"It is a very beautiful face," Desgrez remarked.

Pirot smiled at his friend. "Yes, I suppose it is very beautiful," he admitted hesitantly, and fell silent. Then, a sudden firmness coming into his voice, he said, "That face is terrible. It is a face out of hell."

Desgrez saw that Pirot's hands on the arms of the chair were trembling, and a look of concern came into his eyes. Pirot looked up at him with a brief smile of gratitude, then his gaze turned back to the white roses as he said, "That milk-white skin, that rounded forehead,

those large, radiant eyes that seem to reflect purity and· innocence—
and then that mass of hair with its coppery tints and the crude,
animalistic arch of the cheekbones—cannot the world see that it is
dealing with a demon?"

"So Briancourt said, Edmond."

"Briancourt is a very unfortunate person. I fear for him," Pirot
said mysteriously.

"Why, yes," Desgrez said. "I recall now, you know him because he
studied here. Maître Nivelle considers him a visionary—and not to be
believed."

"Maître Nivelle is a good fellow. I am very fond of him. But he
does not understand these matters. Evil belongs to the realm of the
visionary—that is why people so enjoy hearing about it."

"Do you think, then, that everything Briancourt wrote down is
true?" Desgrez asked, leaning forward eagerly.

"No, not all. But it is true that the marquise murdered her father
and her brothers. Long ago in Senlis I had a premonition of it—that
she was contemplating a frightful crime. Now I know it."

Desgrez sighed. The two men were silent for a long time. The
room was filled with the fragrance of the roses. The street outside the
window was illuminated by the moon, and some distance away
Desgrez saw the towers and oriels of the old Hôtel de Cluny, which
seemed in the white light rather like a spellbound castle out of a
fairytale.

Desgrez thought of the time, now long past, when he had first
made a friend of Edmond Pirot. That had been some twenty years
ago, at the time that the great Doctor Arnauld, the Jansenist and
nephew of the Abbess of Port-Royal des Champs, had been engaged
in his sensational dispute with the Jesuit Fathers. The quarrel had
originally centered around a purely theological problem, but in time,
wider and wider circles among the populace had become involved.
Soon it became clear that what was agitating men's minds was at
bottom not two opposing theological views, but the tendencies in
life from which they had arisen. The representative of Port-Royal
was inflexible, ascetic, austere, moral, rigidly geometric; there was
something of the Stoics and of the primitive Christians about his
mind. The very sight of him gladdened the heart, quickened the
pulsebeat of every economical French paterfamilias. The Jesuit
Fathers, on the other hand, were conciliatory, modernistic, willing

to move with the times and accept the world as it was; they were full of sympathy for human weaknesses. There was a theological licentiousness about them. And everyone sensed that this was the spirit of the court and of the highest nobility, whose members, living in luxury and adultery, in lies and evasions, needed such a lenient view of their sins and therefore chose Jesuits for their father confessors.

Desgrez, twenty years old at the time, had also become involved in this dispute. And because he was of bourgeois origin and still burning with the idealism of youth, he had naturally been on the side of Port-Royal. At that time he had met Edmond Pirot, who was somewhat older than Desgrez and who had taken the position of a mediator in the great debate. But it was not Pirot's conciliatory point of view that had transformed a casual acquaintanceship into a deep friendship. It was the man himself.

Edmond Pirot, often awkward and helpless when confronted with the simplest practical questions, and already ailing and frequently confined to his bed, admired in Desgrez his good will and his clear, cool, rational manner of setting his goals and pursuing them. And it did not take Desgrez long to discover that Pirot possessed a non-logical mind, a *raison de cœur* (in Pascal's phrase), which far surpassed his own mind. Pirot had an instinct for the truth and often possessed a knowledge of things of which rationally he could not know anything. He foresaw long chains of events with the greatest precision and could often describe things that were taking place far away, while he himself lay in his bed. At times Desgrez had the feeling that his friend's senses were not, like those of other men, limited to one time and one place. But there had long existed between them a silent agreement that Pirot's wonderful gifts were not to be used for criminological purposes. Both men felt that these gifts existed on a spiritual plane and could therefore be used only in the service of the spirit.

But such is the case now, Desgrez thought as he looked out upon the Hôtel de Cluny shimmering in the moonlight. That is why I have come.

As so often happens with close friends, Pirot seemed to be following a parallel train of thought to Desgrez's. For now he said quietly in his gentle voice, "I do not know whether I ought to try it. It depends entirely on—"

"You yourself said that she is guilty, Edmond. That settles my last doubt. Criminologically the case has been solved," Desgrez said thoughtfully.

"Would her open confession change the matter?" Pirot asked cautiously.

"No. Do not forget that she has already confessed. Maître Nivelle could talk for ages, but he cannot talk that sheet of paper out of existence."

"Forgive me, François, but would you not feel a certain—let us call it a feeling of triumph if she herself confirms everything you have found out?"

Desgrez smiled. "No," he said. "To me she had already corroborated it all and I did not feel any sense of triumph. On the contrary, I had to fight against the temptation to destroy that sheet of paper. And that is still the case."

"Then is it only for her sake?" Pirot asked, and his black eyes gazed searchingly into Desgrez's face.

"For her sake," Desgrez replied. And then, after a moment's thought, he added in a low voice, "And for my sake."

"François!" Pirot exclaimed softly, as though to remind his friend of something.

Desgrez looked at him. Pirot had lowered his eyes. "Yes, it is so, Edmond," he said firmly. "I love this woman, this murderess, this demon, this monster, this . . . I don't know what. I love her so that for her sake I myself almost committed a crime."

Pirot stood up, swaying. He crossed himself and then slowly lowered himself into his chair again and gazed out into the clear night. "I knew it," he whispered. "Oh, my poor fellow. . . ."

"I know it is madness, Edmond, but that is the way it is. I understand Briancourt now, I understand all the impossible things he wrote about her, and that you, too, should call her a demon and a face out of hell. But it was not that. It was not her beauty, not her mysterious power that made me love her. It was her human misery. I felt sorry for her when I saw her engaged in that agonized battle for her own soul. That was how it began. And then, in her cell, when I rummaged through her poor possessions and held her confession in my hands—Edmond, then I loved her. I saw that she had been close to the point of overcoming her terrible past. At that time she wanted to speak the truth. And it was I, I who prevented her from doing so.

For now she has lapsed completely into her old defiance—her defiance toward God, toward her fellow men, toward her own better self. What is to be gained by cutting off her head? An empty gesture of human justice!"

Desgrez fell silent and looked at his friend, who was still gazing out into the night as though seeking something there that would resolve his doubts. Pirot's temples were white and sunken, and his head, beneath the sparse hair, had something of the delicacy of a child's skull. Desgrez wondered anxiously whether he had not demanded too much of his friend's physical strength, and he began to feel sorry for having burdened him with his still unspoken but, he knew, well-understood request.

A few minutes passed. Then a small clock on a commode whirred, and eleven high, clear strokes broke the silence. "An hour before midnight," Desgrez said. "I must go."

Edmond Pirot turned to face him, his large, dark eyes glowing feverishly. "It is good that you came, François," he said, leaning to one side and taking Desgrez's right hand. "Everyone needs absolute clarity in this matter—she, you, Parliament—in fact all of Paris, all of France. I shall try to obtain it."

"Thank God." Desgrez sighed with relief. He stood up, shook Pirot's hand, and left. But at the open door he paused, latch in hand, and said, "Do you remember, Edmond, how often we used to talk in this room about the relationship between freedom and grace?"

"If only she receives grace—then, only then, François, will she be able to reach absolute freedom of decision."

Desgrez paused another moment. "But Edmond," he said, "how, in a state of grace, can she choose anything but the truth?"

A fleeting smile passed over Pirot's face. "I hear the voice of Port-Royal," he said. "But I do not yield freedom. The relationship of our soul to God stands beyond all causality and can no more be explained mechanistically than can the Resurrection."

Desgrez continued to stand thoughtfully on the threshold. After a while he closed the door quietly behind him. He walked down the corridor and, a faint smile upon his face, passed by the still sleeping concierge and went out into the sweet moonlight of the midsummer night.

⁊ V ⁊

THE ROUND HALL of the Palace of Justice where Parliament was meeting was even more crowded the following morning than it had been on the previous days. The court gentlemen and the masked ladies thronged the gallery, whispering excitedly to one another, so that Monsieur de Lamoignon looked angrily up at them several times as though he were considering whether merely to warn them or perhaps to order them out of the chamber.

Desgrez had taken his usual observation post. He glanced at the audience with contemptuous irritation. Then Briancourt appeared at the side of the prosecutor, modest in his dark semiclerical garb, and took a seat to the right of the councilors. He sat with bowed head and did not look up even when the marquise, accompanied by Nivelle and the prison matron, Madame Duruche, came into the room and sat down to the left of the platform, in the chair where Desgrez had sat meditating the night before.

She was wearing the same dove-gray dress that Desgrez had seen in Liége, but around her shoulders she had wrapped a colored oriental shawl whose stiffness and weight lent her something of the austerely hieratical, semi-Asiatic splendor of one of Phidias' goddesses. Her hair was uncurled; she wore it combed straight back from her frail temples and massed in a bun that was held in place by a tall comb. Her face was white—extremely white. She had obviously powdered herself heavily. Even the base of her breasts, revealed by the low-cut dress, showed a bluish-white tint of powder.

Before she sat down she made a low curtsy, with bowed head, to the platform. De Lamoignon responded to the greeting with a barely perceptible nod. Then he leafed through the papers in front of him and said, "Madame, before we come to the principal matter before us today, will you kindly tell us whether in the past three years you have made confession to anyone—priest or layman."

The marquise had risen when she was addressed. She looked at the president in surprise, but immediately recovered her composure and said in a somewhat husky but perfectly distinct voice, "No, Your Excellency, I have not confessed during those years. Not to anyone."

One of the judges busily wrote something down. De Lamoignon

looked at him, nodded, and asked the marquise, "But perhaps you intended to confess, madame. If that is the case, could you give us the name of the priest whom you had considered as a possible father confessor?"

The marquise reflected briefly. "No, Your Excellency," she said then, "I did not have the intention and cannot give any name."

"That is all," the president said. "You may sit down, madame."

Maître Nivelle stared mournfully into space, the index finger of his right hand slowly stroking his mustache. Desgrez realized quite clearly what bearing this brief bit of testimony by the marquise had on the case. It meant that her confession was not a religious confession nor a preparation for a confession, and hence was legally admissible in evidence. Monsieur de Lamoignon's questions composed into a little masterpiece. But the marquise's answer was strange. Perhaps, since by decision of Parliament she had not been allowed to hear the defense made for her, she had not known of Nivelle's argument and had thought that to admit her confession was religious in character would be to imply that it was true.

Little Palluau, who had been sitting behind Briancourt, hopped up to the platform in his birdlike manner and looked questioningly at the president. "You may begin, Monsieur Palluau," De Lamoignon said. "But limit yourself to only the most necessary questions. And you, too, Maître Nivelle, if you please."

Palluau bowed respectfully. Then he turned to Briancourt, who hesitantly stood up, head still lowered. "Maître Briancourt," Palluau croaked, "kindly repeat once more in the presence of the defendant the confession which she made to you at the end of September 1670 in Louvres-en-Parisis."

"Madame said she was a murderess," Briancourt replied tonelessly.

"What else?" Palluau croaked. "Please speak louder."

"I did not want to believe it." Briancourt raised his voice, but immediately let it drop again as he went on. "I asked Madame not to burden herself with unnecessary self-reproaches. Then Madame laughed and said, 'You do not want to understand me, Nicolas. I have murdered my brother Jacques. And before that my brother Antoine. I have had both of them poisoned, one after the other.'"

"What did the defendant state to have been her motive for these murders, Maître Briancourt?"

"Madame said . . . her brothers had not behaved decently toward her. She said she could not tell me more than that."

Desgrez saw the marquise sitting unmoved, her face stony white. Her mouth was somewhat askew; on one side her lips were firmly compressed, but on the other side the upper lip was raised and the teeth slightly showing, as is sometimes seen in people who are suffering from a painful affliction of the facial nerves. Now she stood up as the president asked her whether she had any comment to make upon Briancourt's testimony.

"It is a lie," she said quietly, mechanically stressing every word, "like everything this contemptible person says." She looked wide-eyed at Briancourt, who shrank from her glance. The president struck the table hard with the gavel. "I request Madame to refrain from passing any moral judgments upon the witness," he said sharply. "Have you anything else to say?"

"Yes, Your Excellency. This person was totally drunk on the evening in question. He had drunk—I believe it was three bottles of wine—behaved improperly, and finally became so importunate that I had to put him out of my room by force."

Briancourt stood like a bundle of misery, his hands dangling limply at his side. "Witness Briancourt," the president snapped at him, "is that true? Answer!"

Briancourt opened his mouth, gasping for air like a fish brought on land. "I . . ." he murmured in a barely audible voice, "I was . . . not . . . quite . . . sober . . ."

A roar of laughter filled the hall. Even the two rigid halberdiers behind the president's chair grinned at each other. "Silence!" the president called out, raising his gavel. The laughter died away, but up in the gallery one lady continued to splutter, her body shaking convulsively, her hand over her mouth.

The marquise had sat down. Nivelle leaned over her shoulder and whispered something in her ear. Her face remained stony and closed, as though she were not listening to her counsel's advice.

Palluau now asked about the proposal to murder Madame Daubray. Briancourt repeated what he had written down in his notes in almost the very same words. Again the marquise denied everything. "The true facts are," she said calmly, "that this person asked me to lend him five thousand livres. He wanted, I believe, to set himself up in an independent practice as a lawyer. I advised him to turn to my sister-in-law in Villequoy since I knew that she needed a secretary acquainted with the law to help her take care of the large sums involved in her husband's, my brother's, legacy. I wanted to help him—and this is my thanks for it."

No matter what Briancourt, guided by Palluau's questions, stated about his knowledge of her crimes, she denied everything. But she did not make her denials in a vehement, excited fashion; she spoke calmly, coldly, considering her replies carefully. Even her indignation at Briancourt, which at the beginning could be sensed in her words, soon disappeared, and she spoke to him and of him in a tone of objective indifference. She reminded Desgrez of the commandant of a fortress hard beset by enemies who refuses to see that his walls have been breached again and again and who firmly and calmly rejects the surrender he should long ago have consented to. Wearing defiance like a cuirass, she stood before the court, a small, almost heroic figure of a woman, assailed from all sides but refusing to lower the tattered banner of her alleged innocence. There was a grandeur in her tenacity, in the stoutness of her defense.

Only once did she cry out, and that was when Briancourt in his shy, hesitant fashion said that she had confessed to him having killed her father for his money. Then she leaped from her chair and threatened the shrinking Briancourt with her clenched fist. "That is not true," she panted. "I did not kill my father for money—not for money! I did not kill him at all. I loved . . . I loved . . . I loved him, my father, as he loved me, his daughter. . . ."

She stood a while longer with raised head, breathing heavily, her fingers clawing at her dress as though she could not get air enough and was on the point of tearing open her gown. It was very quiet in the hall. The audience sat as if petrified, and the president did not call the marquise to order. Only after some time had passed did Palluau break the hushed silence.

"Why, then, Maître Briancourt," he said harshly, reproachfully, "did you keep your peace for so long when you knew of these frightful crimes."

Briancourt bowed his head in silence, so low that his chin touched his chest.

"Answer, Briancourt," the president called out. "Answer the prosecutor."

Briancourt slowly raised his head and looked at the president.

"Because I love her," he said tormentedly. And then he suddenly clapped his hands over his face. His shoulders and his bowed back moved convulsively; his sobbing could be heard to the farthermost corner of the gallery.

The marquise, leaning forward, looked keenly at Briancourt. Her eyes shone and her features froze into that stereotyped smile that Briancourt had called archaic. Without rising she said hoarsely, "You have a weak heart, Briancourt. Shame on you for bawling in the presence of all these gentlemen. I forbid you to love me."

All, especially the president, were so astonished that they sat wordlessly. "Briancourt," the marquise said, and with her forefinger she seemed to fix a point in the air, "you know what you must do after this. Hang yourself."

"This is outrageous," the president exclaimed, pounding with his gavel. "Be silent, defendant! Be silent at once!" And suddenly the painfully restrained excitement of the audience could be restrained no longer. Everyone began talking and calling. Up in the gallery several men climbed on to the benches, and even the prosecutor and the defending counsel were arguing loudly with one another and waving their hands wildly.

It took several minutes before the continual blows of the gavel restored order. "If this happens once more," the president called out, his voice breaking, "I shall have the hall cleared. You, madame, ought to know better than to behave like that before Parliament."

The marquise rose, her face calm again. She curtsied low before the president and said, "I beg the pardon of Your Excellency and all those present. My behavior was improper."

De Lamoignon signaled her with his finger to sit down. Then he spoke at length with Judge le Coigneux, who sat on his right. Palluau touched the hapless Briancourt, who did not seem to have understood what the marquise had called out to him, and with his fingers on his sleeve led him to the witness bench. Briancourt collapsed upon it and resumed his staring at the floor.

Desgrez, up in the gallery, knew that now the time had come for Parliament itself to take an active part in the trial. This highest court of France obeyed no fixed rules of order. In this respect it was entirely sovereign and varied its methods according to events and the character of the cases which the king through his ministers had turned over to it for decision. It had for some time been undecided, Desgrez had learned, whether to allow the marquise a defending counsel, but the final decision had generously permitted Nivelle to assume that role.

Now, however, the prosecutor and the defending counsel, who had hitherto been the chief actors in the drama, were to be shifted from the center of the stage. At a sign from De Lamoignon, the two halberdiers left their place behind the president's seat and led the marquise up to the platform. It was evident to Desgrez, and to everyone else in the room, that from now on the defendant was virtually alone with Parliament. The marquise and the Parliament were confronting one another like personifications of crime and justice.

Of the court judges whom Parliament had selected to fill this temporary office, Le Coigneux was the first to rise. A young man still, whose large, flowing wig did not suit his thin, aristocratic face, he had been one of the intimate friends of Parliamentary Councilor Baron Jacques de Nouars, the marquise's younger brother. In the circles of higher officialdom he enjoyed the reputation of being a witty man of the world, and even at this moment, when he was making an effort to behave with the austere dignity appropriate to a judge, his thin, somewhat uptilted nose gave him a lenient, rather humorous look. "Madame," he said in his modulated, somewhat bored voice, "you have heard the witness Briancourt. It is now up to you to make a full confession."

The marquise looked at him. Her face was so icy that it seemed to Desgrez incredible that she could be the same woman who a moment before had launched out at Briancourt with such fury. "I have nothing to confess, Monsieur le Coigneux." Hastily, she added, "I beg your pardon, I meant to say Your Worship."

"You confessed to the witness Briancourt that you murdered your father and your brothers. Confess to Parliament now, madame. There is no sense in continuing to speak falsehoods."

"Briancourt is lying. I have done nothing," she insisted.

"What about your own confession which you wrote in Liége, madame? Is that not an unequivocal proof of your guilt?"

"I was in a strange land. I was lonely, confused, frightened. I bitterly reproached myself for my behavior toward my father—for my relationship to Sainte-Croix. I was insane when I wrote that—"

"The text indicates that the writer was of sound mind," Le Coigneux interrupted her. "You state unequivocally in it that you had your brothers killed by a lackey, and that you killed your father. No madwoman would write so plainly. We know from the case against La Chaussée that he, a lackey, actually did poison your brothers, in return for payment by Sainte-Croix—a payment which, as we know, was ultimately made by you."

"It is true that I gave Sainte-Croix money. But not that he was to kill my brothers for it."

"The promissory note for thirty thousand livres, madame—was not that payment for the blood of your brothers?"

"No, the creditors were after my money. That is why I made out a note for thirty thousand livres to Sainte-Croix."

"Why did you write, then, that you had your brothers killed and that you killed your father?"

"I did not write it."

"Who else could have written it, madame?"

"The man who found the picture. He is capable of anything. Perhaps he had it written by the agent named Descarrières."

"Why should Lieutenant Desgrez have committed such an incredible forgery? Do you understand at all what you are saying?"

"Because he hates me. Because he is the one who said from the start that I was a murderess. Because he would not rest until he had brought me to this situation in which I, an innocent woman, now am . . . in which I must fight for my very life . . . because he hates me. . . ." She was breathing so heavily that Desgrez, far up in the gallery, could hear her groaning.

"Madame, I can assure you that Lieutenant Desgrez—like all the rest of us here—is interested only in seeing justice done."

"I know what I know," she exclaimed scornfully.

"What do you know, madame?"

"I know that he wants to humiliate me, to tread me into dust— because I am a lady. . . . He is no nobleman, he is a scoundrel, a murderer of women—"

She was interrupted by the president's gavel. "I cannot permit these outbursts of invective. There is not the shadow of a doubt, madame, that you and you alone wrote the confession. Even your counsel admits that. Why do you deny it now?"

She looked vacantly at him as if she did not understand. Her mind was obviously on something else entirely. But after a while she said, less spitefully, "I cannot remember having written anything of the kind."

"But there it lies, black and white," said Le Coigneux, "written in your hand, madame—the same hand that wrote the promissory note."

Desgrez was not disturbed by the accusations and invective she was hurling against him. He was accustomed to being attacked in court by the defendants—it was part of his job. But what nevertheless stunned him was the charge of emotion behind her outburst. He felt once more the close, almost intimate relationship that had existed between him and her in Liége and that had apparently been intensified rather than weakened by the fateful role he had played in her arrest and in discovering her confession. Obviously she could no more get him out of her mind than he could her. Once again he felt stirrings of guilt toward her. For he guessed that her sudden rage was directed not against the detective who had exposed her crimes, but against the man who had betrayed her trust and perhaps her real fondness. He had offended her not as a murderess, but as a woman; he had violated her feminine feelings. That was why she called him a murderer of women. The strange part of it was that he could not help feeling that this monstrous charge was somewhat justified. For in spite of her frightful crimes she struck him as more feminine than any woman he had ever known. Briancourt had had reason to weave around her figure his pagan myth of the goddess of life and death.

Down below, on the platform, she went on with her hopeless struggle. There was a weirdness about her calm and cold composure; only her twisted mouth, her unnaturally chalky face, and, now and then, a faint twitching of the muscles of her cheeks betrayed the tremendous agitation that she was forcibly restraining. She denied everything, no matter what Le Coigneux charged against her. And it was easy to see that the judge, who kept brushing his forehead, was tiring faster than she. Like a dauntless knight of falsehood, she stood unshakable, boldly insisting upon the wildest contradictions and untruths.

She lied impudently, flew in the face of all common sense; but her manner was polite, respectful, and submissive. The other judges, Le Bailleul, De Novion, and De Mandat, relieved Le Coigneux. But it was as though they were riding against a wall of granite on which their lances and arrows blunted and shattered. Admonishments, warnings, pleas to tell the truth at last, threats—everything rebounded from this delicate, white-faced woman with her frail temples. The more the judges tried to reach her conscience, the more there spread over her face that strange frozen smile—a smile not of mockery, but of a diabolic knowingness—which could well be called archaic, for it seemed born of misty abysses which human eyes were never meant to see.

It grew more and more quiet in the hall. Nothing but the weary voices of the judges could be heard, laboring to persuade her, and her husky answers, which involved her ever more deeply in the realm of improbabilities, of fantastically hairbrained justifications.

Finally, after hours had passed vainly, Monsieur de Lamoignon spoke up. His tone was mild and kind. He spoke like a father to her. And he conjured up the figures of her father and her brothers. To more than one person in the assembly it seemed as though the spirits of the murdered men were hovering invisibly in the room, adding their plea for truth to the pleas of the men in the red gowns—pleading that justice at last be allowed to take its course.

The marquise, too, seemed to feel it. Her replies became monosyllabic, her stereotyped grin grew stronger and her mouth twisted more than ever. But she did not yield. It was as if another being, greater than she, strengthened her resistance. Her persistence in falsehood seemed beyond ordinary human strength. Amazed, the audience saw great tears roll down the president's cheeks, and he did not make the effort to wipe them away. More than one of the councilors was weeping. Here and there someone's sobbing marred the silence in which she stood, imperturbably grinning.

"Madame," De Lamoignon said at last, "I was a friend of your father's. He often spoke to me about you. I do not wish you harm. Examine yourself when you are alone. Tomorrow I will come and ask you whether you have anything to say to me. But your judges you will not see again."

She stood silent, with bowed head. Suddenly her right hand clutched at her breast and she said mutedly, "My heart is heavy." Maître Nivelle and Madame Duruche stepped up to her, and her counsel gave her his arm. Thus she left the hall, followed by Madame Duruche. The plump, black-clad matron's face was swollen with weeping.

Monsieur de Lamoignon struck three times with his gavel. "I herewith declare a recess of Parliament until the third hour of the afternoon," he said. "Then, with the public excluded, Parliament will assemble to pass the verdict."

The ladies and gentlemen in the gallery thronged to the stairs, more quietly than on the preceding day, just as the bell of nearby Notre Dame struck one o'clock.

⸙ VI ⸙

THE AFTERNOON of that same day the marquise sat upon a small, three-legged stool in her cell in the top story of the Conciergerie's Montgomery Tower. Her hands were clasped over her drawn-up knees and she was gazing quietly at the small square patches of light which the sun cast through the cross-barred window upon the age-blackened floorboards.

The round, rather spacious cell was divided by a screen, back of which two beds stood. On one of the beds sat Madame Duruche, knitting. Now and then she peered briefly around the screen, and each time she wondered anew at how motionlessly the prisoner could sit. Like so many of the people who came in contact with the marquise, Madame Duruche had fallen a little in love with her. This charming great lady who, as she knew, had once danced with the king, was a remarkable contrast to the women who were usually under her care—prostitutes, thieves, infanticides. When Madame Duruche spoke to the guard at the door, she would refer to the marquise as "the dear child" or "the martyr," although she, like the guard, was firmly convinced of the marquise's guilt.

Before the marquise, a young man from the Latin Quarter had occupied the cell. In a fit of jealousy he had stabbed his mistress, who was a member of the oldest profession, and whose earnings, incidentally, were his sole support. Since he enjoyed the reputation of a poet among the students, his judges had long pondered the question of whether he was accountable for his acts, but in the end they had sentenced him to death after all. Meanwhile the prisoner had passed the time covering the whitewashed walls with more or less obscene drawings and sentences. Madame Duruche, who appreciated such things, had smilingly called the marquise's attention to them.

But as death approached, the thoughts of this poet of the gutters and brothels had turned to a more serious consideration of his situation. He had made an obvious effort to erase the questionable jokes and drawings, though he had only half succeeded, and over them he had written, in heavy black letters, terse sentences of quite a different nature.

"To what has your heart driven you?" was one of these despairing exclamations. "What you thought highest will be the death of you," was written beneath it. And in extremely large letters, covering almost a fourth of the curved wall and framed by two crosses, he had written—no doubt shortly before his execution, "Who knows whether what is called Death may not be Life, and that Life is not Death?"

It was upon this sentence that the marquise fixed her eyes now. She hunched her shoulders, shivering, although the room was hot, for the summer sun fell full upon the lead roofing of the tower.

When the door opened she turned her eyes away. A man dressed in clerical garb, leaning on a cane, approached her and introduced himself as Edmond Pirot. The marquise looked coldly at his thin hair, his sickly face, his worn, shiny cassock, which hung so loosely over his narrow shoulders that it seemed obvious it had been made for a much sturdier person.

"Are you the priest from the Conciergerie—or perhaps the Hôtel de Dieu?" she asked discourteously, without rising.

"Oh no," he said. "I am from the Sorbonne. But you are quite right: I look like the poorhouse. My rector often reproaches me for that— justly, I must say." He smiled at her.

"You're a strange bird," she said. Then she blushed and added quickly, "Forgive me, I should not have said that."

"Why not, madame? I am pleased when people tell me the truth."

She looked suspiciously at him. "I'll wager that Monsieur de Lamoignon has sent you to me . . ."

"Then you have lost your wager, madame. I did have to ask Monsieur de Lamoignon for permission to visit you. But one of your friends has sent me."

"A friend?" she exclaimed.

"I cannot tell you his name—not yet."

"I have no friends. I have had none for a long time," she said defiantly. "They all hate me."

"That is not true. I, for example, do not hate you."

"You don't know me—no more than I know you."

"Oh, but there are others. The matron here," he said, and asked Madame Duruche, who had just thrust her head curiously around the corner of the screen, "do you hate madame?"

"No, I should say not—not a bit," the matron replied, embarrassed, and her head bobbed back out of sight.

"Madame Duruche is an exception," the marquise insisted.

"And Monsieur de Lamoignon and Maître Nivelle and your children and your husband? Do you really believe that they hate you?"

"What do you want of me?" the marquise cried out impatiently, tapping the floor nervously with the toe of her shoe.

He looked at her candidly. "Oh yes, you know, madame," he said in a low, firm voice. "But you do not want to admit it to yourself—no more than you want to admit that you only tell yourself people hate you because . . . because you hate yourself."

She shrank back. Then a look of scorn spread over her face and she said sharply, "I am certain of one thing: that you are interfering with matters that are no concern of yours. You are not such a fool as I thought at first. You are a busybody. I despise you."

Pirot stood still, leaning heavily on his cane and looking at her. It was as though he had not heard her offensive speech but something entirely different, audible perhaps to him alone, which lay behind the words. "Yes," he said softly, "it is difficult to fight him, very difficult."

"Whom?" she asked hastily, throwing a brief, frightened glance over her left shoulder.

"Either he babbles meaningless nonsense and drowns everything in his deluge of stale rationalisms, or else he stands wordless, taciturn, immovable as a rock which a hundred thousand horses cannot move the fraction of an inch from a position once taken. . . ." Pirot went on, speaking ever more softly, so that she no longer could make out what he was saying. His chalky face had taken on an expression of suffering. He began to sway, and the cane dropped from his hand. He would have fallen if she had not leaped up with a cry and thrown both arms around him. "Madame Duruche!" she cried anxiously. "Water! Quick, bring water!"

The plump matron rushed out from behind the screen and hastily filled a glass with water from a pitcher on the floor. She handed it to the marquise, who put it to Pirot's lips so clumsily that nearly half of it spilled over his cassock. Madame Duruche stood by, wringing her plump hands.

The marquise lowered Pirot gently to the stool on which she had been sitting. "There . . . that is better," she said, speaking to him as if he were a child. "Or would you rather lie down, Abbé Pirot?"

Pirot, whose eyes had been wide open and staring during the attack, now closed them. But at last, when the women were beginning to think he had fallen asleep from exhaustion, he opened them again and said with a shy smile, "I beg your pardon, ladies, for making so much trouble for you. I sometimes suffer from this weakness."

"You must not talk now, Abbé Pirot," the marquise said. "Rest quietly for a few minutes."

He obeyed and sat silent, his gaze resting upon the inscription on the wall. Madame Duruche moved another stool up for the marquise and vanished discreetly behind the screen.

The marquise sat down. Elbows on her knees and chin propped in her hand, she studied Pirot, who seemed not to feel her gaze and to be wholly absorbed in his own thoughts. A quarter of an hour passed in silence. From outside could be heard the cooing of the pigeons and the flap of their wings when they rose from the roof gutter. Now and then Madame Duruche's needles made a metallic click; behind her screen she was busily knitting.

"May I speak?" the marquise asked softly.

"Please do, madame," Pirot said without looking at her.

"I don't despise you at all, Abbé Pirot. I just said that before. I was so angry, so annoyed."

"I know. Oh, I know," he said, and still without looking at her he took her hand. After a slight resistance, she let her hand lie in his. The silence returned, and the cooing of the pigeons and the click of needles intensified it.

"Abbé Pirot," she resumed hesitantly after a while, as though reluctant to break the silence. "You referred to something before—" She broke off, struggling with herself, and then exclaimed all in a rush, "Do you believe it exists?"

Pirot turned his head and his black eyes looked penetratingly at her. "That depends entirely," he said, his eyes holding hers, "on what you understand by his existence. Do not forget, he is a spirit, a power in the soul, a demon, an angel—though a fallen one."

She nodded thoughtfully and then said, with an effort, "Sometimes, when I awoke suddenly in the middle of the night, while I was in Liége, it seemed to me that I had seen a fleeting phantom. I always saw it from behind—scurrying away through the closed door— and I should probably have thought it only a night shadow if my heart had not felt heavy as lead, beating so slowly it felt as though it might stand still any moment." She paused, then went on in a lower voice, "I tried to imagine his face—he began coming often, almost every night—and I believed I discovered that he always wore the face of the person I was thinking of at the moment, that behind a thousand masks he had no face of his own. I thought I was sick, feverish. I was afraid I was going mad. Tell me, Abbé Pirot, was that he? Was that he himself?"

Pirot looked down at the floor. "It was then, wasn't it, that you wrote your confession?" he asked.

"Yes," she cried out, shaken.

"And then he vanished and did not come again," Pirot murmured as though to himself. "And you did not see him again until you came here, to Montgomery Tower?"

"Yes!" Her eyes were wide with fright. "How do you know that? I implore you, tell me who it was, Father Pirot!"

"Don't you know? Don't you really know, madame?" he asked.

"No, no," she breathed, and he saw her cheeks flush.

"You do know," Pirot said, fixing her again with his eyes. "But since you are unwilling to admit it, I will tell you who it was, madame."

"No . . . yes . . . tell me," she stammered.

"It is a power of good," he said firmly. "Some call him the Guardian of the Threshold because he stands before the threshold of our consciousness, defending and yet reminding us that we must recognize ourselves as spiritual beings."

"I—I don't understand that," she exclaimed.

"It is not easy to understand," he admitted. "For this power always expresses itself negatively—it is mocking, tormenting, contradictory, violent, threatening—but it's aim is a positive one; it aims to liberate the soul of the person. It is, in other words, the demand of our conscience which in desperate cases appears to us as a shape from the external world. You have seen it, madame. That is good, very good." He was still holding her hand, clasping it so firmly now that the skin over his knuckles was white. He looked at her anxiously, expectantly.

Suddenly, as unexpectedly as a violent gust of wind on a calm day, she uttered a piercing scream and sprang up so furiously that she pulled him up with her. "Let me alone," she screamed, her face contorted. "Let go of me, stop tormenting me!"

He held both her hands with an unexpected strength as she tried vainly to withdraw them from his. Madame Duruche came rushing out from behind the screen, and the bearded guard opened the door. They stood looking perplexed and upset, but, with a glance, Pirot warned them not to interfere.

The marquise went on screaming. She threw herself down on the floor, she writhed convulsively, and like an animal she tried to bite Pirot's hands to force him to release her. "What have I to do with you?" she panted. "You idiot! Damned idiot!"

But he did not yield. His face was shiny with perspiration, but he seemed not to hear the vituperation she poured out upon him in a fading voice. He looked exhausted, but his eyes shone with a mild light. It was as though he were dealing with an adversary who had lain long concealed and now had come out into the open in her outburst of fury.

Involuntarily he smiled as he released her. He sat down and, bending over her as she lay sobbing at his feet, he wordlessly painted the sign of the cross in the air.

Madame Duruche and the guard stood openmouthed. Pirot signed to them to go away. The matron vanished behind the screen, sighing, while the armed guard tiptoed out of the room and closed the door behind him. The marquise was still weeping, almost inaudibly. Finally she fell silent and lay motionless. It was so still that Pirot could hear the persistent buzzing of a fly at the window glass. In the roof a heat-dried rafter creaked softly. Pirot clasped his hands and whispered words in Latin. He was reciting the *Veni Creator*.

Some time passed. Pirot sat silent, his hands clasped, as though he were continuing his prayer. Suddenly the marquise sat up. Her eyes were tearstained and a mocking smile twitched at the corners of her mouth as she asked, "Why doesn't he come himself. Is he afraid of me?"

Pirot probed her face and his eyes were filled with concern as he

said softly, "He hopes that you will achieve reconciliation with yourself, madame. That is his deepest desire."

"What concern is it of him!" she exclaimed bitterly. "He is a policeman, not a priest. But he wants to have everything obey his will.
Even people's souls must dance to his tune."

"You do him an injustice, madame. He wants nothing for himself.
It was to prevent that very error that he has sent me."

She rose and brushed her dress straight. Then she stood still, looking down with a not unfriendly air at Pirot. "Do you see, Father
Pirot," she said with a wan smile, "I knew at once that it was Desgrez
who had asked you to visit me. Forgive me my outburst. I see now
that he has deceived you, too. He is not my friend but my enemy . . .
has always been my deadly enemy."

"But madame . . ."

"No, Father Pirot, please do not say anything. You cannot know;
you are too good to see through him. What he would like best would
be to set his foot upon my neck, the sort of thing we see in old paintings—Don't interrupt me, Father Pirot. I have just thought of something very important." Her smile turned into a grin, then suddenly
gave way to an expression of earnestness, almost of sadness, as she
said, "I am ready, Father Pirot—under one condition."

"That is, madame?" Pirot asked, uncomfortable and distressed.

She sighed. "I know that I can be saved only by death—saved in
your sense, Father Pirot. . . . And please do not think I am making
fun of you. I have become very fond of you. But it is absolutely
essential that I first see Lieutenant Desgrez once more."

"I guessed it," he murmured. "I wanted to tell him the evening he
came to me. But I did not do so, and, to tell the truth, I now believe
it would be better—"

"No," she interrupted him firmly. "It is not a whim on my part,
Father Pirot, but an inner necessity. I am ready to be frank. All
facts must be laid bare, and this fact of Desgrez as well. We Daubrays—that is my father and I—have always liked looking facts in the
face, even when they were . . . were annihilating for us. We were
never sentimental idiots like that frightened fool Briancourt."

He looked at her so thoughtfully that she smiled, at which he
briefly flushed and yielded. "I will speak with Lieutenant Desgrez,
madame," he said. "But I don't know . . ."

"He will come," she said quickly, in a tone of certainty. "He has

many faults, but I do not believe cowardice is one of them." She
broke off for a moment, and her husky voice sounded more ironic as
she added, "Tell him that, Father Pirot. It will please him to hear that
I have so high an opinion of him."

After Abbé Pirot had left, the marquise sat down again on her
stool. Her hands clasped over her drawn-up knees, she sat motionless,
gazing into the gathering dusk. Around her mouth, as though fixed
there, was a malicious smile.

꜀ VII ꜀

AROUND TEN o'clock on the following day, Desgrez entered the cell.
He bowed before the marquise. As he did so he noticed, with a start,
that she was again wearing the patch under her left eye, as she had
done in Liége. "Madame has sent for me," he said.

"Yes," she said dryly. "Let us sit down. Under the circumstances I
cannot offer you an easy chair. As you see, my situation has deterio-
rated since Liége. But I will not take up so much of your valuable
time—not so much as I did then. Abbé Pirot—I like him, by the way,
although I disapprove of his choice of friends—Abbé Pirot has no objection to our speaking candidly with one another." She paused for a
moment and then went on harshly, "To begin with: what business
have you interfering between God and myself? Isn't that going too
far, Lieutenant Desgrez?"

"That has not at all been in question, madame," Desgrez said
placatingly. "Abbé Pirot is, as you know, a priest. And every word—"

"Of course," she interrupted him. "But I don't doubt that you have
a plan, just a cunning little idea of yours, to squeeze one fact or
another out of him. Why did you send him to me, Desgrez? Are *you*
worried about the salvation of my soul?" She laughed bitterly. "No,
no, Desgrez, let us be honest with one another. What you need is a
full confession. Then you will be promoted to your captaincy and
your pay will be increased. But I, I will die. . . . And all the others
. . . everybody will be happy and praise clever Captain Desgrez."
She took a deep, gasping breath. "But it isn't as easy as you imagined,
my dear fellow, not at all. Have you any idea why I sent for you?"

"No, madame."

She smiled scornfully. "Don't look so worried, my dear," she said with affected gentleness. "You're holding all the cards. But I . . . I sent for you only to settle a very small, very unimportant account with you. I've heard that it is well to order one's affairs before death; otherwise it makes such a bad impression upon those who remain. Tell me, Desgrez, and for once speak the truth, were you, at the time you tricked me, convinced of my guilt?"

"Yes, madame. I knew you were guilty the moment I entered your house—when I saw the painting on the vestibule ceiling."

"But that's impossible." She turned pale, and he saw that her hands, resting on her knees, were shaking.

He stared into space, almost forgetting her as the memory rose up. "In chemistry," he said, "there is a strange phenomenon that takes place when a grain of dust falls into a supersaturated solution of a salt. The solution crystallizes; the unformed potentialities are transformed in a few moments into strict geometrical forms. That was what happened within me, madame—and the chance grain that transformed a mere suspicion into an absolute certainty was that painting: Cupid and Psyche."

"But how—how? I don't understand."

"The motive, madame," he said, almost dreamily. "I had been unable to see the motive. Everyone was talking about money, about the Daubrays' three million livres. But that was insufficient for me, although, of course, I saw it as a subsidiary motive. I knew your father well, madame. . . ."

"My father!" she exclaimed softly.

"Your father, madame, and your elder brother. I served under both of them. I knew that they were not motivated by avarice. I knew that their ultimate aim was not wealth but justice—though perhaps in less intense a measure in your brother."

She gave a bitter laugh.

"I knew," he went on thoughtfully, "that your younger brother, the baron, was an aesthete who sought beauty wherever he could find it; that your sister was deeply religious. But then how, I asked myself, can it be possible for the other daughter of this great family to be an insignificant doll concerned only with good living, luxury, and money? Some idea must motivate her, too, I thought. But what idea? I did not know. I guessed at the maternal drive, which is after all the crown of all motives. More than one mother has committed murder for her children. But there, in the vestibule, I suddenly saw the true ideal embodied. It was Eros, madame—it was love. That was what the painting told me—that painting which, as the steward informed me, you had had placed there. And at that moment I knew I was in the home of the murderess. For certain details we had learned pointed to the probability that the ultimate motive of the murders was revenge for offended love."

"You are not human, Desgrez, you are a devil," she said hoarsely, fiercely. "So in the convent you pretended to like me and constructed your trap out of my own weakness." Her eyes glistened with hatred, but her face was remarkably calm.

"I did not want to," he murmured. "I intended only to be pleasant. The liking came of itself. It was not—pretended."

"Desgrez!" she cried out. "You aren't trying to persuade me at this point that you love me!" Her eyes searched his face. He was looking at the floor. "Look at me," she said tensely. "I killed my father and my brothers. My sister-in-law and Briancourt barely escaped me. And I would have killed you, too, if I could have managed it. You know that, don't you?"

"What has that to do with it?" he said quietly.

She stared breathlessly at him and let her hand slide gently over his. They sat in silence for a while. "A pretty pair," she said at last, and the mockery returned to her voice. "Not Cupid and Psyche, but hangman and murderess. So that is the end of my long search!" Her eyes darkened and her weary voice became threatening as she continued, "If you had ever loved me you would have destroyed my confession."

"I thought of that, Marie-Madeleine. It was a tremendous temptation. I struggled with myself. I hesitated. But in the end I could not bring myself to do it. Don't you understand, I would have been dishonored—dishonored for the rest of my life. Sooner or later, I am certain of that, I would have informed on myself. And perhaps . . . perhaps I would one night have suddenly killed you, if we had fled together into the wilderness, or wherever fate led us. Marie-Madeleine, you had a better chance of survival by facing Parliament than by going with me."

"You call me Marie-Madeleine. You would have killed me," she whispered rapturously. "Yes, you still love me, François, but you understand nothing—nothing at all. Don't you realize that I would have offered myself to you willingly—that I would even have sharpened the knife if you had demanded it. You see, François, I always despised Briancourt, but if he had thrust his knife into my throat that night, I would have loved him madly as I died—loved him beyond anything in the world. For that would have made it a great love, not the little sexual excitement, the brief titillation, the swift intoxication from which I always fell back weary and a little disgusted into sobriety. Death is part of the great love—yes, it is true, its sweet core!"

She had jumped up, and now she seemed to him to have grown taller and slenderer. He suddenly felt the mythical, the primitively female quality of her which he had glimpsed only now and then and had mostly put down as one of Briancourt's fantasies. The fine blue veins on her temples, the sweet full mouth, the rounded chin looked womanly enough, but the flashing blue eyes, which seemed to be lidless, were those of a demon.

"Justice!" she cried out, holding her arms imploringly toward him. "Oh, you poor, poor men! You with your government, your morality, your laws and your limited aims. Don't you see, François, that all those are empty, hollow things, products of mere thought. Here!" She gripped her breasts. "Here is where all becomes reality. There has never been but one choice, between justice and love. Even the apostle knew that when he said: 'But love is the greatest among them.' "

"Marie-Madeleine," Desgrez put in quickly, "he spoke of another kind of love."

"Another kind of love! How impious you are, François. If you desire the top of the tree, you must desire the roots also, otherwise it will all fall. Everything stands upon my earth; everything is rooted in my heart." Breathing hard, almost sobbing, she stopped. Her wide-open eyes seemed to be seeing things and relationships that were closed to him, and he felt bitterly the ultimate unbridgeable gulf between them—between man and woman. "Justice! she said, her eyes measuring him scornfully. "Since you abused my affection for the sake of justice, I will give you my justice today. Listen to me, François. You are cunning, you've found me out. Yes, I stood behind Sainte-Croix, behind La Chaussée. They were only my tools. I conceived the murders, I ordered them. . . . But—can you imagine this, François?—I, too, was not the ultimate murderer; behind me, too, there stood someone else." Her eyes were staring fixedly at him, greedily examining him, and her mouth was distorted into that malicious smile.

He looked at her in alarm, thinking for a moment of the marquis, her husband. But he rejected this idea at once. He looked hard at her. She must be out of her mind, he thought.

She read his thoughts from his face. "No," she said roughly, "I am not crazy. We Daubrays never lose our minds. Life perhaps, but not our reason." She looked at him so piercingly that he hunched his shoulders. "Listen to me, François," she said in her hoarse, quivering voice, stressing every word, as though she were speaking to a half-deaf person. "Don't you know that we women always need a mediator, that we are weak creatures, that we always act and live through a man—father, brother, husband, lover, or friend?"

"Why . . . yes," he replied, perplexed. "That is . . ."

"For me, the man was not there!" she cried out accusingly, standing erect before him, her face so contorted by a tragic sorrow that he rose to his feet, shaken. "You, François, were not there! You were hiding. You had other things to do. You did not come to me when as a child I was mistreated, when, barely out of girlhood, I was thrust into a marriage with a libertine at a time when I had not resolved my terrible inner struggle. Oh, I was good, then, better than many other women—but you did not come. And now you claim you love me! It should have been your duty to hasten to me and to help me. Instead you tricked me and turned me over to my enemies —you, François, you who know perfectly well that you are the real author of my crimes. For I murdered in order to find you. . . . You yourself, François, are the true murderer of my father, the true murderer of my brothers."

"I!" Desgez exclaimed, more amazed than dismayed.

"Yes, you! The murderer of the Daubrays. Now I understand why you had me arrested. You wanted to hide behind me. You didn't want anyone to see through you!"

Desgrez swallowed helplessly. He had the dizzy feeling of having pushed forward into a misty world of emotions in which the axioms and conclusions of reason no longer mattered; into a chaos so charged with primitive emotionality that it was nevertheless real— more real, perhaps, than the casual, sensible world in which we move almost all the time. With an effort he pulled himself together and said placatingly, "But Marie-Madeleine, we did not even know one

another. I did not know anything about you, had never heard of
you. Don't you recall that we first met in Liége?"

Strangely, his protest sounded unconvincing in his own ears; it was
as though he were arguing with a force of nature, an avalanche, a
storm, a torrent which was deaf to all reasoning.

"I will not stand for any more of these excuses," she cried out.
"They disgust me because they are unreal." She stopped and he saw
by the fixed look in her eyes that she had temporarily lost all power
to reason. "You yourself say it," she exclaimed. "You recognized me
by the painting. And you recognized me only because you had known
of me long, long before—I mean with that deeper knowledge that
even poor Briancourt occasionally possessed. Don't deny it. That was
why you sought me. But your search came too late."

"I don't know what you are talking about, Marie-Madeleine," he
said.

"Oh yes you do, you know. But you're denying it because you want
to throw off the guilt—your terrible guilt. When you lay there on the
sickbed, you read many books. It was not written in the books, but in
you, in your own heart, François Desgrez. But your heart you did
not dare to read. Oh, how contemptible you are. Sometimes I myself do not understand why I love you. Why did you fail to listen to
the muted inner voice which must have spoken to you, although you
are only a man. . . ."

"What voice?" he asked worriedly.

"The almost inaudible, ever-so-urgent call: There is a woman who
loves me. I must find her. You should have felt compelled to leap
up, to wander through all the streets of the city, to search all the
houses to find her. But not you, François! It did not even occur to
you that it is the task of the man to find his woman. You went on
dreaming over your books and did not waken until the beacon of my
murders flamed over the city. And then it was too late, much too
late. For not the man I had waited for, hoped for, came to me. No,
Sainte-Croix came instead—a mere shadow, a phantom of my yearning, an evil dream. . . ." She sank down on the stool and began
weeping, making no attempt to hide her tears from him.

He looked down at her. "But . . ." he said painfully, "I could not
possibly have known all this." And involuntarily he thought of the
long years when he had had an inkling of such unearthly connections
between human beings. Involuntarily, deep in thought, he reached

out his hand and caressed the mass of her hair, which seemed to crackle under his fingers.

"Don't touch my hair," she cried softly. "It must not be touched."

"No," he said. "I understand." He stood above her, sunk in thought, while she went on weeping softly for a long time. "Marie-Madeleine," he said at last, "I, too, have never believed in chance, in accident. The only possible attitude is humility. And I do not know whether, confronted with these vaster connections among events, I am guilty or innocent. But my heart pronounces me innocent. We had to meet in the way we did meet. Neither you nor I had any choice in that matter."

She looked up at him and he read a timid question in her eyes.

"You are mistaken, Marie-Madeleine," he went on. "You greatly overestimate the importance of my person. If we had met earlier, you might perhaps have been a little happier with me than with Sainte-Croix—or Briancourt. But satisfied, contented? No. The oceanic stillness of the soul that you desired I, too, could not have given you. For believe me, Marie-Madeleine, you expected more, far more, than a mere man, although you yourself might not know it."

"There is nothing else," she said harshly. "Perhaps for my sister, but not for me."

He looked at her for a long time. "You have the power," he said with sudden conviction, "the power of the Daubrays to raise yourself above yourself. Your father—"

"Don't mention him!" she cried out.

"Your father had it, and you have it, too. I see that now," he went on, disregarding her protest. "Your resolution alone matters, the direction in which you set your will. Only weakness, vacillation, lukewarmness—only these you are incapable of, Marie-Madeleine. Ten thousand fathoms deep! Yes, that is it. You must desire all evil or all good. For you there is no middle way."

Once more she had lifted her tear-stained eyes and listened to his words with such breathless attention, such ecstasy, that he blushed. She caught his blush and grinned surreptitiously. "But suppose I desire evil, then," she whispered cunningly, mockingly. "Suppose I want it with every ounce of my strength—perhaps just because it is evil, in order to take my revenge upon you, François Desgrez?"

His face fell. Despairingly, he sensed that his strength was not the match of hers. A phrase he had once heard occurred to him: "Energy

is man's greatest virtue." But suddenly the opposite of that phrase
came to him, in one of those proverbs of the East which he had so
often discussed with his friend the Jesuit missionary, and which in
the course of time had become part of his own being. He murmured
it softly aloud:

> "What has made the rivers and seas kings
> Over all the waters of the valleys?
> That they condescended to descend,
> That has made them kings
> Over all the waters of the valleys."

"What does that mean? What are you getting at?" she whispered,
almost anxiously, as if now she feared that he in his turn had become
unbalanced.

"It means," he said slowly, "that I see where I have been wrong. I
abused your trust, Marie-Madeleine. At the time I did not think of it,
I did so without malice, for the sake of justice, so I believed. But the
fact remains that I tricked you, no matter what the purpose. For
doing that I now beg your forgiveness, Marie-Madeleine."

"What's that!" she exclaimed. "You beg my forgiveness!" Her lips
quivered and a hectic flush spread over her face. Then a bitter laugh
burst from her. "François Desgrez," she said scornfully, "you will stop
at nothing. Even your conscience, even love, are nothing but assistant
police agents which you use for your own purposes. But I see through
you, you and your little verses. If violence does not do it, if treachery
will not work, you will come right out in the open and try humility—
to humble me. But this little Daubray will not let you trick her a
second time. This is one little brook in the valley that will not
acknowledge you as king."

"Oh, I knew it," he said without bitterness. "I, too, am caught in the
net. You cannot believe me. But trust Edmond Pirot, Marie-Madeleine. It is true that he is my friend, but he has never in his life deceived anyone. And he will not deceive you either—never. And now
permit me to leave."

"Yes, go," she said, staring at him. "I hated you, François; now I
despise you. It is a great relief."

He bowed silently and turned to go. He had already reached the
door and was holding the latch in his hand when she called out
suddenly, "François Desgrez!"

He turned. "Yes, Marie-Madeleine?"

"François, in case you really meant that . . . about asking my forgiveness . . . then listen to this: I will not forgive you. Never. Not in all eternity!"

He bowed again and left the room. Outside, the guard looked curiously at him. He had been listening at the door and had heard the marquise's last words. Now he saw to his amazement that there was a smile of relief upon the lieutenant's face. He did not understand it; he had never heard that a too emphatic no is an unacknowledged yes—especially with women.

Madame Duruche behind her screen had also heard some of the conversation. Now she got up, sighing, and stepped into the marquise's part of the cell, intending to chat a bit with her charge in order to distract her, and herself. But the marquise paid no attention to the good-natured, rather vulgar attendant. She paced up and down the room, apparently deep in thought. The matron murmured something about the hot weather, at which the marquise looked at her in such a way that the good dame retreated to her screened-off section of the cell.

Sitting on the bed there, she listened attentively to the sound of the marquise's footsteps. It was uncanny. And that continual pacing back and forth sounded all the more uncanny because the marquise occasionally stood still and murmured words under her breath which Madame Duruche could not quite make out. The matron was ordinarily stout-hearted, but for the first time it occurred to her that she was sitting in the immediate vicinity of a murderess. She felt as though she were shut in with a beast of prey, and her imagination painted in dramatic detail the possibility of her being suddenly murdered, so that her forehead became damp with perspiration. She was glad when the guard came with the noon meal. With an impatient shaking of the head the marquise rejected all thought of food. She withdrew behind the screen and threw herself down on the bed. Hands clasped under her head, eyes fixed on the ceiling, she lay there, as rigidly motionless now as she had been mobile and restive earlier. The matron conversed in whispers with the guard about the strange change in the marquise's behavior—for the lady had been so gracious, so friendly to her before her talk with Lieutenant Desgrez.

⸰ VIII ⸰

WHEN EDMOND PIROT came to see the marquise again late in the afternoon of that same day, he thought he observed that she had been waiting impatiently for him, and her first words confirmed this. "At last," she said, and with a quick gesture invited him to sit down. "I was beginning to think you had had enough of me, Father Pirot, and would not call on me again. Has François—I mean Lieutenant Desgrez—spoken to you about our quarrel?"

"No," Pirot replied, sitting awkwardly down beside her. "He was so thoughtful, and more upset than I have ever seen him. He only said he thought . . . he hoped—" He broke off and looked dubiously at her.

"What?" she asked tensely.

"That you would forgive him although you, of course, he said, would not admit it." Pirot looked at her in surprise. A contented, almost triumphant smile had appeared upon her face.

"Oh, he is clever, very clever," she murmured rapturously. "And he loves me—otherwise he would not have noticed it." Her smile vanished as abruptly as it had appeared. "And yet he has not understood me fully," she went on broodingly. "When I love . . . in the competition of love . . . I am equal to him in that, too." She looked wide-eyed at Pirot. "Listen, Father Pirot," she said firmly, "I know he wanted to remove himself. . . . He knew he was the great obstacle in my way. And that is why—only for that reason did he descend. And I, too, am ready to descend, Father Pirot."

He looked questioningly at her.

"Like the river and the sea," she said, with muted triumph, and he felt in the intonation of her husky voice something of the tremendous energy of that element which always seeks the deepest level. "You were right, yesterday, when you said I hate myself. I have hated myself for a long time. I tried to remove myself from the world." Her voice had suddenly become so mercilessly hard, so fierce, that Pirot looked at her in alarm, although he knew that her cold ruthlessness was directed against herself now. "Once, in Liége, I swallowed splinters of glass, but they did me no harm. I suppose I was being reserved for the scaffold. And farther back, in my home in Paris—

it's true that I was only play-acting to Briancourt in order to move him, but it was half real also. I probably would have poisoned myself if he had not knocked the box out of my hand." She started and touched Pirot's hand gently with her own. "What is the matter with you, Father Pirot? You look so ill again."

"The thought of suicide is unendurable to me," he murmured. She looked at him in amazement. "And yet," she asked abruptly, in a wholly different tone, with the simple, direct thoughtfulness of a ten-year-old girl—"was it not a good impulse that impelled me to suicide, Father Pirot?"

Pirot sighed. "That is what is so strange in this world," he said heavily. "That good also is the root of evil, that back of every great crime are also great virtues—just as back of every error a truth lies hidden. That we ourselves—our weakness, our defiance—make lies out of truth, evil out of good."

"How do you know that?" she burst out, and there was an undertone of menace in her voice.

"How? From knowledge of myself, my daughter." He looked keenly at her. "Do you know," he said reflectively, "I saw you once before. That was, if I am not mistaken, ten years ago, in Senlis. . . ."

"That was the time," she said softly. "Yes, I remember now. . . . My father and I were going to Château Offémont. I was standing at the open window of our inn, looking out and struggling with myself, trying to decide whether or not to do it. And then . . . then a black-clad figure passed across the little market square. He greeted me and gave me such a strange, questioning look, as though he were greatly disturbed—and went by." She looked at him aghast. "Yes," she whispered, "that must have been you, Abbé Pirot."

"It was I," he said tonelessly, with lowered eyes.

"And you knew? You saw it in my face?" she asked with mounting anxiety.

"No, I did not know anything—anything definite," he said, taking her hand. "It was a fine summer morning, and in front of the inn stood a carriage already hitched up and laden with trunks. Then it seemed to me as though a cloud crossed over the face of the sun and shadows settled over the square. I shivered, looked up—the sun was still shining, the day had not changed. And then I saw you standing there. But do not be upset, my daughter. It is nothing supernatural, nothing ghostly. . . . I sometimes suffer from such premonitions; I believe they are related to my illness."

"I am cast out—damned—for all eternity," she whispered, her hand quivering in his.

"You must not say that, my daughter," he said sternly. "Oh, I can understand your feeling it—but don't you see that you, you alone, must now take all responsibility upon yourself." He went on more gently, "All of us, I am sure, pass through these doubts at some time. I have experienced such states. I remember that an older friend once said to me: 'Do not be afraid, Pirot. You would not be seeking God if you had not already found him.' "

She sat with bowed head, pondering. She seemed to be having difficulty understanding the meaning of this sentence. Suddenly she looked up at him and said with childlike amazement, "You and your friends know so much. I have never thought that . . . I mean, these are such mysteries that one scarcely dares to think about them alone. It surprises me that there are people who have not only learned to do so, but also have the courage to frame these mysteries in words and speak of them. . . ."

She sprang lightly from the bed, naïvely shaking her head, and sat down on her stool. He saw that she was struggling with herself, struggling with the desire to say something decisive to him. She regarded her hands, looked up, looked down again. Suddenly she burst out harshly, "It is true—it's all true. Only one thing I do not understand . . . I don't grasp it, I don't believe it." She broke off and stared vacantly for a while. Finally she said, "About the money. I didn't do it for money. . . . That came later, much later, when I thought it all over. Then it seemed so to me. But at first it was something else, something entirely different, Father Pirot." She looked at him, an agonized question in her eyes.

"You loved your father, didn't you?" he said softly. "You loved him deeply, more than any other person in the world. Probably—yes, there is scarcely any doubt of it—you recognized even as a child that your father was good."

"Stop!" she cried out imploringly. Yet her eyes fiercely begged him to go on.

"That must have been so," he continued thoughtfully. "It was against the good that you were rebelling. Your guilt, or perhaps only your sense of guilt—I don't know which—burned you and made his

presence unendurable to you. Perhaps it began by your dreaming of
his death and in your dream enjoying the feeling of relief that his
death would bring you. Then you wished he were dead."

He looked up. Her eyes were gleaming feverishly, her lips were
parted. She was numbed by tension, he saw, as though she had set
not only her conscious will, but all her vital forces upon the solution
of this frightful mystery—this ultimate cause of her misguided life.
Perhaps her emotion informed him that he was close to the truth.
"Now I see it," he exclaimed. "In him you were trying to kill your own
conscience; hardly aware of what you were doing, you tried to silence
it forever." Pirot fell silent, exhausted.

The room was filling with a golden evening light. The marquise
was standing now, an absent expression upon her face. He looked at
her, waiting unhappily. There was a brief twitching at the corners of
her mouth and her eyes looked scornful. But the scorn retreated;
it was replaced by a dull, hopeless sorrow. She seemed to have forgotten Pirot's presence. With short, springy steps she paced the room
like a panther behind the iron bars of its cage. Then she stopped in
front of Pirot and said huskily, "How strange that someone else—
you, Father Pirot—had to say it to me. I have never been a coward.
Yet I ask myself now: did I never summon up the courage to admit
it to myself—or didn't I know it? And yet I must have known. I
even wrote down in my confession that in my feelings I judged
everything by my dead father's standards. That was the first thing I
wrote down. I mean the sin that my brothers committed against me;
that I committed with my brothers. I knew it—but its full meaning
is just beginning to dawn on me now."

Pirot sat with closed eyes. Perhaps he did not want to disturb her
by looking at her, perhaps he saw the truth more distinctly by not
looking at her. It was as though he were blotting himself out, or
making himself an empty vessel into which she could pour her confession.

"Perhaps," she said, "I would have got over it as I matured. Such
faults in our sex are probably not as singular as is generally assumed.
But my father"—she hesitated, and he could sense the choked tears
in her voice as she continued—"my father stood so immeasurably
high above all faults and weaknesses. When I imagined God, as
children sometimes do, He always had my father's face and my
father's voice. My father . . . was inexorable in goodness, like a

prophet of Israel. He believed unconditionally in divine election. And he thought that I, even as a child, was one of the elect. 'You can do what you like,' he often said to me. 'Your name, daughter mine, is inscribed indelibly in the Book of Life in golden letters.' I did not fully understand him, that is true." She paused, reflecting, and then went on. "My father was widowed early—I scarcely knew my mother —and he used to call me his 'angel.' And all the visitors who came to Offémont were so delighted with me—perhaps in order to please my father.

"But then—I remember it so well—something came between us. It must have been this sin, this guilt of mine. I was afraid of him. I avoided him, avoided being alone with him. I was happy when his work kept him from coming to Offémont. I who previously had been really happy only when he was near.

"Years passed. I was married, had children. I felt myself grown-up, responsible only to myself. I was convinced that with my birth, my rank, my wealth and my beauty, which intoxicated even myself, I could permit myself anything. Nothing was forbidden for me. I considered the tenets of morality mere superstition, good for peasants, grocers, and lackeys, but not for me—who was one of the elect.

"But I had reckoned without my father. Suddenly he came and took away from me the man I thought I loved, who at the time seemed to be the whole content of my life. But I see now that it was not his violent intervention, not his paternal authority, that so outraged me that I began wishing he were dead. It must have been the goodness he represented, the constant reproach of his being—as you felt, Father Pirot. It was a choice between him or me; that was the way I began to see it, with terrible clarity."

She fell silent. She did not speak for so long that he opened his eyes and looked questioningly at her. Irresolute, struggling with herself, she passed her trembling hands over her hot forehead. "Let me say it all," she cried out suddenly, and threw herself down on her knees before him.

But she overcame her agitation and began to confess to him with a cold passion. Even in her self-indictment her practical sense of reality did not desert her.

"I begged my name-saint to call him out of this world," she said in her husky voice. "At that time it first occurred to me that his death would bring me not only an unimaginable liberation, but great finan-

cial benefit as well. I don't know whether that was the decisive
factor. I struggled despairingly with myself. But slowly, very slowly,
the decision matured in me—the decision to . . . put him away.

"Several times I was on the point of confessing everything to him—
everything I had hitherto concealed from him. Instead I decided to
travel to escape the growing temptation. But then, quite unexpectedly, he sent for me and asked me to accompany him to Offémont.
He did not feel well, he said, and needed my care. I refused. I even
wept. But he insisted in his unyielding, though kindly, way that it
was my duty as a daughter to be at his side in his illness.

"That seemed like a sign to me, a token from fate. I accompanied
him to Offémont and then . . . then . . . I killed him . . . my
father. . . ."

She looked anxiously up at Pirot, who sat deep in thought, looking
over her head at the small window. But she apparently realized at
once that he had taken in every word, and she seemed to feel that he
understood her better than she understood herself. For she began
speaking more freely, as though the worst obstacle were overcome.
"At first," she said, "I felt relieved, calmed, almost happy. . . . I
avoided thinking about what I had done. But I never succeeded in
entirely forgetting it. It was always there, no matter what I did or
where I was; it undermined everything I thought, said, and did.
I tried to erase all recollection of it, but I have the same good
memory, the same precision and regard for small details that my
father had. I soon realized that the image of my act within myself
could be erased only if I forgot myself.

"It was as though this realization were the breaking of a dam.
Without even desiring it I plunged into depths which I had hitherto
not known—and which few people know, I imagine. A kind of fever
had seized me, I desperately sought for more and more furious ec-
stasies. I lost myself in excesses. One lover no longer nearly sufficed
me. I went as low as I could go. I danced madly, for days and nights;
I gambled away huge sums, just for the sake of the excitement; I
was greedy for more and more wasteful luxury which I could not
even enjoy.

"At the same time I succeeded in throwing a veil over my whole
life. I was considered to be a pleasure-loving, somewhat foolish young
woman, a good mother. No one even faintly suspected what I really

was. I believe my father would have recognized me if he had still been alive.

"In something like three years I ran through three large fortunes—my own, my husband's, and my father's inheritance. I was ruined outwardly now as inwardly I had been ruined long ago.

"Yet I could not change my life. I thought of ways to help myself. There were my brothers, who were rich. And as I thought about it there formed within me the certainty that their fortune by rights belonged to me. I alone of the family had children; more and more I felt myself to be my father's true heir although, or rather because, it was I who had killed him. I and my children, I thought, were destined to come into possession of my father's goods and offices and thus continue a noble family. It was the same feeling that prompted me always to sign my maiden name.

"I know that this will sound like sheer madness to you, Abbé Pirot, but my crime had intensified my arrogance. More than ever I now felt that I was one of the elect—just as now, when I see my guilt, I still cannot get over the thought that some special destiny is reserved for me.

"I hated my brothers—or persuaded myself that I hated them. They were living in peace and prosperity, holding high office, highly respected—Antoine with his wife and Jacques with his literary dilettantism—while I, their sister, sank lower and lower and was now, along with my children, confronted with a financial ruin from which I saw only one way to escape: by their deaths.

"And so I murdered them, too, through a lackey. The thirty thousand livres were in fact the sum I paid for both murders. Sainte-Croix refused to return the promissory note to me. He had begun to be afraid of me and kept the note to safeguard his own life.

"Again two years passed while I continued to live a life of excess. But an irresistible urge to tell someone had taken hold of me. I wanted to cry my crimes to the world—in order to be rid of the pressure of the secret which weighed like a rock upon me. Then Briancourt came to me—and I confessed the murders to him while at the same time I tried to persuade him to attempt a new murder for me.

"The money I had inherited from my brothers was gone. Now I planned to do away with my sister-in-law. But in the end it was not the money but the murder itself I craved. It was not money, it was

the cunning of making plans, the fury of hatred, the excitement of
danger, the triumph of enjoying power over life and death. Murder
had become an end in itself. I had to murder in order to live. I don't
know whom else I would have killed; I was like a scorpion of which
it is said that in the end it stings itself in its fury. I gave a taste of
poison even to my husband and my daughter—but then fate had
mercy; my cup was full."

She fell to weeping aloud, but almost immediately regained command over herself. Yet as she finished her confession the suppressed
sobbing quivered in her voice.

"Sainte-Croix died," she said. "I don't know whether it was from
poison or from the heart disease he had been suffering from of recent
years. The promissory note was still in his possession. I was sure the
police would find it. To escape questioning I went to England.

"La Chaussée was arrested and confessed. My name was mentioned, and soon rumors reached me that Briancourt, questioned
by a police lieutenant named Desgrez, had named me as the murderess of my nearest kin. The police began looking for me, and I fled,
terrified, harried, penniless, and sometimes without bread. But it
was not these trials that brought me again to the verge of suicide,
but the realization, growing in my solitary life, that I must give myself up to the court or I would be lost forever.

"By now I repented my horrible crimes, as I repented my whole
past life. Perhaps I would have given myself up, had it not been for
my arrogance. I thought of my rank, my name, my family, my children—I was still certain that I was one of the elect—and I did not
do it.

"Then there came into my life the man who could have saved
me"—she hesitated a moment—"who might have been able to save
me. There, it seemed to me, lay the cruelest irony of my life, that this
man whom I had to respect as I had in the past respected only my
father—that this man should be my executioner: Lieutenant Desgrez!"

She began to sob. "Oh, my father!" she cried out, "do you realize
what it meant to me at last to feel a pure emotion in my heart? I
threw myself down on the floor of my cell at night and thanked God.
What a miracle that alone was! I felt the dawning of meaning again
in my wasted life.

"How much more terrible the fall was after that. Oh, I know very
well that a parricide has no call to be sensitive—and if he had wanted

to kill me I would have offered myself willingly. But to turn me over
to his policemen like a common thief—that I could not endure.

"I rebelled. I became defiant again. I resolved to fight for my life
by every means at my command, by lies, defamation, silence, mockery, cunning. For my life? Hardly that. I knew the evidence against
me was overwhelming. But no one was ever going to see me weak
again, as he had in Liége. I imagined that I would withstand the
greatest tortures and die in silence like a Daubray, denying everything, despising everything.

"But now it has turned out differently—because of your goodness,
my father. I am glad of that and forgive all my enemies."

Pirot, whose eyes had been probing her face for some time, started.
"It is not for you to forgive, my daughter," he said sternly. "Your
task is, rather, humbly to beg forgiveness. For it is you who have
made yourself the enemy of the whole world. Your only enemy is
yourself."

She looked down at the floor. "That is true," she said after a while.
"May all forgive my crimes—my terrible guilt. May all who once
considered me an enemy find the reconciliation, the peace . . . for
which I long with my whole heart."

"Are you prepared, my daughter, to confess to the world what you
have told me—and to take the punishment freely upon yourself,
whatever it may be, without hatred or reproach for your judges?"

She looked at him, tears sparkling in her eyes. "Oh, father," she
sighed, "if only you had come to me three weeks ago. Then I would
have admitted everything at the beginning of my trial."

Pirot questioned her further about many details of her crimes. She
confessed everything freely. Then he had her say her Confiteor and
gave her absolution.

For a long while Edmond Pirot and the marquise continued to sit
side by side on their stools. Twilight crept into the room; the inscriptions on the walls faded away. Outside the windows, bats flitted
about like restless thoughts. Madame Duruche emerged from behind
her screen and with a low sigh lit the candles on the table, which
consisted of unplaned boards resting on crude sawhorses. Then the
door opened and the guard came with the evening meal of bread,
boiled eggs, salted fish and water.

The candles gave a warm light that conferred an air of sanctity upon the rough peasant faces of the guard and the matron and upon the blue earthenware jug and the glasses. The metal of the armed guard's dagger handle gleamed as though it were not made of iron but of richly gilded bronze. Pirot and the marquise both felt that everything had been transformed as they moved their stools up to the table at Madame Duruche's invitation to share the meal with her and the guard.

There was an embarrassed silence and no one touched his food until Pirot rose and said a brief grace, which the others repeated in low murmurs.

Then they ate. There was an air of benevolence toward one another on all their faces. The marquise sat relaxed and said, smilingly, "It is almost like a picnic in the country. All that is wanting are the games and the voices of children."

"Yes, madame," the matron said, peeling the shell from her egg with the slightly exaggerated care of simple people. "How nice it is to stretch out in the high grass on the bank of the Seine and eat and sing songs until the candles are lit in the houses."

"When I think of the country," the marquise said longingly, "I always see the long lane of poplars at Offémont on an early morning in the summertime. I see myself as a little girl, holding my father's hand and asking what all the whispering and rustling above my head means. And he says, 'That is the west wind that comes from the sea, my child.'"

They chatted about one thing and another, and all that they said was in praise of life.

When the bell of Notre Dame rang out nine o'clock, Pirot rose and said, "I must go now." The marquise was about to ask him to stay longer, but after a glance at his sunken white features she said, "No, you must go."

In the courtyard of the Conciergerie, Desgrez was waiting for Pirot. He had been pacing back and forth for over an hour. "Edmond!" he cried out, gripping his friend's arm. "You look like a ghost. Are you ill?"

Pirot shook his head wearily.

"Was it so very hard?" Desgrez asked.

"No. Or rather, yes, it was not easy. But that isn't the trouble. . . . I keep thinking about tomorrow. It's frightful. . . . This woman could

have done so much with herself. She is of heroic stuff. But now . . ."
There was profound grief in his voice.

"I know," Desgrez replied, and led his friend to a carriage.

A little later they drove across the Pont Saint Michel, in the direction of the Sorbonne. The evening was warm and people sat outside on their housesteps. Groups of young men were talking and laughing together. Children and innumerable dogs raced around wildly in the street. Edmond Pirot was a well-known personality on the Left Bank. He sank down deeper into the carriage so that he would not be recognized. Desgrez sat silently beside him.

That night Pirot was unable to sleep. Before he went to his room he had spoken with his rector, Father de Chevigny, who was shocked by his prostration and offered to take over his spiritual duties with the marquise. But Pirot had asked permission to stay with her to the end, and finally Father Chevigny had reluctantly consented.

Now Pirot sat in his usual chair at the window and looked out into the brightness of the night. He could not get the marquise's face out of his mind. That delicate and yet powerful chalky-white face with its terrified blue eyes, those bare temples and the mass of hair with its coppery glints—that face which he himself had described as a face out of hell now seemed to hover like a phantom out in the shimmering moonlight, an urgent question upon those abnormally tightly shut lips. But it was not the face, which seemed on the point of becoming a vision, but the doubt within himself that so deeply disturbed him.

He struggled with himself, feeling his heart beat slowly and heavily. He struggled for grace, for forgiveness for these terrible murders, for this soul lost in sin. For again and again, no matter how he tried to think of it, her crimes seemed to him beyond mercy, beyond grace.

Tormented, he rose and lay down on his cot. The moonlight flooded the room. By its light he saw that the hands of his clock, which ticked away at the table beside him, stood at three o'clock. He still lay staring; then he noticed that his hands, which he had clasped over his chest, were lying slackly at his sides. He was asleep, not so deeply that he was not aware that he was sleeping.

He did not know how long he had lain this way, between sleeping and waking. Suddenly he felt that his left hand, which he had now unconsciously raised to the pillow, was opening. And in that moment, when he was entirely out of himself and no longer thinking of anything, he felt come over him like a flash of light the certainty that he need no longer worry; the concern which had been oppressing him suddenly disappeared.

He came fully awake at once. Slowly he sat up on the edge of his bed. He looked around him and saw that the atmosphere of the room had changed. The moonlight was paler; the curtains at the window were swaying slightly, blown by a cool breeze.

The doubts that had been tormenting him were gone. More than that, he believed he knew with certainty that the power which can forgive all would in the near future permit him an insight into that secret order by which it saved what, by human understanding, was beyond salvation. He felt that he was about to receive a sign—and the knowledge wonderfully strengthened him. He went to the window and looked out toward the east, where a wavering gray light gave promise of the rising sun. In the garden of the Hôtel Cluny a thrush shyly began to sing, but stopped at once, as though it were still too early for song.

꙳ IX ꙳

Toward seven o'clock in the morning, after he had attended early mass, Edmond Pirot walked from the Sorbonne to the Conciergerie, accompanied by Father de Chevigny. He strode along vigorously and seemed much less frail and ill than usual. It was well known at the Sorbonne, and in fact in all of Paris, that Pirot sometimes had experiences which were called "mystic" and which everyone hesitated to inquire about.

When they were halfway down the Rue de la Harpe a poorly dressed, skinny, dark-haired little girl of about eight approached them. She held out a large peach to Pirot.

"Please take it, monsieur l'abbé," the child said shyly, but with great insistence.

"Thank you, Germaine, but I cannot take your peach."

"It is not for you, monsieur l'abbé," the child said earnestly. "It is for the prisoner."

"Oh, that is kind of you, Germaine," Pirot replied smilingly, and he took the peach. After a moment he asked, "Do you know the marquise, my child?"

"Yes, monsieur l'abbé. My mother used to sew for her, out there in the big house in the Marais. One day when I was sitting in the servants' cellar—I was just a baby then—she came and took my hand and showed me all the pretty rooms and explained the pictures they have on the wall. Then she patted my head and said, 'Always stay as you are, Germaine.' And then she became very sad and I thought she was going to cry. But instead she laughed and gave me an apple and a pretty bowl and said, 'Go to your mummy, darling, and think kindly of me.'"

"Ah, I see," Pirot said, giving Father de Chevigny a questioning look. "But, Germaine, how do you know I am going to see the marquise?"

"Last night I heard Mummy and Papa talking about it. I guess they thought I was asleep, and my papa said, 'I know they're going to clip the head off that lady you used to sew for. There's only one cure for that sort.' And Mama sighed and said, 'She was always nice to me and asked about me and Germaine. She was never like the ladies in the other big houses. Tomorrow I'm going to Saint André des Arts to pray for her. I'm glad she has Abbé Pirot with her at this time.'" The little girl darted a glance at Pirot and murmured, "So when I got the peach this morning I thought . . ." She fell silent, blushing.

"A very good thought it was, Germaine," Pirot said. "You must come again to see me soon. Then I will explain it all to you."

"But is it true? I mean, that they—that they want to do that to her?" the child stammered.

Pirot looked at Father de Chevigny, who was gently shaking his head.

"It's not at all as you think, Germaine," he said. "Haven't you ever heard that doctors must cut a wound open when it becomes foul? That is the way it is—that's all I can tell you about it now."

The child nodded sadly and looked after the two priests as they continued on their way.

As they approached the Pont Saint Michel, where women were busy at the fountain filling pails and jugs with water, Pirot suddenly stood still. "That was it, of course," he exclaimed. He was so moved that he leaned on his cane, both hands trembling.

"What is it? Aren't you well, Father Pirot?" de Chevigny asked anxiously.

"No, no, quite the contrary!" Pirot cried out. In a lower voice he added, "Oh, my father, we live in a world of miracles. . . ."

They walked on. Father de Chevigny, still disquieted, looked questioningly at Pirot. At last Pirot noticed his look and said almost gaily, "You see, it is true: there is some good in every human being—only sometimes it is damned hard to find it!"

"Why, Father Pirot!" de Chevigny exclaimed at the swearword.

"I am quoting my friend Desgrez," Pirot said smilingly. "He is not a priest, but an old soldier."

⌐ X ⌐

THE TWO priests parted in front of the Conciergerie, and Pirot entered Montgomery Tower alone. The marquise was astonished at his changed appearance. "Why Father Pirot," she exclaimed, "you look ten years younger!"

Pirot asked her to sit down beside him. He handed her the peach and explained where it had come from. After a moment's thought she said, "I'd forgotten all about Germaine, but I remember now. Why, it's over four years ago that that happened. And little Germaine hasn't forgotten me. . . . From my own children I have heard no word. Yet I feel sure they, too, will remember me. . . . Oh, my children, what will they think of me some day when they hear what their mother was. And my husband! I have dragged all of them down with me. . . ."

There was nothing he could say to contradict her, and he did not try to console her; instead he advised her to write to her husband, who was staying in Sains with the boys. She went to the table at once and wrote the letter. Then she wrote also to her sister in the Carmelite convent and to her sister-in-law, Madame Daubray, at Villequoy.

"It is so hard," she said as she dried the ink on the letters with a sand-strewer. "They seem to be looking at me so sadly, so questioningly. This short span that our life lasts—this unique opportunity that never returns—what have I made of it? I have been a source of ruin to all who were closest to me—and to myself."

She controlled her breaking voice and went on more composedly, "I know that my husband cares somewhat for me, in spite of all that

I have done. Oh, I am sure he would hurry to me now—but it's better if he stays with the children. My Antoine and the twins—I shall never see their eager, boyish faces again. . . . Why is it, my father, that only on the point of death has the wonder of life begun to dawn on me?" She paused, and her tone hardened. "I must not weaken or complain. I want to die bravely."

This resolution with which she confronted death, the hardening that came over her feminine features, alarmed Edmond Pirot. He felt that it arose from the same ruthless determination that she had used in the planning and execution of her crimes. It seemed to him unchristian, and yet he could not refrain from admiring the quality. For all her repentance there remained a residue of steel in her soul such as few people possess—men like the Caesars, perhaps, he thought, and certainly the saints.

It occurred to him that he himself was perhaps more in need of consolation than this woman. Her enormous energy, which had spent itself upon voluptuousness, murder, and self-laceration, was now reaching out with equal vehemence for death and for spiritual values. He saw suddenly that the steeliness with which she confronted the hereafter was probably the only possible attitude she could master.

Later, too, when she was led into the reception hall of the Conciergerie, where De Lamoignon, De Mandat and Le Coigneux were waiting to interview her, she showed the same stoical matter-of-factness, the objective approach to reality, which had so shocked Briancourt and which had prompted her, in Liége, to write a confession consisting almost entirely of facts and figures. She not only confessed the murders, but she also stated with precision at what times and at what places she had administered the poison to her father. She went farther than the judges in stressing the frightfulness of her crimes, and dwelt on the minutest details, so that Monsieur de Lamoignon's face turned white and he leaned more heavily on his cane.

She spoke of the crimes and of herself with such aloofness, however, that it seemed to her listeners almost as if the whole affair concerned someone else—a past self with whom she no longer identified herself. Several times, though she was obviously perfectly clear in her mind, she confused the first person singular with the third, as small children often do. She would say, for example, "She knew La Chaussée; she knew to what use he could be put," instead of, "I knew La Chaussée," and so on.

The judges were affected unpleasantly by this objectivity, which actually should have pleased them. Pirot could read the distaste in their faces. But he knew well that her factuality came not from a lack of repentance, but from the perception that in the presence of truth (as the Benedictine monk John of Kastl once said) one must not consider either oneself or one's worst sins too important.

When De Lamoignon asked the nature and composition of the poisons she had used, she said with obviously sincere regret that she did not know, since Sainte-Croix had manufactured them. Then De Mandat asked her whether she knew Canon Dulong and his aide, Father Verron. With some surprise she admitted that she knew both casually because both the canon and the father were in close touch with the Carmelite convent on the Rue de l'Enfer where her sister lived.

De Mandat was on the point of asking her another question, but De Lamoignon signaled him with an impatient, nervous gesture to be silent and himself took up the questioning. "Do you know Monsieur de Pennautier, madame?"

"Yes, Your Excellency," she replied. "I know him. I borrowed money from him more than once when I was in need of funds."

"Do you know that Monsieur de Pennautier was engaged in correspondence with Sainte-Croix, madame?"

"I know now. I heard about it for the first time in my cell, here in the Conciergerie. I have also heard that he has been arrested. But I knew nothing about this previously."

"Is it not true, madame, that Sainte-Croix supplied Monsieur Pennautier with poison—poison and probably a hired assassin so that he could have his father-in-law and his predecessor in office killed?"

"I know nothing about that."

"Madame," Monsieur de Lamoignon said, "please consider your situation. You have committed grave crimes against humanity and the state. Now you can do us a great service—and you refuse."

Suddenly she became extremely agitated. "What are you asking of me?" she wailed. "Faced with death as I am, I cannot accuse a person who, as far as my knowledge extends, is innocent. No, I will not do it."

"Speak the truth," Monsieur de Lamoignon said, concealing his uncertainty behind a sternness of tone.

"The truth is that I know nothing whatsoever about it—not a thing."

"You must admit that the circumstances are very suspicious, madame," De Lamoignon insisted.

"I don't know about that either," she replied tormentedly. "It is not for me to judge it."

The gentlemen looked at one another in disappointment.

At this point Monsieur de Lamoignon beckoned a parliamentary attendant, who handed him a roll of parchment from which a gilded seal dangled. Monsieur de Lamoignon unfolded it and read:

"In the name of His Majesty Louis XIV, King of France by God's grace, the Parliament of Paris, obedient to the express command of its beloved supreme Lord and holding justice and truth ever before its eyes, has examined with all care the witnesses and evidence against the Marquise of Brinvilliers, Baroness of Gobelin, née Marie-Madeleine de Dreux Daubray, Countess of Offémont. The Parliament has also given ample opportunity to the defendant and her counsel, Maître Nivelle, to plead for her.

"Hereupon the Parliament of Paris unanimously declares the defendant to be guilty:

"First, of having murdered her father, Antoine de Dreux Daubray, Count of Offémont, in the summer of 1666, by poison.

"Second, of having caused the murder of her brother, Antoine de Dreux Daubray, Count of Offémont, in the spring of 1670, by poison.

"Third, of having caused the murder of her brother, Jacques de Dreux Daubray, Baron de Nouars, in the autumn of 1670, by poison.

"Fourth, of having intended to have murdered by poison her sister-in-law, Marie-Thérèse de Dreux Daubray, widowed Countess of Offémont, née Countess of Mangeau-Villarceau.

"For these crimes the Parliament of Paris sentences her:

"First, to the confiscation of her entire personal fortune, of which 4,000 livres is to be paid to the King as atonement; 10,000 to Madame Marie-Thérèse de Dreux Daubray, whose health has suffered severely under the constant threats to her life; 5,000 livres to the church for masses and prayers for the souls of her victims; the rest to charitable institutions to be designated by Parliament.

"Second, to the confiscation of her home in the Rue Neuve Saint Paul, which is to be given to the merciful sisters of Sainte Marie-Madeleine for the establishment of a lying-in home for women of the poor.

"Third, to public confession and testimony of her repentance in the parvis of Notre Dame, where she will kneel barefoot, dressed only in a beggar's shirt, carrying a two-pound candle in her chained hands and wearing a rope around her neck.

"Fourth, that she is to be driven in a dung cart to the Place Grève, where the executioner of Paris will separate her head from her body on the evening of July 16, 1676—this penalty being prescribed out of leniency, in memory of the great services rendered to France by her murdered kinsmen. Thereupon her body shall be burned on the spot and the ashes scattered into the Seine. In order to demonstrate the especial contemptibility of the murderess, the executioner will be paid for this execution by a levy upon the public prostitutes of Paris.

"God help us and have mercy upon this poor soul.

"Signed: President of the Parliament of Paris: De Lamoignon. Judges: De Coigneux, De Mandat, etc. Paris, Palais de Justice, July 15, 1676. Versailles, July 16, 1676. Confirmed Louis XIV Rex."

She had listened with an attentiveness that bordered on reverence to the passage which proclaimed her fourfold guilt, and she nodded her head slightly in agreement. Her face remained coldly beautiful. Only when De Lamoignon spoke of the penitence and the dung cart had a fleeting flush come over her cheeks, but this vanished immediately. Again the gentlemen of Parliament, who had probably expected some sort of outcry, were astonished by her calm composure. De Lamoignon, who seemed older today than he had during the trial, looked at her with lips involuntarily trembling a little and asked, in a rather kindly way, "Have you anything to say, madame?"

She thought briefly, then said, "I wish to thank Your Excellency and the esteemed councilors of the Parliament of Paris for the trouble you have gone to over me. And I humbly ask forgiveness for the lies with which I made the work of Parliament more difficult."

De Lamoignon bowed confusedly. Then he reached into the pocket of his coat and took out a small medallion attached to a silver chain. He handed it to her and said, "Madame de Lamoignon has asked me to give you this, madame. It is, as you see, a picture of your name-saint, who is also my wife's name-saint. The Holy Father himself blessed the picture when we were in Rome."

Tears filled her eyes. "You are so kind to me, Monsieur de Lamoignon," she sobbed. "Please, please forgive me and thank your wife for me."

The old man, who might have been her father, was so moved that he himself burst into tears and nodded his head without speaking.

⤙ XI ⤚

EARLY THAT afternoon the marquise ate a boiled egg which Madame Duruche had prepared for her. "Well, my poor friend," the marquise said to the fat matron, "soon I will no longer be making trouble for you."

Madame Duruche protested indignantly. Then she vanished behind the screen to leave the marquise alone with the abbé.

Some unknown donor had sent a bottle of red wine, from which the marquise filled two glasses for herself and Pirot. "I have so many friends now," she said smilingly. "You, my father, and little Germaine, and good Madame Duruche, and of course Monsieur de Lamoignon —all have given me something." She looked up slyly at Father Pirot: "It was he who sent the wine, wasn't it?"

"Who, my daughter?" Pirot asked.

"François Desgrez." She was sitting up straight, her eyes on fire.

Pirot looked at her uneasily and said, "You must no longer think of him, my daughter. It is not good—"

"Oh, don't be afraid, my father," she interrupted him. "I have made my peace with all, including François—although that was hardest for me to do."

The door opened. A man still youthful, amiable, possibly too amiable in appearance, entered and bowed with gallantry before the marquise and Abbé Pirot. He introduced himself as Maître Guillaume, Monsieur de Paris.

The marquise and Pirot turned pale. "What? Is it time already?" they stammered.

"Oh no! Oh no," Maître Guillaume replied. "We still have three or four hours. Haste makes waste, I always say. But your wheelwright has just come to me, madame, to complain that he received only three hundred livres for a carriage he built you that was worth fifteen hundred. The poor man was in despair. I really felt sorry for him. So I thought that perhaps Madame would be so kind as to instruct Monsieur le Marquis to pay him."

"Certainly, Monsieur," she said, with a sigh of relief, and got up to write the letter.

Maître Guillaume looked around the cell. "Ah," he remarked contentedly, turning to Pirot, "I see that the inscriptions of my friend Santeuil are still here. He was a fine connoisseur of our French poetry, and wrote rather good verse himself when he was in the mood, though to my taste somewhat too free in form—in the jargon of the people, of course. I've spent many a pleasant hour chatting with him here." Guillaume walked along the wall, stopping here and there with a smile and a shake of his head while he read the inscriptions aloud in a low murmur.

The marquise finished her letter and handed it to Guillaume, who took it with an elegant bow. "Now I will no longer intrude," he said, bowing again, and left.

The marquise looked at the door which had closed slowly behind the visitor. "What a strange man," she said. "I have heard that he owns one of the best collections of paintings in Paris—and yet he follows this profession!" She shuddered involuntarily as though she were cold, and sat down.

"He is a rather odd fellow," Pirot agreed. "Sometimes he turns up at the Sorbonne and listens in on theological disputations. The other members of the audience are usually stunned and give him a wide berth." Pirot fell silent for a while and suddenly, to her surprise, he closed his eyes. He looked tired out again, as he had on the day before. She studied his sickly, sunken face. With the eyes closed, it seemed an insignificant face, the almost inorganic remains of a face whose once handsome features had been washed out by suffering and struggle. She recognized with a woman's unerring instinct that he was not much further from the death of the body than she herself. The bitter foretaste of it seemed to be hovering around his thin, pallid lips.

But now he opened his eyes again, smiled warmly at her, and seemed fresh and without a trace of weariness as he asked, "My daughter, do you know the Holy Scriptures?"

She flushed. "Very slightly," she replied with embarrassment. "When I was a child, my father used to read aloud from the Psalms and Prophets to my brothers and me, and he insisted that we learn some passages by heart. But he had so little time. And later, when I was married, I neglected all that. Not until I was alone again, in

England and in Liége, did I take up the New Testament—" She broke
off, and her lips tightened.

"And?" he asked softly.

"I did not understand it," she exclaimed. "I couldn't grasp what it
meant. . . and I gave it up—" Again she stopped abruptly.

"Would it not be better to speak the truth in this matter as well,
my daughter?" he said insistently.

She looked up at him in surprise, the flush in her cheeks deepening.
He saw her struggling with herself and waited patiently. "You're
right," she exclaimed after some time. "I was afraid—frightfully
afraid. At that time I wrote my confession. I had to write it, at once,
and since I had no paper I wrote it on the back of the picture of the
saint. Then I hid the Book. I even tried to forget where I had hidden
it—under a pile of wood in the cellar. I knew that if I went on
reading it I would give myself up. It was He or I. That was why I hid
Him in the cellar. . . ."

"Are you still afraid, my daughter?"

She looked at him in astonishment, her lips parted. "No," she said,
with happy surprise, as though she were just discovering that she
was not. "I am not afraid at all. The fear is gone. All gone!"

"Then He has done it. Praised be His name," Pirot said. Out of the
pocket of his cassock he took a book bound in black leather with a
gold crucifix on the cover. "The glad tidings which you sought to
escape by such violent means are directed to you, too, and now you
can understand them. Listen, my daughter, listen with your heart.
For that is what distinguishes the Christian—we do not approach
the creative and preserving Spirit through pious fantasies or through
the intellect, which to God, of course, also produces only fantasies.
No, the way, the truth, and the life, the inner light, has appeared in
the flesh among us. The hidden face in the hereafter has also put on a
visible face, one of this world, and the Evangelists have written down
the acts, the Passion, and the words of God so that we may follow in
his footsteps."

He opened the volume, leafed through it for a moment until he
had found the passage he wanted, and began to read:

" 'Now a certain man was sick, named Lazarus, of Bethany, the
town of Mary and her sister Martha. . .' "

He read in an even voice, without emotionalism, like a man of the

people telling about something he has seen, so that the incredible
events of which he read took on a quality of homeliness, familiarity,
naturalness. Like a second Rembrandt he translated the lofty events
of a distant past into the simple present of the cell, yet without
depriving them of their deep, quiet illumination. Here, perhaps, in
the tiny room with its smeared white walls, with its rough table on
which lay the remains of a round loaf of dark bread, a bowl of crude
salt, and the blue earthenware pitcher full of water, this story of a
resurrection took on more distinctness, more radiance, than would
have been possible in the vast gilded space of a cathedral.

He did not break off a single time to offer any explanation or com-
mentary. Edmond Pirot had stepped aside; he had blotted himself
out in order to let one of the Lord's favorite disciples tell of an event
that he had experienced in his youth and was now, an old man of
ninety, thoughtfully recording at Ephesus.

The marquise sat immobile, her hands clasped lightly over her
knees, her face showing tense attentiveness. It was obvious that she
had forgotten everything about her, and herself as well. Behind
Pirot's tranquil voice and the simple words of the disciple, she was,
it was plain, able to hear that other voice which she had struggled
all her life not to hear.

So the hours passed.

⚡ XII ⚡

SLOWY RUMBLING ALONG, often screeching over the rough cobble-
stones, the two-wheeled tumbril moved down the narrow Rue Notre
Dame, drawn by a dirty-white, bony nag which stopped frequently—
whereupon the long-haired, tough-looking fellow who stood on the
shafts would lash him violently into motion again.

Desgrez had posted his men (whom the people out of old habit
still referred to as the Archers of Paris, though they no longer carried
bows) in front of the Hôtel de Dieu, the old hospital dating from the
late Middle Ages. He and Sergeant Cluet were mounted and wearing cuirass and helmet, as was customary on solemn occasions.

Desgrez looked around uneasily. A huge crowd was thronging the
rather small square, so that the dragoons had a hard time keeping a

narrow lane clear for the tumbril. When the cart reached the square, a roar of voices arose. Desgrez could make out curses and vituperation, but expressions of pity as well. He glanced around and saw that the sunken-faced patients, in their rags, had hobbled to the windows of the hospital. An ancient crone, stringy white hair dangling down from her fleshless skull, waved her bony arm threateningly out of the window and shouted in a fury of indignation, "Coupez! Coupez! Cut her throat!"

But suddenly all fell silent. The cart had stopped close up to the cathedral. Now the marquise, barefoot, in a white penitent's garb, a heavy rope around her neck and a huge burning candle in her chained hands, approached the high west portal with its wealth of carved stone figures. Above was the great gleaming, magically blue and tenderly pink rose window, overtopped by the two blunt towers. Notre Dame stood there in the twilight, a tremendous mystery, the life of the soul become stone, the heart of Paris, of the Ile de France, of France itself. And more than that, the symbol of the faith and hope of a whole people.

Many who had often passed indifferently by the cathedral must have sensed the significance of the building as the small white figure knelt down on the lowest step before the center doors of the portal. To her right knelt Edmond Pirot in his black cassock, to her left, Maître Guillaume, wearing, as required by his office, a scarlet cape thrown over his shoulders. The men in the crowd uncovered their heads; the women bowed theirs.

In the soft, fading light, Desgrez could no longer make out the details of the Gothic filigree work in stone. Only here and there, when he looked hard, his eyes could distinguish the pointing fingers of an angel, the ornamented crown of a king of the tribe of Juda, or the long, loose beard of a prophet. But, isolated, more distinctly outlined, solitary, with that frozen smile which he knew from memory rather than saw now, the naked Eva stood above all these mysteries, high above the southern gate of the portal, smaller at her dizzy height than the white-clad penitent below.

Now the two doors of the central gate opened slowly and heavily. The pale light of candles from the high altar, where the Archbishop of Paris was celebrating mass, fell upon the white face of the kneeling woman, who, as a murderess, could not set foot upon the sacred

floor of the cathedral and so had to remain, as it were, outside the
gates of Paradise. She knelt upon the hard stone, worn hollow by the
shoes of churchgoers through the centuries, holding her burning candle. And everyone sensed obscurely that this grand lady of an old
noble line was such only in the world of appearances, and that now
in her repentance she was at last awakening to true reality.

She said something, but so low that Maître Guillaume asked her to
speak louder, so that everyone could hear. Then she spoke up in her
somewhat weary, rather husky voice: "I confess that out of malice
and vengefulness I killed my father and my brothers, and that I
planned to kill my sister-in-law in order to obtain her property. For
these crimes I implore forgiveness from God, from the King, and
from Justice."

Then, accompanied by Maître Guillaume, she once more got into
the cart and sat down in the straw that covered its bottom. Father
Pirot, assisted by the executioner's helpful hand, also swung himself
up into the tumbril. He knelt down beside her as the vehicle, rattling
and screeching, began slowly to move, followed by Desgrez and
Cluet and the Archers of Paris.

In her hand the marquise held the medallion that Monsieur de
Lamoignon had given her. She was perfectly composed. Once she
turned to Pirot and said, "I wish I were suffering more. But I cannot
help myself; I am happy that I must die."

She became uneasy when she caught sight of Desgrez, and asked
Maître Guillaume to place himself between herself and the man. But
as soon as she had made her request she said quickly, "No, no, let be,
I want to see him." And she looked calmly at him as he sat stony-
faced upon his horse.

The procession passed slowly down the Rue Notre Dame and the
Rue de la Lanterne to the Pont Notre Dame. There the throng was
so great that the tumbril became wedged in the crowd on the bridge
and came to a halt. Women of the people, often carrying small
children on their shoulders, thronged around calling out encourage-
ments to the marquise. The crowd of faces, and especially the children, who stared wide-eyed and anxiously at her, so moved her that
she burst into tears. The driver lashed about him with the whip to
clear the way, and accidentally gave Edmond Pirot a painful blow
across the cheek. But still the tumbril was unable to move forward

until Desgrez and Cluet came ahead and the sergeant took the horse by the bridle and led it, holding a drawn saber in his right hand. All along the way the windows were jammed with people. They even sat on the roof gutters like sparrows.

On the Right Bank, in the Rue de la Vannerie, with its medieval buildings, it was just as crowded. At last the tumbril turned into the Place Grève, where the tall, black-draped scaffold rose up in front of the imposing, richly adorned façade of the Hôtel de Ville.

It was almost dark now. Pitch torches were burning on the frame of the scaffold and along the wall of the Hôtel de Ville, where they were stuck at angles into the cast-iron holders. Their light, obscured by clouds of thick black smoke, illuminated a sea of white faces and attentive eyes.

Holding Maître Guillaume's hand, the marquise left the tumbril, and immediately encountered Desgrez, who had dismounted and posted himself in front of the scaffold, drawn sword in hand. The marquise started, but immediately recovered her control. "François Desgrez," she whispered, "can you forgive me?"

He nodded. "I did so long ago, madame," he replied, also in a whisper. "You know that."

"I hoped so," she said. She took his hand, and kissed not the hand, but the cold blade of his sword. Then she mounted the steep flight of steps up to the scaffold.

Once more, as custom required, the verdict of Parliament was read aloud by a herald. The herald then tore the paper in two and handed it to Maître Guillaume, saying, "Do your duty, Monsieur de Paris."

Maître Guillaume bowed and thrust the parchment into his belt. He beckoned to one of his assistants, who set about cutting the marquise's hair. The silence was so profound that the clicking of the shears could be heard. Now and then someone sobbed. There was tremendous tension in the air, and it seemed to grow with the gathering darkness.

"Kneel down, madame," Maître Guillaume said in his pleasant, youthful voice. "And forgive me. For what I do, I do from reverence for the law and without hatred."

"I forgive you, Monsieur de Paris," she whispered. She kissed her medallion and knelt, her face turned toward the Seine and the towers of Notre Dame. Edmond Pirot knelt beside her. "Not so close, my father," Maître Guillaume said, wiping the sweat from his brow.

Pirot prayed. "*Salve Regina, mater misericordiae,*" he prayed. The populace joined, murmuring at first; then the prayer grew louder as it swelled like a dark wave across the square, beneath the smoking torches.

Like a flash Maître Guillaume threw off his coat. The white sleeves of his shirt gleamed in the darkness. With both hands he gripped the huge sword that an assistant held out to him, raised it high up and back over his head, and with a single blow—a masterstroke, he later declared—separated the kneeling woman's head from her body. Spurting blood, the headless trunk fell forward with a low thud.

The populace screamed, groaned, and wailed. One woman laughed piercingly. The laugh went on and on; the woman seemed to go out of her mind as Maître Guillaume lifted the head by the hair and showed it to the people. Desgrez, below the scaffold, noticed that the executioner's shirt was white and unstained. But Edmond Pirot's cheeks were spattered with blood.

The executioner's assistants set alight a large bundle of faggots steeped in tar which lay beside the scaffold. They fanned the fire with cloths. Men and women pressed up to the scaffold to dip bits of rag in the blood; it was a widespread superstition that the freshly spilled blood of a murderess was effective against certain diseases, especially the diseases of women.

Maître Guillaume sat down on a box and circumstantially lit his long-stemmed clay pipe with flint and tinder. His glance fell upon Edmond Pirot, who was standing, now, staring sadly ahead of him. "Come, monsieur l'abbé," he said pleasantly. "Sit down beside me. It is good to rest after work is done, I always say."

"I want to leave," Pirot said tonelessly.

"Not now, not now, monsieur l'abbé," Maître Guillaume said, taking the pipe from his mouth and gesturing with it at the throng. "Later, after the people have scattered. Now you would only be pushed about and troubled with stupid questions. You look tired out, monsieur l'abbé. Would you like a glass of wine? I always carry a bottle with me—on occasions like these."

"Thank you, I could use some," Pirot said. He shook his head and added gloomily, "I will never forget this."

Sighing, Maître Guillaume rummaged in his bundle for the bottle,

while near them the fire flamed higher, producing a sickening smell
of burning hair and singed flesh, which caused the majority of the
populace to flee from the square. Somewhat later Desgrez came for
his friend Pirot. They walked side by side, silently, through streets
crowded with family groups making their way home, most of them
silent and weary, but some singing as if they had just come from a
place of amusement.

The two men crossed the Ile de la Cité, where the cathedral now
lay silent and deserted, its tall west front illuminated by the feeble
light of a single flickering lantern on the corner of the Hôtel de Dieu.
The square was empty, except for a huge, mangy, dangerous-looking
dog that, at intervals, howled a melancholy protest to the smoky
sky. A waning moon, floating among sparse clouds, now and then
cast a diffuse light upon the steep gables, the narrow chimneys, and
the small, opaque windows of the sagging houses. They could still
hear the dog as they crossed the Pont de l'Hôtel de Dieu on to the
Left Bank, and its baying sounded to Desgrez like the hoarse voice
of a wolf.

Dawn was already coming and the birds in the trees on the quays
were striking up their morning song when the executioner's assistants, weary, sleepless, exchanging crude jokes, threw the ashes of
the marquise into the yellow, filthy waters of the Seine, thus carrying
out the verdict of earthly justice to the last point.

⌐ XIII ⌐

IN SEPTEMBER of that same year, 1676, Monsieur de Pennautier,
farmer-general of taxation of Languedoc and of the French Clergy,
was tried on the charge of having murdered his father-in-law and
his predecessor in office by poison, with the aid of Sainte-Croix. He
was found not guilty, for lack of evidence, and released from the
Conciergerie. But the Parisians slyly remarked to one another that
remarkably few guests now came to the gentleman's luxurious table.

The overhanging cloud of the menace of poison was hardly lifted
from Paris and the court of Versailles. A succession of murders, whose
author was found to be a woman of the people named La Voisine

deepened the gloom, so that the king found himself obliged to set up a special court for crimes of this nature. Michel de la Reynie was named presiding judge of this so-called *chambre ardente*, the "Fiery Chamber."

Although this court proceeded with great speed and with extreme cruelty against everyone who came under the slightest suspicion, such Draconian measures did not achieve the desired result. Paris and Versailles continued to feel insecure. A general state of fear prevailed and was, if anything, intensified when Lieutenant Desgrez succeeded in uncovering an attempted murder by poison among the king's most intimate circle.

It was one of the tragicomedies of history, which the conscientious researcher must again and again discover under the deceptive surface of things, that the resplendent France of the glorious Sun King, who apparently stood at the peak of his absolute power, was inwardly rotten. The "great century" of France which had produced heroic conjunctions of great emotion and great intellect in men like Turennes, Colbert, Pascal, Corneille, and Molière was morally finished before its actual temporal end came.

But even in times of crisis and defeat, true men undauntedly obey their sense of duty and strive to fulfill their inner destiny. Such, at any rate, was Lieutenant Desgrez's conviction. And so he continued to work in his profession, solving a large number of remarkable criminal cases. The ingenuity and the determined directness with which he pursued his end and uncovered crimes among the highest persons in the land aroused the admiration of his contemporaries. But what was admired even more than his success was the unmistakable humanity, which led him always to labor to turn the negative into the positive, so that more than once he demonstrated the innocence of men already condemned. He was as zealous in saving men as in bringing the criminal to his punishment.

Thus the Daubray case was, for Desgrez, not closed with the conviction and execution of the marquise. Later he often remarked smilingly, "That case ended with a bachelor who found that experience had fully confirmed his choice of a single life. It would be indiscreet to mention his name. But since he did not wish to be accused of misanthropic inclinations, he set about arranging the weddings of two couples for whom he had to act in place of the brides' deceased fathers."

That was quite true. Villequoy had awakened to new life. In the garden, which even in its neglected state had stirred Desgrez's admiration four years earlier, the weeds had been pulled, the shrubs and trees pruned geometrically, the paths strewn with gravel, and the numerous statues had been given a coat of white paint or replaced. And in the white castle, mustachioed Sergeant Cluet married dark-haired Jeannette, his fiancée of many years and now at last his wife—and a very fine figure of a wife she made.

Madame Daubray, whose lingering pallor was a heritage of the terrors she had passed through, herself gave away the bride and provided her with a considerable dowry. She placed a thatched cottage back of the vegetable garden at the young couple's disposal, and expressed the hope that the sergeant would take over the complete supervision of her estates in the near future.

Desgrez did not have so easy a time of it with the other couple. Briancourt had, as he well realized, become an accomplice in crime as a result of his having concealed the marquise's murders for so many years. But in view of the public service he had rendered by his confession, Parliament had freed him with no more punishment than a sharp admonishment—whereupon Briancourt had returned to Notre Dame des Vertus, apparently to go on struggling with his conscience and his memories.

Both Desgrez and Edmond Pirot were worried by the young man's withdrawal from society. Finally, one windy September day when the brisk chill of autumn was already in the air, they sent for him to come to Desgrez's apartment in the Place Royale.

Briancourt was obviously surprised to find the Sorbonne professor, whom he knew from his student days, in Desgrez's company. "We are old friends," Desgrez explained shortly. "Sit down, Briancourt."

Briancourt sat down and looked nervously around. With a start of surprise he caught sight of the Goujon nymph, over whose bronze skin soft shadows and small flashing reflections of light from the window were passing continually, strangely animating the figure.

"The water witch belongs to my landlady," Desgrez remarked smilingly; he had followed the direction of Briancourt's look. "I don't happen to worship it." Then he grew serious. "You must understand,

Briancourt, that this is not an interrogation. You do not have to answer me if you don't wish to—nor Professor Pirot. This is altogether a private matter. I asked you to come here because it is unpleasant for me when a case I have worked on has not been cleared up to the very end. I don't like to leave loose threads hanging."

"I understand," Briancourt said timidly.

"No, Briancourt, you don't understand." Desgrez stood up and took a longish object covered with wrapping paper from the table. It was a bread knife with a wide blade and wooden handle. Briancourt stared at it incredulously. His lips quivered with barely restrained agitation.

"Isn't it true, Briancourt," Desgrez asked, "that this is the knife with which you did not want to kill the marquise that night?"

"Yes . . . it . . . it is the knife," Briancourt stammered. "But how is it you have it?"

"Very simple, Briancourt. The night we first talked, you surreptitiously put the knife under your coat. I noticed this, but did not at first understand what it meant. Nevertheless, I took it from you that night while you were sleeping in your cell. Take it back now, Briancourt. It belongs to you."

"No, no!" Briancourt cried out, holding out both hands as if to thrust the knife away.

"That is good," Desgrez said. He had been sitting in an oddly tensed attitude. "Then you've changed your mind."

"I . . . I don't want the knife," Briancourt moaned.

Desgrez looked at Edmond Pirot, who cleared his throat and said in his gentle voice, "Briancourt, this business must end once and for all. We know that in the Conciergerie and in Aubervilliers you constantly struggled with the idea of killing yourself—preferably with this knife. You are obsessed with the idea of killing yourself—in memory of her. Perhaps you privately called it sacrificing yourself. . . ."

"Oh my God!" Briancourt cried. "How do you know that?"

"I know. That must suffice you, Briancourt." Suddenly Pirot's voice took on an unexpected harshness. "I forbid you to concern yourself any more with theology. You are not a theologian and never will be one. You have not even grasped the fundamental truth that faith, hope, and love are the prime movers of all true reason—and therefore, above all, of theological reason. You cling to the misshapen products of your fancy, to the unreal, to the nothingness which has almost led you to destroy yourself. I forbid you to go on devoting yourself self-pityingly to your memories of the past. Your outrageous penitences are nothing more than unbelief, despair, and blasphemy. Man, Brian-court, has guts with which he digests food and a reason with which he excretes harmful matter from his memory."

Briancourt had sat down again and was listening to Pirot's harsh scolding with reverent attention and an almost cheerful expression upon his face that contrasted oddly with his previous horror. "But what shall I do, monsieur l'abbé?" he now asked shamefacedly.

Pirot looked at Briancourt and smiled. The young man gave the impression of an earnest but none too bright student. "That you should certainly know best yourself, Briancourt," he said. "Make yourself useful in some way. Go out into life. I have heard that you used to be an assistant to Monsieur Bocager, the lawyer, weren't you?"

Briancourt nodded and looked questioningly at Pirot.

Pirot brushed his forehead and at last said hesitantly, "Finally, it would not be a bad idea if you—" He broke off for a moment. "Let me put it this way—if you would also change your manner of life in another respect."

The young man blushed violently and looked down at the floor. Then, with a quaver of doubt in his voice, he asked, "You mean . . . ?"

"Certainly," Desgrez said with faint irony. "We mean just what you think. We mean a young lady—Mademoiselle Julie de Grangemont."

Briancourt's cheeks flushed again. "But how can I possibly . . . ?" he said feebly. "I mean, after everything that happened there . . ."

"Oh, good Lord," Desgrez groaned, "now that's starting all over again."

"You do me an injustice, Lieutenant Desgrez," Briancourt said firmly, though the quaver in his voice was still just barely perceptible. "Julie has been in my thoughts all this time—how otherwise would I have overcome the . . . the idea about the knife? But I don't know whether she still cares anything about me at all. After all these years, I mean."

Desgrez had stood up and had been pacing back and forth. Now he stopped in front of Briancourt and looked fiercely at him, the furrow deep above his nose. "You know very well, Briancourt. Besides, even if you really do not know, there is a very simple way to find out. Ask her!" He picked up Briancourt's hat and coat and thrust them into his arms. "She lives with her Aunt, Madame de Nadaillac, on the Rue Saint Louis—right near here."

Briancourt stared open-mouthed at Desgrez. Then he jumped up and rushed to the door. There he stopped for a moment and babbled confusedly, "Gentlemen, I quite forgot . . . I mean . . . I want to thank you."

"Go on, go on," Desgrez smilingly ordered him. "You are stealing time from her and yourself."

When the door closed behind Briancourt, the two friends stepped to the window and looked down upon the Place Royale, where children were playing on the grass. In a moment Briancourt appeared, a small, dark figure. Hat in hand, his coat fluttering behind him, he hurried past the bronze equestrian toward the Rue Royale.

"The way it began," Desgrez said thoughtfully. He glanced at his friend out of the corners of his eyes and said, "Tell me, Edmond, how could you know that the young man can never be a theologian? You were quite rough on him, you know."

Pirot turned a smiling face toward Desgrez. Then he asked seriously, "Do you remember the Gnostic hymn which Briancourt thought of in his worst distress—and which Maître Nivelle later quoted in his plea?"

"Of course, Edmond," Desgrez replied, a little surprised. "It sounded to me gloomy, hopeless, a poem of despair."

"That's just it, François," Pirot said. "Briancourt could not pull himself out of despair, not even in the emergency which should have mustered all his energies. He forgot that there is a second part to that hymn on the oppression of the human soul. The second half is concerned with Heaven. It goes:

> "Then the Christ spoke: Father!
> In its temptation to evil upon earth
> The soul removed itself from your spirit.
> The soul seeks to flee the bitterness of chaos
> But does not know what path it shall take.
> Therefore, send me, Father.
> With the seals in my hand I will descend,

Through all aeons I will pass,
Gladly unlock all mysteries
And the hidden Sacred Way which leads
To you, Father, I will proclaim to men."